every move you make

Deborah Bee studied fashion journalism at Central St Martins. She has worked at various magazines and newspapers including *Vogue, Cosmopolitan, The Times* and *Guardian* as a writer, fashion editor and later as an editor. She is married with four sons and lives between London and Somerset.

Also by Deborah Bee

The Last Thing I Remember

every move you make

DEBORAH BEE

ZAFFRE

First published in Great Britain in 2020 by
ZAFFRE
80–81 Wimpole St, London W1G 9RE

This is a work of fiction. Names, places, events and
incidents are either the products of the author's
imagination or used fictitiously. Any resemblance to
actual persons, living or dead, or actual
events is purely coincidental.

A CIP catalogue record for this book is
available from the British Library.

ISBN: 978-1-78576-076-1

Also available as an ebook

1 3 5 7 9 10 8 6 4 2

Typeset by IDSUK (Data Connection) Ltd
Printed and bound in Great Britain by Clays Ltd, Elcograf S.p.A.

Zaffre is an imprint of Bonnier Books UK
www.bonnierbooks.co.uk

*To all the employees and volunteers at bodyandsoulcharity.org,
who are helping to transform the life-threatening
effects of trauma with love.*

One

Coco

Don't know why the woman behind the counter doesn't look up.
    She knows I'm here.
    Throat is burning.
    Can't breathe.
    Lungs about to burst.
    Sweat and rain dripping off my nose.
    Don't know why the woman behind the counter still doesn't
look up.
    Wait.
    Leaving pool of water around my feet.
    Breathe slower.

If you ever go to the police, I will kill you.
    You know that.
    I will kill you and then I will kill your friends.
    Or maybe I will kill your friends first.
    And then I will kill you.

Put fingertips on the counter. Just fingertips. Just to steady
myself.

Leave wet prints. Wipe with sleeve.

Leave a smudgy mark.

Try to rub it out with my fingers.

Leave wet prints.

And another thing.

Shut up talking to Louisa.

Don't let me catch you telling any of your friends anything about me.

Geddit?

NOTHING ABOUT ME.

EVER.

Unless it's good.

They probably want to talk about me.

I see Louisa looking at me.

She wants me. I know she does.

Door shoots open and a massive gust of wind and rain bangs it hard against the waiting room wall. The noticeboard jumps. Notices flutter like frightened birds.

A man shuffles in.

Doesn't look up either.

Woman behind the counter's hidden behind a computer screen. The back of it's facing the waiting room. Black and blue wires where her face should be.

Five minutes I've been here.

Think I have, anyway.

Probably, I have.

If I rest one foot on top of the other, like this, the soles of my feet start to warm up.

For a second.

Line of wet footprints on the carpet tiles.

Leading to me.

Maybe she can't see that my feet are bare.

Perhaps she doesn't realise . . .

'Errrr. Excuse me?' I say.

Babe.

Who were you on the phone to?

You know you're lying.

I can always tell when you're lying because you start to back away.

Stop lying.

COME BACK HERE AND STOP LYING.

Swallow hard.

Throat sore.

Quick, blink.

Stop the tears falling down my cheeks.

Eyes flick sideways from her screen.

Then back again.

I cough.

Words have got stuck.

''Scuse me. Could you help me, please?'

'With you in a second,' says the woman, in a sing-song way.

Like I've asked her for a Big Mac and fries.

I call her a woman.

Can't be much older than me.

Twenty-five?

Maybe.

Dark hair.

Sensible centre-parting.

White shirt.

Short sleeves.

Epaulettes.

You know.

Black-and-white checked scarf thing.

First job.

Probably.

How does someone so young get to be so like this?

'I'd like to, um, maybe talk to someone,' I say, wiping away hot tears with my sleeve. 'Do you have someone I could talk to? Just for a minute?'

Door bangs against the wall again.

I jump.

Notices flutter.

Just another guy.

'With you in a second,' she says again.

Same voice. Doesn't even look at me.

A phone buzzes.

'But,' I say.

'Just a *second*!' she hisses and snatches up the headset in a flash, straightens it over her ear, snaps a button on the keyboard.

'Front desk, Joanna speaking,' she goes. All professional. All smart.

'No problem,' she says. 'I'll have it with you in a second.'

Slips off the headset and hardens her gaze at her screen.

'Here! Joanna,' says a voice behind me.

She jumps.

Makes me jump too.

A man's voice.

'Can I just say? I hope their second don't take as long as her second seems to be taking.'

'What?' says the woman behind the counter, looking behind me, showing her pristine white teeth.

'Oh, shaddup, Barney,' she says, relaxing, looking back at the screen.

Silence.

Throat is getting tighter.

'Is there not somewhere private I could go?' I say.

Sound like I'm whining.

Unwavering gaze at the screen suggests there isn't.

'Um. To talk to someone. You know, privately. Like maybe a private room? You know . . .?'

She tilts her head to one side.

'You do know this is a police station, right? Not a private members' club.'

She says 'private members' really loud.

Is she allowed to talk to me like that?

I think that.

I don't say that.

Babe. You know you won't go to the police.

What would be the point?

Babe?

Babe!
Shut up crying, will you.
Your snivelling totally does my head in.

Legs are beginning to buckle.

''Scuse me,' says a muffled voice behind me.

A thick, gravelly woman's voice. A Liverpool accent.

''Scuse me,' she says again, louder. 'Could I just bother you for one moment, because I was just wondering, if it's at all possible, and if you can spare the time from your very important task, for you to do us all an enormous favour and give this poor girl a break? Would you?'

I turn around.

The row of plastic chairs stuck to the back wall is filled with a collection of dirty old down-and-outs.

Tramps.

They're not even really that old.

You can tell they're not.

Just thin and tired and cold and grey.

Apart from this one.

On the end.

A lady.

Purple anorak.

'Thank you for your interest but this is a police matter,' says the woman behind the counter, hardly moving her lips, like she's sucking on a wasp.

She doesn't look up.

The bloke at the other end of the row of chairs is slumped in his seat, legs outstretched, head buried into his upturned collar, arms folded, like he's trying to keep the world out.

Sole of his trainer is coming away at the side. Frayed.

Pulls his woolly-hatted head out, looks at the woman behind the counter and then at me.

'Feck,' he says, at the exact same time as he sighs.

So, you can't even tell if he really just said that or not.

'And I'd be grateful if you wouldn't swear, Barney, thank you very much', says the woman behind the counter, raising her voice in case he can't hear her under his collar. 'Especially not in front of other visitors.'

'You've finally noticed you've got a visitor then, have ya? Anyway, feck isn't swearing,' he mumbles as his nose dips back inside his collar.

'Feck isn't the same as fuck, you know, Joanna,' says the bloke in the middle. 'Feck is a proper Irish word. Ain't that so, Olly? Been around for centuries. Olly? You awake?' He nudges the coat next to him. It jumps into life.

'Shup up, Ryan,' says Olly, putting his oily old finger on his chin.

'Feck's not swearing though is it, Olly?' says Ryan, nudging him again.

Olly's hands are wrapped in crepe bandages that are grey and torn around his knuckles.

'Let me tink . . .' he says; also Irish.

He taps his chin and looks at the ceiling.

'Guess what, yeah?' he says. 'I don't give a feck, right.'

The line of dirty overcoats shakes up and down.

Just a little.

And a snigger and a cough creep out.

'Pipe down, will you, Olly?' shouts the woman behind the counter. Joanna.

'Now, what is it you would like to report, madam?'

She stresses 'is it' as if whatever it is, it's not worthy of her time or attention.

And she says 'madam' in the most patronising way ever.

She looks at me properly for the first time.

Like I'm shit.

I wish I hadn't come.

I can tell what she thinks of me.

She glances over my shoulder.

She thinks there might be something more worthy of her attention.

Gareth used to do that.

Can I just tell you about your friends?
   They aren't really friends.
   You know that, right?
   They don't even like you.
   You're shit.

'Is it just me, or is there a strange smell in here?' Joanna says, looking at me first, then accusingly at the row of men behind me.

'There's something. Now what is it? Petrol. Barney, have you been drinking petrol again?'

'I think I might need help,' I say, quietly.

She ignores me.

Totally.

'Is it washer fluid?' says Joanna

Then back at me: 'What kind of help is that?' she says, broadcasting it to the room in her loudest voice, pen raised to the lined notepad in front of her.

'Can't you just help me, please?' I say.

I feel the blood rushing around my head, my heartbeat is getting faster and faster.

I'm hot.

The room gets darker and begins to spin.

'Can't you just help me?' I say again, and my legs start to give way under me.

I'm going to be sick.

None of this is my fault.

Gareth says it's all my fault.

I only stay with you because I pity you.

Fix me a drink.

Like NOW, fix me a drink.

Two

Sally

I can't sit here and listen to that nasty little cow a second longer. They shouldn't have girls like her in the force – she gives it a bad name, she really does. Girls like her are more interested in their bleedin' selfies than they are in helping people, that's what I think. Girl at Tesco Express was telling me only last week that it takes her two hours to get her slap on in the morning. And I thought, 'Elizabeth . . .' (her name was on her badge) '. . . Elizabeth, my dear, truly, it ain't worth it. Not with the hand that you've been dealt.' Not that she'd helped herself any. What with her false eyelashes and her lip liner and all that. And you know what she'd gone and done? She's plucked out all her eyebrows so she can draw them back on higher up. Seriously. I'm telling you.

Anyway, this little PC tart, Joanna here, is cut from the exact same cloth if you ask me. She's got drawn-on eyebrows and all.

'What is it with you?' I say to her. 'What is it with you not helping someone like this poor lass, for heaven's sake? Give her a break, will ya?'

I'm being nice, but believe me, I'd sooner knock her stupid, overpainted block off.

I go get the girl from the counter; she's still in her dressing gown, mind, and I put my arm around her scrawny little shoulders and I gets her to sit down with us. Me and the lads who are here for the Drugs Intervention Programme.

'You can sit here, can't she, lads, if we all move up a bit, like?' I say, half picking her up and guiding her across the waiting room. They are waking each other up to shuffle along a bit.

''Scuse me,' I say, over my shoulder. 'I'm not trying to tell you how to do your job or anything' – not much I think – 'but can't you just call Sue Clarke, because I happen to know she'd think this lady needs to be seen very urgently?'

I lower the girl into the chair.

'Do you mean Detective Sergeant Clarke?'

No, I mean the Queen of bloody Sheba, I think to myself.

'I think I'll be the judge of which member of the team needs to be alerted,' she snaps. 'Who are you, anyhow?'

I've told her already, told her when I got here, ages ago.

'I told you, I'm Sally-Ann Parton, to see Detective Sergeant Clarke, 9 a.m. – and for the love of God, why don't you just stop being nasty and help her?'

You know what I think. I think that police stations ain't what they used to be and police reception staff ain't what they used to be either. I know I lost my temper, and I shouldn't have, but little tarts like her need to be put in their place. They don't get taught at school that if you're rude to people, they're going to be rude back.

'Fuck's sake!' she says, under her breath, rolling her eyes.

Three

DS Clarke

When Detective Inspector Bruce Langlands introduced a No Paper Policy in 2017 at Camden Road Police Station, he hadn't bothered to inform Detective Sergeant DS Clarke. If he had, she would have told him straight off that, at the ripe old age of fifty-two, she wasn't about to go kicking and screaming into the twenty-first century, thank you very much.

Now hot-desking had apparently arrived, and she wasn't about to adopt that either.

'Jesus, Livvy. Will you get your filthy chocolate biscuits off Chapman's desk?' she says to PC Olivia Halsall, pink-cheeked with smudges of chocolate in the corners of her lips. Livvy is sipping a mug of coffee – at least, she was – with her laptop and gluten-free Chocolate Hobnobs laid out on what DS Clarke considers to be PC Chapman's desk.

'But—' starts PC Halsall.

'No buts,' says DS Clarke, cupping her hand around the crumbs that are scattered on the surface of the table and moving them to one corner. 'Get rid of these,' she says as she unpacks her laptop.

Halsall gathers the crumbs carefully into her palm and throws them on the floor.

'But DI Langlands said we have to feel free to . . .' She trails off as DS Clarke stares at the crumbs on the carpet. 'DI Langlands said it's the modern way,' she starts again. 'He said that it fosters camaraderie, cohesion and collaboration.'

'Does DI Langlands share his desk?' asks DS Clarke, handing her a tissue and nodding towards the crumbs.

'No, Sarge,' says PC Halsall, stooping to pick them up.

'You see, all animals are born equal, Livvy, but some animals are more equal than others. Especially pigs,' DS Clarke says as she opens her office door.

'I love that film,' says Livvy.

'Which film?'

'*Babe*. Love it. Almost as good as Wallace and Gromit. Oh, there's someone in reception for you. Joanna called just now,' she says, planting her coffee, biscuits and laptop on another vacant desk.

DS Clarke goes into her office, opens the top drawer of a filing cabinet and leafs through the green hanging files; the same files that were supposed to be digitised before the no paper policy arrived and still haven't been. But these date back years, to when reports were handwritten. In pen. In notepads.

Terence Mansfield
57, Aigburth Road, Liverpool.
L17 6BJ
Conviction: Murder of Hayley Thomas and the serious
assault of Mrs Sally-Ann Mansfield.

Sentence: Life
Liverpool Prison
Status: Awaiting Review Board. April 2017
Partner: Sally-Ann Parton (previously Mansfield)

DS Clarke draws in a breath when the *Daily Mail* front page falls open in the file.

HAYLEY THOMAS KILLER GETS LIFE, it says in thick black letters. DS Clarke recognises the picture of the girl underneath – it was on every newspaper front page. Only twenty-two when she was brutally murdered. And Terry's mugshot. Not an ounce of remorse. Not then not ever, that's what they said.

Awaiting Review Board, she thinks. 'Maybe he's found God,' she whispers.

'You called?' says DI Langlands, grinning.

He was likeable enough, DI Langlands. Not the sort of colleague you'd go for a drink with, unless pressed. DS Clarke had never met his wife. She never turned up at the Christmas party. He took her to the office summer party last year though, and according to PC Halsall, who whispered it around the office at the time, she wears orthopaedic shoes. DS Clarke had wiggled her toes in her own orthopaedic shoes, rolled her eyes and smiled.

'I thought we'd banned paper in our new office environment,' says DI Langlands, rattling the filing cabinet in the corner of DS Clarke's office.

'You can ban whatever you like, sir, but as long as I'm here, I'll need paper and an office to read it in. I've got forty-seven thousand domestic violence cases on my books from the past twenty-three years, sir. If you want to digitise them, please, be my guest.'

'What about the rainforests, Sue? Think of the indigenous populations.'

She never could stand him in this kind of mood. Trying to impress the youngsters.

She bustles past him.

'Livvy, call down to reception and tell Joanna to tell Sally-Ann Parton to give me five minutes while I call Liverpool nick. And tell her to make us both a cup of tea.'

'Will do.'

Five minutes was not enough time. DS Clarke is still on hold. The hold music is Elmer Bernstein's original soundtrack for *The Great Escape*. Someone has a sense of humour.

Thinking about it, she could have realised that this was Liverpool nick she was talking about, and getting any sense out of anyone there was like getting blood out of a stone. Herding feral cats. Nailing jelly to a wall . . .

'Did Joanna make me that tea?' says DS Clarke through the open door of her office, as Livvy picks up the internal phone.

'She said "In a second",' she mouths. 'And this is her now, on the phone. She says there's someone here to see you.'

'I know,' says DS Clarke, rolling her eyes.

'No, it's *another* woman.'

There's a pause. *The Great Escape* theme starts over.

'Why does she need to see me?'

'I'll ask her,' says Livvy, and does. Then, 'Joanna says AAOD or DV.'

DS Clarke clamps her hand over her forehead.

'Tell her not to use those acronyms in front of people. In fact, tell her that as a receptionist we don't need her opinions. It's not her job to have opinions. If she uses those words again she'll be disciplined. Tell her, Olivia. Tell her that now. And tell her to get a name and I'll be down there as soon as I can.'

Four

Coco

'Do you think anyone might be coming yet?' I whisper to the man, to the one called Barney.

I'm so tired now.

And so hot.

'Did anyone say they are coming for her yet?' says Barney, in his accent that isn't down-and-out. Wonder where he's from. Sounds London.

'Fuck off,' the woman behind the counter mouths at Barney.

'I thought fuck was swearing,' says Barney, without smiling. 'I need clarity here, Joanna. Is fuck swearing or not? Are we allowed to say fuck, after all?'

He nudges me. Like he's trying to make me laugh. He turns his head and nods at the lady in the anorak.

'Any chance you're related to Dolly Parton?' he says, leaning in towards her.

He nudges me again.

But I'm tired.

So tired.

Babe.

Let's get married.

Let's have babies.

Four babies.

Let's go live by the sea.

Babe?

Wake up.

C'mon wake up!

I blink awake.

The woman behind the counter has her headset on again. She's speaking quietly into it.

She looks up.

At me.

'Name?' she says, out of nowhere.

What?

'What's your naaaame?' she says again

Sounding bored.

Rolling her eyes.

Shaking her head.

'Coco,' I say. 'Coco James,' I say again and cough.

'Coco James,' she says into the phone. Then, 'Do you mean Cocoa like the hot drink?' she says to me.

Flatly.

Staring.

'Cocoa. Like the hot drink?' she repeats as if I'm an idiot.

'C-O-C-O,' I spell it out.

'Yeah, like the hot drink,' she says into the phone.

'That ain't like the hot drink,' says Barney from the inside of his coat. 'Cocoa's got an A on the end. Don't it?'

'That would make it coco-a,' says Ryan.

'Yeah, sure, yeah,' says Joanna, sounding bored again. 'Yeah. Yeah. Like I said. AAOD. Or DV,' she says.

I don't know what that means. The row of coats grumble to themselves.

You fancy that guy don't you?
 I saw you looking at him.
 YOU FANCY HIM!
 You're planning to meet him!
 AREN'T YOU!
 YOU'RE PLANNING TO MEET HIM IN SECRET.

The one called Barney heaves himself up, shuffles over to the water cooler in the corner, pulls a cup off the top of the pile, shakily puts it on the plastic tray underneath the tap.

It looks like he regrets starting all this.

Too much involved.

The bending.

The balancing.

The pouring.

All at the same time.

Giant bubbles glug noisily through the upturned blue bottle.

As he lifts it, the white plastic cup bends out of shape and his hands start to shake.

The water leaks over the rim onto the carpet tiles.

By the time Barney hands me the cup, it's half-full.

Or half-empty.

As it comes to rest in my hand, more water slops over the rim, onto my dressing gown.

'Sorry. I'm sorry. Stupid of me,' he says.

He sits down.

'Thanks so much,' I say.

The dented side of the plastic cup pops out with a crack and the lady in the anorak is holding out a box of tissues she's got from one of the rooms off the reception area.

'All right, love?' she says, putting her arm around my shoulders. 'Can I get you anything, some socks maybe? D'ya have any socks back there?' she asks Joanna.

'We'd like some socks too,' says Ryan, hauling himself out of his chair and shuffling over to the counter. 'Wouldn't we, lads? Wouldn't we all like some socks?'

More sniggers from the row of coats.

'Can you get someone down to help this girl?' he hisses at Joanna, under his breath. He thinks I can't hear him.

'D'ya have a sweater as well, do you, maybe?' says the lady in the anorak.

Hopefully.

Joanna disappears out of the back door of her office.

'Just get that police lady in here!' Barney shouts after her, before slouching back down into the seat next to me, out of breath himself. 'Fuck's sake . . .' he breathes, then turns to the lady in the anorak. 'Honour among thieves, eh?'

'Smells like you spilt some paraffin, there,' he says quietly to me. 'Was it on yourself, was it?'

Keep your head still, bitch.

I can't speak.
   'Must have been,' he says.
   My mouth won't open.
   'You all right, girl?' he says.
   I nod.

I said, KEEP YOUR HEAD STILL!
   Eyes open!
   Bitch.

Joanna returns to her seat behind the desk with a pair of socks, picks up her headset and stabs some numbers into the keypad.
   'You got a jumper for her 'n' all?' says one of the coats. 'She's only got a dressing gown on, for feck's sake.'
   Joanna starts chatting on the phone. About her coffee break. About what time she's on lunch.

It's not a dressing gown, it's a bathrobe.
   Only a total moron says dressing gown.

'Bathrobe,' I say.
   The words get stuck.
   I cough.
   'It's called a bathrobe,' I repeat.
   I'm going to be sick.
   'IT'S CALLED A FUCKING BATHROBE,' I scream.
   My throat hurts.

Hot tears are running down my face, under my nose, into my mouth.

I wipe them with my sleeve.

My sleeve stinks.

Fucking loser bitch.
Mental fucking loser bitch.

One of the coats is standing next to me – his face is red and sweating.

His lips move.

I can't hear what he's saying.

The rest of the coats go quiet.

Five
Sally

Bloody hell, that girl's really upsetting herself now about her dressing gown or bathrobe, or whatever it is you call it these days. Seems an awful lot of fuss to make about a dressing gown, but who am I to criticise? Who am I to judge, eh? None of us is perfect, right? She's drinking water like it's going out of fashion now, which can only do her good, so we can't do too much more till Sue gets down here which, knowing Sue, will be as soon as she can. She's good, Sue. Proper policewoman. Proper integrity, that's Sue. But I can't help thinking an ambulance should be on its way. I can't help looking at the girl's arms. I know I shouldn't but I can't help it, can I?

What a motley crew we have in here today, I mean, what's the world come to, really?

I want you to know right from the start that I don't 'frequent' these places all the time. I'm not common or anything, you know. I mean, it's not like I've ever actually come here before. Apart from last week. That was my first time, in here. I do pass by, occasionally. Well, it is right there on the High Street and you can hardly help but pass by, can you, if you're going up to the shops and everything. But up until last week, I can honestly say that

I don't think I have seen the inside of a police station in, what, twenty years? Not until last week. These lads on the other hand, I see these lads all the time. Can't get away from them, can I? See them in doorways, see them sitting on park benches, messing up the parks for the normal folks, see them sitting on the steps of the United Reformed on Holloway Road, see them in them queues, 8.30 a.m., every single day. I mean it! Every. Single. Day. Ghosts, some of them. Zombies, all the way down Winchmore Road, all the way around the corner into the High Street, some mornings; same at the pharmacy in Parkway, queues and queues of 'em. Sometimes the queue comes all the way past my front door.

I don't mind telling you, I've not seen anything quite like her, though, that girl with the bare feet, that Coco, unless I count myself, back in the day, before you go saying anything! The first I saw of her I thought, well, there's a slip of a thing who's going to keel over if we're all not careful – and considering the company in here, it's not just bad luck that she's nearer death than they are, that's what I think. It's worse than bad luck, I'd say. Well, she looks so to me. I'm no expert, mind; I don't mind admitting I'm no expert.

She's not an addict or anything, you understand, at least I don't think she is. Not AAOD – which is what that cow behind the counter thinks. Another Arsehole on Drugs, that's what that means. I mean, you might think she is, just by looking at her, cos anybody'd think she is, just by looking at her. She acts like she's a proper junkie: strung out on nerves, tapping her foot, drumming her nails – well, she would drum her nails if she could, but since she hasn't any nails ... Never seen such chewed fingers, not in all my life!

And there she goes sighing, heavy sighing, as if it's her last breath, and rubbing her arms cos she's freezing, checking the front door, then checking the front door again, then rubbing her arms again. I mean, I know it's April, but surely she should have a coat on, and shoes for that matter? Heaven's sake. All she's got is a dressing gown, or bathrobe, whatever, and jeans and they won't be doing much. She's got some socks now. That'll help I reckon.

And the way that she came in, that was another thing! It was as if she was blown in, caught in a tornado or something. As if someone kicked her from the bottom of the steps on Camden Road, right through the double doors, right up to the reception desk. Bang! she was breathing so hard.

I'm not here with this lot, either, because if that's what you think, you're quite wrong. Should've made it clear from the start that I'm not here with them! I'm not a junkie. I don't look like a junkie, do I? Say I don't look like one of them junkies.

We're not meant to call them junkies anymore, that's what Sue says. Political correctness gone up the Swanee if you ask me. Not when they're on the Drug Interventions Programme. No, they're 'drug misusers' who may 'benefit from further assessment, treatment or other support'. That's what Sue said last week. It sounded like she'd learnt it off by heart.

'Benefit from support,' I said to Sue, '. . . you're right, most of them need help standing up.'

Sue is Detective Sergeant Sue Clarke, she's my Support Advisor, although she's been my friend for twenty years. I've got a support advisor, at my age! Bleedin' 'ell.

This is how I see it. I say . . . treating these 'drug misusers' with the ' support' of methadone is like putting out a fire with petrol, if you ask me, and I said that to Sue, last week. I did! I said to her, 'I don't care what anyone says, they've gone and spent all that government money on it, all the taxpayers' money on it, and it's never gonna work. I said to her, even some bloke in the paper, who's a lot cleverer than I am, even he said that it was like 'fighting for peace, or fucking for virginity'.

That made me laugh, but he's right, damn right.

She told me to wash my mouth out. I said at the time, it's a quote, for heaven's sake. You can't blame me for swearing if I'm quoting someone else, right?

I have to have these weekly meetings now, with Sue, Detective Sergeant Clarke. I have to call her, from now until Terry gets out. Planning meetings, clarifying-the-situation-meetings, she calls them. That's what they always do when a prisoner comes out after a long stretch.

Six

DS Clarke

DS Clarke is used to summing up a situation quickly and efficiently. She doesn't see the superfluous. She has developed an eye that quickly dismisses the spilt water on the floor, the line of grey-skinned regulars, there for their Repeat Prescription assessment session, the woman in the purple anorak – not the type of anorak worn by those intent on criminal activity – plus it's Sal. She'll catch up with her later. There are wet footprints on the floor leading to the reception desk. The girl next to Sal. Focus on the girl in the dressing gown.

The girl looks to have wet hair, yet the way it's sticking to her head suggests that there is some kind of chemical in it, rather than that it's greasy and unwashed. DS Clarke notices there is also a chemical smell. She breathes in slowly. She can't pinpoint what it is. Something to do with the RP boys? Did the cleaners spill something? She needs to get closer. The door behind her clicks shut. The girl looks up.

She looks to be in her early twenties – give or take, DS Clarke thinks; younger considering her body language; older considering the skin around her eyes and the frown line between her eyebrows. No makeup. No trace of yesterday's makeup either. Unusual for a young woman.

Sal has her arm around the girl, suggesting she is either cold or traumatised, or both. She has an empty plastic cup at her feet, carefully positioned beside her chair, and she is nursing another, so possibly dehydrated. There is evidence of bruising on her wrists and on her neck, small bruises on her neck that could match a handprint. DS Clarke makes a mental note to check the other side of her neck for a thumb print. Usually, the bruising there will be a little bigger, a little darker. The girl has cuts and grazes around her ankles, and the clean socks are out of the office supply and suggest that she arrived at the station without shoes. She has tear stains running down her cheeks and dark rings under her eyes. Drugs or sleep deprivation? DS Clarke can't make a judgement call. Not yet.

She has bruising on the left side of her cheek. Her lips are dry and there are cracks at the corners of her mouth that suggest further dehydration and possibly malnourishment Her figure is obscured by her jeans and dressing gown, but it is clear that the girl is underweight because her head appears oversized compared to her frame but there is no sign of downy facial hair and her teeth look in reasonable condition, so less likely to be an eating disorder. There are reddish- purplish sores on her hands and fingers that suggest chemical burns, and some scarring on the wrists, possibly self-inflicted. The girl is wearing clothing inappropriate for the season – either she left in a hurry, or perhaps she is a runaway. Too old to be a runaway? Possibly.

The girl's twitching and nail-biting are consistent with some-one in a high state of fear. When she looks up and meets DS Clarke's eyes, she looks more relieved than afraid.

DS Clarke's modus operandi for Domestic Violence situations is respectful command. Be courteous, be kind but take control. That's what they want and that's what they need.

'Miss James,' she says, nodding. 'Come this way, why don't you?'

Seven

Coco

I feel sick.

I wonder how far away the toilet is.

I wish I hadn't come.

This woman, holding a bunch of files and a laptop, finally buzzes through a heavy glass door.

Detective Sergeant Clarke she says.

The door clicks behind her.

She's watching us, surveying the line of coats stuck to the wall of the waiting room with a bit of a wry smile.

She must know them all.

Eventually her eyes come to rest on me.

'Miss James?' she says.

I nod.

No one calls me Miss James.

No one has ever called me Miss anything.

She's helping me to get up. She frowns at my feet.

She looks over to Joanna who is behind the counter, busy filing her nails.

Just for a few seconds she looks at her and then she flinches, blinks, as though she's thought something, then dismissed it.

'Coco,' she says.

I nod.

What do you mean, that's not your name?

It suits you.

I chose it for you.

Well, I don't care.

Coco is the name of the sort of girl I go out with.

'I'll have mine with whipped cream, I will,' says Barney.

'And sprinkles,' says Ryan, half coughing, half laughing. Almost slipping off the plastic chair at the end of the row. Then he catches himself by grabbing the leg of the bloke next to him.

It wakes him up and he yells, 'Piss off.'

'Easy, Mr Gullett,' the policewoman says, smiling. 'Do you need some help?' she says to me as she offers me her arm. The down-and-outs and the woman in the anorak all stand up to help.

But all I really need to do is hang on to one person's arm.

'Please ignore our visitors. They'll be leaving shortly,' she says.

'Gentlemen,' she says, nodding at the various members of the line.

'Morning,' she says to the woman in the anorak, who got me the socks.

'Thanks,' I whisper.

'This is our community room,' she says, closing the door behind her. 'It's a good place for a private chat. I'm Detective Sergeant Clarke. I run the Community Safety Unit here at Camden. Why don't you call me Susan?'

Anyone asks, we're married.

Of course we're married!

Anyone can see we were made for each other.

She goes back out to reception.

The door is open and Joanna from behind the counter is getting a telling off.

I don't want to seem unkind, but Susan, DS Clarke, is no oil painting.

She has no wedding ring.

I notice things like that.

But she had lots of other rings: rings with tiny beads; beads that look African or something like that. And a plaited bracelet made of string a bit like the ones we used to make out of rubber bands during school break.

I wouldn't have thought they were allowed to wear string bracelets . . .

'Have you come to make a report?' she says, really quietly and seriously, once she's sat down next to me.

Hand patting my arm.

Head on one side.

Making those affirmative little noises.

Like people do when they are waiting for you to say something.

Why does sympathy make it worse?

I want to cry.

I nod.

I cough.

My voice has gone croaky.

I can feel lumps of sick coming up the back of my throat.

Babe.

 You know what?

 You should give up work.

 You don't need to work.

 Yeah. You should give up work.

 I can earn enough for both of us.

 We can be together all the time.

And then I can't think what to say.

 It's all just disappeared out of my head.

 'I . . .' I say. 'The thing is . . .'

 It's too hot. I wish I wasn't so hot.

I said, you don't need to work.

 BABE!

 Didn't you hear me?

 Put your laptop away.

The back of my neck is stone cold.

 My stomach is turning over and over.

 She hands me another box of tissues.

 It says man-sized on the side of the box.

 Only for man-sized nightmares.

 'Are you injured?' she asks.

 Just like that.

 Am I injured?

Babe.
 Stop pretending.
 Of course it doesn't hurt.
 I'll run you a chamomile bath.
 You know how much you love a chamomile bath.

I check myself from top to bottom.
 Just in my head.
 I do that every morning, soon as I wake up.
 Nothing hurts.
 Nothing majorly hurts.

It's just a tiny bruise, babe.
 Everyone gets bruises.
 You know how you bruise easily.
 Bruise like a peach, babe.

I shake my head.
 I still can't speak.
 'Just to be clear, you're saying you have no injuries at this moment?' she goes.
 I shake my head again.
 I look at my hands folded on my lap.
 The skin is raw around my fingernails.
 Bitten.

Did you, or did you not, bleach this floor?
 I told you to bleach it.

You don't need gloves to bleach a goddam floor.
Well, do it again.
It doesn't look bleached enough.

'I'm sorry to have to ask you this, Coco, but have you been sexually assaulted?'

I shake my head.

She doesn't say anything, just keeps on looking at me.

'Not today,' I whisper.

It's hard to speak.

My mouth has stopped working.

'Not today?' she says.

I shake my head again.

'When was the last time you were assaulted, Coco?'

Did I say you could look at me when I'm talking to you?
Did I?
Do you want another slap?
Do you realise that it's your own fault that you get slapped.
Your stupid ugly face deserves it.
DID I SAY YOU COULD LOOK AT ME WHEN I'M TALKING TO YOU?

'I'm not looking at you,' I whisper.

'Coco?' she says, staring at me.

'What?' I say.

'When was the last time you were assaulted, Coco?'

'Last night,' I whisper.

'Last night,' she says, quietly.

Doesn't she believe me?

'Are you sure?' she says.

'No,' I say. 'But, I think it was last night.'

'OK,' she says.

She sighs.

'It's hard to get the days in the right order.'

Does she think I've done something wrong?

Does she think it's my fault?

I can't really remember much about anything.

No one will believe anything you say.

  You're a drunk and a liar.

My throat feels like it's constricting.

  The room is getting darker.

  I can't breathe.

  'Would you like a cup of tea?' she asks.

  She jumps up and pops her head out of the door and shouts, 'Joanna? Where's that tea got to? Mug of tea. Large mug of tea. And one for Coco while you're at it. Do you take sugar?' she says, looking back at me.

FAT BITCH. I'VE TOLD YOU ABOUT SUGAR!

'NO SUGAR!' I shout at her.

  She looks taken aback.

  She watches me.

'I don't have sugar. Not anymore,' I explain.

I used to have sugar but now I don't have sugar.

You've got fat.

No, my sweet girl, it's got nothing to do with the vitamins.

It's you being greedy.

You do nothing but eat.

You don't understand the meaning of self-control.

I've dated supermodels.

And now I'm stuck with you.

Fat cow.

'Milk?' she says.

'No thank you. Lactose . . .' I say. 'Lactose intolerant.'

I didn't used to be but now I am.

FAT.

COW.

She slides back into the seat, takes a deep breath.

'Two things,' she says, brightly, looking down at her laptop. 'First, we need another police officer here, to help me with all the details because of the sensitivity of your case. That OK?' She looks up. 'And second, we need to think about doing a physical examination. This means I need to take some swabs of saliva, before we do anything else.'

I nod and she gets a box of stuff out of a cupboard.

Giant cotton buds in plastic pouches.

Paper bags with POLICE EVIDENCE written on the side.

A woman appears at the door. She's timid looking, not in a uniform. She's really young. 'This is Alison Boneham, she specialises in sensitive cases like yours. You can call her Ally,' says Susan.

Ally has a burgundy high-necked sweater that looks sweaty and itchy, a swishy wool skirt with flowers on.

They don't look like her clothes.

They look like an old person's clothes.

Like my art teacher.

Mrs Shave.

She's awkward.

Why's she so awkward?

She makes me feel awkward.

Just by the way she looks at me.

Like I'm a specimen.

She asks me to stand up and she pushes the chair I'd been sitting on to the side. She unfolds a large sheet of paper and puts it on the floor, then places the four legs of the chair squarely in the middle of it.

'To catch any evidence,' she says quietly.

She thinks I'm going to moult.

Like I'm a dog.

She asks me to open my mouth, wider, wider. Her glasses have slid down her nose and are squeezing her nostrils together. She wipes one of the giant cotton buds around the inside of my mouth.

Under my tongue.

'Your tongue is blue,' she states.

She looks disgusted.

Dirty on the outside.

Dirty on the inside.

I have a blue tongue.

'Before we start, Coco, is there someone I can call for you? Let them know where you are? Someone who will help you?'

I shake my head.

'A family member? A friend? A colleague?'

No.

'A neighbour?'

I just look at my hands.

'Let's just get started with some easy questions, then, shall we?' Susan says lightly.

I hate false brightness.

She starts to tap onto the screen.

'So it's Coco James. C-O-C-O. J-A –'

'Chambers. My surname is Chambers.'

'Oh. I see. Is James your married name, then?' she says, smiling a smile that is odd when all we are doing is filling out a form.

'We're . . .'

No one would believe that someone like me would marry someone like you.

'Yes. We're . . . I'm not married,' I say.

'That was my next question . . . single, married, divorced, in a rela–' she says, smiling.

'Single,' I interrupt, taking another man-sized tissue.

She looks confused.

'He told all his friends we were married,' I whisper. 'Showed them a ring and everything. He said to say we were married, if anyone asked.'

'But you aren't married?' she questions.

'No, I'm not married. But he'll say we are. He'll say I'm making all this up.'

I'm going to say it was your idea.
   It's the sort of mad shit you would do.

'Who will, Coco? What is it you're supposed to be making up?' she says.

It's too confusing.

All of it.

I can't remember what I'm doing here.

'I don't know,' I say.

And then she's silent for a bit too.

'I'm sorry,' I whisper. 'Can you help me?'

You see, the thing is, babe, now we are married I can do what I like.
   You're mine now.

'Of course, we can help you,' she says, measured, trying not to show anything in her voice, 'but you need to tell us what has happened.'

'I need somewhere safe.'

'And that's because it's not safe at home?'

I nod. 'It's not safe at home,' I repeat back.

'Is that where you've come from. From home?' she says.

I nod.

'Because there's someone there who hurts you?'

I nod.

'Is it your partner?'

I look down.

'And have you been kept inside your home, against your will?'

I nod.

'Can you tell me where it is?'

'The laundry room,' I whisper.

You know where girls go who are bad, don't you?

'You've been locked up in the laundry room of your own home?' she says.

'Yes,' I say.

'I meant can you tell me where your home is?' she asks again.

'It's more of an outhouse,' I say.

'The laundry room?'

I nod.

'In the garden?'

'Yeah, like one of those toilets. From the olden days.'

You're a slut. SLUT. And that's what happens to sluts.

She is staring at me.

I cover my eyes.

I don't want her to see me.

'Can you tell me your partner's name then, Coco?'

Don't say anything.

Shut up.

Don't speak until I tell you to.

'I can't remember . . .'

There is no sound.

Just the humming of the heating system, the clicking of the radiator.

'Coco? Can you tell me where you live? Coco?'

My head starts to swim.

I think I might be sick any second now.

'Do you feel like you're in immediate danger, Coco? From your partner?'

You go to the police and you know I'll get you, don't you?

You can't hide from me.

They can't protect you from me.

I'm cleverer than they are.

'I don't know,' I say, seeing his face at the window.

But it's not his face.

There's no one there.

I wipe my eyes.

Licking my finger and running it under them.

Staring out of the window.

The sun comes out.

Branches with bright green leaves reaching up to the sky.

Blue sky.

He'll be behind that tree.

Waiting.

My finger tastes weird.

'Have you been injured, in the past?'

It's your fault.

You don't know when to shut up.

You'd better stick to the story, babe.

If you don't, you're just going to look even more crazy.

I look at my wrists.

The red marks are still there.

'I don't know.'

The bruise on my calf, hidden under my jeans, is throbbing.

'If I'm correct and you are reporting an incident of domestic violence, I'll need to conduct a Risk Identification Checklist. Is that OK?'

She is looking at me steadily. Ally is also looking at me, her eyes following my eyes.

Looking where I look.

At the floor, if I look at the floor.

At my hands, if I look at my hands.

'This is normal. It's for your own safety. Are you OK, Coco? Do you just want to have a chat for now?'

Just have a chat!

I think I've forgotten how to just have a chat.

I can't speak.

You don't even need to speak.

I can hear what you're thinking.

I know you better than you know yourself.

'Maybe to start with, would it be easier for you to tell us a little bit about yourself and maybe about your relationship? For instance . . .' Susan says, with her eyebrows raised, and her head on one side, like we were talking about fairy cakes or something, '. . . when did you first meet your partner?'

She smiles and nods the way grown-ups do with children when they want them to eat their broccoli.

Joanna appears at the door with three mugs of tea on a tin tray.

She puts the mug with the smiley face on it in front of me.

It's got milk in it.

Lactose intolerant.

I don't say anything.

You're just a silly little girl who's going to look like a liar.

LIAR, LIAR.

I start to cry again.

The gulps of tea take the lumps of sick back down.

When did I first meet him?

That was a different time.

I was sitting in this bar with Louisa.

It was about six weeks after Dad had died, right after Easter. I remember that.

One of the first really warm days of spring, the light streaming through the windows.

The Adelaide, it was called. We used to work there on weekends, while we were at uni. Just off the high street near Boots.

They had live bands on the top floor on Wednesdays. Even after we'd finished uni, we still hung out there. The barman gave us free drinks, whenever he could.

Since my dad died, we'd probably been going more.

I didn't like being at home so much, wasn't used to living on my own, wasn't used to not having to look after someone.

Louisa would come over, even stay sometimes. On the nights she didn't I'd dread opening the front door to a dark empty house.

Louisa told me to sell it, said I could get one of those posh penthouses overlooking the canal for the same money.

She got me all the details from the estate agents in Belsize Park.

And I was thinking about doing that.

I just felt like it was too soon.

It was only a few months after he'd died.

We raised £23K for the cancer unit that Dad was at. We'd been in the local paper, probably because a lot of people knew my dad in the area.

Made a nice story for them.

Front page.

Big picture.

He was only forty-eight.

He was a builder, that's how he knew everyone.

Sat on the town council too.

The people from the paper met us at The Adelaide. They got us to hold a massive cheque and then they took our picture and it went on the front page.

I said that already.

The policewoman puts her hand over mine and nods.

'Go ahead,' she says. 'You can talk to me about anything you like.'

But I'm still thinking about Louisa.

Going on and on like she always did about these new acrylics she'd had done.

The ends were dipped in glitter.

Her nails always looked awesome.

I'd never do acrylics.

It damages your nail beds.

Makes them weak.

Like I could care less about that now.

She's so funny.

She can talk for hours on her own without needing you to say anything back.

I'm the opposite.

I think it's cos she's from a big family and I'm an only child.

She's got seven brothers and sisters.

I wonder what she's doing.

I haven't seen her in two years.

Nearly two years.

Then this man walked in.

To The Adelaide, I mean, when I was with Louisa.

Older.

Like maybe mid-thirties, I thought at the time.

He was a proper man, if you know what I mean.

Not like the boys that me and Louisa were used to dating.

Fumblers, we used to call them.

None of them had a clue.

But this guy!

You could see his muscles under his jacket.

He had hairs creeping out from his shirt collar.

He flopped into a chair, leaned back and looked at the menu.

Then he flipped the menu back onto the table and motioned to the waitress.

'God, Clare,' Louisa had breathed. 'Get an eyeful of that, will you,' she'd said, without moving her lips. 'Did you ever ...' she said as he slipped off his jacket and slung it on the back of the chair.

He was near us. Near enough to hear what we were saying.

But he didn't even notice us.

Well, that's what we'd thought.

Why would he?

We were just a couple of kids.

He didn't look at us once.

The waitress came over and took his order.

She was all smiley with him and he was all smiley back with her.

I can remember thinking 'he really walks the walk and talks the talk.'

Like properly sexy.

Everything about him was confident.

He even had confident hair – thick, wavy, styled perfectly.

I'm sure he knew we were staring at him.

But he just seemed to enjoy that.

Like a cat lying in the sun.

So anyway, his food came.

He had a burger with fries. Lifted off the top bun, rearranged the tomato and gherkin, squared up the slice of cheese, aligned the bottom bun with the burger and replaced the top bun.

'Perfect,' Louisa said sighing.

He was tapping away at his phone the entire time.

Not interested in anyone or anything else.

'And the real trouble with glittery tips,' Louisa was saying, 'is that they like totally shed. All the time! I got blue glitter in my keyboard at work and everything.'

Some of the glitter, she was saying, had got into her eye the previous night and stuck to the inside of her eyelid. She'd spent three hours trying to get it out, and instead just got more glitter in. We were crying with laughter.

She'd wiped a tear away with a finger and then stopped suddenly.

'OMG,' she'd said. 'I've only gone and done it again!'

And we cracked up.

It was a funny story.

So much so that we'd forgotten about the good-looking man.

He put down his cutlery really loudly.

Our heads swivelled in his direction, simultaneously.

He drained his bottle of beer.

Slammed that on the wooden table too.

Motioned to the waitress to bring his bill.

And the entire time, I felt like I was electrified.

I felt like every cell in my body was on high alert.

My heart was beating faster.

The waitress was all smiley. He was all smiley.

Louisa kicked me under the table.

'You luuuurve him,' she said, and started making kissy noises.

Then her eyes widened.

'Shiiiiittttt,' she whispered. 'He's only headed our way,' she said, shutting her eyes like she hoped that the whole scene would just disappear.

'You are actually kidding me,' I said, trying to look out of the corner of my eye without turning my head.

He came up to the table, right next to me, and he leant down to Louisa, who was nearly expiring I can tell you, and he said, 'The trick with debris in your eye?'

He was American.

He said de-bree. '. . . is you fill a sink with water, OK, then you dunk your head into it and open your eyes under the water. Then the debris will just swim right out.'

Louisa was bright red.

She was staring at him.

He was looking at her.

And all I could do was breathe in his warm smell.

Sweat and tobacco.

A real-man smell.

He winked at her, drew himself up and turned to leave.

And I was thinking, don't just leave now. Come back. I'll never see you again.

And he left.

The front door of The Adelaide swung shut with a bang.

Louisa was holding her face, feeling her burning cheeks.

'He is off the scale . . .' she breathed, then stopped.

The doors had swung open again.

He was heading back to our table.

Not really looking at us.

Being really cool and smiling at the waitress again.

And then he handed me a card.

Me.

Not Louisa.

Me.

This was the first time he'd looked at me.

'You should come for a drink with me,' he said. 'This is my number,' he said.

He shrugged at Louisa.

'Sorry,' he said, 'you understand, right?'

She blushed.

And he turned and left again.

'Gareth James,' it said. 'Model/Actor.'

And there was his number.

'Holy cow,' said Louisa.

'But you don't even know my name,' I shouted after him, laughing.

'You're Coco,' he said, not altering his pace

'You're mistaken,' I shouted.

'You're Coco,' he repeated, laughing. 'I know it.'

'I'm not Coco, I'm Clare,' I said to Louisa, as though she didn't know, thinking that he wouldn't hear.

'Not anymore,' he shouted back, just as the doors closed behind him again.

'Coco.'

Detective Sergeant Clarke, is still staring at me.

I jump.

'Coco! Are you OK? You were going to tell me a bit about yourself?'

Wake up' bitch.

I need some food.

I look at the door of the Community Room.

There was a noise.

A noise on the other side of the door.

'It's only Barney,' she says. 'He's always having a barney. Come on now . . . Tell me all about you. How old are you?'

'Twenty-four,' I say.

My hands didn't used to look this old.

'Where do you live?'

Shut your mouth up.

I shake my head.
'Can you hear me?' she says.
I'm not sure I know where I am.

Coco . . .

Eight

Sally

She's in there now, that girl with the bare feet, in there with Sue. I expect Sue'll get the ambulance here right away, because, heavens above, that girl needs it. The boys are still here. Excitement over and probably forgotten, given the state of them.

Known Sue for twenty years, been friends off and on since then, but now I have to call her Sergeant; well, in here, I do. Ever since I came down from Liverpool, I've known her. That was the first time I met her and she didn't have a posh title back then, she was just a plain old PC, like, who made it her business to help DVs. They didn't have swanky women's refuges back then, either, didn't have hardly any at all, and the ones they did have were basic. And when I say basic, I mean dirty thin mattresses on the floor, ten girls to a room, one bathroom per floor and use of a shared kitchen, if you were lucky. There were no TVs and no gardens, no meeting rooms, no CCTV. If we got a break-in, and we got a lot of break-ins let me tell you, we all ganged up together, with whatever we could lay our hands on, and chased them off. I remember Tracey Fernshaw getting rid of one bloke with a squeezy bottle of washing-up liquid and a rolling pin! Seriously, no word of a lie. Mind you, most people would have

run a mile from Tracey Fernshaw, built like a brick shi– outhouse, she was.

They were free in those days too. No one expected you to fork
out for a safe place to put your head down, but you have to pay
these days. I'll be honest, I don't mind giving up £150 a week,
cos it seems a small price to pay for peace of mind.

When Terry gets out, Sue says it's best I go back into a refuge,
just temporary like, until we make sure he's not going to be playing silly buggers, and if he doesn't come looking for me, I can
go right back home again. I've got a nice place now, just behind
that Koko nightclub, on the corner of the High Street; it's what
Camden Palace used to be.

There's a new refuge opened near Regent's Park, someone in
the doctor's was telling me. It's two or three properties knocked
into one or something, in a mansion block that runs the length
of the street, they said. You've got to be off your rocker, I said.
Regent's Park is far too posh for a women's refuge, but apparently there's squats in half the block, the ones up nearest to
Chalk Farm tube; no one wants to live in them, couldn't even
sell them at knock-down prices, so the council got given some
of them. It's all being done up now, with state-of-the-art security
and everything. Whatever that means. Twenty two-bedroom
self-contained flats, all new, and shared use of kitchens, laundry,
TV room and social rooms. Social rooms. Social! In my day no
one wanted to be social, I can tell you. Too busy putting Savlon
on their cuts and concealer on their bruises.

I'm going to tell Sue about it, this new place by Regent's Park
Road, because I may as well go there as anywhere, if it's ready

that is. You're s'posed to go out of your area for a refuge, you know, that's the rule, make it harder for anyone to find you, if you know what I mean. Terry doesn't know I'm in North London, well, I don't think he does anyway, so where I stay's my business. Not unless Terry's brothers have kept track of me over the years, but I doubt that, fat lazy slobs they were. They'll be in their sixties now, for God's sake, even fatter and lazier, I'll bet, with a perma-tan and tattoos, and they'll do all-inclusives on the Costa del Sol, two weeks, twice a year, out of season, when there won't be any kids. I'll bet.

And I should think my Terry has got a lot better things to do getting out of prison after twenty years, than tracking me down. His mum will have been baking for weeks, freezing batches of cheese scones, and coffee and walnut cakes. I always hated coffee and walnut cake. She'll still be alive, you know; at least, she hadn't passed on last I heard. Eighty-one, she is, and she'll have been forcing herself to stay alive just to make those cakes for his coming home.

Some godforsaken young PCSO, wet behind the ears make no mistake, has just gone into the Community Room. They'll be trying to find out what happened to the poor girl.

You know what I think? I think this girl's typical DV if you ask me, all the signs.

What she could do with is a nice hot bath, that'll sort her, and a whole new set of clothes. Sue'll have something, cos they keep stuff here for situations like this. She's a specialist in DV, is Sue, or did I say that already? She's in charge of the Community Safety Unit for the whole of Central and North London.

Come to think of it, Sue'll need her to stay in her own clothes, to start with, if you know what I mean. They always do that with a DV.

Sue comes in to reception and Joanna slaps down her emery board and gives Sue a look like butter wouldn't melt. My mam would have said 'Get off the stage, you little madam, and take your awful sour puss with you.'

And then Sue leans over the desk and says very quietly to her, 'Next time, PC Lee – Joanna – can you make sure that victims take a priority? *Priority*. Understand? Priority over your coffee break, your nail filing, your eyebrows, *everything*! OK?'

Only I could hear, because I was the closest. I don't think the R.P. boys heard. They're all asleep, anyway.

'How am I meant to know she's a victim?' says Joanna, jerking her head around like Little Miss I-Know-Everything, little cow.

'You open your eyes, that's how,' Sue hisses, between her teeth.

Nine

DS Clarke

Over the years DS Clarke has had many hours of training working with DVs, and running the Community Safety Unit for Central and North London. Lately this had included one-to-one cognitive-behavioural therapy with a trained practitioner. She'd sucked her teeth the first time she'd heard about Dialectical Behaviour Therapy – something about integrating the emotional mind with the reasonable mind. Smacked of American do-gooders. And if there's one thing DS Clarke can't stand it's American do-gooders. Billy Graham set her straight on that. And Tom Cruise. She often wonders what happened to Tom Cruise and whether he is still making those action films.

But actually, the premise of DBT was right: allow the emotional mind full rein, then gradually, gradually introduce the reasonable mind to teach rational thinking. Soothe the emotional mind but listen to good sense.

Hence, she always let the emotion burn out of highly charged situations. She'd listen and listen. Only … sometimes her own emotions got the better of her. She was, after all, only human. And, when she found herself getting emotional, she'd remove herself from the situation, let off steam, then – and only then – resume.

The brief conversation with PC Joanna Lee at reception was like a valve slipping off a pressure cooker.

DS Clarke re-enters the Community Room and sits down again opposite Coco. Ally had packed up the forensic kit, the self-seal bags and swabs, so the room looks back to normal. Bland. Except for the girl. She looks up, surprised, as though she hadn't noticed her go and hadn't noticed her come back either. Or worse, DS Clarke thought to herself, she didn't really know who or where she was.

Take respectful command. Be courteous, be kind but take control.

She breathes out, slowly, noticing again the strange chemical smell. Bleach? Turps? She changes the subject.

'Do you have a job at all, Coco?' she says.

The 'at all' DS Clarke employed there is standard waffle to deflect the directness of the question.

DS Clarke's giving the victim the appearance of control. What she's really doing is protecting the individual from events that can't be consciously accessed. Suppressed thoughts that may bring anxiety along with them. DS Clarke often does this without thinking.

Coco's eyes swim with vague memories that eluded her.

'A job . . .' she says. 'I did have a job . . .'

And then her eyes glaze over.

'I can't remember . . .' she says.

'Are you warm enough in your dressing gown?' DS Clarke says, changing the subject again.

And then Coco switches. Just like that.

'Only morons say dressing gown, you thick bitch,' she says.

DS Clarke tries not to show her shock and examines her own nails for a full thirty seconds, before looking up.

'Is that what you think? Or is that what someone else thinks?' says DS Clarke, quietly.

No reply.

'Did someone tell you to say that Coco?'

'What?' says Coco. What did I just say?

Ten

Coco

'You're doing OK,' Susan says.

That policewoman.

Smiling.

Nodding.

'Look, I know it may not feel like it right now, but you're safe here,' she says, taking a slurp of tea.

I have a sip.

I can't decide if it's the milk that makes me feel sick or if I just feel sick anyway. Maybe it's the lactose intolerance.

'So,' she says. 'If you're ready, we can start the Risk Assessment.'

I nod.

'And we can stop at any time.'

I nod.

'You hold the reins on this.'

I don't know what she's talking about.

I nod.

'So, all you need to say is "Yes", "No" or "Don't know". OK?'

'Yes,' I whisper.

'OK, are you injured at this moment?' she says.

I shake my head.

'Is that a no?' Susan says.

'No,' I say.

She taps the screen.

'But my dressing gown,' I say.

*I'VE TOLD YOU, ONLY MORONS SAY DRESSING GOWN,
YOU THICK BITCH.*

'I did accidentally get paraffin on my dre – bathrobe.'

'Paraffin?'

'Yes, it's called a bathrobe.'

'How did you get the paraffin on your bathrobe?'

'It was soaked, you see. But it's dried. Evaporated. But it was soaked.'

I looked down the V of the dressing gown. Red bra.

ALL UNDERWEAR RED, FROM NOW ON, GOT IT?

Put it on.

Now.

Put it on.

PUT.

IT.

ON.

Now, guess what?

I'm going to have to fuck you all over again.

The paraffin has stained it blue.

'How did you get the paraffin on your bathrobe?' she repeats.

He probably didn't really mean to do it. He was having one of those black days. Like people do sometimes. My dad had black days.

But not like Gareth's.

'Did someone pour the paraffin on your bathrobe?' she says.

'I don't know,' I say.

She doesn't say anything.

She just waits.

Like she likes waiting.

Big, empty pauses.

'It dripped down, you see,' I say.

'Was someone intending to injure you?'

'I'm not sure,' I say.

A corner of skin on the side of my thumb is beginning to peel off.

It's bleeding.

My index fingernail is too broken to pick it.

I try to chew it off.

'I remember it went in my hair and dripped down.'

It's always bleeding.

This thumb and the other one.

It tastes of bleach.

And paraffin.

'How did it get in your hair?' she asks.

Coco.

'Did someone pour it over your head?' she asks.

Coco.

   Answer me.

   Stop pretending.

'Did your partner pour it on you?' she asks.

Coco.

   Wake up.

'Was it intentional?' she asks.

Coco.

   Stop pretending.

   I'm hungry.

'How did you escape further injury?' she asks.

Coco.

   Get up!

She lets out a long sigh and stops asking.

   'He ran out of matches,' I say.

   'What do you mean?' she says.

   'You asked how I escaped further injury,' I whisper.

   She nods.

   'Well, he ran out of matches,' I say.

   She looks at me, confused.

'Matches?'

'He was flicking the matches at me and then they ran out.'

She looks at me hard.

Staring.

Not blinking.

Then she stares at the floor.

'I think we should say yes to that then,' says Susan. 'To the question, I mean. Yes, it was intentional.'

She scribbles something else down.

'I hid the other box,' I say. 'I think I did. Don't remember where, though.'

DS Clarke breathes out sharply.

'You hid the other box,' she says. 'Look, I'm sorry I have to ask you this stuff.'

I nod.

'I'm here to help you,' she says.

And she pauses for a second, then looks down.

'Question number two. Are you frightened? Yes, no or don't know.'

'Don't know,' I say.

'What are you afraid of,' she says, 'violence or injury?'

Violence or injury?

'Aren't they the same thing?' I say.

Well aren't they?

Violence always ends in injury, doesn't it?

Does for me.

'Is it usual, Coco . . .'

'Clare,' I say. 'Can you call me Clare?'

I told you.

    Your name is Coco.

    Because I said so, that's why.

'I thought . . .' she says.

    'Clare,' I say. 'He says Coco. But I'm Clare. My name is Clare.'

    'Clare Chambers,' she says, retyping the name at the top of the screen.

    She stares at me for just a second too long.

    And I think I can see a tear welling up in her eye.

    I wonder what the hell she's crying for.

    'Is it usual, Clare, for, um, violence to end in injury.'

    'Yes, that's how it happens,' I say. 'His moods . . . I make him cross . . . I get so tired. And clumsy.'

    'Sometimes it feels like I'm watching a film. Like it's not really me. That I've remembered it all wrong. It is actually all my fault. I try to be the right person for . . .'

How do you always manage to do everything wrong, bitch?

'It's not your fault,' she says.

    Smiling.

    Nodding.

This floor is NOT CLEAN.

    You've not done it properly.

    It doesn't meet my standards.

    YOU TOTALLY ASKED FOR THIS.

'It's not,' she's saying.

Smiling.

Shaking her head.

'I'm sorry,' I say.

'I'll do better next time.'

The tea.

The heat.

The questions.

Him screaming in my head.

'Who are you talking to?' Sue says.

There's a noise in reception.

The door handle moves.

The sky has gone dark.

He's out there, I can feel it.

The tree has got closer.

The branches are brushing against the window.

My feet.

The sweat.

The stench of paraffin.

The sick rises up again, silently but violently, and suddenly I vomit over my dressing gown and jeans.

A splat sound as it hits the floor.

And I slide off the chair.

Coco, my darling.

You do know I love you.

DON'T YOU?

Babe.

Wake up.

Eleven

Sally

Out of nowhere, Sue yanks open the door and starts yelling her head off like the world is about to end.

'Get an ambulance,' she screams. 'Joanna!'

The boys and me, we've got no bloody idea what's going on, but police appear through every door, and it feels like it's an episode of *Prime Suspect* or something and I wouldn't have been a bit surprised if Dame Helen Mirren didn't skip through the door at any second, it's that mad. And the lads are all panicking, backs pressed against their chairs, cos they think they've got done for something, and for once they haven't.

'Get the ambulance on the phone. Ring ahead to the hospital. Tell them we've got suspected ingestion of chemicals,' she shouts to Joanna. 'Young woman. Early twenties. Unconscious. Breathing. And someone get me water and tissue. Quickly!'

In the toilet, I yank a thick pile of paper towels out of the dispenser and Ryan has found his senses and filled up a couple of cups with water. The girl is lying on the floor and Sue is washing the sick off her face, gently dousing her in water.

Next to her head, there's a spreading pool of blue sick, yeah blue sick, mixed with brown tea and bubbles.

Then the paramedics arrive, a couple of nice-looking lads in green uniforms and they have her sorted in no time. Done her vitals, put a drip in, and next thing, they stretcher her out; she's coming round but we can't see her face cos it's covered in these gauze bandages and, as the stretcher comes right by us, I can see her fingers moving, picking at the skin on the side of her thumb. They've put a silver foil sheet around her and a blanket on top of that to warm her up.

Sue follows, nodding quickly at me as she goes. We understand each other. Ingestion of chemicals, no wonder she was shaking.

Once they've all gone it's weirdly quiet.

Calm after the storm.

And, now everything's properly late and I'm still sitting here and Sue has disappeared into that side room with what looks like a DV caseworker – you know the type, all tea and tampons.

And guess what, the lads still haven't gone in yet either. They're in for one of them assessment sessions with the CJIT. That's the Criminal Justice Integrated Team in case you didn't know. Fancy-shmancy.

This is how it's supposed to work. They get pulled in for something like, I don't know, shoplifting, breaking and entering, you know – something they've done to buy their heroin, and now, instead of charging them, they get put on these Drug Intervention Programmes. They have to go to these assessment sessions and if they don't turn up, or turn up late, or have the wrong attitude or something, then they get charged for the crime, but if they do as they're told, go the pharmacist, stick on the methadone programme, and attend the 'information and education session on drugs and drug related issues' with the CJIT worker, then they don't get charged. In theory, it gets them off the heroin and keeps them out of prison.

This is how it really works. They get the meth from the pharmacist, and instead of swallowing it they store it in the side of their cheek or under their tongue, then soon as they get out, they spit it into a pot and sell it on . . . to buy more heroin with. Seriously. And in case you want to know, that's called 'spit meth'. It's a bit cheaper than meth – but not by much. And it comes with extra phlegm.

Sue says the Drug Intervention Programme makes the police look better because it lowers the arrest statistics. She said that, not me. Instead of getting charged for theft and possession or whatever, they get a conditional caution and 'an individual care plan'. It's very popular. You can see by the queues.

'What'd you say to her?' I whispered to Barney, as I nod towards Joanna. He's half asleep next to me.

I know Barney, right? Barnaby Pickard, he's called. He's all right, for an R.P. boy. He was a bouncer, back in the day – ran the security at Camden Palace. Used to see him, on my way back from the shops and the like. Always said hello, always had a smile. Nice enough bloke he was then, right up until they did him for GBH and he lost his job. Not his fault, if you ask me. I mean, if you're a bouncer you gotta expect to have to bounce some people, every now and again, right? Anyhow, seems like he'd ejected some lairy, drunk teenager who was the son of someone-or-other who's posh or something, and the next thing he's fired and his wife's kicked him out. So then he doesn't have a job, doesn't see his wife, doesn't see his kids, nowhere to live. There but for the grace of God, that's what I think.

'When?' he mumbles.

'Before,' I say. 'What'd you say to her before?'

'You heard,' he says.

'Not that, the other thing, the thing you mouthed at her, I saw you do it.'

'Mind yer own,' he says, without even opening his eyes.

'Go on,' I say, nudging his arm.

'I told her I know where she lives.'

'Did ya?'

I laugh out loud.

'Yeah.'

'Really?' I say, still laughing.

'Yeah.'

'Do ya?' I say, cos you know what, he's a nice sort of bloke underneath all that shit.

'Nah,' he says.

We go quiet.

'What d'ya say it for then?' I ask, dabbing at my eyes with a bit of hanky.

'Cos she's a hard-nosed bitch and you can always find out where someone lives, can't you. That poor kid. She don't deserve to be treated like that.'

Shite, it's gone eleven! I've been here over two hours and I just got to wait, cos what on earth else am I s'posed to do? Said she'd always try to see me right away, Sue did, cos she doesn't want me hanging around her waiting room, where there are loads of crims all the time.

'Last thing we want is for someone to identify you to one of Terry's lot,' she said.

I don't know why everybody's getting paranoid all of a sudden. I mean, he's not even out yet, not till sometime next month, Sue says.

'It all depends on what she is given to swallow,' I say to Barney, who was still upset about the girl and the sick and everything.

'How'd you know she didn't swallow it herself?' he goes.

'Nah,' I say. 'This is a DV, for sure.' And then I say, 'I s'pose she might have drunk it herself,' thinking back to how many times over the years, stuck on my own in London, I'd considered the same thing, on account of Terry and everything.

'They'll pump her out,' I say, 'then they'll phone around for her, find where there's a space for her to stay. Not round here, mind; somewhere really far away so he won't be able to find her. That's what they usually do. They put me in one round here, and I was from Liverpool.'

'No shit. Would never've known.'

'All the best people are Scousers. Aigburth Road, that's the posh bit, best place in the world, no word of a lie.'

'You like it so much, what you still doing here?'

I don't answer, cos I like him and all, and I've known him for years, and he's never even asked, and I respect someone for that, you know. And anyway, what am I going say to him? Seriously? That I married a murdering psychopath and I've been hiding most of my life since? So I pretend to look for something in my handbag.

He doesn't notice, though. Well, I don't think he does, cos his nose is still buried in his coat collar.

'They're not bad these refuges,' I say more to myself than anyone, cos Barney's well away. 'Straightaway, they'll put her in a refuge,' I say.

He still doesn't reply.

'You get your own room, you get use of a kitchen, there's television rooms. There's a new one up Regent's Park way, very modern and everything, with CCTV and you get therapy things there now you know, like talking therapies – they're good, talking therapies. Not that I need them, but the CCTV wouldn't go amiss, that's for sure. If I can get a place.'

Not listening.

It's bloody boiling in here, I'm not surprised everyone's asleep. I'm dog tired myself, after last night, when I didn't sleep a wink the entire bloomin' night.

'How'd you know?' Barney goes. 'It might not be DV. She could've got beaten up by a stranger.' He shuts up then, while I'm thinking how I know it's got to be a domestic. And just when I'm about to give him an answer I hear his breathing go slow and deeper.

The girl behind the counter, Joanna, is still filing her nails. She's staring at the clock as it ticks by and Ryan is snoring.

'I thought she'd done something with paraffin,' Barney goes. 'Did you?'

'I could smell it on her. Just putting it out there,' he says. 'Felt it in my bones.'

'Who're you then, Sherlock Holmes?' I say.

His head bobs back down, meaning all the jungle juice lads are now fully fast asleep.

A police officer pushes through the double doors; he's only young, tall and lanky, you know, like a string bean, face-full of spots and not the full shilling, if you ask me. He's clinging on to a clipboard like it's a swimming float.

'Mr Pickard,' he says in the quietest voice known to mankind, no word of a lie.

The line of grey overcoats barely moves, just a tiny up, down, up, down in time with the breathing.

'Mr Pickard. Barney Pickard,' he says a fraction more loudly, and Ryan, down at the end, starts snoring hard like an old hog.

'C'mere to me,' I say to him and he edges my way as though he thinks I'm going to take a bite out of him. 'This is Mr Pickard,' I say and I jab my thumb into Barney's chest.

Barney jumps up, jolted awake.

'Is it my turn already? I've only been here what, two days? Be time for my next assessment by the time I get outta here,' he says, pushing his hands on his knees to lever himself up. 'Will I be seeing you around, Sally-Ann?' he says to me.

'Call me Sal,' I mumble. 'Maybe, maybe not,' I say a little louder.

He's nice. I know what you're thinking, but for a meth addict, he's nice. He deserves a break.

'Excuse me, Joanna?' I say, going up to the counter where Little Miss Misery Guts still looks like she's sucking on a wasp. 'Can I just go into the Community Room while I wait for Sue?'

'You think it's a private club an' all?' says Joanna, without missing a beat, same bored expression she used for the DV girl.

'Anyone needs it, I'll get out the way,' I say.

Shit, it smells bad in the Community Room, what with the petrol or whatever it is, and the sick; not a nice combination, I can tell you. And it's so unbelievably hot, I'll need to take off my anorak.

'God, Sal. I'm so sorry. I completely forgot about you,' says Sue, rushing through the door, slamming it behind her, enough to give me a heart attack. 'Christ, the smell in here! Sorry to have kept you.'

'Don't worry yourself, Sue, I've been fine. That girl get to the hospital, did she?' I say.

'She's out of danger. Well, stable, they said. Bit of a wait-and-see while that stuff goes through her system.'

'Petrol or paraffin or something, is it?'

'Well, it's not confirmed but yes, looks like it.'

'Poor little kid,' I say.

'If they call,' she says, picking up her mobile, 'you won't mind?'

'No! No, love. Course not.'

'So, you all ready for next month? You want some tea?' she goes, then, 'Joanna,' she shouts, opening the door a crack, 'do us a couple of teas again? Just knock me when they're ready.' She closes the door.

'Christ, it really stinks in here,' she says.

'It's not in my job description to make everyone tea,' shouts Joanna, through the door.

'Remind me to add it in,' Sue shouts back.

She reaches for her laptop and starts tapping on the keyboard.

'So, the latest update. Where's your file ... There you are.' Click. 'Parton. Sally-Ann Parton.' Click. 'You've decided not to change your name, right? You've always stuck with your maiden name? Click. 'Terry Mansfield.' Click.

'The methadone lads said I've got a lot in common with Dolly Parton,' I say, smirking a bit. 'Still got it, right!'

'If we ever had it,' says Sue, putting down the laptop as Joanna yells that the tea's outside.

'Speak for yourself, Sue. They'd be queueing up, if there were any good men left in the world,' I say.

'You looked thick as thieves with Barney when I walked through this morning,' she goes, suddenly serious like. 'You should be careful there.'

'Do me a favour!' I say.

'I am doing you a favour telling you to be careful,' she goes. 'He's an addict, Sal. However nice addicts seem, they will always shop you for a hit.'

'Don't be feckin' ridiculous, there's nothing going on with Barney. Known him for years and he's a good bloke, s'all. Deserves a break. I thought you were the one that was always going on about giving them the benefit of the doubt? That's what you said, your exact words!'

'Benefit of the doubt is not necking with him.'

'Oh, shut up, Sue, get off the stage, will ya? You're just trying to wind me up.'

Her phone buzzes and she looks at me and I nod and stare into my tea so it looks like I'm not listening, though obviously I can't help but bloomin' listen.

'Well, tell them to wait until she wakes up,' she goes and then she pauses, 'when she *next* wakes up then.' She sighs. 'Has anyone been round to the house?' She listens. 'Yes, we've got the address. Just see if he's at home. Make him nervous.' She listens again. 'Just go and have a look at him. See if there's anything unusual.' She puts the handset down on the table and looks at it for a bit, like she's concentrating, then she remembers that I'm there and she looks back at the laptop.

'Still not properly confirmed,' she says. 'Sometime this month though. I don't think you should come here next week – he could have people out looking for you, for all we know.'

'There's this new refuge near Regent's Park' I say, knowing that she'll think I should go out of the area, but I may as well give it a try, since it's new.

'I saw it last week,' she says. 'It's nice. You'll like it. All self-contained flats. And the security is beyond ridiculous. State-of-the-art. Apparently. CCTV everywhere. Internal locking system like Fort Knox. They even have a direct line to the station.'

'Like Batman?'

'Like Batman!'

'So, you're not worried I should leave the area?'

'Of course, you should. But if it were me . . . Right by the zoo? Apparently, you can hear the wolves howling at night.'

'Great.'

'Have you told work?'

'Yeah, they were fine about it, no difference to them, where I am. External examiners all work from home anyway. It's just all the boring AQA meetings that you have to go in for, and I'm not sorry to be missing them, I can tell you. It's not busy right now, either. I've told the head and they'll email stuff to me.'

'You should avoid Camden Town altogether, though, if you do go out, just till we see where he goes. We'll have him tagged the first couple of weeks, anyway. I bet he'll just go home. Old stomping ground. See his mother. She's still alive, right? That's the address he's given.'

'What do you mean, tagged?' I say.

'Police monitoring ankle bracelet. To keep an eye on where he is.'

'That's not normal, is it? I thought they just did that with young kids.'

'On violent offenders, sometimes.'

'You mean ones that aren't sorry? Do they work?'

'Tags? Of course, they bloody work! We wouldn't have them if they didn't work, would we?'

Her phone buzzes again. She lifts the headset to her ear. 'Hang on a minute, Mark,' she goes. 'Listen, I'll call you,' she whispers to me. 'I'll get in touch with them and find out the exact day he's being released and call you. Don't come here next week, though, Sal. Let me visit you in your new flat, if you're in it by then.'

She's already packing up her stuff, with her phone pressed against her ear.

'Catch you later,' she mouths at me. 'Yes, try Yorkshire!' she says into the phone. 'Of course it's cold. It's cold anywhere north of Watford.'

I go for a pee. It's even hotter in the ladies loo than it is in the waiting room. My scalp is sweating and my hair's gone flat.

'Excuse me, Sally-Ann,' says Joanna, the bitch PC with the miserable face shouts through the toilet door. 'D S Clarke just asked you to come back in. The release date you were talking about has been brought forward, apparently.'

Twelve

DS Clarke

DS Clarke takes one of the standard unmarked police vehicles from the underground car park in Lyme Street, to drive to the Royal Free Hospital. The queues on Kentish Town Road are mental as usual, so against her better judgement (and Met rules), she blue lights it down the bus lane. Just as she pulls into Camden Street, Livvy from the office puts through the second call she'd had that morning from the governor of Liverpool nick.

She can and does recite Terry Mansfield's prison number off by heart, again, for Governor Morris, who seems confused by his own long-term prisoner release protocol. Yes, of course he's tagged. Yes, of course he will be required to visit his local station or release officer once per week. Yes, he has had the requisite psychological assessment.

'So, he is already released, Governor Morris?'

'I believe so.'

'You believe so, or you *know* so?'

'I know so.'

'And you're sure?'

'You are beginning to try my patience, sergeant.'

'Governor Morris. It has greatly tested *my* patience that you have released a prisoner without following any kind of protocol. Anyone convicted of a violent offence, serving a sentence—'

'Are you trying to tell me my job, DS Clarke?'

'It sounds as though I need to, Governor Morris. I would have thought—'

'Langlands is your boss, is that correct? I'm sure—'

'Governor Morris, may I ask if you have followed procedure for Home Detention Curfew or—'

'Sergeant! Enough!'

'Has he shown any remorse at all, Governor Morris?'

There's a silence.

'Sorry, DS Clarke?'

'Does he regret what he did?' DS Clarke says, with a sigh.

'I'm not at liberty, DS Clarke, to give you that information.'

'Then would you kindly put me through to someone that is,' she says.

'DS Clarke – would you kindly—'

'Stop messing with me, Mr Morris. Is he a danger to his ex-wife? That's all I want to know.'

Governor Morris ends the conversation by slamming the phone down.

Sal's was one of a few cases that has stuck with DS Clarke over the years, probably because, as a young PC, she'd not been so close to such a violent killing before, nor experienced the tangible fear of young women all over the UK who, overnight, became afraid of such an apparently motiveless crime. Even in London.

Only it wasn't.

TERRY MANSFIELD.
Prisoner number 127963
Committed to life imprisonment in HMP Liverpool.
Mandatory tariff of 20 years for the murder of Hayley
Thomas and the serious assault of Mrs Sally-Ann
Mansfield.

DS Clarke remarks to herself that twenty years have flown by and wonders how Sal, who is similarly committed to a life unencumbered by full-time male partners, has managed to pull herself together, on her own. She was only twenty-one at the time. Not so different to our new girl. Clare. Coco. Whatever she calls herself.

DS Clarke rates Clare's chances, as she tended to do with all her cases, in order to prioritise. She gives her fifty-fifty. She hadn't got enough of a picture of the damage done by the paraffin, or the extent of her psychological state. So PTSD at best.

She calls Livvy back from the car phone. She wants to know if anyone has reported Clare missing.

No one has.

She locks the car and walks up from the car park next to A & E.

Images of the girl keep appearing in her head. Her almost transparent skin, fine and dry as paper; the blue veins rippling over the thin bones in her hands, making her look older, more broken.

How come no one has reported her missing? There must have been *someone* missing her. There must be other members of the family. Friends. Colleagues. Someone.

Not missed this morning.

Not missed for two years.

She goes over the details again.

> *CLARE CHAMBERS (also known as Coco James).*
> *DOB 26/3/1996*
> *ADDRESS: 289, Oval Road, Camden. NW1 4BS*
> *Reported: grievous bodily harm by partner Mr Gareth James. With intent to cause serious injury.*
> *Incident report: collapsed at the station. Believed to have ingested toxic chemicals.*
> *INJURIES: chemical and thermal burns.*

She needs more from the hospital.

As she arrives at the doors of A & E, she opens a text from PC Halsall who has submitted a report on the Oval Road Property: RKNR.

Repeated. Knocking. No. Reply.

She tuts to herself.

What do they expect, she thinks – some kind of sodding welcoming committee?

Thirteen

Clare

Babe. Let me help you up.
  Babe.
  Come on.
  Give me your hand.
  Come on.
  You can trust me.
  Oh shoot!
  I've got real butterfingers today.
  Now look what you've made me do.
  I've accidentally gone and kicked you in the fucking head.
  Jee-sus.
  Be more careful where you're putting your head next time.

Breathe.
  I'm not sure where I am.
  Slowly.
  I'm on a bed.
  There's a thin nylon curtain with pink and purple flowers decorating it.
  Daisies, I think.

Calm.

There's a plastic mask over my nose and mouth, attached by little bits of elastic.

The elastic is digging into my cheeks.

Pressing my ears.

A bag of clear liquid is strapped up to a metal stand next to me.

A tube runs into my hand.

Dripping.

The end is hidden under a plaster.

I have a gown on.

Through the curtain I can see the shadow of a person.

A man.

Coco. Open your eyes.

Wake up, babe.

No, you don't need to go to the hospital.

Stop making a fuss.

I sit up, too quickly.

My head starts to swim.

I edge myself back down.

'We just need her to take things very slowly,' a man's voice says. 'She's had a rough time.'

'We need a statement,' says another voice.

A woman.

Impatient.

I feel my heart start to race.

I hear the words 'ingestion of chemicals,' but the blood is rushing around my head so fast, I can't think straight.

The curtain is pulled back.

The metal hooks scrape on the rail.

I shut my eyes quick.

A shadow leans over me.

'Can't you give her something?' says the woman.

'We have. That's why you can't talk to her.'

'I meant so we can talk to her!'

'I know what you meant,' says the man.

The doctor.

'All you detectives are the same. Just leave her alone for a while. A few hours. You stay in the corridor outside.'

There's the sound of footsteps.

'And who are you?' says the doctor, sighing.

'I'm Celia Barrett,' says another voice, 'DV caseworker from Camden.'

'Oh good. From the station? She knows you, right?'

'No, I haven't met her yet. She collapsed before I got there. Sorry I'm late. Traffic was bad. How is she?'

'Well, she's stable.'

I hear a pen scratching on paper.

Clean on the inside.

'It doesn't actually look like it's as serious as we had first thought. She has significant thermal burns on her shoulders, upper thighs, stomach, labia.'

Scratching pen.

'She has some skin irritation and chemical burning on her upper arms and upper legs. Paraffin, by the smell of it. She has pigment lightening and permanent tissue damage on her hands.'

He stops writing.

'If I had to guess, I'd say her hands have been over-exposed to bleach. Seen something similar before in Queensland.'

He continues writing.

'She has bruising. There's swelling on the back of her head and an abrasion that's also been irritated by paraffin. The abrasion is probably a month old.'

He stabs the paper with a full stop and there's the sound of metal meeting metal and I watch between half-closed eyes as he clips the board to the end of the bed.

'Would have been nasty at the time. Doesn't look like it was properly treated.'

He lowers his voice to nearly a whisper.

Professional discretion.

'I believe there are several signs of long-term abuse and she's significantly malnourished. She could do with gaining weight. At least ten kilos. You'll need to get the nutritionist down to see her.'

Between my eyelashes I can see his outline against the curtain.

His hands are on his hips.

'She's been catheterised and had gastric suction. Whatever she ejected at the station is being tested. We won't know what damage has been done until she wakes up. Everything else, so far normal, we're waiting until we get her bloods back.'

'Has she been washed? The sergeant at the station mentioned the paraffin.'

'Yes, it's been noted. She still needs to be examined by the police doctor. We need to record all her injuries.'

'What time will that be?'

'They're setting it up now. She seems to have been lucky.'

'Lucky!' says the woman, letting out a cry.

He sighs.

A heavy sigh, like the weight of the world is on his shoulders.

'I don't mean that. You know what I mean!'

He sounds tired.

Exhausted.

'The burns on her body aren't so bad. They'll blister over the next forty-eight hours. And she may not be able to taste much, depending on what it was she actually drank. If she has oesophageal burning it will hurt like hell for a while. But probably, hopefully nothing long-term. Someone gave her some tea at the station, apparently. The milk might have helped. Reduces the acid.'

There's the sound of tidying, bin lid flipping open and shut.

'People can get addicted to paraffin, you know. Saw a girl last year who'd been drinking it for years – you can develop a tolerance over time. We only found out because she collapsed and we investigated why her stomach was so distended.'

'What! You don't actually think this girl drank the paraffin intentionally?' says the woman, sounding affronted. Like she's about to jump on her feminist soapbox.

'I didn't say it was definitively paraffin, did I?' he hisses. 'No. I didn't. And I'm a doctor not a psychic.'

He's annoyed with her, tight-lipped suddenly.

'I'll be back later. Keep an eye on her and let me know if there's anything. You know. If she gets agitated . . .'

'She could be in shock, could she?'

'You don't wake up every day, in hospital covered in burns, with an infected head wound and suspected oesophageal scarring. She's still too sick to talk. She *shouldn't* talk. Do you get that? So don't let that PC in, no matter how much she insists. Not yet.'

'Yes, OK,' the woman says.

'And don't you go trying to get statements out of her either.'

The door clicks open and shut.

I don't want to hear your voice, right!
  Shut the fuck up.

Later, I open my eyes and the woman is sitting in the chair next to me, wearing a home-made cardigan, holding a leaflet.

It's an armchair with a high back, made of grey plastic. Wipeable.

I can't read what it says on the leaflet.

She's tapping her right forefinger on the wooden arm.

'Hello, Coco,' she says, noticing I'm looking at her.

Smiling, nodding.

Is smiling and nodding at the same time part of the training?

'I mean Clare.' She blushes. 'Sorry, some confusion on the top of your form.'

I blink. I've got bandages around my neck and mouth.

'I'm Celia,' she says. 'I'm your caseworker. I'm here to help you through this period of distress.'

In a home-made cardigan like my nan used to wear.

'I'm part of a support team that helps women like you get their lives back on track. Victims of domestic violence. Do you understand. Just blink if you do. Don't try to talk.'

She puts her hand on my shoulder, in a caring way.

I wish she wouldn't.

Why shouldn't I touch you?

You're my wife now.

I'll touch you whenever I like.

'Clare, you're in hospital,' she says. 'Blink if you understand.'

I blink.

'You collapsed in the police station. Do you remember?'

I blink again.

'You're in good hands, here. The doctor says you're doing very well, but you mustn't try to talk.'

Smiling, nodding.

I feel a tear trickle past my temple and into my hair.

'It's OK, dear. We're going to get you all sorted.'

She mops the side of my head with a tissue, looks at the leaflet.

'I'm going to tell you what we can help happen next. If there's anything you don't understand, it's OK, I can go through it all again later, if you want me to. Is that OK for you?'

I'm sure she means well.

'Everything we are about to talk about is in this leaflet,' she says, showing me the leaflet she'd been holding earlier.

It says on the front 'Information for victims of crime'.

It's just a form in black and white.

No smiley pictures.

No jokey cartoons.

No sugar-coating.

'I'm going to leave it here for you so you can read it at any time,' she says.

Nodding again and smiling.

Smiling and nodding.

'So there are two parts to this. Firstly, we want you to get better and be safe.'

I'll find you anywhere.

You know I will.

You will never be safe.

You know that.

'Secondly, we want to follow up with an investigation so that we can prevent any more of what's been going on. We'll have to ask you some more questions that you might find uncomfortable. Do you understand that, Clare?'

I nod.

The bandages on my neck pull.

'A police doctor would need to examine you. Properly. You know. But only if you give your permission.'

I nod again.

'They need to record the evidence. They will need to take pictures.'

Pictures?

What for?

What do they need pictures for?

'And a detective will be appointed to your case and will come and take a statement from you. That might mean you have to answer the same questions again, Clare, but it's necessary. We need to get enough evidence so we can prosecute, so she'll need your full cooperation. She's waiting outside.'

Evidence.

Prosecute.

'Evidence?'

I mouth the word.

No sound comes out.

She's smiling, nodding, smiling, nodding.

'Prosecute?'

'Your partner. Whoever did this to you,' she says.

YOU ASKED FOR THIS, BITCH!

Silence.

Dark.

'Clare, can you hear me?'

The caseworker in the homemade cardigan has gone.

There's another woman. A different one. Grey hair. Pink blouse. Broken veins on her cheeks. Wild hair.

'Do you know where you are?'

I half nod.

'I'd like you to sit up now. Just slowly. That's it.'

She presses a remote control, staring out of the window, as though she's thinking about something else.

There's a click, and the top half of the bed starts to hum and rattle me into an upright position. The remote's joined to the side of the bed by a springy spiral cord.

The pillows behind my head slip a little and there's a wet patch under my neck; the bandages across my chin are dragging on the corner of my mouth.

The oxygen mask has gone.

She clips the remote back on the bed frame.

It's a private room with views of the sky down one wall, a windowsill in front.

Some water in a plastic jug, a plastic glass and an orange.

Just one orange.

On its own.

Black plastic cushions for somewhere to sit.

The sky is a rectangle of flat grey.

No discernible clouds.

No blue.

The occasional bird, nothing else.

There's a window to my left as well, with blinds. Through the slats I can see into the corridor. There's a row of chairs with a policewoman sitting at one end, speaking into her phone. She has a black-and-white checked scarf fanning out from under her white collar.

Her lipstick makes her mouth look mean.

She's watching me out of the corner of her eye.

Pretending not to.

Eyes down.

I'm covered with a sheet but there's some kind of box under the sheet where my feet should be.

The woman with the broken veins on her face seems more interested in the sky.

'It's for your leg,' she says, flicking her eyes my way. 'You have severe bruising on your right calf.'

See this piece of wood.

    How hard do you think this piece of wood is?

    Go on, Coco.

    Have a guess.

    It's a game.

    Have a guess.

    I said HAVE A GUESS.

    Oh no.

    Sorry.

    I bet it's harder than you thought, right?

    Is it harder than you thought?

    Is it?

'Probably done in the last week or so,' she says, without asking.

    I shrug.

'I'm a police doctor, Clare. Do you know what that is?'

    I nod.

'I'm making a report regarding your injuries. I have already examined you, I expect Celia your caseworker already explained to you but just in case I'll explain it again.'

She washes her hands in the sink and examines her teeth in the mirror.

'I'm a doctor, but I also work for the police.' She switches focus and looks at me in the mirror and shakes her hands dry. 'Part of my job is to record injuries so that there is evidence that might be useful in a prosecution.

'Part of the examination involves me taking photographs. I will also have to ask you some questions. From there, I will write a report that can be used in court.'

I nod again. She's leafing through the pages stuck to the clipboard, reading at the same time as talking.

It's like she's on automatic pilot.

'So now, we'd like you to try to have something to eat.' She looks up and smiles. 'And a drink.' She nods. 'Be good to get some food inside you. Right? Will you have some ice cream? I know that sounds like an odd thing to have but I think you might find it soothing.'

I nod.

A nurse is standing with her head through the door. She's so new her uniform looks like it's wearing her. It's stiff and the shoulder seams sit beyond where her arms start. She looks so worried she might cry. She wipes her nose on the back of her thumb, nods and closes the door.

'Do you remember the last time you ate anything, Clare,' she says, looking at the metal clipboard she's picked up from the end of the bed. 'Your glucose levels are remarkably low.'

'Yesterday,' I whisper. 'I had something yesterday.'

I'm sure I did.

'Sixty-four milligrams. Hypoglycaemia,' she says to herself. 'You're not diabetic, Clare, are you?'

I frown.

'Any history of diabetes in your family?'

I shrug.

'How much do you usually drink? Alcohol, I mean.'

I shake my head. The bandage snags on my lip.

'What, not ever?'

'No,' I whisper.

'If only there were more people like you in the world the NHS would go out of business.'

She laughs at her own joke.

Celia comes in.

My caseworker.

Same cardigan.

'Hi, Clare, remember me?' she says, smiling, nodding. 'You fainted, nothing to worry about, really.'

She sits by the bed on the grey plastic armchair again. There's a yellow blanket folded over the arm and she busies herself, folds the handles of her handbag carefully inside it and pushes it into the corner of the windowsill. Then she folds her cardigan over the top of the bag and makes the whole parcel as small as humanly possible.

A bit OCD.

She pours some water into the cup, raises her eyebrows at me and offers me the cup, which I take. She switches on a lamp behind the headboard.

The sky has got darker.

She folds her arms and stares, with her back to me, at the grey terraced rooftops and flickering orange street lights.

I wonder what she's thinking.

'Do you remember exactly what you ate yesterday?' asks the doctor. 'Clare? That might help us understand why your glucose level is so low. It's not uncommon in situations like this . . .'

Your tits are saggy.

You need surgery.

You look old.

Ignorant bitch.

SLAP.

'I had some Diet Coke and some rice cakes.'

Drink this.

It will clean your insides out.

'What, that's it?' says the doctor, looking at me like I'm stupid. 'You girls are all addicted to Diet Coke and rice cakes. What about some potatoes? Green vegetables? Some bread? Or rice? Brown rice is much nicer than everyone says it is.'

Celia puts her hand up to her neck and catches the doctor's eye.

The doctor raises her eyebrows.

The nurse comes back with a tray.

There's a polystyrene bowl with a scoop of yellow ice cream in and a glass of milk.

'I'll come back in an hour,' says the doctor. 'Enjoy!' she says as she shuts the door behind her.

'I'm Dr Ridley, by the way,' she says, as she pokes her head back through the door again. 'Nice ice cream?'

'Delicious,' I whisper, as I quietly spit it into a paper towel.

Celia is watching my reflection in the window.

'That policewoman sitting outside is DC Walker. She's been assigned to your case. Would you like to speak to her yet?'

I shake my head.

'She's going to stay right there until she's had a chance to have a chat with you, if that's OK. We need a signed statement before we can go ahead any further.'

There's an awkward silence.

'How many more police are here?'

She looks blankly at me.

'For my protection?' I whisper.

She shakes her head.

'I need police protection. That's what I went to the police station for.'

My throat is burning.

'They're sending someone to your house,' she says. 'To see if he's there.'

'My house!' I whisper, tears spilling down my face. 'What if they tell him where I am? He said he will kill me, and kill my friends. He said he will kill them first and make me watch.'

'You don't have to worry. No one's going to tell anyone anything, Clare. I promise you that.

'Now, have some more ice cream. It'll help,' smiling and nodding.

'But he'll know where I am . . . He'll know that I'm sick . . .'

There's a sound from the corridor. A phone ringing. DC Walker presses a mobile to her ear. At the same time, there's a sharp clang as metal hits metal. Through the blinds I can see the policewoman stand up, suddenly.

A bed is wheeled past.

Just a bed.

Calm.

That's all.

Just a bed.

Breathe.

The policewoman sits back down, still talking on the phone, she laughing now.

Breathe.

Next to a man.

Babe.

It's him!

Coco.

He's here.

Sharp gulp of air.

Hurting my throat.

He's here.

I'll be watching you, even when you think I won't.

Looking at me through the window.

Quick. Turn my face away.

He's here.

Staring right at me in the reflection in the window.

Smiling.

Scramble off the bed.

Staring.

Laughing.

Laughing at me.

Behind the bed.

The catheter bag is tangled up in the spiral cord.

'Clare! What are you doing?'

Hide.

Hide.

Hide.

Hide.

'Clare, get back into bed. You can't do . . .'

'Get away, get away, get away . . .'

Can't breathe.

Rocking.

Back and forth.

Back and forth.

He's singing.

Every move you make
  Every vow you break
  Every smile you fake
  Every claim you stake
  I'll be watching you.

Fourteen

Sally

Last time I looked, they were supposed to be welcoming in women's refuges, kind, empathetic, that sort of thing, that's what I thought anyway.

'I don't know what you are getting upset about, Sally,' says Mrs Henry. Mrs Henry is the woman who runs the place. 'Most women don't bring anything with them. They are quite happy to simply select some clothes from the garment wardrobe. Everything is clean, you know.'

And I don't know why this woman is getting so arsey with me, honest I don't. Back in the day, they didn't used to be bossy.

'Look, no offence, Mrs Henry,' I say back, 'but what's the sodding point of borrowing clothes when my bags are packed and sitting right by my front door like Sue said "in case you have to move fast", like, not ten minutes from here? We just need to go and get 'em!'

Sue had got a call from some bloke at that Liverpool nick, who said that the Governor was an arse and it looked like Terry was out after all. Sue had gone green, Livvy'd said. She'd been more worried than I was.

PC Chapman, nice lass, blonde hair up in a high ponytail, was to take me up York Gate.

'York Gate?' I'd said.

'The refuge they're just doing up,' she'd said. 'I know it's not ideal, but we're desperate – we've checked and they've got space.'

'Oh, that place in Regent's Park. State-of-the-art. What 'bout my bags?' I'd said.

'Later,' she'd said. 'Can't waste any time. Let's just get there.'

So that's why I'm here, and no bags.

She's huffing and puffing like a steam train, Mrs Henry, up this corridor, down that corridor, up these stairs, and round that corner. Is it just me, or are women like her a pain in the backside?

'If DS Clarke had thought it was a good idea for you to go back to your flat, then someone would have taken you back to your flat. Fact is, she didn't. Fact is, she said you were an emergency admission. So, hello. You're here now,' she says. 'Make the best of it.' She marches off down yet another magnolia-painted corridor ahead of me.

Hell, she's one of those army wives, you know the type, tweed and twinset, has had to find things to busy herself with while her husband's away driving tanks in Afghanistan or something.

'Mrs Henry, I've got the clothes I stand in,' I say, trying to appeal to her on a human level, 'to be very specific, I am wearing the one pair of pants I have with me. I do not want charity pants, thank you very much.'

'Everyone else manages with the garment wardrobe, Mrs Parton,' she says, coming to a halt outside the front door of flat 9, and twisting the Yale key in the lock.

'Miss; it's Miss Parton,' I go.

I bet she doesn't have charity pants on; she'll have a 24-hour girdle. Do they still make 24-hour girdles? I bet you could find one in the back of a Saga catalogue.

'Someone can easily go down to Marks tomorrow and buy you some new pants.'

Or I can just go and get my godforsaken bags, I think to myself. I mean, Terry's not exactly the four horsemen of the apocalypse, is he! Is it four or is it seven? I don't know. And he won't have access to a private jet either, now will he? Sue is being cautious, that's all, and maybe she feels a bit responsible for not knowing that Terry was due for release already, like gone already, wires crossed somewhere between here and Liverpool.

'Do you want to tell me a little bit about yourself, Sally?' says Mrs Henry, drawing some tired-out looking curtains in the tiny little sitting room. 'Your room is just through there,' she says, pointing. This is probably around the time I would put my bags on my bed, I think to myself, if I had any bags.

'Well, as you know, I'm here on the advice of the police,' I start. Mrs Henry has her back to me, checking the insides of the cupboards in the sitting room.

'There's rodent activity in here,' she says. 'You afraid of rats?'

'Not the four-legged kind,' I say.

'God knows how they get in. Must have wings,' she says. 'Slippery little fellows, rats. Sorry you were saying . . .?'

'My ex-husband was put inside twenty years ago. I was a witness for the prosecution. My evidence rubber-stamped his conviction; well, he thought that at any rate, and if you ask me, he's not wrong.'

She nods.

'He always was a bit of an angry man, born that way.' I grin a grin I don't really intend, it's what I always do, to make people feel less awkward, if you know what I mean.

'Well, you'll be very safe here,' she says. The 'very' makes me suspicious. 'Very' safe, she says, you're either safe or you're not, right?

'We have state–'

'–of-the-art-security,' I finish for her. 'So I hear.'

'The police have a silent intruder alarm connected to the station, twenty-four hours a day, seven days a week.'

'What about a noisy intruder alarm?' I say.

'We haven't had any of those yet either, Sally,' she says, choosing to ignore the joke. She winks and clatters down the stairs. 'Why they don't put lifts into these buildings, I just don't know,' she's saying.

From my third-floor sitting-room (and I use the term loosely) window you can see way up the railway line, halfway to Euston station, I reckon, eight tracks that snake across the mud and stones, between weed bushes and walls of meaningless graffiti. Well, I think it's meaningless, I don't know about you; maybe you understand this stuff: 'Adore & Endure' sprayed in pink with a swirling raspberry ripple ice-cream cone; 'FML' in red and yellow lightning strikes; 'Vapour' in electric blue, all turned ugly shades of orange by the street lights.

He got twenty years in prison, Terry, for killing Hayley; twenty years, that's all, for stealing a life, and she was a good girl. White-wine Hayley, we used to call her. We'd be knocking back pints of lager top, or rum and black, or Bacardi and Coke, but white-wine Hayley only ever had white wine.

'Another white wine, Hayl?' we'd yell and she'd nod till she was half falling over. On her way home she'd regularly fall asleep in people's front gardens. She regularly fell asleep in her own front garden too; she did that more than twice and her mam nearly killed her.

I've spent the last twenty years looking over my shoulder, on my own – no family, no friends, not really. Apart from a few colleagues from work, oh, and Sue, but she was only every month or so. You ask me, it's the exact same as prison, right? You're not actually locked up, but you don't have contact with the people you want have contact with. You ask me, I'd rather have spent it with my mam, with Jake, with Dawn and Beth and Jan and Charmian – the crew. And Hayley.

Seems like Terry got off scot free compared to me, and the day the bastard comes out I have to go in to this. It's so hot in this sweaty little room, so I try to open the window, but the metal frames have been painted over with cheap white gloss, all over the pane too, and the latch is stuck fast, with globules of dried paint dripping through the notches in the handle. There's not a breath of air, and someone's put the heating on full blast, like they do in old people's homes and nursery schools, warming up the low hum of urine accidents.

I pick up the packet of teabags and a pint of skimmed milk that Mrs H has given me and lock up.

There's no stair carpet; there are marks where a stair carpet used to be, but no stair carpet. Not yet, anyway, so your feet can't help but clatter.

On every landing, behind other locked doors, children are shouting and babies are crying, TVs are blaring and women are silently blaming themselves for absolutely everything. That's what we do.

I pass two of them on the stairs, Indian ladies, hollow eyes that don't meet mine.

There's a big colourful sign running across the top of the noticeboard stating that this is The York Gate Women's Refuge and there's a map pinned underneath. It's at the other end of Camden from my flat, and up here they'll call my area 'King's Cross', and down there, we call this area 'Regent's Park', so by my reckoning that makes actual Camden about as wide as the High Street, and that's it.

'It's one of those buildings that was made for the servants of the big houses around the park. Edwardian,' Mrs H had said. She also said that, at that time, if there weren't enough servants around, they let 'Johnny foreigners' live there, and the jury's out on whether she was trying to be funny or not.

The block takes up one side of the whole road and faces a row of little tiny Victorian cottages, with quaint little front gardens, picket fences, and pointy gables on the roofs, the sort of houses that every Londoner dreams of owning, except if they are bang opposite a red-brick block, half full of squatters.

The end of the block nearest the park and the posh houses and the croissant shops and small-volumes-of-French-poetry-bookshops, towards Primrose Hill, has new front doors, all painted white with a choice of a million buzzers for each flat. The end nearest the railway line doesn't, that's for sure – the doors there are hanging off their hinges, there's seven loads of shite in the front gardens, like shopping trollies and plastic hat-stands and paddling pools covered in dog poo – that's the end that's full of squatters, apparently, so Mrs H says. York Gate Women's Refuge is somewhere in the middle, gifted to Camden Council she said, for a pound or something, so they'd get it all done up.

It's just two double-fronted blocks, you know, in a terrace, with central front doors in each block and stairs going right up the middle of each, if you know what I mean. So they've gone and blocked off one door, right, for security I s'pose, completely blocked it off, with a sign and a big arrow pointing towards the other door.

So, you go in the other door, and first you have to buzz, then you have to look in a camera thing, then you get through that door. So far, so Fort Knox, right?

Then you're in this kind of lobby with a thick glass screen like you used to get in the taxis in Liverpool, and you talk through that to a security guard, (mostly glowering ex-coppers but there's one smiley one who gives me a wink), where you explain what you are doing there and everything. Someone's there, day and night, they said, but you're not gonna get in after ten, are you? Not unless you are a resident, or the police, or the fire brigade or something, any of the emergency services, which presumably you'd want to come in for whatever the emergency was that was going on. But your residents, they get these key fobs, so your residents can come in and out like they want, like normal folks.

But I have to tell you, I got the impression that they don't really want you out and about after ten, because who are we kidding, it's not like any of this is normal, right? Staying out clubbing or something it's gotta be asking for trouble, yeah?

So, then the receptionist lady, and IT MIGHT NOT BE A LADY – I know! I'm all for sexual equality and all that, believe me – the receptionist PERSON lets you through the lobby doors, and then you're into the main hall. That's it. And then all the rooms go off that and the stairs, so it would have been four flats on that ground floor but they've all been turned into the communal areas. There's a big kitchen for each block and a laundry room, and a dining room that looks out onto the garden so you can sit and have your coffee looking out, then there's two TV rooms and little smaller rooms for therapy and the suchlike. There's one big room at the back with no TV, and that's used for group activities, Mrs H said. I dread to think what that's all about. Seriously, group silences, I bet – apart from them, social workers'll talk the hind leg off a donkey given half a chance.

The kitchen over this side, my side as it turns out, looks like the sort of kitchen you used to get in schools back when they had kitchens in schools. It's all easily wipe-downable stainless-steel basic. The fridge is the size of a house but not new – second-hand from a restaurant or something – cos it's got scratches on the door from where it maybe, once upon a time, smacked into a wall. It's got a million shelves but hardly any food in it, 'cept for a few plastic boxes with people's names written on, in permanent marker, which I had to laugh at: lacks a bit of that optimism if you ask me. There are at least ten open cartons of milk in the door as well as an open tub of humus, half a squeezed lemon, half an avocado gone black, not covered with cling film. What is it with people not using cling film? Makes food last longer; don't they watch the ads on TV? Who wants half an avocado that's just been sitting in a fridge for days with other people spilling their off-milk all over it?

I switch on the kettle and look for a mug. There are Muppet mugs and Barbie mugs and Camden Graphics mugs and Nationwide Building Society mugs, all donated very kindly I'm sure, and all stained brown from years and years of half-drunk tea that was supposed to make you feel better and didn't. Go on, have a nice cuppa tea, make you feel better. Not.

The kettle shoots steam out the spout and clicks off.

You know what? This place ain't what it's cracked up to be. It's new, yeah, sure it's new, and it's in a nicer area – well, nicer than you usually get any rate – but inside, Jesus Christ, it's just like any other women's refuge. There's nothing like relying on pity for your décor; stuff that nobody wants is always stuff that nobody wants, however much you try and spruce it up, kid yourself.

Nothing's nice here, really, not at all. I don't know what they were doing, spending all the money on poshing-up the building but forgetting to make it comfy. I mean, really! It's shabby, that's what my mam would have said, shabby! The sofas are either modern and plastic shabby, as if they come out of an office waiting room or something, or pink velour shabby, from house clearances. The dining chairs are all scratched and wonky and nothing matches, and it's not like anyone has even had a stab at making anything match. There are pictures on the walls that have got to have come from a second-hand shop, no glass like, just amateur people's paintings – scenes from somebody else's holiday. Almost makes it worse, doesn't it?

And then some halfwit has bought some posters. You can hear someone thinking, 'Oh I know what'll cheer the place up, a load of posters!' So they've gone off and spent a fiver on some clearance shite posters, and then they go and stick them to the freshly painted walls, with Sellotape. I mean, WTF, really?

'Today is a new day.'

Do me a bloomin' favour.

'Today is a new day,' in pink letters on a pink gingham background, like a housewife's pinny.

Jesus. Someone has gone and got a permanent marker and scribbled in the corner, 'BUT TOTALLY THE SAME SHIT' and I think, ain't that the truth?

Fifteen

DS Clarke

'Hello. Yes. It's DS Susan Clarke from Camden, London. I'm calling in regard to a prisoner you have recently released, a Mr Terry Mansfield. Yes, I can hold.'

DS Clarke is back at her desk on the first floor of Camden Road Police Station, deleting spam emails, and cursing the lack of IT to deal with the shite firewall. Livvy had fetched her a prawn sandwich from M&S, the one with brown bread and low-fat mayonnaise, but this week she's on the 5:2 diet, and can only drink a pink plastic container of blended kale, blueberries and chia seeds. So, she's skipping lunch altogether.

'No. No,' she says into the phone.

Heavy sigh.

'No, I don't know of his whereabouts.'

She picks up a pencil and starts tapping it on the desk. She does that sometimes.

Heavier sigh.

'Yes, I'm calling from the Community Safety Unit, Central and North London. Yes, I can hold.'

She fires off an email to Livvy, asking her to secure a place for Clare at the Regent's Park refuge. It's only a temporary measure, for her own safety. She wants Clare close by – she's got more she wants to ask her. If she needs to, she can get her moved further away once she's got some answers. She puts her wallet and ID into the side pocket of her Zara bag that is slung on the back of her chair.

The officer on the other end of the phone is back.

'Hmm,' DS Clarke says, trying to hold her anger in check. 'Look, young man, why do you want to know if *I* know of Mr Mansfield's whereabouts? Aren't you supposed to know where he is? I thought he was tagged. Your Governor told me this morning that he was tagged.'

This time she throws the phone down.

DS Clarke sends yet another email to the Governor of Liverpool Prison, formally asking for more information regarding the premature release of Mr Terry Mansfield, prisoner number 127963, and pointing out the ineptitude of his long-term release protocol, and his officers along with it.

She picks up the report on her desk, a very short report she notices, about the Oval Road Repeated Knocking, No Response. She checks the address and grabs her bag.

'If a job's worth doing . . .' she thinks to herself, as she straps into the Volvo.

PC Olivia Halsall is running down the back steps of the station, waving at her to stop.

'Shall I join you, sarge?' she says. 'If you're going back to the property?'

She climbs in, pulling her skirt down over her knees. DS Clarke wonders why these girls wear their skirts so short. It's not a beauty contest, it's a job.

'So, Livvy, nothing at the property?' she says.

What happens next perfectly demonstrates to DS Clarke why some women aren't particularly suited to certain aspects of policing. The gathering of data. The bigger picture, the finer details. Some female minds always get caught up in what people feel and how they feel it, rather than fact. What are the facts PC Halsall? she wants to scream, but she doesn't!

'We spoke to a neighbour. A Mrs Vocking. She's an older lady and can't remember much about the couple next door except that he seemed like a nice chap,' says Livvy, gazing out of the window.

'How old is older?' says DS Clarke, knowing the answer won't impress her. Eighty is old, she thought to herself. Or ninety.

'Oh, I don't know, about forty-five or fifty. And she said that the young gentleman was an attractive man.'

'Has she seen them recently?'

'She said she couldn't remember seeing Clare, but that there was some banging last night, around midnight, and that she noticed some bin bags in the front garden this morning. But she said they don't take building refuse, or garden refuse, in the Camden area, because that's for the council to deal with and she finds that a bit unfair given that she's there alone and doesn't generate a lot of refuse herself, but she could really use some help with the garden refuse because she doesn't drive herself you see.'

'And did you look in the bin bags, Livvy?' DS Clarke says, as the nervous twitch in her right cheek sets off.

'Oh no, they'd gone by then. It's bin day, you see.'

DS Clarke shakes her head imperceptibly, but Livvy wouldn't have seen it even if she had been facing that way.

And DS Clarke thinks to herself, any refuse worth having will be halfway to Dover by now, in a container.

The terraced houses in Oval Road are not your typical London two-up, two-down Victorian style. DS Clarke didn't know much about architecture but she guessed that these were built before that. They're four storeys, grey brick, with arched windows on the second floor, and mostly black or white front doors. This is the fancy end of Camden, where the artists and poets used to hang out. Jasper Conran used to live two roads down. And Stephen Fry. Or was it David Hockney? Or Alan Bennett? Some of the gardens towards the High Street are overgrown, front rooms spilling onto the windowsills, spider plants in plastic pots, china figurines, yellowing books.

Number 289 Oval Road was, from the outside, well kept. The front door had been recently painted black, and the curtains were drawn so there was no possibility of seeing inside. The side gate was locked, bolted from the inside top and bottom and padlocked from the front.

While DS Clarke knocks on the front door, PC Halsall goes to see if Mrs Vocking next door is available. DS Clarke concerns herself with Clare – getting her out of hospital and into a secure unit, and wonders how that would work, considering Clare had not yet made a formal complaint. On her third attempt at knocking, DS Clarke's phone buzzes.

'Hi, Celia. What news on Clare Chambers? Slow down . . . No, slow down, Celia, you're going too fast . . . OK, so there *was* a man outside her room – was it Gareth? *Celia!* Stop screeching . . . So, there wasn't a man outside her room? Well, *was there or wasn't there*? Who's down there with you? No, I'm coming now . . . Stay where you are. Don't leave her room.'

DS Clarke shouts as she runs for the car. 'Livvy, there's a suspected intruder outside her room.' Livvy runs down the front steps and jumps in the car beside DS Clarke.

'He's not been identified,' DS Clarke says, half to herself. 'Livvy, find out what Walker's been doing – she's supposed to be watching the ward. And put PC Hall outside her room for the night – we'll get another team down to do a search of the building. And get on to the hospital for the CCTV records. Let's find him!'

Sixteen

Clare

I can hear breathing.

That's how I know there's someone there.

I open my eyes.

It's the policewoman.

The same one that was at the police station, not the one sat outside my room in the corridor.

She's staring out the window.

It's morning.

She sees me watching her.

'There's no one there, Clare,' she says, seeing my eyes flick towards the closed blinds.

I can't see the row of chairs outside the door.

'Did you get him?' I say to her. My voice is still croaky.

'Not yet, Clare, but we will,' she says.

Like it's going to be easy.

She's clasping her hands together. It's odd when people hold their own hands.

'Why?' I whisper. 'He was right here!'

'We're looking into it, Clare. You can leave that to us. You can trust us.'

'I need police protection,' I whisper.

'I understand that,' she says. 'We've organised for you to go to a women's refuge.'

'Can't I stay here, until I go home?'

'It's simply not practical to have officers here around the clock. The women's refuge is totally safe.'

I want to go home.

Why don't they just arrest him?

Make him go away?

Isn't that what they're supposed to do?

They don't know what they're dealing with.

Who they're dealing with.

I say nothing.

'We have not yet located the whereabouts of Mr Gareth James. As soon as we can locate him . . .' she says, tailing off at the end of the sentence.

He could still be here.

You know I'll always find you, don't you, babe.

I wish I could just disappear completely.

'You'll be going to the new women's refuge in Regent's Park. It's totally safe. You'll be safer there than anywhere else, even here, Clare. We'll escort you in a taxi. You can trust me,' she says, putting her hand on my arm.

Why do people always do that?

I move my arm away.

It's not you I don't trust. It's him.

I think that.

I don't say that.

And then I think, actually, I don't trust you either.

'How do you know he's not still here?' I say. 'He could be sitting right there.' I nod towards the door.

'Celia, your caseworker will come with us in the taxi and settle you in. The doctor says you are fine to go, provided you don't feel too woozy.'

I wish she'd go away.

I wish they'd all go away.

'Maybe I wouldn't be woozy if they hadn't knocked me out.'

'You were in a very agitated state, Clare. It's standard procedure for patients who are agitated.'

It's standard procedure for people to get agitated when they think they are about to get murdered.

I didn't say that out loud either.

The caseworker, Celia, knocks on the door and looks through the windowpane.

'Good night?' she says, hopefully.

Like it will make her day if I've had a good night.

Fake.

I nod and look away.

'Ready to go?' she says, looking at DS Clarke. She looks at me. 'I've brought you some things to wear,' says Celia, holding up a navy fleece and some trainers. 'I think they'll fit. You can give them back to me when you've got your own things. If you tell me exactly what you want, I can go over to your house and pick them up if DS Clarke says I can. Do you have a key?'

Like I'd have a key!

No, I don't have a key.

I haven't had a key in months.

Years.

For your own safety, babe.

Don't want you getting lost!

'It's cold today,' says DS Clarke, looking out of the window. 'Colder than yesterday.'

Shouldn't she be thinking about how to catch Gareth, not commenting on the weather? Isn't that her job?

'Really,' I say, looking at the ceiling.

Not trying to be rude.

'Is there still a policewoman out there?' I say.

'Yes, Clare,' she says, trying not to sigh but sighing anyway.

She sits down on the edge of the bed, checking with her eyes that I don't mind.

'What happened to your leg?' she says, looking at the box thing.

'Just a bruise,' I say.

'Quite a bad bruise it says on the medical report.'

'All right, just quite a bad bruise,' I say.

'Look, Clare. I don't know why we're getting off on the wrong foot here, do you?'

I look out of the window.

'Clare, we are trying to help you.'

'You don't believe me, do you? You don't believe that Gareth was here, do you? He was right there. Laughing at me.'

None of them believe me.

'I haven't said I don't believe you. However, I can tell you that the police officer assigned to your safety and welfare, who was outside your room the whole time, did not see a man matching the description of Mr Gareth James. The key is, I believe, that you believe that you saw him. But as I say, DC Walker says that she was alone there the entire time. I'm checking the CCTV. We've got your description. I will check it and double check it. I assure you.'

'She must be blind. He was there, clear as day. I saw him with my own eyes. She was too busy on the phone.'

'She was on the phone?'

'Yeah, she was laughing. Wasn't she supposed to be looking out for me?'

She frowns to herself, that way teachers do when they're trying to show you what a pain you are instead of just telling you what a pain you are.

She puts her hands together, like she's saying a prayer or something.

He was standing RIGHT NEXT TO THE POLICEWOMAN. I'm screaming in my own head.

'Let's step back a bit,' she says. 'We still don't have a signed statement from you, Clare. Have you decided that you don't want to make a formal report about, er, Gareth?'

'Please don't say his name.'

'Your partner, then.'

'He's not my partner.'

Coco.

   Angel.

No one ever gets the better of me.

She huffs a bit, like she's trying to keep a lid on it. 'What would you like me to call him, Clare?'

'Him is fine.'

'OK.' She sighs a long sigh, then breathes in. 'OK. Have you decided you don't want to press charges against him?'

'I never want to see him again. Or hear anything about him. I just want him to be gone. Why haven't you arrested him yet?'

'You know why. But when we do, we will need something from you in writing to back all this up. We need proof.'

'You've got proof. Wanna see my leg?' I say, whipping the sheet off my calf. The purple bit is going green around the edges.

'Just quite a bad bruise, Clare, as you say.'

I can't believe she just said that.

'Don't turn that one on me,' I say.

God, what a witch.

'Listen! We can't lock someone up for a bruise. You're going to have to give us more than that. Work with us, please.'

I don't know what to say.

I don't know what to do.

I don't know anything.

Shhhhhh.

Babe.

It's all gonna be fine.

You know I'll make it all better.

Babe.

Roll over this way.

'Have some water, Clare,' she says, stretching out her hand to give me a plastic cup.

'I don't want any water.'

I said, ROLL OVER THIS WAY.

I need to get my exercise.

I fling a cup across the floor where it skids under a chair.

DS Clarke slowly walks over to the sink and pulls out some paper towels from the dispenser.

'You keep forgetting, Clare,' she says, wiping up the water. 'We're trying to help you.'

'You've got a medical report! Isn't that enough?'

'It's not conclusive, Clare, unless you give us some evidence. A jury would say you could have done all this to yourself.'

'Who purposely bashes their own leg in? Who purposely douses themselves in paraffin? Who purposely drinks paraffin?'

'People do strange things.'

'You're saying I could've done this, are you?' I say. 'You should have been there.'

'I wasn't there, Clare. That's the point. You need to tell me. The jury will need to hear it from you.'

Have you been a naughty girl again?

I can't catch my breath.

YOU HAVE, HAVEN'T YOU?

'Why don't you go to my house, then? Go to my house. Look in the laundry room.'

I'm too hot.

'Look in the laundry room and count the markers on the plaster behind the door.'

I feel like I'm going to be sick again.

'That's how many days I've spent in that room.'

I pick up the cardboard sick bowl from the top of the bedside cabinet and hold it under my chin.

'Wanna know how many days?' I say into the bottom of the bowl.

My voice sounds loud and low.

She looks at me.

Pity.

I hate pity.

'One hundred and twenty-seven. That's how many days.'

My stomach heaves and bubbly swirls of ice cream mixed with mucus and milk come back.

I cough.

'He wouldn't even let me out to go to the toilet,' I whisper. 'You'll find proof of that too!'

My throat is burning.

Not until you say that I fuck you better than you ever got fucked in your life.

Say it.

SAY IT.

She hands me a paper towel so I can wipe my mouth.

Then she hands me the cup she's picked up from the floor and refilled with water.

She doesn't have any pity on her face now.

Not a flicker of anything.

'If you don't press charges, he'll get away with that,' she says.

'I can just hide.'

'Your whole life?' she says more forcefully.

She puts the sick bowl into the bin by the sink. The lid slams shut.

'Can you check outside?' I say.

She walks over to the door and looks through the small pane of glass.

'Just PC Mark Hall. Did you meet Mark. Did he say hello?'

'We said hello. He sat in here. In that chair. Stayed half the night. So I could sleep,' I say.

Whose number is this in your phone?

I bet I know whose number.

Filthy whore.

'He's a good lad, Mark.'

She sits down.

'Let's go back to the beginning, shall we. Tell me what happened in the beginning. Tell me about your dad.'

My dad.

'My dad died in September 2014. The twenty-first.'

She takes out a pad.

'Can I?' she goes, holding up her pen.

I nod.

'We weren't even there.'

'Who wasn't?'

'Me. And Louisa.'

She frowns at me.

'Louisa is my best friend.

Was my best friend.'

I'm your best friend now.

You don't need Louisa.

She's only your friend because she wants your money.

And she wants me.

Have you seen the way she looks at me?

'What do you mean, Clare? I don't understand.'

'We weren't there when my dad died. We were raising money for Cancer Research. For all the help they were giving my dad.'

Getting pissed in China, more like.

'We'd gone to China. To walk seven hundred miles along the wall. We got loads of sponsors. And then I got this phone call to say that Dad had got an infection from a drain they'd put in his stomach. And that because he had an infection, he couldn't have his chemo. And he died.'

On his own. While I was having a good time.

'I'm sure he was very proud of you for trying to raise money.'

He could see through me. He knew it was an excuse to get away for a bit.

'We raised twenty-three grand. "BRAVE BAR GIRLS RAISE £23K FOR CHARITY BUT DAD DIES". We were in the paper. In the *Camden Gazette*. It was a while after Dad died. After the funeral and everything.'

'But it's amazing to have raised so much.'

'Not for him, it wasn't. Too late for him. I didn't have any other family. Once he died, that was it. My gran died when I was ten and my mum committed suicide when I was sixteen. So I was on my own.'

'You had friends, though. You had Louisa. And a boyfriend maybe?'

'I didn't have a boyfriend. I'd never had a proper boyfriend. Louisa stayed over a bit to start with. It's not a big house, three bedrooms but small, better for a family with little kids. It's in a nice area. Expensive area. But it's old and creaky. It was creepy by myself.'

'So, then what happened?'

'Then he happened.'

'Him?'

'He moved in. Almost straightaway. Like a month or so after Dad died. Just after we were in the paper. I met him in a bar one day. The one that Louisa and I used to work in at weekends. It's where they photographed us for the paper. We'd gone there for a drink and he sat down at the next table. And he asked me out. *Kind* of asked me out. We met for a drink the next day. And the day after that, he told me that his place was being decorated so could he stay over at mine. And I was like, well, it's not ideal, cos

I hardly knew him, but I couldn't say no, could I? I mean, you can't say no when people know you've got a spare room. Two spare rooms really.

'And to start with it was fine. It was great. He helped me clear out the house and we sold loads of stuff. Dad's old stuff. And I still had my job. And it was still going well. I'd get home in the evenings and he'd have cooked a meal and tidied up.

'He was really kind. At first he was. He was really smart with money. Used to help me sort out with all the bills. He even took over sorting the finances in the end. When I got a bit over-whelmed. That's what he called it. "Overwhelmed". That's what he would tell people.'

'So the relationship was good at the start?' she says, scribbling something down on her pad.

'It was amazing. Seemed like he was crazy about me. Couldn't get enough of me. I mean, he'd been out with supermodels. Anyone could see I was lucky to get with him.'

'Lucky?'

'He's a model you know.'

'Is he?' she says.

Well, he said he was a model.

I thought that.

I didn't say that.

'But then, little things would start to annoy him. There were flashes of anger. He'd blow up over something really trivial. And then be fine again. In a second. He got jealous of the weirdest things.'

'Like what?'

'Louisa. He used to cut her off when she phoned.'

She never liked him, from the start.

'Or, if someone called me from work. He would tell them to fuck off. Like literally say "fuck off". He went through my emails, found all the addresses of my male colleagues.

'And told them they weren't allowed to talk to me.'

'And did they stop talking to you?'

'What do you think? He threatened to kill them. He broke Simon Quinn's arm.'

'Who's Simon Quinn?'

'Just an Irish guy at work. He's nice.'

'And did Gareth know you thought he was nice?'

I don't know why you fancy someone who looks like a fucking emu.

I shrug.

'I guess . . .'

'And did Simon Quinn report him to the police?'

'I doubt it. I don't know. I left my job shortly after that. They let me go, I'd become so flaky. Not turning up, always on the phone to him. He'd call me a million times a day.'

'Where is your phone now, Clare? Your mobile. You didn't have anything with you yesterday.'

'I don't have one.'

He took it away.

Said I didn't need a phone.

Said I didn't have any friends.

'No phone?'

'No. I don't go out.'

'Never?'

'Not alone. Till yesterday.'

She tapped her pen on her pad.

'Where do you think he would go, Clare, once he discovered you had gone?'

You can't live without me now.

You can't even wake up without me telling you to.

'He's here somewhere. Watching. Waiting to get me. I told you.'

I'll set fire to you, you little whore.

I need to get rid of you.

You're weighing me down.

'The kitchen looked like a bomb had gone off. I ran into the laundry room before he could throw me in there. He locked me in later.'

Susan's busy scribbling it all down.

'So how did you get away?'

'I fell asleep, against the tumbler dryer. I always put it on to keep me warm. There's no heating in the outhouse. And when I woke up, the door was open. He'd taken the padlock off.'

'Is that usual?'

'His conscience gets the better of him when he's pissed. Sometimes.'

'So he's done that before, opened the door but not woken you up?'

I nod.

'And this time was different because . . .?'

'Because he'd left the side gate open too.'

'And had he done that before?'

'And why would he have done that this time?'

'I don't know.'

'Maybe he wanted you to run away?'

'Want me to run away. Why?'

'I don't know. Why do you think?'

'I didn't say he did. *You* did.'

Tap, tap, tap goes the pen on the pad.

'Clare, do you have a phone number for him?'

'I don't have a phone.'

'But you used to,' Susan says, gently.

'Can you remember his number from before?'

She's trying to be really nice.

'He changes his number all the time.'

And his phone.

Smashes them, mostly.

'He never pays his bill on time so they cut him off.'

'I'm sorry to press you, Clare,' she says, 'but how do you get in contact with him if you don't have his number?'

'When he goes out, he locks me in the house.'

Susan nods slowly, like she's finally starting to understand what I'm talking about.

'What about family? Did he talk about his parents? Brothers, sisters? Did he phone or email them?'

'No, nothing. Every time I asked him about his family, he said I didn't want to know. He said he didn't need family now cos he had me.'

'So Gareth was happy with you?'

'Sometimes he was happy. Next minute he would be furious. Then happy again. You couldn't predict his moods. Anything could set him off.

'He'll say I'm lying,' I say. 'He'll say I'm a drunk. He'll say I get drunk and do all this to myself. He'll say I'm depressed. He'll say I'm bipolar. He always makes stuff up. And most of the time, everyone believes him, he's so convincing.'

'We went to the house yesterday,' she says, 'looking for him, you know.' She taps the end of her pen on her pad again, like she's thinking. 'Clare, he's not there. No one's there.'

'Is the car there?' I say.

She looks at the pad, then at me.

She doesn't know. And she knows she should.

Seventeen

Sally

There's nothing like waking up at five o'clock in the morning in a strange place, in a shite bed, with horrible nylon sheets and a pillow that's like a bit of foam pretending to be a pillow, but that's all it is, let me tell you – it doesn't do anything to cushion your head, cos it's thinner than a bloomin' crispbread, and then you remember you're in the exact same clothes you were wearing the night before, and the day before as well, by the way.

And another thing while you're at it. There's nothing like waking up at five o'clock in the morning because the sodding curtains aren't really sodding curtains either. Oh yeah, they look like curtains all right. But they don't act like curtains when you need them to. They do nothing to shut out the light. Make no mistake about that. May as well have some kind of interrogation torch in your face. And then there's the endless trains coming in and out, in and out, in and out of Euston. Who goes to work that early? I mean, is it really necessary? Not surprising no one wants to live in this block but squatters and down-and-outs. Probably the only way to get to sleep is if you're off your bloomin' head.

The sink and bath are tinned-salmon coloured, honest – not pink, not orange, tinned salmon. Very 1972, and already stained a beautiful mint green where the water drips down from the leaky taps. So much for state-of-the-art. When you turn on the hot tap – either of them, the sink or the bath – the boiler in the airing cupboard sounds like there's a psycho on the inside with a very large spanner, trying to get out of it.

I don't have my toilet bag because, guess what, that's also in one of my bags by my front door, so my teeth are warm and furry. I hate that. I stare in the mirror and give up. If Prince Charming gives me a second glance today, he's gonna get a full-on coronary. Call the paramedics, someone.

My phone buzzes.

'Sue, if you're not calling me to say you're picking up my bags . . .'

'I'm not,' she says. She's on hands-free so it sounds like she's calling from the bottom of a toilet.

'If you're not calling to tell me that Terry has been found dead . . .'

'Not that either,' she says. 'I need a favour.'

'I'm not sure what pills you're on, Sue, but whatever, I'll have some.'

'What?' she goes.

'The best I got here favour-wise is a stained mattress, or a cup of builder's tea in a mug that's never seen hide nor hair of a Finish Quantum Max tablet.'

'I'm serious,' she says. 'Oh, fuck off!' she shouts. 'Sorry!' she says to me. 'Some wanker trying to tell me I'm in the wrong lane. *I'm a police officer, you little shit,*' she yells.

'Favours only granted here if you bring me my bags,' I say. 'They're right by my front door.'

'Can I do that later? I'm on my way to you now.'

'Yeah, fine. What's the favour? Nothing to do with Terry, then?'

'See you in five,' she says and clicks her phone off, so I nearly bust my bloomin' eardrum. She always does that, Sue, rings me when she's five minutes away. She thinks that's normal.

In the kitchen, a toddler with a nappy half round his knees is trailing around his bottle, holding it by the teat, spilling mini jets of milk onto the lino.

'You all right there?' I say. He stares up at me, blinking, big brown eyes, big brown mop of curls, turquoise and white pyjamas, flowery.

'I'm not a girl,' he goes, staring at his grubby little brown fingers and poking at the flowers on his tummy.

'Boys can like flowers too,' I say, smiling.

'I like trains,' he says and smiles. Then he frowns for a bit, concentrating hard. 'And I like chewy sweets.' He's smiling again.

'I like trains and chewy sweets – and I like flowers,' I go.

'You is a girl, then,' he says and pitter-patters off down the corridor, his bare feet slapping on the lino. It's warm here, for dirty little bare feet.

I stick the kettle on and examine the mug selection for the least-stained offender. Sue'll have something to say, I'll bet you.

There's a buzz at the front door and from the kitchen I can look down the corridor and see the black-and-white uniforms standing in the lobby, chatting away to the receptionist behind the glass. There's someone wrapped in one of the silver space blankets, the kind they gave Coco. They have them on *Holby City* when there's been an accident and someone is in shock or something. Don't look as though they'd keep you warm at all, just a bit of foil.

There's this Indian lady who was in the kitchen, in a blue sari that looks as if it belongs somewhere else – the sari I mean – somewhere more exotic than this place, and she darts into the laundry room then closes the door to just a crack and presses her eye against it. That's how all newbies are, don't believe they are safe, don't trust their own shadow, some of them, and maybe they never will. She's not done anything wrong, she just thinks she must have, that's how it is.

It's the girl from the police station. She's got trainers on now, and a navy fleece over her dressing gown. Her hair is tucked into the neck of her top as though she put it on in a hurry. Mrs H is shaking her by the hand – more welcoming to her than she was to an oldie like me, I can tell you. Next to Mrs H the girl looks even smaller, tiny bird, keeps touching her face, hiding her mouth behind her fingers.

'All of our flats are two-bedroom, so you'll be sharing. But you'll have your privacy too,' I hear her say.

The girl just stares back, wide-eyed, barely registering, let alone understanding.

Sue's there, craning her neck, looking for something and she eventually clocks me down the end of the corridor and I hold up the mug and she shakes her head and holds up her five fingers, then mouths the words, 'See you in a sec, OK?'

I nod and keep on making my tea.

'It's quite hard getting anything out of her,' says Sue, curling her lip up at the stains on the *Frozen* mug. Clare's on the guided tour with Mrs H.

'Don't you go judging that mug, should've seen it before I got to it,' I say.

'I mean, I know it's perfectly normal not to trust anyone after an ordeal like hers. Has this got sugar in?'

'Here,' I say, passing her the sugar cubes in a box that looks like it's pre-World War Two. 'So, you want me to talk to her, is that what you're saying?'

'Well, not obviously. But if she says anything, that might help. You know. We don't even know his real name – the name she gave us doesn't check out.'

'What d'ya mean, it doesn't check out?'

'There's no one registered under that name. We're contacting Interpol.' She's sipping at her tea like it's maybe poisoned or something.

'Well, I don't know why she'd tell me if she don't want to tell you. I'd've thought she wanted him caught.'

'It's not what she says, necessarily – it's how she behaves. But she's not stupid. There's something odd about her, about her story. Something I can't put my finger on. You're her room-mate! Gain her trust.'

'Room-mate! You're kidding, right?'

'Hey, roomie!' She laughs.

'Fuck off, you're not kidding, are you?'

She laughs again and takes another slurp of tea.

'I'm paid for this, being an informer, am I?' I say.

'I'll pay you in custard creams. Or digestives. Something to mop up this shit tea.'

'You can get my bags, that's what you can do.'

'Give us your keys, then. I'll get Chapman over there later. Listen,' she says, putting her cup by the sink, as I pull the keys out of my pocket and hand them over, 'I don't think you should tell her that we know each other.'

'Why the hell not?'

'Call it police instinct,' she goes, winking.

'What if she recognises me from the station?'

'She won't because she won't remember. She could barely stand up . . .'

'It'll be a bit of a bugger if she does.'

'She won't. I'll speak to Mrs Henry.'

'Blimey, do *you* have to call her Mrs Henry and all? It's like sodding boarding school, this.'

'I'll phone you,' she says.

'Bags!' I shout after her.

It's nearly lunchtime and the women's refuge kitchen starts filling up with women; they shuffle as if they're in a daze, like you'd expect patients in a mental home. They look down at their feet; they do everything slowly, quietly, like they don't want to risk upsetting anyone.

''Scuse me,' and 'Sorry,' and 'Could I just ...?' Whispers between sounds of glass and china chinking on metal.

I need someone to do a shop for me so I look for Mrs H. She's standing by the noticeboard, pinning up a sign about cleaning rotas, because apparently everyone gets to have a go at mopping the floors, sterilising the work surfaces, hoovering out the social areas. Great.

'Do you think anyone will be going to the shops any time soon?' I say. 'I'm still on a bit of a lockdown.'

'Put your name down here,' she says, pointing to a different sign, without looking at me, trying to push a drawing pin in. 'It's a favour exchange,' she goes.

The sign is that important it's been laminated.

'SWAP-A-SKILL' has been written in wavy writing using one of those shite clip-art programmes they get on computers. Pink smiley faces all over, flowers with smiley faces, watering cans with smiley faces, even the bloomin' sun has a smiley face.

'Write your name and room number in the first column,' says Mrs H, putting all her weight behind the dry old thumbnail, 'what you need – i.e., food shopping – in the second column, then your skills in the final column.' She leans back and the drawing pin plops to the floor.

'Skills?' I say. 'What skills?'

'Aren't you a teacher?'

'No, absolutely not. I work for the AQA. The board of examiners. Freelance. Part-time. Consultant, they call it these days.'

'But you used to be a teacher, it says in your notes ...'

'GCSE science students – what fifteen years ago.'

She looks surprised, Mrs H does.

'You don't seem the type,' she says.

Bloody cheek.

'Have you never met a common scientist?'

She returns to the pinboard.

'I was quite good at school. Top in all the sciences. But then I met boys. I went back to school, after, you know, everything. And got my teaching degree. But it was a brief career,' I say. 'The profession of AQA external examiners is over-run with teachers who have quickly realised they fundamentally can't stand sodding children. I'm going to be fairly useless when it comes to skill swapping I'm afraid.'

'Oh, I don't know,' she says, turning and looking at me up and down. 'What about mending clothes? Knitting . . . can you knit? Always looking for knitters.'

Seriously. I'm forty-one years old. Do I look like a granny? Hand me a sodding shotgun.

'I can knit,' says a girl, leaning against the wall in reception, examining the ends of her long blonde hair. She's got one of those enormous dirty knitted hats on that only really suit Rastas, which pretty girls wear sometimes, because the hats are so ugly they make them look even prettier.

'My gran taught me,' she says, to no one in particular, still staring at her hair. 'I used to sit by her feet and watch her. By the fire. And she'd help me when I did it wrong.'

'What can you knit, Kitty dear?' says Mrs H.

'I knitted a square once. Is that a word, knitted? Or is it knut?' she says, suddenly more interested, looking up at Mrs H.

'Knitted is the word,' says Mrs H, leaning over to pick up the drawing pin.

'I can't knit,' I say to Mrs H.

'Well, read to children then,' she says, matter-of-factly.

'The C word!' I say.

'You read, don't you?' she says.

'Doesn't mean I read to children.'

'Do you want any shopping or not?'

'I would go myself . . .'

'You can't go yourself, now can you? Detective Sergeant Clarke explained everything to me.' And she nods and I nod, just once, and we understand each other.

The girl is watching.

'Listen,' says Mrs H, 'there's a load of charity stuff needs washing in the laundry room. It's the stuff in the yellow bags. I was going to do it but you make a start on that and I'll get your shopping myself. Leave a list on front reception. Five minutes. Nothing too heavy.'

I dig around in the bottom of my bag to get a pen and a bit of paper and I sit down opposite the girl, Kitty.

'Don't bother getting a load of stuff. It all gets nicked,' she says, still examining her hair, like she's looking for split ends. 'Sarah Murray ate my Cadbury's Creme Egg yesterday. She's the fat one with no neck and dark hair – looks like that big one out of the Addams Family. The bloke, not the woman. Big shoulders. Stupid shiny high heels, short skirt, no tights.'

Kitty is one of those girls who spells trouble. That's the thing with being judgmental – you just can't help yourself, right?

There's me thinking she's being a bit mean, really, and that the poor neckless Sarah Murray probably can't even afford tights, or her own Cadbury's Creme Egg for that matter, and then I'm thinking, at the exact same time, that Kitty is far too young to be in a women's refuge and surely there were worthier women in more desperate circumstances, and I don't even know anything about her, other than she can't really knit, not properly, even though she says she can, and that she likes to eat Cadbury's Creme Eggs when she's got one. There's something not right about that girl.

I go up to my room to get my purse.

Clare is curled up in the arm of the sofa, under her dressing gown, still totally reeking of paraffin.

'Who are you?' she goes.

'I'm Sally, your room-mate,' I say, sticking out my hand for her to shake. 'Well, not exactly room-mate. We share the flat. That's your room and that's mine,' I say, pointing. 'We share the living room and the bathroom.'

She nods and looks out of the window and ignores my hand.

'I'm getting some shopping. You want anything? Hula hoops? Snickers? Five sugar-coated jam doughnuts.'

'No,' she says.

'How about I get some anyway?' I say. 'In case you change your mind.'

She shrugs.

'See you later,' I say, turning on my heel, with the cash for Mrs H.

'Have I met you somewhere?' she goes, still looking out the window.

'Nah, don't think so,' I say. 'But I guess we are going to get to know each other.'

'I'm temporary,' she says.

I don't know about that, I think.

Eighteen

DS Clarke

DS Clarke is looking for PC Halsall's original Oval Road site-visit report to see if a car was mentioned, and it wasn't. At the back of the station, the gated windows look out on the car park and DS Clarke can see DC Walker chatting to PC Halsall; she wonders first at their relaxed familiarity and, second, at their distinct lack of urgency.

She watches PC Halsall pull a face at DC Walker when she looks at her phone and sees who the call is coming from.

'Sarge,' she says.

'Quit blabbering to Walker and get in here, Livvy, before I decide to write your appraisal early.'

Something is bothering DS Clarke about her latest victim. Just when she is convinced by the veracity of Clare's ordeal, something pops up to undermine it. For someone who's been locked up in a laundry room, on and off, for the best part of two years, she's a bit too sassy, she thinks. And then she thinks that maybe it's a generational thing as Livvy walks through the door.

'PC Halsall!' she says. 'Are we running some kind of youth camp?'

A gamut of emotions pass one by one over PC Halsall's face, from confusion to understanding, innocence to stammering embarrassment.

DS Clarke feels a prick of embarrassment herself.

'Can I just ask, was the car belonging to the alleged perpetrator still outside the property?'

'Um. Wait. Oh yes! It was! A silver Lexus.'

'But not in the report?'

'No, sarge.'

'And that didn't lead you to believe that, perhaps, Mr James was home?'

'No.'

'No? Why not?'

'Well, he could've taken the bus.'

'He could've taken the bus?'

'Yeah. The 24 goes practically to the front door of the Royal Free. What is it, four stops?'

Shame, thought DS Clarke, that her policing education doesn't match her knowledge of the London bus network.

'I don't believe Gareth was at the hospital,' DS Clarke says to herself. Actually, she says it out loud. She does that sometimes. 'She's either lying, she's telling the truth or she's seeing things.'

'Sarge?'

'Dismissed, PC Halsall,' says DS Clarke, having forgotten she was there.

In DS Clarke's experience, in most cases like this, the perpetrator most often disappears off the face of the earth, only resurfacing when they think the police have got bored of looking.

The CCTV report is due early evening. It takes that long with so many cameras, but early reports suggest that he wasn't there.

Not there.

'So just where are you Gareth?' she thinks aloud to no one in particular.

Her email pings.

Dr Ridley's police medical report is through.

Bruising consistent with abuse including to the thighs, abdomen, buttocks, cheeks & neck.

Bruising consistent with trauma including to the knees and shins.

Superficial cuts and grazes.

Malnourished.

Ingestion of hazardous liquids – not confirmed.

Thermal & chemical burns – confirmed.

May have a propensity to self-harm.

DS Clarke snaps her laptop shut.

Experts piss her off.

But Ridley *really* pisses her off.

What good is a report, she fumes to herself, that starts 'bruising consistent with abuse' then finishes with 'propensity to self-harm'.

DS Clarke picks up her phone and dials.

'So you've confirmed the thermal and chemical burns?' she barks down the phone at Ridley.

'Hi, Sue, and how are you?'

'Bruising, trauma, cuts and grazes?'

'Yes, you've got my report, then.'

'So, you are confirming abuse?'

'I'm confirming abuse as best I can,' says Ridley. 'The facts speak for themselves – but I wasn't there. Still, it's hard to fake that kind of abuse.'

'And then you say she self-harms,' says DS Clarke, still barking.

'I didn't say she had self-harmed,' says Dr Ridley, offended.

'Well, it looks like it says that to me.'

'I said she *may* have a propensity to self-harm.'

'When I last looked, propensity meant "a natural tendency to behave in a certain way".'

'She may have developed a habit of self-harming.'

'"Develop" and "have" mean different things. Very different things.'

'Well, if she didn't have it before, she'll have it now. I think you might be splitting hairs, DS Clarke.'

'I think you might be generalising, Dr Ridley.'

'If you police officers are so damn clever, why do you consult with experts?'

'I often ask myself the very same thing.'

'Jesus, Sue, you're on massively good form tonight. What happened? One of the cats run away?'

'More generalising, Dr Ridley?'

'Look, Sue, all I'll say is this: keep an eye on her. Or get someone else to. Any lethal means in the vicinity – you know the drill. No sharp objects, lighters, matches, hazardous liquids – any means of deliberate self-harm.'

'She may have had enough hazardous liquids for one lifetime. And matches.'

'Hmmmm.'

'What's "hmmmm" mean?'

'We'll see about that. Meanwhile, make sure she's not self-administering her meds – and keep her out of the kitchen/laundry.'

'OK.'

'And I hope the cats are all OK . . .'

Nineteen

Clare

I don't know why there has to be so much talking.

I've decided to move back to New York.

Police.

    Caseworkers.

    Doctors.

    Nurses.

    More police.

    Therapists.

    And now apparently, a room-mate.

    Why can't they all just leave me alone?

I've been invited to sing at Carnegie Hall Festival.

Oh my God. Now there's someone shouting through the door.

    'Hi, Clare. It's just Mrs Henry. I've got a man here to look in some cupboards. Pest Control.'

    I open it.

    She has the key in her hand. Don't know why they didn't just come in.

'This is Mr Spencer, my dear, from Pest Control. He's come to put out some lovely bait,' she says.

All jolly hockey sticks. As though she's talking about Crufts or something.

'How about you come downstairs and have a look through the garment wardrobe?'

'No thanks.'

'How about a coffee then?'

'I don't drink coffee.'

'Diet Coke?'

'I'm not thirsty. Really.'

'Clare, can you please come downstairs with me for five minutes while Mr Spencer checks for rats?' she says, getting edgy.

She could've just said.

I pick up my key.

Put it in the pocket of my dressing gown.

Bathrobe.

Loads of artists made their name at Carnegie.

Judy Garland.

Benny Goodman.

You've never heard of Benny Goodman!

You're so dumb.

'I'd really like you to meet your room-mate but she's in a meeting. How about we just have a quick look at the garment wardrobe?'

Already met her.

What's the point?

I shrug.

'If the police were doing their job properly, I could go home today,' I say.

'Celia will be here shortly. Your caseworker from Camden. She also works here so she can continue looking out for you. Are you happy with that?'

'What for?' I say.

I mean, what are they making such a big deal for. Once they've got him, I can go home.

You can loan me the ticket, right?
It's only like a thousand bucks.
That's not even First class.
Business.

'Hi, Clare!'

Celia's back.

Again.

'We've got a meeting booked in now. Is that OK? I would have called to check but . . .'

I nod.

She's annoying.

But I guess it goes with the job.

'We need to go over a range of practical issues that I can support you with,' she says.

I nod again.

'Shall we go into Cerise?'

All the rooms have pink names – Cerise, Rose, Magenta, Fuchsia . . .

I hate pink.

Didn't used to.

Pink and red.

The nice policewoman is still here.

Susan.

She *is* nice.

Genuinely.

Even if she doesn't believe me about the hospital.

She's talking to someone in the kitchen at the end of the corridor, drinking out of a *Frozen* mug. I can see Elsa from here.

Wouldn't have had her down as the type.

Not for fairy tales.

Celia drags out a ripped black plastic chair for me opposite her ripped black plastic chair, then firmly closes the door.

The walls are lined with grey spongy tiles; vile, half picked-away grey spongy tiles.

'They cut down on sound,' she says, nodding at the walls and smiling like they all do. 'We like our ladies to be able to speak freely.'

Ladies!

I nod.

'I'm preparing a welcome pack for you. Just the basics, you know, tea, coffee, soap. If there's anything you want, in particular, we can put a request in!'

She raises her eyebrows and smiles.

Mock excitement.

At least the policewoman is real.

'Is there anything you can think of that you need?'

'No,' I say.

She's reading from a ring binder.

Not as modern as at the police station.

It's got lots of loose sheets of paper in.

A report.

'We're still waiting for more information from the hospital. The police doctor suggests that you set up a regular appointment with your GP. But she's going to follow-up, said she'd pop in on her way home just to make sure that the blistering doesn't go septic and the thermal burns may need re-dressing. And we have to have a talk about your weight. 'Do you have a GP in the area, Clare?' she says, looking up.

I shake my head.

'No?' she says.

Like I'm lying.

'But you used to live around here, right?'

'I still live around here,' I say.

Why would I lie?

'Of course, you do,' she says, blushing.

'I used to have a GP but I haven't been in ages. The only doctor I've seen is one in Harley Street, but that was just for vitamin shots.'

She nods and writes something down.

'Have you found him yet?' I say.

'Who?' she says.

Genuinely. She said who.

Who else am I going to be talking about?

I think that.

I don't say that.

'The police are getting on with it,' she says.

She must have just read my face.

'Why don't you get on with it too, then?' I say, quietly. 'Why don't you stop wasting your time talking to me about tea and coffee?'

I'm not having a go or anything. I don't even like tea and coffee . . .

'I'm a caseworker, Clare. I don't go around hunting for criminals. I support victims.'

'I don't need your support, Celia. I just want to go home.'

Please go and find the bastard so I can go home.

'As I say,' she says, taking a deep breath,' I'm here to support you with a range of practical issues . . .'

I stop listening.

I need to think.

She's saying something about registering with a GP. Getting welfare benefits. Contacting a solicitor. Counselling. Weight-gaining shakes.

I nod occasionally.

And if that gets a confused response, I shake my head. You can usually tell what someone wants you to say.

He's never left the side gate open before.

He often unlocks the laundry room when he's totally hammered and tries to get me to go in the house with him.

But he never left the side gate open before.

I never hit you.

You just get pissed and fall over.

That's what I tell anyone.

Not that anyone cares.

It's just you and me, babe.

He's always sorry at that point.

I usually pretend to be asleep.

Going inside with him mostly ends up being worse than staying outside . . .

'I understand what you've been through,' says Celia, passing me a tissue.

I doubt it.

I'm not being unkind.

I'm just doubt it.

For example.

Hey, Coco, I got this great game off the internet. Wanna play? It's got all the instructions.

The Matches Game.

Let me read it to you . . .

Method:

First of all, overpower the victim.

Tie the victim's wrists together and secure them to the handle of a low cupboard or drawer.

Take one bottle of Paraffin, 250ml available from most hardware stores.

Do not be tempted to use petrol.

Paraffin is a less volatile combustible hydrocarbon liquid that takes time to catch.

Once the victim is secured, pour paraffin over the victim's head.

Slowly is better if you want to really put the shits up them.

Limit head movement so that paraffin goes in eyes.

Dispense enough paraffin for the victim to be sitting in a pool of it, yet not enough to run out of control across the floor.

Sit opposite victim.

Support your lower back against kitchen cupboard, for comfort.

Ensure source of beer/wine/whisky is accessible. Add ice to beer/wine/whisky to prolong personal consciousness.

Take one box of matches, large family-sized, making sure not to get the box damp. Lie box of matches on its side, strike side up, between knees to prevent slippage. With the tip of index finger of left hand, hold match perpendicular to the box, head down against strike, then, with your right hand, tuck your index finger under your thumb, then flick the side of the match.

Flick with meaning.

Half-hearted flicks will not ignite.

Observations:

Babe? Are you listening?

Going low on the match will attain maximum uplift, targeting hair, face, breasts, shoulders.

Going high on the match will attain minimum uplift targeting feet, legs, pubic hair, labia.

Conclusion:

The matches game is an effective and compelling way to strip a victim of pride and dignity, forcing the victim to feel inferior. It is a profoundly violent and disturbing act that leaves the victim with long-term psychological wounds.

Do you have any pride and dignity, Coco?

Shall we see?

What do you mean you don't want to play?

'Clare. Clare, are you OK?'

Celia is still here, mumbling on.

Focus.

'All of the women here have experienced some form of domestic abuse. It might be psychological, physical, emotional, or all of those. A refuge is not an institution. It's a house where women should feel safe.'

Celia is still on script.

'It can be difficult leaving your home and adjusting to life in a new environment. But other women . . .'

'Look. Can I stop you, Celia?' I say. 'Do you mind?'

'Clare, yes of course.' She smiles brightly, aware that she's finally got my full attention. 'Did you want to ask a question?

'Can I go now? I want to sleep.'

'Um yes, of course. We can pick this up later.'

I get up and walk out.

Sally has her back to me when I walk into our sitting room.

She doesn't even look round even though she must have heard me come in.

Staring out the window at the railway tracks.

Eight tracks.

Eight tracks out of here.

The room is hot.

'Can you open the damn window?' I say.

'I tried. They're painted shut. I'll get a screwdriver,' she says, quietly, without moving her head.

No way out of here.

I wonder if she's thinking what I was thinking earlier.

There's a crisp brown bag on the coffee table.

It's the size of five doughnuts, in a line.

But I don't want to eat.

I don't want anything or anyone.

I move towards my bedroom door.

She still doesn't move.

Like she is stuck in a dream.

She's quite nice, Sally. Not pushy like the rest of them.

'You all right?' I say.

'Fine,' she says.

Like I would say fine.

Which means, why don't you just leave me alone.

Someone's put a duvet on my bed.

And a pillow.

Sally, probably.

There's a sheet now covering the stained mattress. And a folded nightie like the sort my gran used to wear.

I don't bother with that.

Just sleep in my clothes.

It's two hours later when I wake up.

It's after lunch.

I still haven't eaten anything.

Someone's knocking on the door.

'Need to check the baiting stations!' says a man's voice.

'Come back later,' I shout.

'It's Mr Spencer, from Pest Control. I—'

'Come back later,' I say again.

'I'm not here later, Miss,' he says. 'I'll be five minutes. Promise.'

The lad can't be more than seventeen.

Seriously.

Bet he wishes he'd listened in class, done his homework, sat his GCSEs.

Instead of having to deal with rats all day long.

I shiver.

'Don't you worry yourself. They can't get through to here now. Blocked up the 'oles,' he says. 'Worst you'll get is a bad smell of dead mouse.'

'Mice,' I correct him.

'Well, yes, there is more than one,' he says, his skin turning the same colour as his spots.

If you won't loan it to me, how about you just take some cash out of your savings.

I mean, that's what it's there for right?

Twenty

Sally

Mrs H has bought me a selection of meals for one, and all I can think is, bloody hell, how depressing is that? I've always avoided meals for one. People who buy meals for one have obviously come to terms with being alone – I haven't, not me.

I'm toying with a macaroni cheese that I microwaved, put out onto a plate because, who eats out of plastic containers, right, then noticed the plate is covered in bits of old food, so now I'm wishing I had eaten it out of the plastic container. I don't know why I care that it looks cheap, it's not like the manners police are out on the loose. I wouldn't do it at home, eat out of a container, I mean, I'd have it off a plate at home.

When you're in here, you can't let your standards slip, feel sorry for yourself and let things go. Things like don't forget to wash your hair, or clean your teeth, don't put your micro-meal on a proper plate. I think everybody looks at everybody else and wonders, 'how come I ended up here?' and 'I'm better than all this'. To start with they do. But we're none of us better than this. Sometimes I look in the mirror and wonder where on earth I got to, at what point did I leave the room and this old person came in.

There is nothing to hold on to here, nothing normal, you know. S'like being in a rowing boat in the middle of an ocean in a storm, looking for land, with waves and rain and you know, killer sharks and stuff, and no oars.

Clare is asleep, still. I made up her bed, you know, put out a nightie for her, made her laugh more than anything. Winceyette. Do you remember winceyette, all furry on the outside, and furry on the inside?

'Thanks for doing that washing,' says Mrs H, sitting down opposite me in the dining room. I'd sat close to the back in the hope of avoiding people, by the window overlooking the garden. Two little Indian girls are digging in the flower bed, and they've got anoraks over coral pink leggings and pink wellington boots, and they're chattering between them, like they haven't got a care in the world.

'Those are Prashi's girls,' goes Mrs H. 'She arrived last week. She could use a friend.'

Oh God, here she goes.

'Goes without saying, we could all use a friend, Mrs H,' I say, 'but the thing is, there's not a lot of point, is there?'

'You know the score around here,' she says. 'You're an old hand.'

'Thanks. Not for years and not this one specifically,' I say sarcastically, thinking thanks very much – charming, that is.

'Will you come to the house meeting later?'

Oh my good gawd, a house meeting.

'What for?' I say. 'I'm not even here that long.'

'Everyone says that,' she says, biting on a broken nail, then picking at it to break it off, and chewing on it.

'You know my circumstances. I'm different,' I say.

'Everyone says that too,' she says. 'You could really help.'

And now I'm staff all of a sudden.

'I seem to be doing a lot of helping here,' I say.

She gives me a look. A 'get a life' kind of a look.

'OK, fine, I'll come to the meeting,' I say. 'But I'm not saying anything.'

'Great attitude.'

'Look, Mrs H, I'm not here to have a great attitude, that's what *you've* chosen to do with your life. It's not what I've chosen to do with my life. I'm here to avoid being attacked by a psychopath. Just because I'm not twenty doesn't mean I've suddenly turned into Mother Teresa.'

'Have you met with your support worker yet?'

'No, but . . .'

'I think you're on Lucy Walker's list, she's one of our best support workers. She might be able to get you some counselling or get you on a mindfulness course. You'll like her.'

'Right,' I say. But I don't mean right. And because, just this once, I don't want to piss on her firework I'm not going to give Mrs H any attitude.

Counselling! Like a) I haven't got time for counselling and b) it ain't me that needs it, it's my ex-husband. He's the psycho.

Counselling!

When my ex-husband crashes through the patio doors with a machete, I'll remember to say, 'Hang on a minute, darling, while I try a little mindfulness, would you?' Perhaps I can ask him to 'reframe his thoughts and feelings'. Yeah, good idea. No, this is it; I'll tell him that I have reframed my thoughts, so don't attack me, there's a good lad! That'll do it.

'What time's the meeting?' I say.

'Three, in Magenta, the big room at the back. Will you bring Clare?'

'If she wants. Have you asked her?'

'No, I thought . . .'

'Well, why don't you ask her then,' I say, and gather up the tray and cutlery, 'cos remember, I don't actually work here, do I.' Rhetorical question. 'Oh, and while you're here. What's with the plastic cutlery?'

'Precaution,' she says.

'Precaution against what?' I say, to her back, as she disappears down the hallway.

PC Chapman is here with my bags and I'm not lying, I've never been so pleased to see two suitcases in my whole entire life, and she's dangling my door keys at me and smiling.

'Thanks so, so much,' I say, 'I can't wait to change my pants.'

'TMI,' she says and laughs.

'Nothing to report,' she goes. 'No criminal activity. Apart from the pint of milk you left on the side, which has stunk the whole kitchen out. I got your post too,' she says. 'Do you want a hand with anything?' she says.

'No, I'm fine,' I put the keys and letters in my bag, and pick up the suitcases, 'exercise'll do me good. Thanks again, and for sorting the milk.'

'No worries.'

The suitcases started out all right, but by the time I had got halfway up the stairs they had literally doubled in weight. I was dreaming of one of the Stannah stairlift thingies they have on the telly, which would've whizzed me up in no time, while I could just sit with my cases on my knee, smiling away like they always do, in the ads, in a nice cosy pink dressing gown. By the time I get to the second-floor landing I can no longer feel my fingers.

'You got lucky with the third floor,' says a voice.

It's the blonde girl. Kitty. She picks up one of my bags.

'Everyone always wants to be high up,' I wheeze, between gasps, wondering if I'm going to need life support.

'Best views,' she goes.

Best views! You have got to be kidding me.

'I had a third-floor room but they moved me down, cos they said you had to be in it.'

'Most women in refuges want the highest floor cos it's far-thest away from the front door,' I say. 'Won't necessarily save 'em, but it helps them sleep at night.'

Best views! I can hardly breathe.

'From this floor you can get up onto the roof. But shhh, don't tell Commandant Henry.'

'How do you know?'

'I saw the door when the rat man was here. . .'

I wonder what she's on about and give her a look.

'Sunbathing!' she goes. 'I got my bikini here. I got two bikinis here. No, hang on, I got three!'

It's not the first thing I'd think of packing for a trip to a women's refuge; clean underwear, teabags, Nurofen, and oh yeah, three bikinis.

Like I say, there's something not right about that girl.

'Can I meet your roomie?' she goes.

'Not now,' I say. 'She's asleep.'

'Can't you see if she's awake?'

'She said she doesn't want to be disturbed.'

'Did she actually say that?' she asks, a bit nasty like.

'Yeah, she did actually say that,' I say, pulling the cases through the front door and slamming it.

'Thanks!' she shouts through the door, insulted.

'No problem,' I shout back.

'Yeah, right,' she mutters, thundering down the stairs as loud as she can.

'Who was that?' says Clare, standing behind the door where she'd been looking through the gap in the hinges. I nearly crap my pants.

'Kitty, another resident.'

'Is that what we call ourselves, residents?'

'"Resident" sounds better than "inmate". "Inmate" sounds better than "victim". I s'pose we could go for "guest" – but that sounds like we asked for it,' I say.

She grabs a case and hauls it into my bedroom.

'Thanks for making my bed,' she goes. 'I gave the nightie a miss.'

'Thought it might give you a laugh,' I say, unzipping the first case. 'There's some quite nice stuff in the garment wardrobe,'

I say and I think, oh my good gawd, I'm institutionalised already. 'You can wash your own stuff too, if you want, in the laundry room next to the kitchen. You could just borrow something out of the garment wardrobe, for now, cos it's all clean, I know, because I washed it myself.'

'I'm all right,' she goes.

'That dressing gown smells like it might combust on its own.'

'I don't notice the smell anymore,' she goes, wrapping it around her even more tightly.

There's a jar of hot chocolate tucked in the corner of my suitcase, which I'd forgotten about completely and I suddenly have a craving for a mug.

'Fancy some?' I say, holding up the jar, and I can see her arguing with herself in her own head cos half of her wants it and half of her's thinking that she'd rather not talk to anyone or see anyone.

'I'm not ...' She stops. 'Yeah, OK,' she says, 'why not?' As we go down to the kitchen she whispers, 'What's that Kitty all about?'

'You make your own mind up about that one,' I say. 'She's not the full ticket, if you ask me, but each to their own, that's what I always say.'

'Is there a type in here, do you think?' she says.

'Not according to Mrs H,' I say. 'But yeah, I think there's a type.'

'Naive and stupid.' She looks at the stained mugs in the cupboard, as though they have toxic waste on them or something.

'Trusting and kind,' I say. 'And naive and stupid.'

She giggles, which is the first time I've seen her smile.

'There's a house meeting this afternoon,' I say.

'What's that?'

'It's for all the residents, to chat.'

'I don't do chat.'

'Me neither,' I say. 'I'm not sure many will want to, apart from the social workers – they'll want to chat, a lot, they always do.' I stir the chocolate powder into boiling water. 'Actually, I'm being unfair, it's part of the process, meeting other people who are in the same situation as you are – we both are.'

'I doubt they've been in the same situation as me,' she says mockingly, deliberately copying the way I said it, which is weird because I haven't seen that side of her.

'You shouldn't be like that,' I say. 'You'd be surprised. Most of the women here will have been systematically abused, that's what they call it.'

'What's that mean?' she says.

'It means no one's here after a one-off beating. They've all had a situation that's gone on for a while, getting worse and worse, same as you.'

'How'd you know about me?' she goes, looking spiky.

'You hide behind doors, you refuse to speak, you're afraid of your own shadow . . . I've been there too.'

'Well, I'm still not saying anything,' she says, blowing over the top of the chocolatey froth so that some of it lands on the table and she wipes it off with the palm of her hand, quickly, too quickly, nervously, looking over her shoulder. Her hands are raw and pink, and they look like they must sting.

'You don't have to say anything, it'll still help,' I say.

'I don't see how.'

'Knowing you're not the only one helps,' I say, thinking of Hayley, the blood gushing out of her neck and soaking into her long blonde highlights.

All different colours and shapes of chairs are arranged in a horseshoe, all different colours and shapes of women take their seats, apart from the lady at the front. That's the lady from Women's Aid, and you can pretty much spot a lady from Women's Aid a mile off. I wonder if the wardrobe comes with the job or the job attracts the type of person who likes to wear tie-dyed skirts to the floor and novelty earrings.

Some of the women in the room look like they actually want to be there; they've brought bits of paper and pens, to take notes, and some of the women look totally bored and we haven't even started yet, and some of them look broken, as though they can't take one more thing.

Kitty is leaning against the door frame, looking as if she doesn't belong with these women, doesn't *want* to belong with these women. She can sneak out, around the corner, in a second if she wants to and she sees me watching her and she smirks to herself, like she's glad that I'm looking at her because she thinks I think she's interesting. Which I don't; I just don't think she's right for here. S'all.

'Here at York Gate we aim to empower women and children through support,' says Mrs Women's Aid. Ho hum. The Indian lady just wrote down what she said. Prashi, the one with the two girls. There's a woman next to her, in a hijab, and she's writing everything down too. Jesus wept. Or do I mean Allah?

'We're here to enable women to realise the new opportunity they have created for themselves, so that they can live their lives free from domestic violence.'

'What opportunity is that?' says the big girl in the leather jacket by the window. She has a surprisingly low voice, and a surprisingly loud voice, compared to Mrs Women's Aid. She's thirty-ish, dyed blonde bob, dirty roots, long, perfect, turquoise nails filed to a point.

'Hello, you're quite new, aren't you?' says Mrs Women's Aid.

'Debbie,' says Debbie. I think she might be the one who ate the Cadbury's Creme Egg, cos I'll be honest, she looks like she's had a few. Or maybe it was the other big one. I mean, I'm not slim myself, I'm no Kate Moss, I'm not. Just saying. Just so you know.

'Got here two weeks ago when it first opened . . . Was here last week and the week before,' she goes as if she's accusing Mrs Women's Aid of not noticing her, like that was possible.

'Welcome, Debbie,' goes Mrs Women's Aid, looking around the room expectantly.

'Welcome, Debbie,' says everyone, apart from me and Clare, who catch on too late. Clare widens her eyes at me and half bites her lip. We couldn't get seats together, so she's parked just one away from Mrs Women's Aid, which means I can't look at Mrs Women's Aid without seeing Clare trying not to laugh.

'Debbie has brought up an interesting thought,' says Mrs Women's Aid. 'Would anyone else like to comment?'

No one says anything. It's like the French lessons we used to have at school when they'd ask for someone to read out loud. '*Qui veut lire? Une voluntaire?*' No one wanted to speak then, either.

'Who would like to talk about opportunity? About how being here presents an opportunity?' She's smiling like a Cheshire cat and all. Holy sodding cow, this is worse than embarrassing.

'I would have thought,' says Big Debbie, sounding like an articulated truck driver, 'that, up until now, most of us have been denied opportunity. So, we don't have something new, do we, really? We just have something that got robbed off us, that we should've had in the first place.'

Prashi's not sure. Should she write it down or not? The woman in the hijab goes for it and begins scribbling, apparently word for word.

'Aiysha, you seem to find that concept interesting. Would you like to share your view?' says Mrs Women's Aid.

Aiysha stops in her tracks, like a rabbit in the headlights, and shakes her hijab and carries on writing, like it's really important to get every single word down.

It's all gone hideously quiet. No one is saying anything at all.

'And while we're on the subject of stuff that got robbed off us – where's the fucking cutlery gone? You can't cut a piece of toast with a sodding plastic knife,' says Big Debbie.

'I'm sure there's an excellent and valid reason that the cutlery has been replaced. However. Shall we leave cutlery for now and go back to opportunity?' says Mrs Women's Aid.

'Where's the usual cutlery?' says Aiysha, looking concerned. 'Did someone steal the cutlery? It wasn't me if that's what anyone thinks. I haven't stolen anything. I can see you all think I did, but I . . .'

'Oh, be quiet, Aiysha,' says Prashi. 'No one thinks you've stolen anything . . .'

'I think you're all talking shit,' interrupts Big Debbie, suddenly, loudly.

There's a bit of a gasp from the group. Kitty settles her back against the wall and folds her arms, like the group meeting has finally got interesting.

'I don't think we need to swear, Debbie,' says Mrs Women's Aid, getting a bit hot under the collar.

'You asked me what I thought,' says Debbie. 'I think you're talking shit.'

Clare coughs but I swear it was a snort that turned into a cough halfway through.

'You're right to feel aggrieved, Debbie,' says Mrs Women's Aid. Don't you just hate it when people do that whole thing with your name, like they're trying to prove to everyone that they're so damn caring that they can remember everybody's names? Like God or something.

'You're right, Debbie, it's not normal to have your opportunities taken away from you, by perhaps someone stronger, more powerful, more convincing, more . . .'

'What's normal?' says Big Debbie, getting properly annoyed. 'You're now trying to tell me what's normal and what's not normal. I'll tell you what's normal. *Nothing's* normal. That's what's normal. Nothing. This isn't fucking normal, is it?' she says, heaving her and her leather jacket out of the ripped plastic chair. 'Sitting around here like a herd of fucking dairy cows is not fucking normal.' And she waddles out, her yellow flip-flops slapping against the lino.

Clare is biting her lip so hard it looks like she might bite it off. Mrs Women's Aid is boiling all over her tie-dyed skirt and novelty earrings. Mrs H bustles in and sits down, taking Big Debbie's empty chair.

'Marina,' she says to the thin woman the other side of me, pretty girl, olive skin, Greek, maybe. 'Would you like to talk a little bit about opportunity?' she says. 'You've been in various refuges over a number of years. We've got a few new recruits and I'd love it if you could help to explain what we do here at York Gate, to support our residents and prepare them for a new life, full of opportunities.'

Marina nods around the room. 'I'm Marina,' she says, and I sat there thinking that I'd never have turned out that confident, not even if nothing had ever happened to me.

'Welcome, Marina,' everyone replies in unison. Clare and I are late again. Kitty, I notice, looks like she's shut down. No expression.

'I'm from Cyprus.' Her voice sounds more American than Greek, but who am I to judge? 'Some of you know me,' she says, smiling at an older lady sitting two away from Clare. 'I lived in the United States since I was seven. I have a degree from Harvard Business School in International Economics. After I moved to the UK with my husband – without my family, you understand – I lost my freedom and my independence. My now ex-husband was unable to find a job and became very angry, to the point that he was often violent and controlling.

'When I first went into a refuge, the one in Kentish Town, I was unable to think straight; I was so used to being told what I could and couldn't do that I no longer had the ability to make a decision. I found it hard to get up in the morning without being told I could get up. My body no longer knew when I was tired or hungry or thirsty.

'Since then, I have had behavioural therapy. I've learned to reframe my past experiences and move forward. Don't underestimate how powerful therapy can be, both one-on-one and group,' she says, looking specifically at Mrs Women's Aid. 'You don't know how grateful I am. I don't think anyone knows yet,' she continues, 'but I'm leaving next week. I've got a flat. Just in Hackney, not far, and I've found a job in the city. Not as high up as I was before, five years ago, but it's well-paid. My mum is coming over to live nearby with my little sister, and I'm going to come back here as a volunteer, to help other women in my position, or in a similar position to mine, no two positions are the same.' And she tips her head to one side and smiles a wide smile, gums and all.

No one is writing now. Aiysha and Prashi are staring, openmouthed.

'Grab the opportunity with both hands.' Marina shrugs, looking like butter wouldn't melt.

Everyone looks as if they've just had some kind of religious experience, except me and Clare, and of course, Kitty.

Kitty looks like someone just told her to eat her greens. She can't hide her grimace as she stares at Marina. After a while she also tips her head to one side, and smiles, but her attempt at a really wide smile, gums and all, looks almost violent.

Twenty-One

DS Clarke

DS Clarke has seen her fair share of DV cases; in fact, more than her fair share of DV cases, and something about Clare's didn't add up.

She tends to go with her gut. Prided herself on always going with her gut. However, when her instinct was in overdrive, sometimes she needed a sounding board, a grown-up conversation, with insightful dialogue, which is why she decided to invite caseworker Celia in – just for an informal.

But apparently, and DS Clarke remembers and quite literally kicks herself about three seconds into the conversation, social workers try not to hold opinions. Not when there is utter vagueness to cling on to. How could she have forgotten such a thing?

'I think Clare may be having a hard time managing her emotions.'

Really, thinks DS Clarke, mentally rolling her eyes.

'She may be? Or she is?'

'She may be,' repeats Celia, nodding furiously to the point that DS Clarke worried for her neck.

'So, you believe her?'

'Clare?'

A few seconds pass while Celia thinks.

'Of course I believe her. Emotions are very real, DS Clarke.'

'Right. Most of the DVs we see have a hard time managing their emotions, Celia.'

'Clare's experiences are more intense, I think, than many that we deal with.'

'In what way?'

'I think most DV victims spend at least some part of their everyday in a non-threatening environment. Maybe when the kids are home from school. The hours when the partner is out of the house, at work. Or the hours when they themselves are at work.'

'Go on.'

'Clare has been living under the control of another person, twenty-four hours a day. No let-up. No non-threatening environment. Even when he wasn't at home, he could come back at any time. He played with her like a cat plays with a mouse.'

'So that means . . .?'

'That means that now she's out, she's not able to acclimatise. She's used to being controlled. Now she can make her own mind up, she can't decide what to do, who to listen to. She'll be prone to losing control of her anger, exploding at well-meaning people, erratic moods. She might be crying one minute and lashing out the next.'

'Why would she get so upset by a question about who her GP is?'

'We're awaiting her assessment by Emma Tudor, the community psychiatric nurse. She'll be able to help with all this.'

'So, you're not sure what it was about the GP?'

'No. I'd say she's suspicious, negative and paranoid about other people's motives. She twists her hands together. She avoids eye contact. She shuts us out when it gets too terrifying.'

'She's terrified of her GP?'

'No, she's terrified of trusting anyone. Especially anyone who is kind. I'd say it's typical of someone who has suffered intensive long-term abuse by a partner. It's like PTSD on a massive scale.'

'So, nothing calculated?'

'Calculated?'

'She couldn't be making it all up?'

'Well, I doubt it. She dissociated at the end of the last session. She just froze. Couldn't seem to hear what we were saying to her at all.'

Dissociated. Interesting word, thinks DS Clarke. Didn't she terminate the interview, she thought. Didn't she simply walk out? That's what it seemed like to me, she thinks.

'I can only give you my observations, of course,' says Celia, with a smile. 'I don't have an opinion, only observations.'

DS Clarke thanks Celia for her insightful observations and, for once, Celia Barrett leaves, not looking like a woman expecting the end of the world. DS Clarke imagines there was not a lot of joy in social work.

DS Clarke imagines she was Clare. Walk in the victim's shoes. She imagines she was sitting opposite Celia, in Cerise, staring down at her burnt, bitten fingers, smelling the stench of paraffin on her dressing gown and the dull pain in her leg and the back of her head. She imagines how tired she might be.

After everything. And all the questions. And the hospital. After two years living with a monster.

Or after telling the police a pack of lies, for whatever reason. She imagines she'd be very tired. And if the questions got too close to uncovering her lies . . .

'Tell you what,' she says out loud. 'I'd dissociate if I had something to hide. I mean, all you do is sit there in a daze. Wait for an opportunity. And run.'

DS Clarke smiles, glad to have some insightful dialogue with herself.

Twenty-Two

Clare

I'm not sure I've laughed that hard for years.

'It was when Aiysha started writing down all that stuff Big Debbie was saying,' Sally says, when she could finally get the words out. 'Do you think she actually wrote down, "I think you're talking shit"?'

We're back in our sitting room, half-whispering in case anyone hears us laughing.

'I nearly exploded at that point,' I say. 'It was like being in school assembly all over again.'

'I couldn't even look at you,' Sally says.

'What a bunch of misfits,' I say. 'But I'm including me in that. I'm not saying . . .'

Sally nods.

She's funny for an older person. Most people her age don't find stuff like that funny. And they don't swear or anything anymore.

Not women.

My dad swore.

'You wanna doughnut?' she says, holding up the bag.

'No,' I say.

'You eaten today?' she says.

'No. I've got to see the doctor again at six. The one from the Royal Free. She's coming here, for a follow-up appointment.'

'You'd better eat something, then, or your glucose will be through the floor.'

'God, she kept going on about glucose.'

'I'll get a plate,' Sally says, and disappears out of the sitting room.

Coco!

   Coco!

   Coco!

   What have we said about sugar?

Wonder what he's doing right now.

Driving around, searching, going to my work, I bet. Louisa's moved away so he can't try her.

Down to the canal, see if I've thrown myself in.

That would have suited him.

Babe, you're just weighing me down.

She's cutting one of the doughnuts in half and handing me the plate with both halves on.

She's takes a bite of one herself.

'Do you know who all the other women are?' I say. 'They don't exactly talk much.'

'I only arrived just before you,' she says, 'so no, not really. Prashi is the Indian lady with the two girls. Big Debbie is well,

Big Debbie; don't know her story. Marina's the one from Cyprus who leaves next week, and the one who looks like Debbie, only with dark hair is Sarah, I think, but I'm not sure. She's the one who steals Cadbury's Creme Eggs.'

'The other big one?' I say. 'Not that I'm fat-ist . . .'

'Me neither,' she says. 'And just to prove that point . . .'

She dips her hand into the bag of doughnuts again.

I've eaten both halves of doughnut on my plate. I kind of wish I hadn't.

You really need to cut down on sugar, babe.

You don't wanna see how big your ass looks from behind.

She throws me the bag across the crooked IKEA coffee table.

'Cut it in half. It never feels so bad if it's in halves,' she says, licking sugar off her lips, and gazing out of the window again.

'What's your story, then?' I ask because she looks sad. Lonely, like I am. Wishing she was somewhere else. Just like I wish I was somewhere else.

'I'm from round here . . . well, now I am, but I didn't used to be,' she says. 'I came down from Liverpool twenty years ago. My ex was a bad lot and I gave evidence against him, got him put away for twenty years, but now he's out and we don't know what he's up to and until we do, I'm stuck here.'

'Who's we? You got family?' I say, mouth full.

'We is me and the police. I had family,' she says, 'but after he went inside, the police advised me to start all over – new place, new job, new everything, so his family wouldn't come after me.

It's like witness protection but it wasn't called that then and, if I'm honest I'm not sure it was worth it.'

The bandages on my shoulders and legs are starting to itch.

'You shouldn't scratch,' she says. 'It means it's getting better.'

I stop scratching.

'What about you,' she says.

'Me?' I say, stalling.

Wonder what I should tell her.

'My "partner",' I spit the word out. 'My "partner" turned into a monster.'

He didn't start out a monster.

Tell me what you want.

Babies?

Four!

That's how many I want.

OMG. Same.

Four babies and we'll live in the country.

OK! By the sea. I love the ocean. I've always loved the ocean.

You won't need to work, babe.

I'll work for both of us.

We'd get a ton for this place.

We could get something amazing outside of London.

On a cliff.

OK, on a beach.

I love dogs too!

We can have loads of dogs. We can have a whole pack of dogs.

And a whole pack of babies.

'He used to get so excited. Said he wanted babies. And dogs. To live by the sea.'

'And is that what you wanted?' Sally says, tucking her feet up on the sofa.

'It is exactly what I wanted. I mean, not right then. Not when I was twenty-one. But in a few years.'

'And did he change his mind?'

'No, I don't think so. I don't think he really meant it. When he said it, even, he didn't mean it. None of it. I think he just pretended that he wanted what I wanted.'

'Why would he?'

'I don't know. To reel me in, I guess. I don't even know why he was interested in me in the first place. He was so good-looking. I was a geek compared to him.'

I don't like talking about this stuff.

I want to change the subject.

I don't know why he lied.

He always lied.

'He had some issues with his childhood. But he would never admit that. He's not the sort of person to ever admit there was anything wrong with him.'

'Lots of people have bad childhoods, doesn't mean they beat up women.'

'Yeah, but he lost his mum. Imagine how hard it is to lose your mum, when you're really young. I was sixteen when mine died and that was bad enough.'

'Didn't turn you into a raging psycho though, right?' says Sally.

'That was different. You know what boys are like with their mums. Can I tell you something? Something not to tell anyone.'

Sally's nodding.

'He was like two different people. One second he was crazy about me. Buying me underwear. Desperate to have sex with me. Telling me I was his princess. The next minute, I'd only gone and poured him the wrong soda water, hadn't I! And it was like a bomb had gone off in his head.'

Who were you talking to?

When I came in.

Who were you on the phone to?

Why were you talking about me?

I don't care if she's your friend.

DON'T YOU DARE TALK ABOUT ME.

NOT EVER.

Give me your phone.

Give me your fucking phone.

NO MORE PHONE CALLS.

'He wouldn't let me talk to my friends. He wouldn't let me go to work. In the end, he wouldn't even let me go out of the house.'

Not alone.

Only with him. To the doctor's.

He wouldn't let me drive. Nothing.

It was my car and he wouldn't let me drive.

'But you got away,' Sally says. 'And you're here now and you're safe and you can put all of that stuff behind you and start thinking what you're going to do next. A brand-new start, right?'

'I only got away because he made a mistake.'

I knew he would one day.

He lost control.

Wrecked the entire house because he was that drunk.

You should have heard him crashing around the house after he'd locked me away. Sounded like a tornado had hit it.

'I've been waiting and waiting for him to lose total control. And he did and he slipped up. Waiting and waiting.'

There's a noise outside the door.

'Clare, the doctor from the Royal Free is here to see you,' says Mrs Henry.

'At least you can say you've eaten,' says Sally. 'Come on. You're going to be fine.'

'Will you tell them I'll be two seconds, just need to go to the toilet,' I say.

'Hi, Clare,' the doctor says, scrutinising my face for too long. 'Remember me? Doctor Ridley. I saw you yesterday.'

She has a backpack. She starts unpacking it on the table. Clear plastic pouches with cotton wool in them, dressings, scissors, and tape.

'Clare, I'll catch you in a second,' says Sue, from the door.

She's nice.

'Give you some privacy.'

There's a lock on the inside of the door.

And a grey blind that unrolls to cover over the narrow window.

'How are you feeling now, Clare?' says Doctor Ridley, ripping open the pouches. 'Will you take off your top for me.'

I wonder why they always add 'for me' at the end of those sentences.

I take off the fleece and pull up my T-shirt.

The T-shirt is out of the garment wardrobe.

Garment wardrobe!

'If I take these dressings off and put some waterproof ones on, you can have a shower,' she says. 'It'll be good for you to feel clean.'

I'm going to run you a nice bath.
  That's what you need.
  That'll make you feel better.
  It'll only hurt a little when you first get in.

I wonder how bad I smell.

'Did you eat lunch?' she says.

'I just had doughnuts,' I say. 'Does that count?'

'Sure does,' she says, writing something down on a sheet attached to a clipboard. 'Rice? Pasta?'

'Working up to that,' I say.

She changes the dressings. Takes my blood pressure. Looks in my mouth.

I say 'ahhhhh' while she presses my tongue down with a big lolly stick.

She stares at the backs of my hands.

Then the fronts.

She pulls down my lower eyelids then looks in my ears with a torch.

She stares at the door while she listens to my chest.

She stares at the floor while she counts my heartbeat.

She holds out my forearm.

'We're going to have to reset this at some point,' she says. 'You didn't get it looked at when it was broken?'

'No,' I say.

'Any point asking why?'

'No,' I say, shaking my head.

'Well, you're nearly good as new,' she says. 'On the outside. How's the inside going?'

Dirty bitch.

Dirty on the outside.

Dirty on the inside.

A fraction too early to tell?

I think that.

I don't say that.

It's only been a day or so . . .

A day compared to two years.

'I'll be OK once I'm home,' I say. 'Do you know if he's been locked up yet?'

'You'll have to talk to the police about that,' says Doctor Ridley. 'I'm just a doctor. I'm paid to stick you back together again, nothing more. Clare, I need to ask you something,' she says, looking at me so directly in the eye that it's like she's trying to see into my brain.

Or my soul.

What does she want?

I feel myself start to blush.

Like I've done something.

'We're waiting for detailed tox reports on the contents of your stomach, but I wondered if you know what it was that you drank?'

'The blue liquid?'

'Yes, the blue liquid?'

I can't remember. I don't want to remember.

He said I had to drink it. Said I was dirty.

Dirty on the inside.

'I think you said it was possibly paraffin. You were certainly covered in it. But do you think you'd *drunk* paraffin as well?'

Clear plastic bottle.

CAUTION KEEP OUT OF REACH OF CHILDREN

Blue label

DO NOT SWALLOW

Red writing

FLAMMABLE LIQUID

Black screw cap

DANGER! COMBUSTIBLE LIQUID AND VAPOUR

HARMFUL OR FATAL IF SWALLOWED

Drink it, you little bitch.

'It wasn't paraffin, was it?' she repeats.

It's not a question.

'Not paraffin,' I say.

It's like trying to remember a dream.

Touching my hair.

Smelling my fingers.

'Something else?' I say.

'Something else,' she agrees.

I can't think straight.

I start to cry.

Not because I feel sorry for myself.

Not because I want sympathy from her either.

I just want to be away from all this.

'If it was paraffin it would probably have killed you. Especially when you were sick. If it gets into the lungs . . .'

Drink it up, babe.

You'll be nice and clean by morning.

Twenty-Three

Sally

'What's the gossip?' Sue goes, like I'd have gossip, stuck in here. She's standing by the door to the main hall, turning her nose up at the coffee before I've even made it and keeping her eyes half on the stairs, in case someone comes in and sees us chatting.

'None,' I say. 'Clare's typical DV, Sue, shit-scared and embarrassed to be a victim – and guess what? She'd probably take him back in a heartbeat.'

'You've got to be kidding me!'

'Well, no. Maybe. Half the women here would take their partners back if they came knocking. You should get your head out of those text books, Sue, and listen to what women are saying to you, cos she's no different from any of them. Trouble with women is they think they can fix anything, including raging psychos. Love 'em enough and you'll fix 'em, can't help who you love, see.'

'I have more self-respect than that,' Sue says, looking back at the door again.

'You have no idea, Sue, really you don't,' I say, slamming the plastic cutlery drawer shut. Sometimes professionals are so thick; thick about life, I mean.

'Well, whatever. Chapman's due here in five minutes and we'll finally be able to get a full statement out of her.'

'Why aren't you doing it yourself?'

'I've got to see Langlands. That idiot in Liverpool has made a formal complaint against me.'

'Talking of total wankers,' I say, 'how is Terry?'

She tuts and takes out her laptop.

'According to the highly professional team at Liverpool nick – bunch of tossers – Terry spent his first twenty-four hours of freedom at . . . his mother's. His second twenty-four hours of freedom at . . . his mother's. And if we had to guess, his third twenty-four hours of freedom at . . .'

'. . . his mother's,' I finish. 'And you get all that off the tag device, do you?'

'They get a report every twelve hours. To confirm his whereabouts. If he goes more than one hundred feet from her house, it sets off an alarm. Or so it says here.' She puts away her laptop. 'Did she say anything to you about drinking paraffin?'

'She said something about it last night, after she saw the doctor. She was crying cos the doctor was having a go at her. That's what she said. So, what was it then, if it wasn't paraffin?'

'I thought she said it was, originally. We'll have to listen to the tape again to be sure.'

'She can't remember much about the night before. And she certainly can't remember being at the police station. So, it wasn't paraffin then?'

'It was a mix of stuff. But not paraffin. Do you think he gave it to her to drink or she drank it herself?'

''Christ's sake Sue, I've told you – she can't remember. So far, all I've managed to do is get her to eat two doughnuts.'

'She ate them?'

'She swallowed them down. Not sure if they stayed down, if you know what I mean.'

'No, what do you mean?'

'Sue, she's bound to have some eating issues, after being abused for two years.'

'So she says . . .' Sue looks away.

'Give her time, Sue. After what she's been through, even *she's* not sure if she's a nut job.'

Sue sighs. 'She didn't say anything else?'

'She said she could vaguely remember him getting drunk and losing control, wrecking the house, then locking her in the laundry room. Said he drank too much and slipped up, so she managed to get away. She thinks he's a psycho. Oh and his mum died when he was a kid.'

'Well, that's a whole lot more than two doughnuts, Sal,' she says. 'We're going to the house again this afternoon. We've got a warrant. If I go myself, we might actually find something. That Halsall wouldn't only miss a needle, she'd miss the sodding haystack and all. We're going to get inside and get some of her stuff, if she wants us to. We can have a good look around.'

'You're sure he's not there? How'd you know he's not hiding?'

'We've got a neighbour on the lookout. Some woman. Said she heard some noises the night before. Said she thought it was maybe someone doing DIY.'

'Who's doing DIY?' says Kitty, snaking through the door in that daft big woolly hat of hers and Sue flashes me a look, as if she's wondering how much Kitty had just overheard.

'Detective Sergeant Clarke,' says Sue, who's not in uniform so she looks like she could be anyone. 'And you are . . .?'

'. . . minding my own business,' says Kitty and snakes out again.

Sue raises an eyebrow and I shake my head. 'Bit of a loon,' I mouth at Sue.

'Young to be in here,' she mouths back. 'You know anything about her?'

'She brought three bikinis in with her so she can sunbathe on the roof,' I say, ''nuff said.'

'LEAST I CAN GET INTO A BIKINI,' shouts Kitty, skipping down the hall.

Sue shuts her eyes, shakes her head slowly, and she sighs.

'Go and wake Clare up, will you?'

'You go and wake her up,' I say. 'I'm her mate.'

'Just tell her I'm here,' she says and sighs. 'Go on, Sal. For me! I wanna say hello before I go.'

'There's a couple of policewomen downstairs to see you,' I say, walking into Clare's room and talking to an empty bed.

'Tell her to come back later,' she says, from under the bed. She's actually sleeping under the bed!

'What are you doing?' I say.

'Nothing,' she goes.

'Why are you under the bed, then?'

'Just tell her to come back later,' she goes, like she's mumbling and still asleep.

'Somehow, I don't think that's how the police work,' I say. 'Last time I looked they were a bit more demanding, know what I mean? You want me to wash this for you?' I say, holding up her dressing gown that's lying on the floor. 'Doesn't half smell bad.'

'What?' she says, not moving from under the bed. As though I'd just said, 'Can I kill your pet kitten with my bare hands?' or something.

'This dressing gown, you want me to wash it?'

'Why don't you fuck off, Sally,' she says, red-faced, puffy eyes, crawling out and grabbing the dressing gown, rolling it into a ball and stuffing it under her chin.

'I was only trying—' I start.

'Don't try anything with me!' she yells. 'I don't need anything from you or anyone else. Understand?'

'I thought we—'

'You don't know anything about me, Sally. Get the fuck out of my room – and don't let me catch you touching my stuff again.'

'Can we get this into perspective, Clare?' I shout back. 'I just kindly offered to sodding help you by washing your sodding dressing gown, so why don't you just fuck off instead?' I slam her door and go into my own room and slam that door too, for good measure.

I hear her in the bathroom – my toothpaste, no doubt – and I hear her in the sitting room, slamming around, and I hear her close the door and go down the stairs, mad bitch.

I don't ever get angry, you know, not anymore, no one to get angry with. Apart from the queues in Starbucks, and people who walk slowly. Hang on, changing lines at Green Park tube station, that gets me really angry, knock-me-down-dead angry; because it's so bloody far, you may as well have walked to wherever it is you're going. And there's people dawdling all over the bloody place; nearly drives me up the sodding wall.

When I stop breathing so hard, I decide to have a bath and then sort out my stuff, put it all away, you know, properly, and then I think I could go and get some towels later from the garment wardrobe and hang them over that ugly great metal curtain rail to cut out the light in the mornings. The trouble is, I can't get Clare out of my head. The bath is supposed to be relaxing but all I can think about is how angry she got. She seemed to snap. She was like a different person.

I can't be bothered to go and get something to eat. At least I've got all my own things here. I push my suitcases under the bed and pull open my handbag, find the bunch of letters that PC Chapman picked up. As per usual, they are mainly bills.

Water rates, electricity, pension update – yeah, I know, I've got a pension, all right, calm down – and then at the bottom there's this handwritten white envelope, no stamp or anything, addressed to Mrs Sally-Ann Mansfield. And I know that handwriting. I'd know it anywhere. My hands start to shake as I tear open the back and unfold the piece of paper inside.

My Sal,

   I've been waiting here for you. Maybe you've gone on your holidays . . . but you left your case in the hall. I was hoping we could meet. It's been a long time, girl.

   Nothing's changed for me Sal. That's why I came to see you. Before I did anything else. I've spent the last twenty years dreaming of this moment.

   Nothing's changed.

   You know what's coming. x

A cross at the bottom. A kiss. The kiss at the end kills me.

I put the letter carefully back into the envelope, and place the envelope into my bag. I slowly walk to the bathroom and kneel in front of the toilet, like I always do, bringing up the contents of my stomach quickly and silently without even coughing.

I haven't forgotten.

I send a text to Sue.

'*I need to see you urgently.*'

I can hardly see the buttons.

'*He's back.*'

Twenty-Four

DS Clarke

DS Clarke is fifty-two. A young fifty-two, she likes to think. Young enough to go hill walking in Scotland, take a spinning class once a week, pass the advanced driving course, find an alternative career. One day. However, also older than the mothers of most of her team. She misses Liz. Liz retired last year to a croft in Durness, in Sutherland, Scotland. Where no one knows she's a retired policewoman, so no one bothers her with petty crime problems or possible insurgent sightings. Since Liz retired, DS Clarke has had no sounding board. Liz was the best sounding board. DS Clarke does have a white board, a famous white board. Liz always used to call it a wipe board, swore it was called a wipe board. DS Clarke once had to Google it for her to prove that she was wrong.

DS Clarke lines up the white board perpendicular to her desk. No one else has arrived for the early shift, and the overnighters are drifting off home, grey from tiredness, gathering up their coats. Someone has borrowed the white board and scribbled all over it, something about internal comms; HR probably. And now the board rubber is missing which annoys her all the more. She goes to get kitchen roll.

The kitchen area on her floor is always chaos, despite her nagging emails asking people to clean out the fridge, wash up after themselves, load and unload the dishwasher, wipe the side down, etc. Today it's worse. And no kitchen roll.

Toilet roll would have to do, then.

She flicks the switch on the kettle, picks up three mugs before she finds one without dried-on scum left by the dishwasher, and spoons in two teaspoons of coffee granules. She unlocks the stationery cupboard and gathers up a selection of marker pens and a new board rubber.

While she waits for the kettle to boil, she thinks back to her training.

'*Put yourself in the position of the victim.*' That was the key message of her training.

She picks up the internal phone.

'Joanna. Can you look for my mobile? It's the one with the green cover. It might be in the breakout area. I think I left it there earlier. No, not my work one. The other one.'

She dreaded admitting that she'd lost her mobile. Again. It was like an admission of her own senility. She knew they all laughed about it. Sometimes before she's even known she's lost it.

'Try ringing it, will you?'

'What's your number?'

'Joanna . . .'

'All right, all right!'

'Ask everyone if they've seen it. I'm past caring. Send an email!'

*

PC Chapman was the next to arrive at the station. Bright and breezy, high blonde ponytail, bustling in from the cold.

'Dawn. Come into my office when you've got a sec.'

'How was Langlands?'

'Oh, fine. The dick from Liverpool is retracting his complaint. For now! No, it's about Clare.'

'You've seen the statement I got from her?' she says, taking off her uniform jacket.

'You want a coffee?' says DS Clarke, searching for another mug without scum.

Chapman nods.

'Yup I saw the statement,' says DS Clarke, pouring the boiling water over the coffee. 'It doesn't tell us anything we didn't already know.'

'I know, but it's a signed statement at least.'

Chapman adds some milk.

'She refused the video?'

'Yes, but we got audio.'

'How was she?'

'Same. Defensive. Nervous. Erratic. Emotional. What you'd expect.'

Chapman had been briefed to keep to the facts. Nothing too speculative. She perched on the side of DS Clarke's desk.

'She didn't get violent?'

'No, but she's angry. She obviously thinks we're shit. Thinks we missed Gareth at the hospital.'

'What do you think?'

'I think we should start again with the CCTV. Maybe we missed him.'

'Fuck. You think she's innocent?'

Chapman nods. Emphatically, professional. 'Of course, she's innocent,' she says. 'What could she be guilty of?'

Chapman was watches DS Clarke suspiciously over the rim of her mug. DS Clarke is hard to read; she comes at life from a different angle. That's why she wanted to work with her.

'Put yourself in the position of the victim,' said DS Clarke.

'OK, where am I?'

'You're on the floor of the kitchen. You're naked except for a bra.'

Chapman's navy pen squeaks across the surface of the white board.

KITCHEN, she writes.

UNDERWEAR, she writes.

'That I've been forced to wear?' says Chapman. 'And cuffed to the door handle of a kitchen cupboard?'

'Yes, that's it,' says DS Clarke.

FORCIBLY RESTRAINED, she writes.

'Am I blindfolded?' asks Chapman. 'She mentioned something about that.'

'She said that it happened sometimes. That he liked it when he could see her fear. But it didn't happen that night.'

'OK, so not blindfolded.'

'No. He's poured paraffin in your hair. And you're sitting in a pool of it.'

PARAFFIN, she writes.

'Why paraffin. Why not petrol? Easier to get hold of?'

'Less combustible. If it'd been petrol she'd have gone up like a rocket. And that would be no fun for him, either. He wants to see her fear. So how do you feel?'

'I'm terrified.'

'And now he tells you to drink something.'

'What is it?'

'Paraffin. Maybe.'

'Is it in a paraffin bottle?'

PARAFFIN BOTTLE, she wrote.

'Yes.'

'Why would I think it was anything but paraffin?'

'Good point.'

'So, would you drink it?'

'Do I have a choice?'

'You could refuse. Why don't you spit it out?'

DS Clarke clatters her mug down on her desk, like she's irritated.

Chapman treads carefully.

'Not if you were half-naked, chained up to a cupboard door, being set alight. You'd do what you were told, wouldn't you?'

'I wouldn't. I'd rip his fucking throat out.'

'Would you? How? If you were chained up and after two years of putting up with all that shit? I'd be petrified.'

'You're better at this role play than I am, Dawn. You're right.'

DS Clarke draws a line under the points so far and divides the lower part of the board into two columns. At the top of the right-hand column she writes:

SUBMISSION, and underlines it. And underneath that she writes:

FEARS – FIRE/ BURNS/ ASSAULT/ CHEMICAL BURNS/ STARVATION/ POISONING/ HISTORY OF INTIMIDATION AND ABUSE.

At the top of the second column DS Clarke writes:

ESCAPE

She straightens up and, tapping her chin with the end of the marker pen, looks at PC Chapman.

'So, what would make you stay, Chapman? Think like a victim,' says DS Clarke.

'Well, he's clearly threatened her enough times.' She picks up her laptop and starts scrolling through the statement.

'He said he will kill me, kill my friends, kill anyone I care about. And then he said he will kill them first and make me watch,' she reads.

'OK – so try this,' says DS Clarke. 'You've been held captive by a controlling psychopath for two years. He's abused you . . .'

DS Clarke stops. She picks up the board rubber and wipes everything off that she's just written.

'I've been coming at this wrong,' she says. She continues, 'He's abused you, sexually, physically, psychologically. He's beaten you, denied you food, and treated you worse than an animal. What's more important?' She draws two columns and begins to write again. FIGHT OR FLIGHT she writes across the top.

'What would make someone fight back and what would make someone run away?'

'Depends . . .'

'Depends on what, Dawn?'

'Depends on the person. If it were me, flight.'

'Go on.'

'I'd be so afraid of getting caught that I would be in escape mode. Just get away as fast as I can to the safest place possible.'

'Get to a police station,' says DS Clarke, and writes it on the board, under FLIGHT.

'And if it were me?' says DS Clarke, giving her a wink.

'If it were you? Fight.'

'How well you know me!' DS Clarke writes, 'Get rid of the threat' on the board under FIGHT.

'Clare's not you or me, though,' says Chapman.

'No, she's not,' says DS Clarke, thinking.

'She's weak,' says Chapman.

'Physically, certainly. But she's got a strong character. And she's sharp as a knife. She misses nothing. And she wants her life back,' says DS Clarke. 'But she's got no family left, and no friends who seem to care.'

'So, the threat of killing them is a bit thin?' says PC Chapman.

'Not thin as much as it's less immediate. Less pressing. He doesn't even know who her friends are, anymore. And neither does she.'

Joanna has arrived, smirking.

'Here's your phone DS Clarke. It was in the ladies' toilet.'

'Thanks, Joanna, do knock next time.'

'I thought you wanted your phone back!'

'I did . . .'

PC Chapman is staring at the board.

'Well? What do you think?' says DS Clarke. 'What made Clare decide between fight or flight? Why didn't she fight?'

This is the time that Liz would always come up with something brilliant. Something no one had thought of.

'I don't know. She's too weak. Her only choice was to come to the station.'

'She came to the station, but what did she do before she came to the station?'

'She still can't remember. Celia says that's totally normal. It's just too traumatic for her to remember. Same as if you are in a car crash. You forget everything.'

DS Clarke rubs out the line between FIGHT and FLIGHT on the board and writes a plus instead, adding a question mark on the end.

'What?' says PC Chapman. She looks at the board again. 'Both?'

'Yeah. Well maybe. I mean, she's smart enough.'

DS Clarke looks down at her phone. She'd had a text, then a missed call from Sal.

'Shit, Dawn,' she says. 'Send Halsall to pick up Sal. Urgent. We need to get her into court to get an injunction. We've told the solicitor she's coming. You get back to Clare. Push her. Don't let her pull any stunts. Ask her again about the paraffin. Read her face. She's not that smart.'

DS Clarke scrolls through her call log and puts her phone to her ear.

Twenty-Five

Clare

I'm back in Cerise.

I feel like I'm going mad.

'Are you sure it was paraffin?'

'I don't know."

'Did it say paraffin on the outside of the bottle?'

'Yes, I think so. That's why I thought it was paraffin.'

'How much paraffin was in the bottle?'

'I can't remember,' I say.

How would I know? And why does the stupid policewoman keep calling it paraffin if she thinks it wasn't paraffin?

I can tell she hates me.

I hate her.

She was nicer than this before.

'Was the liquid in the bottle the same liquid he was pouring over you?' PC Chapman says.

I'm trying to think.

'I don't think I could see,' I say.

'Why not? Why couldn't you see, Clare? What prevented you from seeing?'

I wasn't blindfolded.

Sometimes he did that. Blindfolded me so I couldn't see where the matches were going to land. So I'd cry out more.

Coco.
   Coco.
   Time to play.

To start out with, that's what I did. Cry out.

But then I realised that's what he got off on.

Sometimes it was more fun for him to see me watch them land and ignite. Then fizzle out. Sometimes he would let them burn. For a few seconds.

Naughty match hurting naughty Coco.

The smell of burning hair mixed with burning paraffin . . .

'Maybe I had my eyes shut,' I say. 'Maybe it was going in my eyes. It always used to go in my eyes.'

'So, you previously said you thought you were drinking out of a paraffin bottle?' she says. 'But you don't know that it was paraffin you were actually drinking.'

'Look, I don't remember, right.'

He'd not made me drink anything before.

This was new.

Panic.

You're holding me back now? Coco.
   Holding me back.

'Did it smell, Clare,' PC Chapman asks. 'When you drank it, did it burn your mouth, your tongue?'

'I can't remember.'

'Did it burn when it was in your mouth?'

PC Chapman looks like she's losing her patience.

'I don't know,' I whisper.

She'd have drunk it. I bet she would. People always think they know better.

She hands me a tissue.

Not kindly.

More like she just wants me to shut up crying and tell her more things.

'It was mouthwash,' she says.

'What was mouthwash?'

'The liquid that you drank. The tox report on the ingested chemicals shows that it was mouthwash. Blue mouthwash, but you said you didn't know that.'

'I didn't know what it was. I know my sick was blue. That's all I can remember.'

She doesn't believe me.

I start to feel hot.

'It looked like paraffin. It was in a paraffin bottle.'

'And did it taste like paraffin?'

'How would I know what paraffin tastes like?'

'I see,' she says.

I can tell she doesn't see.

'I'm going over to your house later, Clare. Is there anything you would like me to bring you?'

'He smashed it up. The house, I mean,' I say. 'He'll say I did, though.'

'Is there anything you would like me to bring you?' she repeats, as though she can't hear me. Like she's losing patience with me.

'I don't know. Wait, in the front bedroom, on the left side of the bed, there's a chest of drawers. In the bottom drawer, just bring me the clothes from there. Leggings and jumpers, I don't have much. And some underwear, plain white, just bring the plain white underwear, nothing else. Do you think I'm going to be here a while?'

PC Chapman's expression softened.

'We do need you to stay here, Clare. You're OK though, right? They're good people?'

I nod.

'And my shoes. My trainers. I've only got one pair. They're by the stairs. Well, they were by the stairs.'

Babe. You know I don't like you in sneakers.

Just heels for me.

Let's make those stubby little legs as long as we can, shall we.

Her phone buzzes.

She nods at me. 'Excuse me, I just need to . . .' she says and disappears through the door clicking it shut behind her.

'He'll tell you I'm mad, that I'm mental and I made all of it up,' I say, but she won't hear me. 'He'll say I'm always drunk, but I'm not. And I'm not mad.'

I watch her walking down the hallway, half running.

Coco.

Come on, Coco.

Don't pass out on me now.

I don't want you to miss out on all the fun.

When I go upstairs Sally has gone and there's the smell of sick coming from the bathroom.

I wonder if I made her do that.

Now I feel bad . . .

Sally's not in the kitchen.

Or any of the social rooms.

Or the laundry room.

I ask Mrs Henry and she says she's gone to the police station. Something about her ex.

Mrs Henry makes me some onion soup out of a packet and there are lumps of powder in it where she hasn't stirred it. There's a bread roll next to the bowl but I'm not hungry for either.

I go up to my flat and slump on the bed, looking in all the empty drawers.

Someone has lined them with 70s wallpaper.

I hang my dressing gown/bathrobe – whatever it is – in the wardrobe, on the only hanger. It's one of those metal ones from the dry cleaners.

I take the dressing gown off the hanger and fold it into a drawer.

I look out of the window at the trains leaving London.

I could have disappeared.

Found a town by the sea.

Somewhere in the north.

Got a job in a café and a bedsit overlooking a bay.

I could've got a dog, taken it for walks in the morning when the sky and rock pools glow pink, our feet leaving tracks in the sand.

I fall asleep dreaming of making tea for old people.

Folding paper napkins.

Reading a book with my dog snoring by my feet.

When I wake up, it's getting dark.

Walking into the shared lounge, I can see the street lights are flickering to life. Proving there's life out there.

While I'm stuck in here, watching the trains.

Maybe I shouldn't have shouted at Sally.

She's right, I should wash the bathrobe. It's a fire hazard.

There's a knock at the front door.

I figure if I don't answer then whoever it is will just go away.

I like it here.

Sitting here, in the dark.

There's another knock and I still don't answer.

Then the sound of a key in the lock.

The girl with the blonde hair comes through the door, silently, and shuts it behind her.

Quietly.

Like a proper burglar. One you see on the telly.

She doesn't see me because it's dark.

'What do you want?' I say.

Just like that. Not even nasty.

'Oh!' she jumps. 'You're here! Hi! I did knock!'

'Where'd you get the key?' I say.

'This used to be my flat. I made a mistake. Sorry,' she says, turning to leave.

'Do you usually knock on your own door before you go in?' I say. 'How come you still have a key?'

'Look, I made a mistake, OK? Sorry,' she says angrily not looking in the slightest bit sorry. 'I'm Kitty!' She smiles at me, but stops when I don't reply. 'What's under your plasters?' She points to my chin and neck. 'Did you hurt yourself, did you? They said you hurt yourself.'

'I didn't hurt myself.'

'They said you did.'

'Who's they?'

'Look, I'm not saying you're a cutter or anything.'

'A cutter?'

'A self-harmer. I'm not saying you are,' she's talking too fast. Filling in the gaps. 'It's just they said you'd hurt yourself. Burnt yourself and stuff. That's why they took all our knives away. Plastic cutlery. Didn't you notice? We all noticed. Can't even cut a piece of fucking toast with a plastic fucking knife.'

I breathe.

I count to ten.

I'm hot.

They'll spot you a mile off, babe.

They'll have you sussed from the start.

'Just go back to why you were breaking in to our flat again . . .'

She looks around her. Thinking, thinking.

'Can I be honest with you?' Kitty asks.

That's always a prelude to a lie, at least it was in Gareth's case.

'I liked being up here. Better than on the second floor . . . Feels safer being further from the front door. Helps me sleep better.'

'OK, you can go. Leave the key,' I say, getting up from the sofa with my palm outstretched.

She hands over the key.

'Ask to be moved next door, if you're that bothered,' I say, edging her out and shutting the door behind her.

I wouldn't like her, even if she was telling the truth. Which she wasn't.

Downstairs, there's a group of women watching *Midsomer Murders* on the telly in one of the social rooms.

Not Sally.

No lights on.

Just the telly lighting the room.

They've all got blue faces.

They're all staring.

Not saying anything.

Arms folded.

Some of them resting mugs on their stomachs with their feet on the coffee table.

Well, Big Debbie and Sarah are.

'I prefer this new Inspector Barnaby,' says Big Debbie.

'So do I,' says Sarah.

'Shut. Up! He's not a patch on the old one,' says Abigail, laughing.

'What do you mean? What old one?' says Sarah, confused.

'Why did you say . . .' starts Big Debbie, but gives up.

'Your little one's awake, Prashi,' another woman says, poking her head around the door.

Prashi pushes herself up and out of her seat. 'Night, ladies. Tomorrow is another day.'

'For Pete's sake,' shouts Big Debbie at the telly, 'you don't get a black eye walking into a door. What a fucking cliché.'

'She's just saying that to cover up. I'll bet the husband did it,' says Abigail.

'It's *always* the husband who did it,' says Sian, a quiet woman who's sitting in the corner reading a copy of the latest *Hello!* magazine. 'That's why there's no point watching these shit dramas.'

'I thought she did it by accident,' says Sarah. 'She said she walked into a door.'

They all look at Sarah like she's a halfwit.

'Trevor Eve wouldn't be playing the husband if it wasn't a juicy part. It must be him,' says Abigail. 'Do you remember him in *Shoestring*? I used to love him in that show.'

'The point is,' says Big Debbie, getting up and pulling out her box of fags, 'whoever wrote it, the scriptwriter, should have come up with something a bit more original than "I walked into a door, doctor". Doctors ain't stupid. If you went into casualty with a black eye and said, "Oh yeah, doctor, I just walked into a door", they'd laugh you out the place.'

'It's a TV detective series,' says Sian. 'You don't get Albert Fucking Einstein writing the script.'

'Albert Einstein didn't write scripts,' says Abigail.

'But if he had of,' says Sian, 'the husband wouldn't have done it every time, right?'

'If he had of, we wouldn't understand a sodding word of *Midsomer Murders*,' goes Big Debbie. 'I know!' she says. 'Let's play excuses for injuries.'

We all look up at her, not quite sure what she means.

'Like, my first time, at the hospital, when my husband tried to strangle me with a bit of garden twine, I told 'em I got my head caught in the bit you pull the blinds up with. The cord, like. Like that's definitely possible!'

We all start to giggle.

'I mean, what my head can 'ave been doing I just don't know,' she says, starting to really laugh.

'When my husband threw me down the stairs,' says Sian, 'I said I was doing my trainer up, at the top of the stairs, and fell headfirst. When they said it didn't sound like a very safe place to do a trainer up, I said it weren't my fault that that's where it'd come undone.'

Mrs Henry is coming out of the office to see what the noise is about. She's smiling, glad we're all getting along.

'You know you can't smoke . . .' she says to Big Debbie.

'I'm going out the back in a minute,' says Big Debbie.

'I said I'd fallen out of a tree when my husband broke my nose,' says one of the Indian ladies, the one who had been entirely silent up until that point. We all stop laughing and gape at her. 'I can't imagine why I said it. I could see them all thinking, "what's a middle-aged Indian woman doing up a tree in the first place". It was just the first thing that came into my head. I thought about changing the story once I'd realised, you know, that it wasn't very believable, but then I thought they'd just lock me up in a lunatic asylum. It would have been all right, but I had a wedding sari on at the time. All gold embroidery and bells.'

We all hoot with laughter. So does she.

'They asked how high the tree was and I said "forty foot". And then they said, "where was the wedding?" and I said "Grosvenor House Hotel" and the doctor said "that sounds rather incredible to me" and I said, "Indian weddings are always incredible."

'Did they actually believe you then?' says Sarah.

Big Debbie shakes her head. 'To my mind,' she says, 'the more unbelievable the better. 'I walked into a door' just don't cut it no more.'

It was like we were all a bit pissed. Soon as someone piped up with another story, we'd fall about.

'When I told my doctor I'd stood on a hockey stick,' says Abigail, 'she said that my story was about as believable as this bloke who'd come in with a hoover attachment stuck to the end of his willy. Said he'd been advised to hoover naked because of a dust allergy and that during the process he had become "inexplicably fatigued" and stopped to "take a nap" while the hoover was left running, and while asleep his penis had flopped into the vacuum hose.'

'Did he actually say "take a nap"?' shouts Sian, wiping tears from under her eyes.

We shriek.

'And "flopped"?' I say.

'Was it a Henry?' shouts Big Debbie. 'Was he wheeling Henry along behind him?'

We shriek some more.

'Or a Hettie' says Sian.

Sally walks in, just before ten and we were starting to calm down a bit.

'You see? I guessed it was Trevor Eve that did it, all along,' says Sarah, really loudly, as the credits start to roll.

'We *all* said it was Trevor Eve that did it,' says Big Debbie, coming in from the garden in a cloud of Marlborough smoke.

'He's not going to play a bit part, is he?' says Abigail. 'He was Shoestring.'

'He was something else as well,' says Sian.

'But he was mainly Shoestring,' says Abigail.

I nod at Sally.

She nods back.

She's been crying.

'Wanna a hot chocolate?' I say.

'You bet,' she replies. 'Can I have the *Frozen* mug. I've always wanted to be a princess,' she says.

'Sorry,' I say.

'Me too,' she says.

Twenty-Six

Sally

There was so much noise coming out of the TV room that I don't think that Kitty heard me get buzzed through reception, or close the lobby door behind me, she was so busy staring into the mirror at herself, listening to the other women talking, hanging on their every word, but out of sight of them, so they couldn't see her.

One of them was saying something about falling out of a tree, and there was a conversation about Henry vacuum cleaners, you know, the one that's got a face drawn on it and there's a pink one too. Anyway, they were laughing, screaming with laughter, some of them.

It reminded me of when I was last at a refuge; the women were like that there too, sometimes. Well, just a few times, a bit like when you used to go on Girl Guides camp or hen nights, when everyone forgets themselves, stops trying to be someone else, someone more impressive, just for a minute.

I had my back to the door and I was just breathing slowly for a minute, pulling myself together; what with Terry and everything, I didn't really feel like joining in. It's not really my type of thing.

Then I thought I heard Clare's voice and I was surprised, cos I wouldn't have thought it was her kind of thing either.

That's when I notice Kitty. She's listening to what's being said. That wasn't strange in itself, but then she's laughing about it, and watching herself laughing in the mirror, silently laughing, great big laughs but no volume. Another burst of giggles escapes from the TV room and ripples down the hall.

Kitty turns to face the far end of the corridor and looks at herself over her shoulder, and giggles like you would if you were flirting with someone. Mischievous giggles.

She stops and she juts her chin into the mirror, examines her teeth, frowns, rubs her teeth hard with her finger, then fluffs out her hair and smiles a big cheesy smile.

Then she shakes her head as if she really can't understand what everyone is going on about and nods, as if she is agreeing with herself.

Then she sees me and narrows her eyes; or maybe she didn't narrow her eyes, maybe she's just short-sighted, and maybe she didn't have her lenses in. I don't know, all I'm saying is it looked to me like she narrowed her eyes.

She's staring at me now, and I am not going to move and I am not going to change my expression – she can go to hell before I crack.

She can't decide if I've seen her or not, that's what's holding her up, and cos I'm not giving she decides her best option is to go all innocent, like butter wouldn't melt.

'You like my new hair?' she goes, holding up the ends for me to see as I walk towards her, then staring at her reflection again.

'It's called "graduated",' she says, pronouncing it grad-u-ated, like it's a word she's never even heard before.

'In England, it's called "grad-u-ated", in France it's called "ombre", and in New York it's called "degradé". It's all over Instagram.'

'Degradé sounds a bit like degraded,' I say.

'Does it?' says Kitty, not in the least bit interested in what I think. 'I think it sounds . . . exotic.'

We've made hot chocolates, me and Clare, and we've taken them to our flat so that we don't have to mind out for long noses, Kitty's long nose, specifically.

'So, what does a criminal injunction stop him doing?' says Clare.

I've just told her about Terry, about leaving the letter in my house, using my notepaper as well. I wonder what else he looked at, and touched, it feels like I've been violated.

'Coming within one hundred feet of me,' I say, trying to work out in my head how far that is. 'How far is one hundred feet anyway?' I say.

'Well, I'm five foot, so it's . . . twenty of me,' she says.

We both fall silent.

'That doesn't sound right,' I say.

'Twenty times five is one hundred,' she goes.

'Yeah, it's not that,' I say. 'I can't do feet and inches. Only metres. That's what comes of being a science teacher. What's one hundred feet in metres?'

'Thirty,' she goes, blowing on her hot chocolate, 'it's definitely about thirty.'

'My solicitor . . .' I say.

'. . . oh, sol-ic-i-tooooor,' she says, imitating a posh voice. 'How did you get one of those?'

'You can get one,' I say, 'and an injunction. Anyone who feels threatened can get one, so my solicitor Jane says; she's only young, got newborn twins.'

'So, you had to go to court?' Clare says, licking the froth off a spoon.

'Yeah, I was half expecting Terry to turn up, but he didn't. That would be typical him. No, PC Halsall took me, then it was just me and the judge and Jane, you know. All seemed a bit much really, like I was massively overreacting, or like I was making it all up. You know how your voice goes a bit sort of echoey sometimes, so you can hear yourself speaking. To be quite honest, I've said all that stuff so many times I've almost stopped believing it myself, and we were in and out like a factory line. You get given a copy of the order, and you give that to the police station, and then they've got what's called "powers of arrest".'

'Gareth's too smart to get arrested. He knows people everywhere. They pull strings for him.'

'Thought you said he was American?'

'He is. He just knows everyone. Charms everyone. It's cos he's good-looking.'

'Terry hasn't got the looks and he hasn't two brain cells to rub together either, that's the truth, but he still gets what he wants.

Not through charm though, that's for sure. Took five coppers to arrest him – first time around.'

'So now what?' she says, spooning the hot chocolate into her mouth.

'I stay in here, don't go anywhere, wait and see where he turns up and get the tagging done on him properly.'

'Tagging?' she says.

'They put these devices on long-term prisoners who get out on release, on their ankles, and it's like satnav on their legs. No, not satnavs – what do I mean, those tracking signals, and the police know where they are, what they're up to, all the time.'

'Sounds like a good plan,' says Clare.

'You'd think, right? It would be a good plan if the government hadn't given the contract to a bunch of crooks.'

'What do you mean?'

'Rather than the police putting on the devices, as they're meant to, they get an outside contractor to put them on, cos they're way too busy filling out forms and filing their nails, and then they wonder why it doesn't work. The whole thing's corrupt. Seems that half the cons don't get tagged in the first place. And the other half get what's called "loose tags". Seriously, it's a proper name. The cons pay £400 to get the tag put on loose, so they can slip it off. They reckon Terry went to his mum's for some coffee and walnut cake, and then he just left his tag there. Took it off and left it in her house. Bloody idiots.'

'You are actually shitting me!'

'Nope. The cons take them off and then they put them on someone else – so it's moving around the house and everything.'

'Loose tags,' Clare says, half smiling. 'That's really something!'

'There's a story about some bloke who was in his seventies who strapped it on his cat. They found out cos they could track him hopping over all the garden fences in his street. Then this other bloke, he got them to put the tag on his wooden leg, then he detached that, left it in the corner of his bedroom and put on his spare. It'd be funny if it wasn't terrible.'

She snorted into the remains of her hot chocolate.

'The police are a bit shit, aren't they? Really. I mean, what have they done for you?'

'They've got us both in here,' I say.

'But how safe are we in here?' Clare says.

'Safer than we were out there,' I say.

'I'm going to wash my hair,' Clare says suddenly. 'Will you stay?'

'Stay where?' I say.

'Just stay outside the door. So I can hear you,' she says, looking embarrassed.

I nod.

'I get nervous in the shower. Used to love long showers. Could spend all day. But Gareth . . . Can I use your shampoo?' she says. 'I was going to earlier but I didn't want to without asking.'

'You're on the mend,' I say. 'Of course, you can. Did you eat today?'

'Mrs Henry made me onion soup. Out of a packet.'

'We can get some fruit tomorrow,' I call to her in the bathroom, 'and maybe we can get you some supplements from the health food shop, like vitamins. Did that doctor bring you any of those weight-gaining shakes?'

'I hate those drinks. They make me want to throw up just thinking about them. And I'm not sure those vitamin supplement things work,' she calls, switching on the shower and putting her hand under it, waiting for it to heat up. 'Gareth told me that my moods were erratic and that I needed some vitamin shots. Saw this American doctor in Harley Street. Some friend of his. Had these shots every month or six weeks. I can't really remember. And medication. Gareth said I'd be full of energy. I couldn't see any difference. Didn't feel any fitter at all. If anything, the tablets made me feel worse.'

'Worse how?' I shout through the door, not wanting to sound too interested.

'Depressed. Tired. Generally hopeless. But living with a psychopath has its side effects. Gareth swore by vitamins. I used to *pretend* to take them, in the end, he got so weird about it. Said I needed them to help calm me down. It was all I could do to get up in the mornings. Look, can I use your shower gel too. I'm going to get all this stuff tomorrow.'

'Anything you want,' I shout.

'I think I lost my bearings in the end,' she calls above the noise of the shower. 'Stopped caring about my work and my friends. After I got fired, they stopped calling.'

I hear her turn the water off.

'Will you help me wash this dressing gown tomorrow?' she says as she walks back into the sitting room, wrapping it tightly around her. 'And have you got any nail scissors?' she asks, staring down at her toes.

'In the green toilet bag on the windowsill. Help yourself,' I say.

'Did I tell you that Kitty was in here earlier?' Clare says, coming back a bit later, toothbrush in her mouth.

'She's been dying to get in here. What did she want?'

'No, I mean, she had a key, and let herself in.'

'What the . . .?'

'Exactly.'

'What was she doing?'

'She looked like she was hoping to nick something,' she says, between brushing.

'You bet she was,' I say. Not that I've got anything much worth nicking.

Clare goes back into the bathroom to spit out the toothpaste.

'She's very pretty,' she says, drying her hair with a towel.

'Pretty people often seem so much more convincing. Use their charms . . .' I say, thinking about the way Kitty was practising her laughing face earlier.

'Tell me about it,' she says. 'Gareth's a model. Part-time actor and model. Not that he has ever done a single job the entire time I've known him. But anyway. Whenever we went anywhere, especially at the beginning, when I first met him, all the women would fall over themselves to say hi. He used to get this look on his face . . .' She does a kind of trout pout. 'One that said, "Look at me, I'm the hottest guy in the room", and they'd all melt. Right in front of him. Like he was Harry Styles or something. Trouble was, he *was* the hottest guy in the room. Women couldn't take their eyes off him. He'd say, "See her. Over there. That's Beth. The one with the body like a supermodel. She is 1000 per cent in the looks department, don't you think?" And then Beth would come over and be all over him, like a rash. And I'd say, "Do you have any idea how all this makes me feel?" And he'd go, "I'm worth it though, right?" And I'd say, "Why do I feel like I'm the only one working at this relationship?" And then he'd tell me to work harder. And, later, he'd make me swear on my best friend's life that he was the best fuck I'd ever had.'

She pauses, I think because she's glad it's all over. But then she gets this wistful look in her eyes and I wonder if a part of her was wishing that the hottest guy in the room was still with her, in that mad way that DVs do.

She snaps back to the present.

'Like I say, I think I lost my bearings. I thought he was doing me a favour,' Clare says.

'And *was* he the best fuck you ever had?'

'Well, here's the joke,' she says, wiping her face with a ball of cotton wool, covered in my moisturiser, 'He was the only fuck I ever had. I was a virgin when I met him.'

'REALLY?' I shout, loudly. 'Sorry,' I say, quietly. 'That came out wrong.'

'Yes, really,' she goes. 'But then, he didn't like that either. Said I should have told him. Said that because I'd already fucked him, I was no longer a virgin and therefore technically no longer marriage material.'

'What! That's mental,' I say.

She snorts.

'Anyway, did you get the key back off Kitty?' I ask.

'It's here,' she says.

'Wonder what she thought she was after.'

'She said she feels safer further away from the front door.'

'And don't tell me, it helps her sleep at night.'

'She did say exactly that too.'

Twenty-Seven

DS Clarke

There's a selection of plant pots on the outside ground floor windowsill, and more along the sides of the three steps leading up to the black front door. Some of the pots are terracotta and have cracked so that pools of soil sit around their bases. Some are black plastic and intact. None contain plants. The only evidence of plants having been there is the faded, muddy labels stuck to the sides of the pots. DS Clarke notes to herself: an unloved house.

A young police officer is waiting for her by the open front door.

'Afternoon, Detective Sergeant, I'm PC Corkett!' he says officiously, fresh from training.

'Corkett.' She nods, thinking this one is even younger and more of a wanker than usual. 'Anything to report so far?'

'Not immediately, sir. I mean, sarge.' He blushes right up to his hat rim. 'It's your average house. Perhaps tidier than we might have expected, judging by the report. PCs Chapman and Walker are inside.'

When DS Clarke steps over the polished silver front doorstep, her overriding impression is that she's entering a show home. Not a speck of dust anywhere. Gleaming, with a hint of lavender furniture polish. Her mind goes back to the plant pots outside the front door.

'Out of sight, out of mind,' she thinks, making a mental note of something else that didn't add up, the hallway tiles. Black-and-white ceramics like you get in posh hallways.

Clare's father was a builder, DS Clarke reminds herself.

The stairs are carpeted in grey wool from edge to edge. The walls decorated with a matt paint, an expensive shade of green, perhaps Farrow & Ball. There are two reception rooms, the first is carpeted in bottle-green wool and freshly vacuumed, judging by the wheel marks. It has a polished fireplace, inside and out.

Chapman skips down the stairs with the confidence of someone who has been up and down them a few times already.

'You might want to keep downstairs for now, sarge. The forensics team are up there.'

DS Clarke thinks she should have put the blue plastic shoe covers on, but since her back has been playing up this week, she decides to let it go.

'Halsall told me that Sally-Anne got the injunction OK yesterday?' PC Chapman says, following her into the dining room.

'Yes, I spoke to her this morning. We were half expecting him to show up but he didn't. Fucking tags. What do you see, Chapman?'

DS Clarke faces each wall of the dining room in turn and stares and stares, from top left to bottom left, at every skirting board and dado rail, every doorknob and lock.

'I see a laptop. Open. People never leave their laptops open. There's also a mobile. People never leave them behind. Nor do they leave their car keys, like those over there,' she says, pointing to the side table.

'Unless they had to leave in a hurry.'

She shrugs.

'Have you checked the fridge yet? Any food? Checked the dishwasher?'

People often forget the dishwasher. DS Clarke had found more evidence in dishwashers than she'd care to count.

'Both empty. The whole place is forensically clean.'

'It'd better not be.'

DS Clarke knows PC Chapman is right, even after just five minutes. The downstairs toilet floor is clean enough to eat off. DC Walker comes thundering down the stairs.

'No one home,' she says, brightly.

'I think we all know there is no one home, Walker. You are supposed to be gathering evidence.'

'Of what?'

She actually looks surprised. Surprised!

'You're a detective. Go detect.'

'There's a lot of new clobber in the wardrobe,' Walker says, rolling her eyes.

'There you are, you can detect! And?'

'Well, that doesn't exactly stack up, does it?'

'Why not?'

'She said she only had a few items of clothes, tops and sweat-pants, didn't she?'

'You're saying it's women's clothing?'

'Yeah, I said! Clobber.'

'I'm sorry, I obviously didn't understand the nuances of your colloquialisms. Clobber is female?'

PC Corkett, who hears the exchange from the front door, is staring at his shoes.

'Come along, Chapman,' DS Clarke says, leading the way up the stairs.

The landing looks like every landing of a middle-class, middle-income, middle England estate. There's pretend posh art, a five-pound print that's been clipped inside a silvered frame. Off to the left there's a family bathroom. The pedestal mat and bath mat are matching. The guest bedroom has plumped-up scatter cushions and flowery curtains that don't look used.

DS Clarke walks over to the window overlooking the back garden. It's dirty, the window, but only on the outside. She traces a finger over the inside and it's spotless.

The garden is knee-high in nettles that have started to go to seed.

The rotary washing line is broken with pegs still clipped to it.

There's an outhouse.

And a side gate.

'It's all Net-a-Porter. Stupid money,' Chapman calls from the front bedroom.

'You ever bought anything on Net-a-Porter, Chapman?' asks DS Clarke, wondering who did.

'Not on public sector wages, I haven't.'

'This is Chanel. Looks expensive,' says Walker, mispronouncing Chanel as channel.

'Walker, are you the only person on the planet not to have heard of Chanel?'

'What, the perfume?'

The master bedroom is overly feminine. That was DS Clarke's first thought. Master bedrooms give a lot away about the power in a relationship. Dark and imposing suggests a male-dominated home. Comfortable and messy is nurturing. This she hasn't seen before. Pristine fitted wardrobes. A mirrored dressing table hung with scarves and strings of pearls. An old-fashioned powder puff and silver hairbrush. A silk dressing gown and designer perfumes. The overwhelming impression was 'pampered princess'. And the wardrobes were stuffed with designer dresses.

In the en suite there was a row of nail polishes in every shade of purple. Twenty of them. More.

But she has no nails, thought DS Clarke. When does she wear nail varnish?

In the cabinet behind a mirror there are vitamins, minerals, healthy stuff.

And a receipt. For bleach. Stuffed at the back, behind a shampoo bottle. Strange place to keep a receipt, thought DS Clarke.

'Have you checked outside, Chapman?'

'The laundry room? Yup. It's clean. It's smart. It's not what she said. It smells newly painted.'

'So, it could have been done up? Show me.'

'Oh, there's an attic. It's only storage.'

'OK, you look up there, Chapman. We'll do the laundry. Walker! Come on.'

DS Clarke glances at the forensics team, packing up their stuff into plastic toolboxes.

In the living room, there's a sofa she recognises from the Sofa Workshop ads, with two matching tub chairs. The cushions are lined up, puffed up in a geometric pattern in grey and cream. All very tasteful – like some kind of show home on a brand-new estate.

A wedding photo, over the mantlepiece. Wedding photo?

Clare is there, in white, alongside a man who is presumably Gareth.

The picture is quite close-up, not full-length. Their faces are glowing, with his head over her shoulder. She's wearing a white lace veil and the dress has got a silk ruffle neck. She's wearing diamond earrings.

He's going in for a kiss, his hand protectively around her shoulders, looking like the happiest man alive.

'Chapman. CHAPMAN. HERE! Walker, get Chapman down here,' says DS Clarke as she steps back to get the whole picture into the photo she's taking on her phone.

'Lovely, isn't it? Scrubs up well, Clare, doesn't she?' says Walker.

DS Clarke's phone goes before she can say anything.

'I need to get back. You lot finish up here.'

Show home, thinks DS Clarke. Designed to give the very best possible impression.

Twenty-Eight

Clare

Celia, my caseworker, has brought Emma Tudor to see me. Emma is a CPN.

'It stands for Community Psychiatric Nurse,' says Celia, getting breathy.

Emma is standing in reception, wearing an Indian print blouse and cropped jeans. She's also wearing tiny gold ballet flats that she could probably have got from a children's department. Emma Tudor is very small and very, very quiet.

To the point that I can't hear what she's saying.

'Hi,' I think she says.

That's what it looked like she said.

'She will visit you here, and if you'd like, can continue seeing you, even when you move on from here,' Celia says.

'Provided you don't move to Cuba, or something,' whispers Emma, winking.

She has very long eyelashes and a beauty spot above her lip like Marilyn Monroe.

'I'll leave you two here,' Celia says, mainly to Emma.

We're in one of those grey soundproof rooms again with pink names. There are two chairs – scuffed plastic ones like you get in school, and a round plastic table with a pot plant on. The pot plant has chunky leaves and tiny yellow flowers. It looks like a cactus or something.

The room has no window.

No air.

'I'm going to check in with the station to see if they've picked up your belongings, Clare, and try and get you some shopping,' says Celia.

She's trying to close the door as slowly and quietly as is humanly possible.

I don't know why.

'Thanks, Celia,' says Emma, hugging her laptop to her chest and leaning back in her chair.

Watching me.

'How are you feeling today, Clare?'

She sounds breezy.

Given the circumstances.

'This must all feel slightly surreal after everything you've been through.'

There are long pauses between her sentences.

'Can I just ask how you know what I've been through?' I say. 'Not being funny or anything. I just wondered.'

'I've been through your case file. I've spoken to DS Clarke. I've seen your tox report and the police doctor's report and I've talked it through with Celia.'

'A lot of homework,' I say.

She thinks she knows everything about me.

I can't even remember her name.

No one will believe you.

Look at you!

Do you look like a reliable witness?

'Did they get Gareth yet?' I ask.

She doesn't reply.

'Can I get a police injunction?'

She's one of those people who lets you talk and doesn't interrupt. They get trained to be like that.

It's not normal.

Her lips are pursed. The frosty pink lipstick gluing her mouth together.

She waits a bit longer.

Then she says, 'I'm here to talk about you, Clare, not Gareth. Do you mind if I call him Gareth? I've heard you can find his name disturbing?'

'No, it's fine.'

If I find out you're talking to your friends about me, you'll get it.

Understand?

She really does know everything.

'I'm here to make a psychiatric assessment, which sounds scary, and as though I'm here to judge you. But that's not the point at all. OK? I'm not here to judge you.'

'Yes. Sure. That's OK,' I say.

'If and when your case comes to court, this assessment can be used in evidence against the accused. It's like an official evaluation of your mental state. Same as the physical one the police doctor did at the hospital, only this is about how well your mind is, not your body.'

She pulls up her chair to the table and flips open her laptop.

'It's easier if I type it in – I hope that doesn't feel too impersonal,' she says, very, very quietly. 'Bit of housekeeping first. Bit of background.'

Oh, background. I thought she meant she was going to get a duster out or something.

Must remember to tell Sally that one.

'I'm a qualified psychotherapist. I specialise in behavioural disorders, specifically in BPD, Borderline Personality Disorder, and PTSD, post-traumatic stress disorder. Just to be clear, we're here to do a psychiatric evaluation with a two-fold purpose. Firstly, so we can produce an accurate assessment for the court of your current state of mind and, secondly, so we can agree, you and I, on a course of treatment to help you moving forward.'

'I get the first bit,' I say. 'But the best course of treatment for me going forward is to live my life without Gareth. Once he has gone, I'll be fine. I can get my job back. Get my friends, my house, back.'

She waits for like ten seconds.

Long enough for it to feel uncomfortable.

'We can come back to that point,' she says.

I don't want to come back to that point.

For me that is the only point.

I think that, but I don't say that.

'Shall we begin?' she says.

I don't know what's going to happen.

I nod.

'Can you tell me how you got the injuries that you presented at Camden Police Station on the tenth of April 2018.'

Haven't we been through all this already?

'Yes,' I say.

She tips her head to one side.

'Oh, I see. Yes, I was attacked by my former partner, Gareth James.'

'Can you remind me what your injuries were?' she says, tapping away.

'They will all be in the police doctor's report,' I say.

'Yes, but I was hoping you would be able to tell me.'

'Well, OK. I had match burns and chemical burns. On my shoulders,' I say, moving the neck of my T-shirt, so she can see.

She nods her head and smiles sympathetically.

'And on my legs; I have burns there too. I have an infection where I cracked the back of my head open,' I say, touching the bandage under my hair. 'I've got bruising. I swallowed something that made me sick. I cut the soles of my feet on the way to the police station, but I don't think that really counts?'

She smiles the same smile, but says nothing.

'What about your weight?' she says.

I feel my ribs through my bathrobe, dressing gown.

'I've lost weight,' I say. 'I don't have scales. I don't weigh myself.'

'And how did you acquire all those injuries?' she goes. 'Include the weight loss in that if you can,' she says.

Acquire. Like I bought them from Harrods or something.

'You know how,' I say.

'I need you to tell me how,' she says.

'Gareth is a psycho. That's how,' I say.

'So, Gareth is responsible for all the injuries?'

'What, do you think I did them to myself?' I say. 'People don't go around setting fire to themselves. Not normal people anyway. I'm getting a bit fed up . . .'

'It's all part of the assessment, Clare. I have to ask you these things. I know it's difficult.'

She pauses.

'Shall we?' she says.

Emma is a miserable cow. I can see that.

She carries on.

'Do you suffer from flashbacks or nightmares?' she says.

'No, my life is one long nightmare,' I say. 'Going to sleep couldn't be any worse than being awake.'

I start to cry.

Because I'd never thought of that before, and now I have, it seems all the more tragic.

'Do you worry about being alone?'

'No, I like being alone.'

Although I never knew how long he was going to be, so being happy didn't last long because I would start to dread him coming back.

'OK,' she says.

'Do you sometimes lose your temper with your friends and say things you don't really mean?' she says.

I was, like, what are you talking about?

I didn't say that though.

'Do you think you have the right document there, Emma?' I say. 'Do you know the last time I saw any of my friends? It was over eighteen months ago. When I lost my job.'

She says nothing.

Then she says, 'If you can think back to a time when you were with your friends, or contacting your friends, let's say, was there ever a time when you lost your temper and said something, perhaps, that you later regretted?'

'No,' I say. 'But Gareth sent them some shit messages telling them not to contact me. You can ask him when you arrest him!'

'Would you like some tea, Clare? You're getting a bit overwrought,' she says. 'How about some water? I think that will really help. It often works that if you reduce the temperature . . .' her voice trails off as she goes out of the room towards the kitchen.

Sally walks past, casually.

'You OK?' she says, wrinkling her nose. 'You look like you're gonna kill someone.'

'She's asking me such dumb questions,' I whisper.

'They always do,' she whispers back. 'Just keep calm and factual. They are actually on your side – they're just so used to dealing with complete nutters that they treat *everyone* like complete nutters.'

I take in a very deep breath and let it out slowly.

'I ordered a pizza for lunch. Hurry up and get this over and done with,' she whispers as Emma comes back with a glass of water. She doesn't notice Sally wandering in the opposite direction.

'What about the weight-loss, Clare? You say you've noticed that you are underweight? Are you satisfied with your eating patterns?'

'I am aware that I've lost weight,' I say. 'And I didn't control my eating patterns. Gareth controlled them. Again, ask him!' I say.

'Does your weight affect the way you feel about yourself?'

'I don't know what you mean. I don't know my own weight so how could it affect the way I feel?'

'Have any members of your family suffered with an eating disorder?'

'No.'

'No?' she says, like I'm deliberately hiding something.

'I don't have any family to ask,' I say.

'Your mother,' she says, 'did she have any kind of eating . . .'

'I don't know. Don't know. Don't *know*.'

She pauses, more for my benefit than hers I think. She has a patronising look on her face.

'Do you think you will resume normal calorific intake now that you are outside of the influence of Gareth? I ask because I understand that when you were at the hospital, you spat out the ice cream you were given.'

Hmmmm.

'I did spit it out. I remember spitting it out. I'm lactose intolerant, you know.'

'We've estimated that on the day you were in hospital you had 347 calories. You need to be pushing 1500. Are you accepting this as a future goal?'

'Yes,' I say, calmly.

'Have you ever self-harmed, Clare. In the past?'

'No,' I say. 'I've been too busy self-saving. It's an occupational hazard when you live with a psychopath.'

She frowns at her screen.

'Could you class anything in your recent behaviour as reckless?'

'Reckless?' I say. 'I'm not sure what's more reckless, Emma, staying with a man who wants to kill you, or running away from a man who wants to kill you. What would you say?'

She looks at her screen and taps.

She doesn't answer.

She doesn't look at me.

She just taps.

What's she saying about me?

That I'm mad?

That I deserve this?

That I asked for it?

'*Emma!*' I scream. '*What would you say?*'

She closes her laptop.

'Shall we have a break?' she says.

'I don't want a break. I want to finish,' I say, very quietly. 'I want to go to my room.'

'There's only a couple of questions left,' she says. 'I guess we could carry on, if you're happy to continue.'

I nod.

'Mood swings. Do you have mood swings, do you think?'

'No.'

'Have you ever been prescribed anything for mood swings,' she says, 'in the past?'

'I had vitamin shots. Gareth insisted because he'd had some vitamin shots and they gave him back all his energy. Made him feel younger.'

'So, you had vitamin shots for mood swings?'

'Yes, but I never thought I had mood swings. Gareth said I did. Said I needed cheering up. So, we went to see this American doctor in Harley Street, one of Gareth's mates from Delaware or something, I think, and he gave me shots and these tablets. Gareth used to get them from the pharmacy in reception, while I waited in the car.'

'And you went there more than once.'

'Yes. We went once a month. Ish.'

'In your car?'

'I don't know why this is interesting,' I say.

She says nothing.

She just taps.

'I'm trying to understand what your life has been like, Clare.'

'We went there maybe ten times. In my car. But he always drove. We ended up having massive rows because he never wanted to pay for the parking meter. Or he'd pay for twenty minutes and we'd be like half an hour, so I'd have to race down to the car and sit in it and wait for him.'

'So, you never collected the tablets. He took charge of that?'

'Yes, while I made sure we didn't get a ticket. He hated traffic wardens. Anyone telling him what to do. One time, he got down to the car and there was this warden about to issue us with a ticket and Gareth went mental at him so the guy started dialling the police and saying he wanted Gareth's full name so he could report him.'

'When was this?' Emma interrupts.

'I'm not sure.' I can't remember. It feels like the last few months are a real jumble.

'Was it recently?'

'I don't know.'

'But it was when you went to visit the doctor?'

'Yes,' I say. But I'm not sure.

'So, what happened?'

'He was shouting at the guy. Told him he wouldn't show him his licence. Told me to climb over to the driver's seat. And then he got in the car. He was so angry. Like he gets with me. And I watched him wrap his jacket around his fist. While I was starting the engine. And I looked over my shoulder to reverse. And he was just winding it round and round. And just as I pulled out of the space he punched me in the side of the head. I blacked out, I guess for just a second, and the car stalled. So he punched me again. I was trying to find the keys to switch the engine on, but every time I reached forward, he hit me. The last time he hit me so hard I banged my head on the side window. Blood was dripping through my eyebrow. He told me to fucking hurry up. Just fucking hurry up.'

'Was it his car then, Clare?'

'No, it was my car. But he liked to drive it. On our second date, he pointed at the car keys and put his hand out. He didn't even say anything. He'd done this course for stunt driving. There was nothing he didn't know about driving.'

'OK. So let's move on,' she says. 'Just five more minutes, Clare. Do you think you could pinpoint for me how you are feeling right now? I mean, *right* now. In the present. How do you feel, in the present?'

'I don't know. Relieved maybe?' I say. 'Well, I will be when he's been locked up.'

'Anything else?' she says.

'Embarrassed. That I fell for it all in the first place.'

'Many victims say that.'

'Useless, I suppose, a bit,' I say, 'kind of empty.'

'Empty?'

'Yeah, like I can't decide what to do. I'm so used to, you know . . .'

'That's very understandable,' she says. 'And does that make you angry at all?'

'No, not really. Not angry.'

'You haven't threatened anyone here.'

'No!'

'Perhaps, overreacted to something harmless?'

'No! I don't think I've even really spoken to anyone.'

'Kitty, for example. Did you have a misunderstanding with Kitty?'

'Kitty? No! Why, what'd she say?'

'She said that you invited her into your flat and then threatened her.'

'She had a key. She broke in.'

'Why did she break in if she had a key?'

'No, you don't understand, she had a key but then she . . .'

'The details of it don't matter, Clare. What matters is whether you got angry and threatened her.'

'I asked her to leave, yes! But I wasn't threatening. Did she say I was threatening? Did she?'

'She said that you frightened her. She wants your verbal abuse recorded. On file.'

'Fucking bitch!'

'Why do you say that?'

'You people! Why do you *think* I say that? She just totally made that up.'

'Did she, Clare?'

'Yes, for fuck's sake.'

'Or do you think you just remember it differently to her?'

'You people!'

Is she just trying to wind me up?

Because she is.

This is exactly what Gareth used to do to me.

I need to get out of here.'

'Do you often find you're unable to control your anger?' says Emma, quietly.

You're the fucking mental ones.

My glass shatters as it hits the wall behind her.

Twenty-Nine

Sally

She didn't eat much of the pizza, Clare didn't, barely touched it, and I'd ordered a Vegerama one, which, let me tell you, is a bloody long way from a Meat Feast with extra jalapeños. What is the point of artichokes on a pizza?

If I'd known she weren't going to eat anything . . . Anyway, she's gone for a lie-down, and she looks like she needs a lie-down.

'You want anything from Tesco?' asks Prashi. She's got the girls all bundled up in their anoraks and scarves, and they're arguing about who gets to wear the pink scarf.

'Why don't I look for another pink scarf while you're out?' I say. 'Maybe I can find you another one.'

'I want a new one,' says the older girl, taking off the pink scarf she'd tied around her neck and throwing it at her sister.

'*I* want a new one,' says the shorter girl, throwing the scarf on the floor.

And that's why I didn't have children.

The garment wardrobe is a room off the main hall, next to the noticeboard and it's jammed with rails, like a jumble sale, filled with women's and children's clothes and then there's plastic storage boxes underneath with badly spelled name tags; SCARFS, SOCKS AND TIGHTS, PANTS AND NICKERS.

Kitty comes in, quiet as a mouse, silently closing the door behind her like she's a cat burglar or something.

'Didn't see you there,' she says, looking at me as if I shouldn't be in the room. 'I'm looking for some leg warmers.'

'Didn't they go out of fashion in the eighties?' I say, smiling, trying to be nice. I mean, she can't help it, can she, if she's mental?

'I wasn't even born in the eighties,' she says without smiling, as though she thinks time didn't exist before she did.

'Something like this?' I say, showing her a pair of over-the-knee lurex socks. 'You could cut the feet off?'

'Are they new?' she says. 'I don't want them if they're second-hand.'

'Everything in here is second-hand.' I laugh, because honestly, where does she think she is, Harvey Nichols?

'Some of it was given by the shops. Old stock,' she goes. 'That's what Mrs H said.'

'Well, you can look,' I say.

'I wouldn't wanna wear dead people's clothes, would I?' she says, shivering at the thought.

'I draw the line at pants,' I say, more as a joke than anything.

'You're kidding, right? There are pants here? Oh my God, I wouldn't wear dead people's pants, not even if you paid me.'

'I know what you mean, but I guess the pants are just pants and they don't know they used to belong to someone dead.'

I feel sick.

I'm supposed to meet Jane, the solicitor, about the exclusion order, because apparently there's no sign of Terry anywhere so they can't actually tell him about the injunction. This means it's not actually legal yet, and because he's not got the stupid device thing on, he's in breach of his release conditions or something. Anyway, he's not at his mother's or at any of his mates, and he's not been round mine again, so they say – although I doubt they're sitting outside my flat day and night, right?

Sue sent me a text and said I should talk to Jane, but she wants to talk to me too, cos there's some photofits she wants me to look at of Terry's brothers. And on the one hand she says she doesn't want me coming out of here unless it's absolutely necessary, for my own safety and everything, and then on the other she wants me down at the station so I can talk to her about Clare, because she also doesn't want to be seen talking to me, in case Clare sees us, you know, or that other mental cow, Kitty. She says she'll send me a car with blacked-out windows, like I'm a gangster or the sodding Queen. I'd feel a lot more comfortable if I wasn't snitching on Clare; I mean, I don't even know why Sue thinks she's not telling the truth.

She's kind of counting on me, I think, just too much. I mean, I've got enough on my plate, and Clare, she's just a young girl, a kid really, and let's face it, she's been through a right traumatic time. The police should talk to her directly 'stead of coming through me all the time.

'You might change your mind about that,' Sue says, when I tell her that later back at the police station, after I've signed more forms at the solicitors. 'It's just not adding up,' she says.

'What's not?' We're back in the community room. 'Cos it's not like you don't have physical proof. You only had to take one look at that girl to realise that she was a DV.'

'It's the house,' she says, leafing through my file at the same time. 'She thought she heard Gareth smashing it up. That after he'd poured paraffin on her he'd lost it. That he was drunk.'

'Yeah?' I say, wondering if any of this has to do with me.

'The house was spotless. Like a show house.'

'Really? Spotless? And no sign of Gareth?'

'No, we even checked with the neighbours. They said he's a nice guy, really charming. They say they haven't seen much of either of them for months. Him out in the car a bit. But not her.'

'And didn't you say that same neighbour thought he was doing DIY in the middle of the night?'

'Clare said he was trashing the place.'

'Well I guess, if she thought he was off his head, she'd have thought DIY noises were trashing-the-joint noises. It's possible.'

' "Used to hear a bit of arguing but not so much recently",' Sue read from Halsall's notes from the neighbour.

'So he's not there and the house is tidy; maybe he cleaned up before he buggered off to live in Cuba or something.'

'Well, OK, here's the other thing. All the stuff you would expect someone to take? Laptop, keys, phone? All still there. No one goes away anywhere without their phone, right?'

'Maybe he left in a hurry. Soon as he saw she'd escaped, he'd have guessed she was going to go straight to the police and he'd have scarpered, fast as he could.'

'Exactly. So, he wouldn't redecorate the laundry room.'

'What?'

'She told me that he'd regularly lock her in the laundry room and that she had scratched how many times she's been in there, on the wall, in the plaster.'

'Right?'

'It's newly-painted.'

'You got the right house, yeah?' I say, giving her a bit of a look.

'Course I got the right house! I'm seeing Clare tomorrow but you'll talk to her too, right?'

'I'll talk to her,' I say. 'But I'm not promising you anything; it's up to her what she says. I'm not the prying type – and that Emma gave her a hard time yesterday; sounds like she was tough on her.'

'She's a mental health expert. She was just doing her job. Clare has a bit of a habit of hating people she thinks are giving her a hard time.'

'Perhaps Clare just remembers it differently.'

'She has a habit for that too. Seems to me Clare remembers an awful lot of things differently.'

'Seems to me you've made up your mind,' I say.

Sue ignores me.

'And watch out for that Kitty Bryers,' she goes.

'What, our Kitty? The blonde bimbo? I don't think we need to worry about her.'

'She was sectioned last year. Only out because it was a children's unit. Kept crying rape and then she actually was raped.'

'Sectioned for what?'

'APD. Anti-social personality disorder.'

'Bloody hell, there's a personality disorder for everything these days.'

'Kitty's trouble. She definitely told you she's not married, right?'

'What! Kitty's married?'

'No, I'm talking about Clare.'

'Oh, Clare. Yeah, she said that he just pretended they were married so that other men didn't go after her, so that he owned her.'

'That's what she said to me too.'

'Why?'

'Because there's a bloody great big wedding photo over the fireplace.'

When I get back, there's a problem.

Prashi had been gone since two and was only booked out until four, and now it is six. That's what you do, you book out so people know when to expect you back. I'd only been back myself for about five minutes when PC Chapman races through the front door to get the details from Mrs H.

'Can you give me a description of what the girls were wearing?' she's saying to Mrs H in the hallway. There's a group of women standing around her. One of the other Indian ladies is holding her hands together tightly and keeps looking at her watch.

'They had on those purple anoraks,' I say. 'But it's quite a warm day. They might have taken them off.'

'Did she say where she was going?' asks Chapman.

'Just to Burger King in Parkway. The girls are collecting the trolls you get in Happy Meals,' says Abigail.

'That's McDonalds,' says Sian. 'They do the Happy Meals, not Burger King.'

'So, it's just Prashi and the two girls who are missing, no one else was with them?' says Chapman. 'Let me go down to Parkway now. I've got backup coming.'

Clare's standing still, looking pale.

Everyone there's imagining it was them, that's why they all look so shit-scared. Everyone dreads being 'found'.

'Her ex is from Bradford. How's he going to find her down here?' says Sian.

'Exes do have a nasty habit of turning up,' says Abigail.

'Did she know not to use Facebook?' asks Sian.

'What's wrong with using Facebook?' says Sarah.

'Of course, you can't use Facebook, you mong! He'd be able to trace her. You totally do my head in,' says Big Debbie.

'I don't know why you always say things like that,' says Sarah. 'I used to be head of human resources at a very big company. I was in charge of eight and a half thousand staff.' She stomps off.

'And your husband is an out-of-work brickie who tried to rearrange your facial features with his fist,' Big Debbie calls after her. 'Frankly, I can totally see why.'

'Can I speak to you, Debbie? Please, in my office?' says Mrs H.

'What! I only said mong. Everyone says mong. Doesn't everyone say mong?' Big Debbie says to everyone.

'I've not heard mong,' says Clare, walking into the kitchen.

'It's not a good word. It's a bit like the C word. You don't go there,' I say, following behind.

'What is a mong, though?' she says.

'I'm not sure. Since political correctness went apeshit, don't know anymore. Let's just say it's someone who's from Mongolia.'

'Mongolia? Is Sarah from Mongolia? Is she?'

Big Debbie is trudging up the hall with her head hung in shame.

'Definitely,' she says, under her breath.

'I'm making chicken,' Clare says to me. 'You want some?'

'I'd love some,' I say, thinking it's good she's eating. 'I had to see the solicitor about the injunction, Terry has gone AWOL.'

Kitty is in the kitchen making toast. The timer is ticking and she's jumped onto the stainless steel worktop and tucked her feet under her crossed knees, like you do in yoga, or like little kids do in assembly. The butter and knife are waiting and she's playing with her multi-coloured gem rings and woven thread bracelets, not nervous, you understand, just like she doesn't give an actual shit. She doesn't even register that we're in the room.

'Why'd you say I threatened you?' says Clare, out of the blue.

'What, me?' I say.

'No, her. Kitty. Why'd you say I threatened you?'

'Cos, you did,' she says, not even looking at Clare.

'You know I didn't,' she goes. 'You know I didn't.'

'Maybe we just remember it differently.' Kitty's still twiddling with her bracelets, not even bothered.

'You broke into our room!' says Clare.

'You're not remembering it right.'

'Why are you so weird?' says Clare.

'You're the self-harmer,' responds Kitty.

'What the—' starts Clare, but the front buzzer goes and everybody runs into the hallway, including Mrs H and Big Debbie, to see Prashi and the girls being herded in by PC Chapman, and they all have ice lollies, including Chapman, and the girls have orange lolly stains down their chins, and their T-shirts.

'I'm so sorry, we lost track of time!' says Prashi. 'We worried you! I'm sorry.' The girls are beaming, happy to be the centre of attention, enjoying the hugs.

It's a bit of a Jesus moment, if you know what I mean, everybody cooing over the kids and putting their arms around Prashi as though she's been rescued from the arms of the devil, even though they'd only been in the park. And Mrs H looks dead proud to be head of a group of women so kind, supportive, all those things a women's refuge is supposed to be.

'They were by the zoo,' says Chapman.

'False alarm,' says Mrs H, smiling.

The smoke detector goes off in the kitchen, at almost exactly the same time as she says false alarm.

'Chicken!' shrieks Clare, laughing, and I run after her. The chicken in the oven is actually on fire, and Clare's jumping from one foot to the other, holding the baking tray with the oven gloves, the half chicken filling the kitchen and hall with clouds of grey smoke.

I turn on the tap and shove the whole tray into the sink, where it sizzles and goes out. By now there's a crowd standing at the door, including Prashi and the girls, all screaming with laughter.

'Errrr, Helllllooooo,' says Mrs H to the girls. 'Enough excitement for one day. Here's the takeaway menu, Clare. They only take twenty minutes. Let me know what you want. Prashi, get those girls into bed.'

Clare picks up the burnt chicken from the bottom of the sink and flips open the top of the bin as I pull my specs off the top of my head and start to read through the takeaway menu. Kitty is still sitting on the side, finishing her toast. She hasn't moved since she began eating it, feet still tucked under, playing with her bracelets, not giving a shit about Prashi and her kids or the chicken being on fire, not interested in anything but her toast. She didn't even seem to notice the smoke.

Thirty

DS Clarke

DS Clarke is on autopilot, taking her usual route to work from her one-bedroom flat in Belsize Park, a sixties concrete block that wouldn't get past the planning these days. She snakes around Primrose Hill, down into Regent's Park Road then takes a right off Parkway to the back car park. On a good day it takes her twenty minutes. On a bad day, forty. On a bad day she could walk it faster.

DS Clarke never listens to the radio in her car. She keeps the ear out for local police reports, sure, but driving down the back roads of North London, she takes time to think. It's her form of meditation, she tells herself, although she's not emptying her mind as much as focusing it. She likes to call it 'finding holes'.

The hole that she is wrestling with today? Who tidied up the house? She admonishes and immediately forgives herself for her sexist attitude, because, frankly, she can't help but think that it would take a woman to clean a house to that degree. Or a gay man. She bites her lip. Now she's worried she's being homophobic.

But if it wasn't Gareth, then it must have been Clare. Unless there was someone else involved . . .

But who?

Why would Clare say the house was a mess if it wasn't? Why would Clare clear up the house, then say that it was a mess?

To cast doubt on Gareth – he's the mad one?

To implicate Gareth – he had something to hide?

DS Clarke needs her white board.

At 8.04 the children (that's how she thinks of her junior team), are beginning to slope in. Frankly, it wouldn't have surprised her to see their mums standing at the gate handing over plastic lunch boxes.

What adds up? It might be easier to say what doesn't.

She divides the board into two.

On the left – FACT. On the right – CONJECTURE.

Under FACT she writes:

Clare is injured.

Gareth is missing.

Clare is in the Regent's Park Road Refuge.

They both lived at 289 Oval Road.

Clare has no job.

Clare's father died in September 2014.

Under CONJECTURE she writes:

Clare is the victim.

Gareth is the perpetrator.

Gareth is in hiding.

Gareth has done a runner.

Clare is telling the truth.

Gareth is the victim.

Clare is the perpetrator.

Clare is lying.

'What do you think?' she asks PC Chapman, as she wanders in with her Starbucks coffee and begins to take off her coat.

'I don't know anymore. Every time I'm with Clare, I'm convinced she's telling me the truth. Then you see the wedding photo, and his phone, laptop and keys on the table and you think – this is a crime scene, but what is the crime?'

DS Clarke takes a step back from the board and looks hard at PC Chapman. Like she's seeing her for the first time. PC Chapman blushes but DS Clarke doesn't notice. She turns to look at her white board and taps the end of the marker pen on her chin.

'Good fucking point,' she says to PC Chapman. 'Good fucking point.'

The evidence retained from 289 Oval Road has been catalogued and an inventory has been produced. DS Clarke is frankly loath to ask DC Walker anything, but buzzes through to her.

'I'm doing it now,' says DC Walker.

'And you've logged the pictures?'

'They're on the hard drive.'

'Can you forward the wedding picture to my phone? The one I took is blurred.'

'Will do.'

'Anything interesting happen after I left?'

'No, nothing. There was nothing incriminating in the house.'

DS Clarke sighs inwardly. She's watched far too many police dramas, she thinks.

'Apart from . . . the tidiness, the posh clothes, the laptop, the keys and the wedding picture?' she says.

'None of that incriminates Gareth James. If anything, it incriminates Clare Chambers. It proves she's been lying all along.'

'Does it?' says DS Clarke.

'Yes, sarge, it does.'

DS Clarke has neither the time nor the inclination to remind DC Walker of the first principles of the British judicial system.

'Anything else?' says DS Clarke.

'Oh, we did find his journal.'

'What's a journal?'

'It's a jumped-up way of saying diary.'

'Gareth kept a diary?'

'Looks like it. Minute-by-minute account of his life over the past two years.'

'Can you get that to my office – now, please!'

'Yes, sarge. I already put it on Chapman's desk. I'll ask her to bring it over.'

DS Clarke can see the diary from where she's sitting. It's one of those desk jobbies, black leather with a silky ribbon, and silvered edges to the pages. She walks over to Chapman's desk. The diary is in a clear plastic evidence bag and there are traces of powder on the outside cover. The forensics team has been all over it.

She opens the evidence bag, pulling on protective gloves and flipping back the cover. The end papers are marbled. Posh. She leafs through to the middle.

'. . . had a restless night. She has frantic episodes where she begs me not to leave her, even though I have no intention of doing so. She refuses to leave the house now and . . .'

It's not an actual diary, just a book with blank pages and each one has been filled out with carefully scripted handwriting, done with a fountain pen, black ink, italic nib.

'. . . I am more concerned than ever about Coco. When I came back from the supermarket, she had been self-abusing by stubbing cigarettes out in her skin. I've applied some burn cream to her forearms but she keeps ripping off the bandages to . . .'

The words on the opening pages are sweeping, elaborate. Towards the end of the book, the writing becomes sloppier, with smudged ink obscuring some of the words as though the ink was still wet when the page was turned.

'. . . transient, stress-related paranoid ideation or severe disso-ciative symptoms usually associated with Borderline Personality Disorder . . .'

'What do you think?' says Chapman, peering over DS Clarke's shoulder.

'I've only just opened it,' she replies. 'Have you had time . . .'

'Basically, it says he's been putting up with a monster for the past two years. A narcissistic, profligate, violent, drug addict, self-harmer. Shall I go on?'

'And what does it say about him?'

'That he's a martyr. Do-anything-for-his-lovely-wife type thing.'

'Really?'

'He's *that* type of guy!' says PC Chapman, turning on her heel and heading back to her own desk. 'I used to go out with one like that. He was a wanker. Anyway, it doesn't mean anything.'

'It's a diary,' says DS Clarke. Juries respond well to diaries, DS Clarke knows that. Ridiculous as it might seem, she thinks to herself, the mugs tend to believe it if it's written down.

'Well, he's obviously made it all up,' says PC Chapman.

'Has he, Chapman? How do you know that?'

'I believe Clare.'

'We'd all like to believe Clare. Did Walker track down this Quinn bloke?'

'Yes, she saw him last night.'

'And . . .?' says DS Clarke, arms folded, expecting the worst.

'Quinn said, and I think these are his exact words . . . "I can't remember how I broke my arm last year! I think I was drunk. Sorry not to be of more help."'

'Perfect,' breathed DS Clarke. 'So, where is Gareth, then? If he's not at the house, where's he gone? Maybe he did go to the hospital after all? Still nothing on the CCTV?'

Chapman shrugs.

'Go back and look at it again. He's devious. Oh, and look for any traffic or parking violations in the past six months for Clare's car. We need to find someone to corroborate Clare's story.'

The police doctor's report is through and includes all the photos. DS Clarke has requested a hard copy and it's now lying unopened on her desk. She needs to wait till the children are busy. Sometimes the photographic evidence is hard to look at.

The case briefing meeting begins in Meeting Room 1. The children wander in with their mugs. DS Clarke has some time.

She closes her office door and slices through the seal of the envelope.

Medical Police Report – Clare Chambers. Case Number 4267819DV

Each point in Ridley's report is matched by a photo of a part of Clare's body.

DS Clarke flips open the first pages.

Ingestion of hazardous liquids – not confirmed

The photo shows close-ups of Clare's tongue, blue, and some red sore patches around the mouth. Tox reports on the contents of Clare's stomach are referred to. The initial hospital report is included. So, thinks DS Clarke, just mouthwash after all that.

Thermal & chemical burns – confirmed

Shots of skin, charred in places, angry red in others. The inside of the thighs are criss-crossed with black and brown scorch marks. Old scorch marks suggesting ongoing abuse.

Bruising consistent with abuse including to the thighs, abdomen, buttocks, cheeks & neck.

Grey skin mottled with yellow, green, blue and purple bruises – all sizes, all shapes. The differences in colour indicate when the bruises were caused.

Bruising consistent with significant trauma including to the knees and shins.

Superficial cuts and grazes

The biggest, angriest bruise on the thin right leg – barely any fat or muscle.

Malnourished.

Bony shoulders and a spine so sharply defined it looks like it could pierce through the skin.

May have a propensity to self-harm.

The last photo makes DS Clarke take a sharp breath. A tear-stained Clare, naked from the waist up, lying on a hospital bed, apparently unconscious, the palms of her hands facing up. She looks like a starving, hopeless child from one of those charity appeal films that's impossible to watch.

DS Clarke remembers what Dr Ridley said,

'It's hard to fake that kind of abuse.'

Thirty-One

Clare

I'm not sure why I'm eating.

Mrs H is standing guard half in the kitchen and half in the dining room.

I honestly don't think she'll go until I've eaten every last crumb of breakfast.

I'm also not sure why I'm eating granola (gluten) or yoghurt (lactose) but I guess I'm not intolerant to either after all.

So much for Gareth's nutrition tips.

Babe, I know everything about nutrition.
 Really.
 There's nothing I don't know about nutrition.
 Did you have your vitamin supplements today?
 Let me see you take them.
 In your mouth.
 Swallow.
 Now open wide.
 Let me see they're gone.

Kitty is dipping rice cakes into humus and swigging out of a Diet Coke can.

I'm trying not to hate her for lying about me.

Mrs Henry is listening in.

She's got glittery leg warmers on. Kitty, that is.

'You like my new hair?' she says, staring out of the window.

Gareth used to do that. Ask me things, then not be interested in the reply.

'Yeah,' I say, not really sure what's different.

'It's graduated. That's what they call it. Got it done in Parkway. The guy there, the colour-specialist, he said I had quite a good face.'

'Nice,' I say.

'I think I'm going to get scouted soon. By an agency. Like Cara Delevingne. They look for people all the time. Storm Models is the best one. But I think Elite are quite good too.'

'Why don't you go and see them, if that's what you want to do?'

'I'm not going to ask them! They have to ask me! That way you hold all the cards in the relationship. That's what Kate Moss did.'

'Wasn't Kate Moss ten or something when she got scouted?' I say, chewing on unchewable bird seed or something.

'Yeah. At an international airport. If I was going through international airports all the time, I'd have been scouted already. She came from a privileged background. It was easy for her.'

I thought she was from Croydon.

I think that.

I don't say that.

'You should come to my dance class,' Kitty says, examining the ends of her hair.

'No,' I say. 'Thanks, though.'

'It's Jazz and Contemporary. Everyone is pretty rubbish. I should be in the senior group but they said they're full up.'

'Is it safe for you to go out?' I say. I mean, I don't even know what her story is. But if I ask she's bound to ask about mine.

I'll find you wherever you go.
  I promise you, babe.
  I'll be behind every wall, every tree.

'Yeah, it's fine. I was groomed,' she says, lowering her voice so Mrs Henry can't hear, 'by a gang. The police are all over it. They've arrested fourteen of the wankers already. Come on! Get your stuff. I can loan you some shoes if you haven't got any. I've got a spare pair.'

'I don't think . . .' I start.

'You don't have to think,' she interrupts. 'You deserve some fun, don't you? And you ain't gonna get any around here.'

'Morning, Clare,' says Sally, coming in.

She's all dressed and ready for action.

Even got lipstick on.

'I don't know why I'm eating again,' I say, 'I'm still full from last night.'

'You off to your dance class?' Sally says to Kitty.

Kitty doesn't reply.

She slides off the table and picks up her bag.

'See ya. Wouldn't wanna be ya,' she says to me.

'The rubbish, Kitty. In the bin please,' says Mrs Henry, winking at me behind Kitty's back.

She huffs like a three-year-old.

Drops her bag in the middle of the floor.

Picks up the Diet Coke can and the humus pot and slams them in the bin.

Picks up her bag again.

Swings her hair.

Saunters off.

Proper little madam.

'I had a call from DS Clarke,' Mrs Henry whispers to me. 'She'd like to see you today. And she's got a bag of your clothes.'

'You're kidding me! I can take off this crap?'

'And we can wash that dressing gown,' says Sally, waiting for me to have a hissy.

'She said she'd be in this morning. You're here, right?' says Mrs Henry.

'Actually, I have an appointment with the Queen of England,' I say. 'She's going to have to wait her turn.'

Mrs Henry laughs.

So does Sally.

And then I thought they looked at each other kind of funny.

I don't know.

Just something I thought.

Maybe not.

'How come Kitty goes out all the time?' Sally says to Mrs Henry.

She shrugs. 'It's a refuge, not a prison. Quite a few of the residents have classes, or jobs, appointments, whatever. It's up to you what you do. I wouldn't recommend that either of you go out, though. But I can only recommend. You have to make your own decisions.'

She clocks my empty bowl.

She doesn't say anything though.

It's not surprising you're so fat, babe.

You gotta drop a few pounds.

'This won't get the baby a new bonnet,' Mrs Henry says and sighs. 'I'll let you know when Susan gets here. She's bringing Celia.'

'Kitty invited me to her dance class,' I say, when Mrs H has gone.

'I hope you told her where to go,' says Sally.

She's got no time at all for Kitty, since she complained about me.

'She was groomed,' I say. 'By men, a gang she said.'

'Nearest she got to grooming was getting her hair dip-dyed,' says Sally.

'No, really. She was groomed and the police have arrested fourteen wankers,' I say. 'That's what she said. Fourteen wankers.'

'Everything's larger than life for Kitty,' Sally says.

'I'm not sure what you mean.'

'I mean she makes stuff up,' says Sally. 'You know that. So, shall we wash that dressing gown, then?'

'Bathrobe,' I say. 'Gareth says . . .'

'Dressing gown,' says Sally.

'Dressing gown,' I repeat.

I don't know why everyone is looking so serious.

'Can I put these on now?' I say, holding up my favourite pyjama bottoms.

Brushed cotton.

Pink rabbits.

The only ones that Gareth didn't find and throw out.

They're in the Sainsbury's bag that Susan has brought me. Two T-shirts. Trainers. Sweatpants. Knickers and a bra. White. Plain.

Only French underwear for you, my love.

Detective Sergeant Clarke doesn't smile like she usually does.

'We need to talk first, Clare,' she says.

Very official.

'It's all going to be OK,' says Celia, putting her arm around my shoulders.

'What is?' I say.

'This is,' she says, looking at Susan.

'You found him!' I blurt out. 'What happened?'

'We haven't found him, Clare. We're going to do a full forensic on the house,' says Susan.

'What's a full forensic?' I say.

'We need to check it out,' says Susan. 'Things aren't quite adding up.'

'What's not adding up? What's she mean?' I say to Celia.

She shakes her head, looking at Susan.

'Gareth seems to have disappeared,' she says.

'Disappeared?' I say. 'Well, he's not going to just sit there and wait for you to arrest him, is he?'

I'm a master of disguise.

Did I tell you that, babe?

One of my best friends works for the CIA.

I know everything about international intelligence.

I do actually work for the CIA but I'm a sleeper.

I just come when called.

Like a dog.

A superhuman dog.

When they have a top operation that they want handled the 'Lone Wolf' way, that's when they call me.

'None of his stuff has gone, Clare. His laptop. His keys. His phone. His journal . . .'

'What journal?'

'The diary he kept . . .'

'Gareth never kept a journal. Or a diary. Or whatever it is you want to call it. He was far too shallow to have anything to write down.'

'Was,' says Susan. 'You said "was".'

'*Is*,' I say, turning red.

I don't know why. It's not like I've done anything.

There's a long silence.

No one says anything.

But everyone seems to be thinking a lot.

'Why are you trying to make me feel bad?' I say.

Celia looks at Susan as if she needs permission to speak.

'That's not at all what we're here for,' says Celia, patting my hand.

'I'm going to be absolutely straight with you, Clare, so you can be absolutely straight back,' says Susan.

I nod.

'I have been straight, though,' I say to her. 'I have . . .' but she interrupts.

'First of all, your clothes, Clare.'

'What about my clothes. They were in the drawers, next to the bed, right?'

'There were a few clothes there, Clare. But the majority of your, let's call it, "extensive" wardrobe, don't look like these. There are a lot of designer clothes.'

'They're not mine,' I say, shaking my head, looking at Celia.

Waiting for her to smile and nod.

Nod and smile.

'Cashmere sweaters. Joseph skirts and trousers. Silk shirts in ten colours.'

'Those aren't mine!' I say. 'I haven't bought any clothes in two years. You're making this up. You're trying to make me go mad. Gareth says . . .'

Babe, you're remembering everything all wrong. Take a pill or something.

'The laundry room,' Susan interrupts again, 'the one with all the scratches on the wall, you said?'

I nod slowly.

'There are no signs of anything unusual there, Clare. It's a nicely painted room, with about a hundred pairs of women's shoes in. Size thirty-eight, that's your size, right?'

'I'm a thirty-eight.' I shake my head in disbelief. 'I have one pair of trainers, by the stairs,' I say.

Celia fishes them out of the Sainsbury's bag.

I snatch them off her.

'The house is spotless, Clare. Nothing broken. Nothing smashed. No bottles in the recycling. No paraffin bottles in the bin. No matches on the floor. And the laundry room has no lock on it. It's much nicer than you made out.'

'Made out?' I say. 'You don't believe me. Do you? You're saying "made out" but you mean "made-up". Bitch.'

'What did you say, Clare?'

'Nothing.'

'Did you call me a bitch, Clare?'
'No.'

Babe, you're losing it again.

'There's a picture over the mantelpiece, Clare. Can you tell us about that?'

'The painting? The fields? It's an oil painting. A country scene. Yellow and green. My dad bought it at an auction. For one hundred pounds, he said. Always used to joke that it was a lost Constable and would make us our fortune.'

'Not this, then?' Susan holds up her phone for me to see a photo.

In a frame. Above the mantelpiece.

My sitting room.

My home.

It's me, with Gareth.

It's from the day we went to the wedding-dress shop.

I rang him from work one day.

Three or four months in.

Said I just wasn't really sure anymore.

Would he mind moving out?

Just for a bit, while I sorted out what I wanted to do.

What was best for both of us.

Still getting over my dad.

Missing my friends.

I'd waited till lunchtime.

So we could talk privately.

Then locked myself in the boardroom.

Knew no one would come in.

I told him I thought it was over.

We were over.

Said I couldn't do it anymore.

And he seemed fine about it.

Just asked me to make him a promise.

Babe, look it's fine with me.

I understand.

I'm too much for you.

Way too much for you.

I get it.

You're punching way above your weight, we both know that, don't we, babe?

Make me this promise, though, Coco.

Never call me.

Get rid of my number from your phone.

And if I see you walking down the street, I'm not going to know you.

Do you understand?

I won't even blink, babe.

Not a blink.

We were never anything, OK?

For me you don't exist.

'We broke up. He made me promise not to contact him. Told me I didn't exist.'

I keep looking in Susan's eyes. I can see she doesn't believe me.

'Then three hours later he called. To tell me that he'd met another girl. That he'd fucked her brains out all afternoon.'

Sorry to have to tell you, babe, but she was a 1000 per cent in the looks department. Body like a fucking goddess.

Tears streaming down my face.

'So, I slammed the phone down. And then he called me back. All afternoon he called me back. Called and called. Said he would keep calling. Until I said I was sorry.'

Twisting the tissue in my hand.

'So I said I was sorry. I couldn't bear to think of him with someone else. I loved him. I think I loved him more than I've ever loved anyone.'

Sip of water.

Blow nose.

Susan glares at Celia as if to say 'let her go on, don't interrupt'. I clocked it.

'And he came and collected me from work. Told me we were getting married. And he drove me to that wedding shop. That one in Chiswick. Chiswick High Road. He said I could have any dress I liked.'

I run a finger under my eyes to wipe away the smudged mascara.

'And he said he would wait and tell me which one suited me best because he knew about fashion. Knew everything about fashion because one of his best friends was a fashion editor for *Vogue Italia*.'

Sip of water.

'So, I tried on one dress after another. I loved it for a minute. They were a bit big. They didn't have smaller sizes. But the lady was so kind. Pinched in the waist at the back with pins. Kept fiddling with the veils and the folds of skirt, like I was a princess.'

I stop crying.

'But they were all wrong. They got worse and worse.'

Another tissue.

'And on the last one, he came into the changing room. His body took up all of the space. Asked the lady to leave us alone for a second. And he got his hand behind my neck. Under the veil. Pressing it. Pinching it between his thumb and forefinger. And he did a picture of us both. With my phone. Told me to smile my best smile or we'd be playing with the matches when we got home. He took loads. Said my smile was too fake. Told me to imagine how happy I was gonna be when we got married. With my neck between his fingers.'

Twisting the tissue.

'And then he said that leaving him was the worst thing I had ever done. *Ever*. And when we got home, he took my phone to download the pictures. And I never even saw them.'

'You're quite sure that's how it happened, Clare?' says Susan, looking at the twisted tissues on the table in front of me, then at the photo again.

Celia is looking at the floor.

'You look perfectly happy here,' says Susan.

'When we were leaving the shop, I saw this picture of a dress in the window, on a model. And I was looking at it and he said,

"I went out with her for three years. In Australia she's a super-model." And that night, when he was fucking me, he whispered in my ear 'By the way, babe, I didn't really fuck anyone else.'"

By the way, babe . . .

I'm not certain if Susan or Celia believe me.

One of them hands me another tissue. I'm so busy crying I can't see who it is.

'Do you think she could have a break, DS Clarke?' says Celia.

'Not right now,' says Susan. 'We've got a lot to get through. Clare, can we continue?'

I nod.

I don't want to continue.

I want them to go away.

But I figure they will just come back.

I'll never leave you, babe.

'Are you sure there's not more you can tell us about Gareth, Clare. Give us some background. So we can try to work out where he's gone. Relatives? Work colleagues?'

All the time Susan's saying stuff, I'm shaking my head.

'By the way,' she says. 'That work colleague of yours, Simon Quinn? He doesn't confirm your story about getting his arm broken. Said he can't remember how he did it. That he was drunk. Said he was sorry not to be able to help. Asked after you,' she says.

'Drunk?'

'He says you must have got confused.'

You know what, babe, you're getting really forgetful.

We went to the shops yesterday.

Did you forget?

You must have.

Take another tablet.

That's what Stephen said to do.

Whenever you get forgetful, take another vitamin. Up your energy levels.

'What about Gareth's old friends?'

'I asked him about his past and he always said it wasn't interesting. He said he had friends all over the place. But there was no one he kept in contact with regularly. Told me he was the type of guy who liked to sip Cristal 'as and when'. Said that's all I needed to know: he was an 'as and when' guy, always prepared for his next adventure.

'I think that's why he always had a bag packed. A suitcase. Just small. On the top shelf of the wardrobe which he thinks I don't know about, and guesses I can't reach.'

Looked inside.

Quickly.

Packed.

All his old stuff.

Old jeans he used to wear.

Shirts and sweaters he wore when I first met him.

Not the designer stuff he's bought since.

'There's all this stuff he orders online then keeps locked in a cupboard. I can smell it. New, expensive clothes. Comes in smart black boxes with ribbons and tissue paper. Most of that hasn't even been opened. And there was a passport too – his photo but in someone else's name. An old tin box full of stuff. Papers and jewellery and old photos.'

Susan is scribbling everything down.

Celia is supplying tissues.

'Do you remember the name on the passport?' Susan says.

'I didn't get that far. I had to be quick.'

'Was the first name even Gareth?' says Susan impatiently.

'I don't know. It was an American passport, I do remember that. He said he worked for the CIA. But then again, he also said that he was a concert pianist. And that he could give Robbie Williams a run for his money.'

'Did he not do any work?'

'He had been doing modelling.'

'So what were you living off?'

'I had money, my inheritance from when my dad died. I had my cards. He used them for everything.'

It's not fair if you have money and I don't.

Our lifestyles need to be the same if this relationship is going to work.

Everyone knows that.

'And no exes calling him?' says Susan.

I shake my head.

'I never knew who he was speaking to. We did bump into this girl, one time,' I say. 'In a bar. Mayfair. We'd been to some drinks party with this guy he'd worked with in Miami. We're sipping Cristal, and this girl comes in, and he points her out. Says she was with him for six months. He wasn't with her, you understand. She was "with him". Big difference in Gareth's world. And I watched him rearrange his face. Properly rearrange it into a sneer. And she totally blanked him. To the point that I doubted he even knew her.

'Maybe she just looks like the girl you went out with,' I said, trying to make him feel better.'

I need a shower.

'He said he needed a shower. Right in front of all the people we were standing with. Like suddenly. In the middle of the party. Really loud.

'And I said, "What now?" because I was totally confused. Why would anyone, in the middle of a party, suddenly announce that they needed a shower?'

You can either come with me now and wash me, or I'll see you when I'm next in town.

'And he said that I could either go and wash him now, or he'd see me when he was next in town. He said that to the entire room.'

'And what did you say?' says Susan, lost in the story.

'He was living in my house, at the time,' I say. 'I couldn't work out what was going on at all. When we got back to the house, he kissed me suddenly, urgently, and said "I want you to take that off", pointing at my dress. "And those", pointing to my bra and pants.'

'How did that make you feel?' Susan said.

'Well, I felt cheap. I did. But I guess it was thrilling, too. To be desired like that. I said to him "You can fuck me any way you want," I said. '"I want whatever you want."'

'And what did he say?' says Susan.

'He said, "I know." And he fucked me so hard, and so violently, I couldn't walk for three days.'

Thirty-Two

Sally

Whenever anyone says 'official', you know, official with a big fat capital 'O', it always makes me wonder. It's like, 'here's some total shit for you, and meanwhile, the unofficial version – which, by the way, is what actually happened, and which, by the way, totally implicates us – *that* version we're too embarrassed to tell you.' So, they're going to issue an 'official apology', and I'm thinking, go on then, what really happened?

'The tagging company was told by the probation service about the release of Terry Mansfield, Prisoner number 127963 after 3p.m. and was therefore unable to get to the offender before the following day. The offender was permitted to spend his first night under the care of his mother at her registered address, without being monitored.'

Jane is reading an email. She's come to visit and we're one along from Clare who's in Rose – God, I really can't stand these pink names, couldn't they have just numbered them? – with Sue and Celia, who looks a lot like a God-botherer if you ask me, what with the big old crucifix and the buck teeth. Do you think God-botherers spend so much time with their eyes shut praying that they don't notice their own buck teeth, or facial hair for that matter, and I'm talking about excess facial hair on women, by the way, not a regular beard or moustache on a man?

A gay guy once said to me that if *you* can see your facial hair, *everyone* can see your facial hair.

'*When the tagging company arrived at 415 Grafton Road, Liverpool . . .*'

'Street' I interrupt.

'Quite,' she says. '*When the tagging company arrived at 415 Grafton Road, they discovered that Mr Terence Mansfield, the offender, was not known at this address.*'

'Isn't that New Brighton way, Grafton Road?' I say, thinking. 'Yes, Wirral,' I remember.

She shrugs. '*When the tagging company contacted the probation officers, they were told that it was the tagging company who were responsible for sorting out the problem. But the tagging company had been given the address by the probation officers.*'

'You couldn't make it up, could you?' I say to Jane. 'They couldn't manage a piss-up in a brewery, this crowd.'

'It gets better,' she says. 'A court official had put a "*handwritten notification on an obsolete form, with a misspelt address and the incorrect postcode, indicating that an illegal 12-hour curfew was received*".'

'What's that mean?' I ask.

'I think your piss-up in a brewery analogy sums it up,' she says.

'Orgy in a brothel?' I say.

'Yup,' she says, nodding.

'Bun fight in a bakery,' I say.

'Totally. Under normal circumstances an offender who had avoided curfew for more than twelve hours would be taken back to prison. But since this case is regarded as an official miscommunication . . .'

'And unofficially a giant cock up,' I interrupt.

'. . . the offender can make himself known to the local probation officer within the following twenty-four hours, who will then inform the tagging company, without penalty.'

'And he didn't do that.'

'No.'

'Because no one at the probationary service noticed that the tagging company still hadn't put the tag on and the records showed that Terry was still at the registered address of his mother. It kept showing up as that.'

'So, he's still on the loose.'

'They have no idea where he is.'

'Terrific,' I say. 'Anyone looking?'

'Well, strictly speaking because he's in breach of his release terms, he's wanted for arrest.'

'But . . .?'

'It's probably not a priority, if I had to guess.'

'Why isn't it a priority?'

'No one likes to admit a mistake.'

'Not a priority. Doubly terrific. Fancy a cuppa?'

'Always,' she says, not knowing about the mugs, obviously.

*

Prashi offered to go down the shops for me, after I found her another pink scarf in the garment wardrobe, which actually shut up her girls for about three and a half minutes, so I asked her to get me a bottle of Sauvignon Blanc. Prashi's never drunk a sip of wine before, let alone bought an entire bottle, cos her mother told her 'Indian women can't handle their drink', and then she'd read in the *The Times of India* that 'Women go crazy taking selfies when they are drunk', and that's put the fear of God in her even more – even though her phone doesn't even take photos.

When Prashi staggers up the stairs to my flat later in the afternoon, she's totally cock-a-hoop that she's bought her first-ever bottle of wine, and she's managed to get what I'd asked her for, even though she'd just handed over the bit of paper it was written on at Tesco Express.

'Will you stay and have a glass?' I say to Prashi.

'No! I will be sick.'

'You won't be sick,' I say. 'Not on one glass.'

'I will become a woman of loose morals,' she says, laughing. She just doesn't want a glass of wine, and really she's taking the mick out of me for caring that she won't.

'Are you saying . . .' I shout down the stairs after her.

'Indeed, I am,' she shouts back, shrieking with laughter.

Kitty is on the way up.

'Hear you've been getting Prashi to supply your alcohol habit,' she goes.

You just want to kick her, she's so fucking full of herself.

'Nice time tap-dancing?' I say.

She curls her lip and we both turn our backs on each other, although it doesn't get past me that she's now moved flat again, to next door to us, our floor, now that Marina's gone off to live in her place in Hackney with her mum and her sister. Good for her, that's what I think; Marina, not Kitty.

I can hear Clare coming up the stairs too. She's got her clothes – they look like her clothes – in an orange carrier bag, but you'd think she was carrying the weight of the world on her shoulders, the amount of time she's taking.

'You want the good news or the bad news?' I say.

'I don't think there can possibly be any more bad news,' Clare goes, with a sigh, as she reaches the top step. 'Go on.'

'We have wine,' I say, 'special thanks to our lady of the loose morals, Prashi.'

'Well, I don't drink much, but I agree it's not bad news. So, what's the bad news?'

'No corkscrew.'

'I thought they all had screw tops these days?'

'Not this one.'

'Can't you ask Mrs Henry?'

'Drinking's not allowed,' I say. 'Well, they say it's "tolerated" but because there's so many drug dependencies in the building, they prefer it if we don't have it. But today being a special day . . .'

'How come?' she goes.

'The police have admitted that Terry's officially gone missing. The police are after him for breaking his release agreement.

I mean, he does twenty years and then he's gone and done something else before he's even had chance to warm up his bed.'

'Well, I guess we do have something to celebrate. Gareth's still missing too. I don't know what he's up to. Something, that's for sure.'

'Like what?'

'Gareth is always up to some scam or other. The house is spotless, Susan says. That's unheard of for him. He never cleans up. She says the laundry room is newly painted. Like properly nice. Says there's nothing broken. No bottles. No paraffin. And a bloody big wedding picture that he must've got done ages ago. Why do I get the impression that Susan hates me? She certainly doesn't believe anything I say.'

'What do you mean?'

'I don't know. I'm not sure of anything anymore. Even I don't believe me. Sometimes I wonder if he had this planned all along,' she says, 'totally set me up and now he's just done a runner with all my money.'

'If you had any,' I say and laugh, thinking of the state of my savings account.

'My dad had loads of friends in insurance,' she goes, 'and I think that when they all started he tried to help them by taking out life assurance policies.'

'So?'

'So, when he died, I inherited the house, the car, all his savings – and two million pounds in insurance claims.'

'What the fuck!' I say. Jesus, what I could do with £2 million. 'But Gareth didn't know that when he met you, did he?'

'No. I mean, I didn't blurt it out straight away, did I?'

'You've got two million quid? Wow. I've never met a millionaire.'

'I *used* to have two million quid. I don't know what I've got now.'

'How come?'

'I think I signed stuff. I know I shouldn't have. I can't remember. I don't know what's real and what's a bad dream. I know some days I felt so ill I couldn't even get out of bed and it was days like those that he'd say I needed to sign things in case anything happened to me.'

'But didn't you see a doctor?'

'Gareth said it was normal to have mood swings and just to keep taking the vitamin supplements.'

'And did you?'

'I told you. They just made me worse.'

'You definitely didn't tell him you had two million quid when you met him, though, right? I mean, he wasn't just some freeloader?'

'No, I definitely didn't to start with. But I wonder if he'd read the article in the paper. And put two and two together. I mean, it did kind of spell it out. Poor little orphan. No relatives. Well-off local builder.'

'You don't think . . .' I start but she wanders off into her bedroom with her stuff and then when she comes back she's in pink rabbit pyjamas and chucks a pen at me.

'The old pen trick,' she says. 'I'll get some glasses from downstairs.'

I'm worrying about her bare feet on the floorboards but she comes back with two plastic children's beakers.

'No glasses. They're banned like the cutlery.' She shrugs. 'First time I met Gareth, he gave me his card and told me I must meet him for a drink. Not, would you like to go for a drink? It was an order.'

I push the pen through the foil top and start to press down on the cork. Clare comes and holds the bottle steady on the floor.

'So, the next day I called him, right, and it was like he had no idea who I was. He kept saying "Who? Who? Who is it?" down the phone. 'And I said, "Clare. You know, from The Adelaide pub. Coco, you called me Coco." He used to call me Coco. All the time, Coco. Like Clare was too prosaic or something.'

The pen suddenly shoots the cork into the bottle and a large glug of Sauvignon Blanc spurts onto the carpet.

'Clare's prosaic, is it?' I say.

'Common, he said.'

'Should have got a load of me then, shouldn't he,' I say giggling into my drink.

'Finally, when he twigged who it was,' she says, swigging from her My Little Pony plastic beaker, 'he said he might be able to meet me later. "Might", only if he had time. And he started asking me all these questions like . . . Where was I? Who was I with? How old was I? What kind of work did I do? Who pays the bills? Who do I live with? Where's my house? What number house, even. And I was back-footed by that, if you know what I mean. I was just handing over all these details. Like I was stupid or something. I don't even know why. And then he says "Gotta go" and hangs up. Just like that.'

She tops up her beaker.

'When we did meet, maybe a couple of days later, I was all over the place. He was so good-looking and everyone was staring at him. All these women, like bees round a honey pot. He kept staring over my shoulder the entire time, asking me questions, but never really caring what I answered because there was always something way more interesting behind me. So, in the end, I got up to leave. I'd had enough of being humiliated.

'"You're quite pretty," he said, while I was putting my coat on. He looked quite surprised. He stood up too and stared down into my eyes, and for some reason I felt dizzy, like I was drunk on him looking at me. "You have beautiful eyes," he said. "I can see your fear in them."

'That was the point I should have run. That exact point. I look back and think that was the first time he did it; flatter me and shatter me in the same sentence.'

'Look, I know this sounds mean,' I say, slopping some more wine into my cup, 'but if he was like that on your first date, how come you didn't see it all coming?'

'I don't know. By the time I realised he was a proper psycho, I was in too deep. Don't judge me, Sally,' she says, drawing her eyes away from the window and looking at me like she is so ashamed. 'Please don't judge me. If you're really my friend, you won't. Even though he was stealing my money, controlling me to the point that I was his slave, starving me, raping me. I was too in love. I was so afraid he would leave me. I was like one of those dogs that gets kicked and kicked and kicked but still ends up loyal to their master. I would do anything he said. I loved him and hated him. Half of me just wanted to die for him. The other half wanted to kill him. Sometimes I used to dream about killing him.'

Thirty-Three

DS Clarke

DS Clarke prides herself on running a tight ship.

When she hears of any figure in a senior position described as 'firm but fair' she likes to think that that's how she would also be described.

Calm, but tenacious.

Approachable, yet professional.

After the case briefing meeting, she picks up the phone and dials reception.

'Joanna,' she barks. 'This witness report, you just emailed through.'

'Yes.'

'You mean, yes, sarge,' she barks again. 'Come up to my office and tell me about it.'

There is a photo of Terry, looking older, fatter but as tight-lipped as you'd expect him to look.

'*Do not approach . . .*' it says next to the image. '*Report any sighting immediately to Camden Road Police.*'

The email accompanying the ID said:

A PHOTOFIT ID OF MR TERENCE MANSFIELD WAS POSTED AROUND THE CAMDEN HIGH STREET/ CAMDEN LOCK / PARKWAY AREA AT 3 P.M. ON 13th APRIL.

DS Clarke's landline starts ringing as PC Joanna Lee sidles into the chair facing her.

'Hi? DS Clarke, it's Celia Barrett.'

'Celia, yes.'

'I'm just following up on our meeting with Clare Chambers.'

'I see. Thank you for that. How did you feel the meeting went?'

'I'm concerned, Detective Sergeant, that Clare is becoming more emotionally unstable.'

'And why do you think that is?'

'She seems . . .'

'No, sorry, what I meant was, Celia – she is indeed becoming more emotional, but that emotion is most probably anxiety. She is getting more anxious, and I'm not in the least bit surprised that she's anxious, Celia, because if I was her, I would also be getting more anxious. Her story is unravelling before our eyes, wouldn't you say?'

'No, DS Clarke, sorry, I didn't mean she was anxious. I meant more that she seems disturbed and disorientated. Periods when she appears to dissociate.'

I think 'dissociate' has become my favourite word ever, thinks DS Clarke to herself. *I think if I dissociated more often I wouldn't get so stressed.*

'Did you also notice,' DS Clarke says aloud, 'how much she blushed when she accidentally said "was" instead of "is"? Seems like she's written Gareth off, don't you think?'

'I know that she—'

'What about her clothes, Celia? Don't you think that's a bit strange? All that new stuff. Clobber.'

'I'm talking about the periods when she wasn't speaking, DS Clarke. When she seemed to be reliving the past. This is dissociative behaviour that we would normally—'

'And she was very quick to dismiss the subject of the clothes, wasn't she,' she says. 'And you heard her call me a bitch. I'm not sure even Clare knows which side she's on anymore.'

'I think, in these circumstances that it's important for you to evaluate the state of—'

'Thanks, Celia. I'm very well aware of what's important for me to evaluate.'

'But—'

'You can go, Celia.'

'What?'

'You can go. You heard.'

And DS Clarke smacks the phone down.

PC Lee is still sitting opposite DS Clarke, examining her new acrylics, looking like she would rather be just about anywhere.

DS Clarke has only just noticed her.

'Joanna? What is it?'

'You asked to see me about the witness statement?' says PC Lee, curling her fingernails underneath her laptop.

'Which witness statement?'

'The one you just rang me about?'

'I do work on more than one case at a time, Joanna,' says DS Clarke, breathing out slowly.

'The photo ID of Mr Terry Mansfield, case number 423145,' PC Lee reads from her laptop.

'Yes, what about it?'

'Well . . .' begins PC Lee.

'When did the ID go out?' barks DS Clarke.

'Didn't you see it? I thought you approved its release.'

'If I'd approved its release, I wouldn't be asking you about it.'

'Oh, look, it says here that Detective Walker signed it off. Yup, it says so here.'

'Right! Next question. Who is Mrs Carol Pringle, the witness, and when did she come in?'

'Oooh, was it about an hour ago?'

DS Clarke is trying hard not to sigh audibly.

'Who is she?'

'Who is she?' PC Lee repeats back. She refers to her laptop again. 'She lives in, um, Oak Road. Says so here.'

'Your name is on the statement, Joanna. Did you take the statement?'

'I do a lot of reports.'

'This one was an hour ago! Can't you remember back that far?'

'Oh, that one. Yeah, Carol Pringle. Actually, Rach and I did that one together.'

'Rach?'

'Detective Walker.'

Ah, the utterly stupid leading the utterly stupid.

'Do you think you could ask Rach to come in to fill in the gaps?'

'I think she may have popped out.'

'Do you want to ask her to pop back?'

PC Lee starts tapping away at her phone.

'On her way.' She smiles, hopefully.

DS Clarke is trying hard not to lose her mind.

'So, Walker, you met Carol Pringle, did you?' says DS Clarke when DC Walker eventually drifts into her office.

'Yes, sarge. She presented as a witness at the station this morning. She claims to have seen a man matching the description of Mr Terry Mansfield at the Sheephaven Bay pub, the one on the corner of Mornington Crescent, at 20.00 hours on the thirteenth of April.'

'What else did she say?'

'Sarge, it says it all in the statement. She saw him approach a group of blokes outside the pub and he bought them all a drink. They were all sat outside for a while. She thought they might be louts. You know, homeless.'

'Do you have her contact details? Either of you?'

They are looking at each other. Gormless.

'Neither of you.'

PC Lee blushes.

'I didn't actually meet her, sarge,' Joanna says. 'I was only sending out the report for Rach cos she—'

'What you throwing me under the fucking bus for?' says DC Walker, furious.

'So, you didn't even meet her, Joanna, despite your name being on the report?'

DS Clarke is tapping her index finger rapidly on her desk.

'No.'

'You can go. Expect a disciplinary. DC Walker, you can stay, and perhaps you'd like to describe Mrs Pringle? Old, young? Short, tall?'

'She was around fifty, I guess. Brown hair. Wearing sweat pants. Adidas. She mentioned she had a daughter.'

'Well, that's good,' says DS Clarke, smiling. 'That should make it an awful lot easier to find her. We need more on Terry. Oak Road is only a mile long. Door to door. Get a move on. Oh, and when you're done, can you go back to the house in Oval Road and photograph the laundry room again. Before it gets dark. And then can you go over to the shop where they bought the wedding dress and find out if the shop staff remember Clare and Gareth. We are getting absolutely fucking nowhere here.'

That wedding photo is beginning to get right up my arse, DS Clarke thinks to herself.

Just one of those days.

Thirty-Four

Clare

I go down for breakfast.

Kitty is there again.

She's got an apron on over her black Topshop jeans with busted out knees. I used to have some like that.

And she's got rubber gloves on.

She's waving a can of kitchen bleach.

Bleach makes me shudder.

And a pan scrubber.

'Only use the left-hand-side of the kitchen for now,' she says to no one in particular, 'I'm doing a deep-clean.'

'What's a deep-clean?' I say, thinking of Gareth and his love of sterilising.

A love of me sterilising.

He never did anything.

That is so typical of you.

Half do the job.

If you're not going to bleach it properly, don't bother.

Because you'll just end up having to do it again.

Not with gloves on.
You can't do it properly if you've got gloves on.

'I'm doing it properly for a change,' she says, marching about and slamming stuff.

She slams the cutlery drawer so all the plastic cutlery rattles.

She smacks the mugs and tumblers so hard on the side you'd think they'd break.

'Can you NOT . . .?' she shouts at Prashi as she goes to put something in the dishwasher. 'I'm doing a deep-clean.'

'Looks to me like it's less of a deep-clean and more of a fucking big song and dance about it being your turn on the rota,' growls Big Debbie.

She stomps over the kitchen floor, on the right side, and puts her plate in the dishwasher.

You've got to love Big Debbie.

'If everyone bothered as much as I do, properly sterilised all the surfaces, then I wouldn't even need to do a deep-clean. People should do it every day. Keep up with it.'

'That's what the fucking rota's for,' says Big Debbie, stomping back again.

She lets the kitchen door slam behind her as she leaves the room.

'I just want to make a black coffee,' says Sarah. 'I won't get in anyone's way. I never bother with breakfast, Just a black coffee. That's all.'

'What you mean is, you never have any MORE breakfast after the Sausage and Egg McMuffin you crawl out for every morning at seven,' shouts Kitty.

She's got her back to Sarah.

She's not even looking at her.

She's not even bothered what her reaction will be.

She's just polishing the fridge door.

Like she's trying to prove something.

No one knows what it is.

We all keep half giggling.

Sarah's not.

Sarah has turned the colour of tomato ketchup.

'I don't . . . I think . . . YOU'RE A LIAR!' she says.

She gives up on the coffee, slamming the spoon down on the counter.

'Listen, Sarah,' says Kitty, before she's had chance to go.

She puts her cloth down. Takes off her Marigolds. Gives her hands some air. Flexes her fingers.

'No one actually gives a fuck what you eat. Apart from you, Sarah Fat Murray. That's what we all call you. Sarah Fat Murray. Sarah Lard-Arse Murray. You go around telling everyone that you have a hormonal imbalance. You tell everyone that you don't eat enough to keep a sparrow alive. You say you can't have fat. And you can't have carbs. And you can't have sugar. And then you go off and binge on chocolate and McDonald's. You eat chocolate in bed, for fuck's sake. Who eats chocolate in bed? Chocolate plus McDonald's equals shit diet. And guess what, Sarah Fat Murray? That's why you're fat! Nothing to do with hormones. Nothing to do with imbalance. It's called eating too much shit. *Geddit*?'

She snaps her gloves back on.

'I'm leptin resistant,' says Sarah. 'You don't understand the biology, you nasty little freak. I've been seeing specialists for years. I don't get how you think it's OK to speak to me like this. I've run the entire HR department of a large British retail—'

'IF ANYONE IS IN ANY DOUBT AT ALL ABOUT WHETHER OR NOT SARAH HAD A SAUSAGE AND EGG MCMUFFIN THIS MORNING, PLEASE CHECK OUT THE BIN IN ROSE, WHERE SARAH PUT THE WRAPPERS TWO HOURS AGO!' shouts Kitty.

She switches on the tap full blast.

The water hits the stainless steel with a roar.

She couldn't care less what Sarah has to say.

'That's not even mine,' says Sarah, running from the room. OK, waddling. 'It's not mine!'

'Now what?' says Mrs Henry, flying in.

'I'm doing a deep-clean,' shouts Kitty from the sink.

'Turn the water off, Kitty,' says Mrs Henry, flicking off the tap for her. 'Clare, what are *you* doing?' she says, turning her attention to me.

Like I've done something.

I can tell she hates me too.

'I'm hoping to get some granola but without interfering with Kitty's deep-clean,' I say.

'Thaaaank yooooou ...' sings Kitty in an American-diner waitress accent.

She snaps her gloves again and winks at me.

'We have a group session today that I'd like you all to attend,' says Mrs Henry.

Abigail and Sian are standing at the counter in the kitchen, spoons hovering midway between their bowls of muesli and their mouths. Sian has an old copy of *Vogue* open on the counter at an article about Oprah Winfrey.

'Another one!' says Abigail.

She puts the spoon in her mouth.

She's got that look on her face.

'I've got an appointment,' says Sian. 'Unchangeable. Moved it three times already.'

'Beautiful day,' says Sally, arriving in full war paint as usual. 'Anyone fancy a walk in the park in the sunshine? I mean, it's beautiful out there, right?'

She sees us all staring.

'I'm doing a deep-clean,' says Kitty.

'Good that you've got a free day, Sally, and since you're on lock down, you'll be able to come along to the group session that we have arranged for this afternoon. And I think you would also benefit, Kitty. Today we are covering Mindful Eating.'

'I think—' Kitty gets interrupted.

'I think you would find it useful to learn some empathy,' says Mrs Henry, before Kitty can start.

'You are actually kidding,' says Sally. 'What in God's name is mindful eating?'

'You'll find out all about it at two. In the workout room at the back. With Mr Bulsara,' she says and whisks out like a headteacher.

'CAN YOU NOT PUT YOUR BOWL ON THE SIDE,' shouts Kitty, at Sian.

'What are you supposed to wear?' I say to Sally.

'I don't know. It's utter nonsense. But I guess it's something to do,' she says.

'Do you think we have to hum?' I say.

'Have you called Sue?' she asks.

'Sue who?' I say.

'You know, DS Clarke. I think you ought to tell her about the money. You were going to tell her about the money, weren't you? It could explain why he's disappeared, right? He's just done a runner with the cash.'

'DS Clarke. Yeah, I could call her.'

'You want the money back, right? I mean, don't ya?' she says. Like she's amazed.

'I don't expect to get anything back,' I say.

I kind of wish I hadn't told her about the money. Everyone will think I'm a total moron.

'Seems like a small price to pay . . .' I say.

'True,' she says, and gives me a hug.

'Can't remember the last time someone gave me a proper hug,' I say.

'Here, wear your dressing gown to the session. I washed it. It's got this massive hole in the hem – I mean, it's not that massive, but you did know about it, right? Tell me I didn't do it?'

'Oh yeah, I did know about it. It smells back to normal,' I say, smiling and taking in a big breath.

'Do you have a needle and thread so I can mend it?' she says.

I was hiding the locket in the hem.

Took it out yesterday.

I'm not going to put the locket back in the hem, though.

It's safer where it is.

No one would ever think of looking there.

'I must have caught it on the door.'

'That's funny. It looks as though it was cut.'

'No, it was definitely the door. Do you think we have to hum?'
I say again.

Mr Bulsara is a small, wiry man with olive skin and a thick black moustache.

It's mysteriously straight.

Like it doesn't follow the contours of his face.

Not at all.

I don't know if he's Indian or not but he looks like he's Indian.

He has Freddie Mercury's accent.

British.

Clipped.

With a hint of Indian.

'Thank you, ladies, for attending,' he says, quietly.

So, you have to listen really hard to hear.

'We are coming now to sit,' he says.

He's cross-legged on a blue yoga mat.

He extends his arms slowly, as though in an invisible embrace with someone very large.

'We are coming now to sit,' he says again.

Seriously slowly.

'Coming now to sit,' he says.

We all look for somewhere to sit.

'Making ourselves comfortable. On a cushion. On a mat. On a stool. On a chair.'

Sally is mouthing at me, 'On a toilet . . .'

'Is this Mindfulness McDonald's?' shouts Big Debbie from the door. 'Kitty just said it was Mindfulness McDonald's in here and that we all had to come in.'

Mrs Henry shuts her eyes and points at a chair by the window.

Big Debbie marches over bodies on cushions and mats.

'We'll be sitting for two hours in this session,' he says.

'Kin'ell,' says Big Debbie.

'So, making yourself comfortable,' he whispers.

Big Debbie slumps back in her chair and folds her arms.

'And if you're sitting on a chair . . . coming away from the back of the chair . . . so that your spine can be self-supporting . . . so that your baaaack and neeeeck and head are in liiiiinne . . . in an erect posture . . . in toooouch with this mommmment . . . and letting your eyes close . . .'

'Fuck a duck,' says Big Debbie.

Mr Bulsara suddenly stands up. In that way that incredibly bendy people stand up without putting their hands out.

'Today we are going to be looking at Mindful Eating,' he begins, looking at his spiral notepad. 'Mind-ful ea-ting,' he says, annunciating each syllable as if we are foreign students.

We all look at Big Debbie out of the corner of our eyes.

Her eyes widen.

'Fuckin' Kitty . . .' she growls.

'The structure of these sessions is as follows: firstly, we will welcome each other,' he says, looking at his pad. 'Then we will discuss the session structure. Then we will do a homework review, though of course, not this week as this is our first session. Then we will conduct some mindfulness exercises, followed by a group exercise. Then we will set some homework.'

Sally is in one of the armchairs by the door.

'Get me out of here,' she whispers.

'Let us be welcoming of each other,' says Mr Bulsara.

He sinks back down to his mat, cross-legged in one movement.

'We are now getting in touch with this moment ... Letting our eyes close ...' he whispers.

We all pretend to close our eyes.

Mr Bulsara takes a lime green plastic lunchbox out of a Tesco Express bag.

We're all thinking he's about to have his lunch.

Inside is a miniature glockenspiel – with eight rainbow-coloured bars, and a wooden stick with rubber balls on each end.

He places it before him.

He straightens it.

By now everyone has given up pretending to shut their eyes, apart from Big Debbie who looks like she's having a snooze.

He closes his eyes and strikes the red bar with the wooden stick.

PING, it goes.

Someone's phone buzzes.

'We're coming now to focus on your breathing ... focusing on feeling your breath coming innnnnn and ouuuuut of your boddddddy.'

There's a long pause in which, I guess, we are supposed to be noticing sensations.

I think I need to pee.

'Allowing the breath to anchor you in the present moment . . . and bringing your mind baaaaack to the breath and baaaaack to the present moment . . . whenever you notice it has waaaaan-dered away.'

I need to find a needle and thread.

I wonder why D S Clarke doesn't like me.

I wonder where Gareth is.

'And this may happen maaaaany, maaaaany times. And just as often as it happens, then very gently, bringing it back . . . because sometimes the mind waaaaanders, for a few moments . . .'

This is bullshit.

Jesus Christ.

'And it's possible to find yourself, judging and criticising, criticising and judging . . .'

Can he actually hear my thoughts?

You're dragging me down, babe.
Holding me back now.

I didn't know what Gareth meant back then.

Started on about a month ago.

Right after he got me to remortgage the house.

I don't want to hear your voice right now, Coco.
You just stay in here.

Don't put your fingers inside the door babe, or they'll get trapped again.

I think I knew for a while he was planning to go.

But I just couldn't think what to do.

The signs were all there.

I just didn't want to believe it.

Didn't want to be left alone again.

Like after Dad.

I felt so ill.

The whole time.

I can't even remember stuff.

'PING.'

'Coming back to being aware of the body as a whole . . . sitting here, in this moment . . . and in this moment . . . and in this moment.'

PING.

Can't remember half of the last year.

'And nooooow . . . letting go of all particular intentions to focus on anything at all, the breeeeeath or the boddddddy . . . and allow yourself to sit here . . . resting in awareness itself . : . and taking this sense of spaciousness . . .'

Please don't cry, babe.

Please don't make that noise.

Babe.

You know what will happen.

Babe.
I can't hear myself think.
SHUT UP YOUR FUCKING NOISE.

'... Awareness of this present moment ... into the next activities of your day ... and remembering that this sense of being present is available to you at any moment of your day. Day by day. And moment by moment ...'

PING.

SHUT UP YOUR FUCKING NOISE, YOU FUCKING WHORE.
Slap.
Crunch.
WELL, OF COURSE YOU ARE GOING TO HURT YOUR FUCKING HEAD IF YOU PUT IT IN THE FUCKING DOOR.

Thirty-Five

Sally

I don't mind telling you, if Clare hadn't got up and left, I'd have gone myself, right off, I would've. I'd have feigned something. She got a phone call, she had an excuse. Jesus, Mary and Joseph! Excuse me, but seriously, I don't know who Mahatma Gandhi thinks he is, but if he whips out a loincloth and a turban I won't bat an eyelid, not for one second I won't.

I didn't watch her go because, guess why, I have my eyes shut because I am allowing myself to be 'resting in awareness itself' . . . not forgetting to be 'acknowledging this sense of spaciousness' . . .

Why does everything end in ing? That gets on my nerves and that's before we even start to talk about the Australasian query inflection. Does my head in at the best of times.

I see Kitty hasn't bothered, or Sarah, for that matter – not that I'm in the least bit surprised about Sarah, because she's probably crapping herself that Kitty's gonna bring up the whole McDonald's thing again, which I for one didn't think was true, but then Kitty showed Clare the wrappers and I honestly don't know who else would have gone out at 7 a.m. to do anything at all, let alone get a Sausage and Egg McMuffin, apart from

Sarah, who, let's face it doesn't have a resistance to leptin any more than I've got a resistance to bacon sandwiches. I don't even know what leptin is, but I'm delighted – no, *honoured* – to tell you that I do know what a raisin is, and I am being asked to take one off a small tea plate with yellow flowers on, being held out by Mr Mahatma.

'I want us to start by placing the raisin in the palm of your hand.' He's speaking slowly again, like preachers in churches do who are only preachers in churches cos they like the sounds of their own voices.

Big Debbie's head nearly swivels off her neck she's so busy trying to see if everybody is doing exactly as instructed and laying a single sodding raisin in the palm of their hand.

'Now I would like you to set your intention to bring a non-judgmental attitude to your moment-to-moment awareness of the raisin.'

'Could you say that again?' goes Sian, looking suspicious under her fringe.

'Excuse me, can I get another raisin?' says Big Debbie. 'I've been that non-judgmental, I ate it.'

We all start to snigger until Mrs H tuts and looks away.

'Whenever you lose sight of your intention to bring a non-judgmental attitude to your moment-to-moment awareness of the raisin, see if you can recommit to paying mindful attention to the raisin.'

'Fuuuuuuuu,' says Big Debbie.

Abigail drops her raisin on the floor.

'Excuse me,' she says, from her cushion. 'EXCUSE ME!' She puts her hand up. 'Are we going to have to eat these raisins at some point, because, you see, I just dropped mine and I know this floor isn't clean because they had Zumba in here yesterday and everyone apart from me was barefoot,' she says, without taking a breath.

'Now, focusing on seeing the raisin as if you've never seen one before, using your beginner's mind, noticing the shape, size, and colour of the raisin, turning it around in your fingers, noticing the folds and where the surface reflects light, bringing an attitude of curiosity to seeing all aspects of the raisin.'

He's ignoring all of us and Mrs H catches me winking at Prashi.

'Whenever you are yourself thinking about anything other than the raisin, or you are noticing thoughts about the raisin, such as "It's so wrinkly or I wish I had a bigger one," you are gently redirecting your attention to seeing the raisin, allowing your experience to be, exactly as it is, in this moment.'

'I've never met a man who didn't wish he 'ad a bigger one,' stage-whispers Big Debbie.

Abigail explodes and Sian snorts and Prashi clamps her hand over her nose and mouth and Mr Mahatma is holding his raisin high in his right hand and is fondling it between his fingers.

'Nah,' says Big Debbie, scraping the legs of her chair as she stands up, freed from the eagle eye of Mrs H. 'Nah, it's no good. This is crazy, so I'm going to fuck right off now. Goodbye, Mr Mercury. It's nice to see you've been reincarnated into a mumbo-jumbo gym-teacher, and thank you so much for a fascinating insight into how people waste their fucking lives more than I could ever have thought possible.' And off she goes, picking her way across the bodies on the floor, just missing Sian who is falling off her cushion.

And just as we are all wondering how on earth a mindfulness mood can be rediscovered, the fire alarm goes off. Nick of time, that's what I'd call it.

There's a massive alarm system behind the glass in the lobby by reception where security sit, and when something sets off the fire alarm it shows where it is so they can sort it out faster and direct the police and fire brigade. It rings the fire brigade at the same time as it goes off, state-of-the-art, so just as we all start filing out of the workout room, the sirens from the fire engines start mixing in with the wailing of the alarm in the hallway. The alarm system shows it's coming from the third floor, my floor, which means I've probably gone and left my curling tongs on again and they'll have set fire to that cheap-shite chest of drawers by the mirror. Then Kitty and Clare come clattering down the stairs like they'd been set upon by a pack of starving wolves.

'It was my aerosol, that's all,' says Kitty, laughing.

'It's not funny, Kitty,' Mrs H shouts down the hall. 'The Fire Brigade is on its way, because of your hairspray.'

'Didn't say hairspray. Said aerosol.' Kitty shrugs. Clare looks like she's trying to distance herself from the whole thing.

'Clare, what do you have to say for yourself?' says Mrs H.

'I don't need to say anything, Mrs H, because it wasn't my aerosol,' she says, and goes and sits in one of the meeting rooms on her own, even though everyone else is standing around trying to work out what to do while all the time the bleeding alarm is going off and Mr Mahatma is still sitting on his mat with a plate of raisins.

'What's up with you?' I say to Clare, cos it's not like her to be rude to people.

'Nothing,' she goes. 'I'm not going to lie, though.'

'Lie about what?'

'We were smoking. Out the window. My bedroom window. I don't see what's so bad about that. It's not like we're underage.'

'How'd you manage to open the window? They're jammed shut. And there's nothing bad about it, except there's a no-smoking rule in the house, which is why they have a designated smoking area out the back, which you know all about. Let's back up one moment, because pardon me if I state the blindingly obvious, *you don't smoke!*'

'Kitty had some cigarettes.'

'And?'

'It just seemed like a good idea at the time. She unjammed the window with a penknife she had in her bag.'

'And you thought you'd just hang out of the window now it was open and start smoking even though you don't?'

'Not now, Sally, OK?'

'When, then?'

'Just leave me alone, would you? You're not my mother.'

I don't know what she's on about, but she looks like shit.

'Come on. Let's go up,' I say to her. 'Let's get some tea or something.'

'Did you see me go for the phone call?'

'I heard them come to get you. Wish they'd come to get me!' I say. 'Why, what'd they want?'

'Susan left a message for me to call her. Said she had something urgent to talk to me about.'

'Oh yeah?' I say, thinking that I haven't phoned her today. We're through our front door, and Clare flops down onto the sofa with her dressing gown drawn up over her knees.

'So I call her back and she says she's got a load of names for me – from some emails that they've found. Wants to know if I know any of them.'

'And did you?'

'Never heard of any of them. But then she said they'd found a T-shirt. The forensics people. Wanted to know if I was missing one. Or if I'd had an accident wearing a T-shirt. An injury to the neck or something.'

'And did you.'

'D'ya know what, Sally? I could have done. I'm not sure of anything anymore. I guess not recently. My injuries tend to be burns and bruises.'

She said that so matter-of-factly, it was shocking. I looked away. She's just a kid.

'Man's or woman's T-shirt?' I say.

'I dunno! I couldn't understand what she was on about.'

'What does she mean, "injury to the neck"?' I say.

'That's just what she said. She said they've been bleached away, the stains. But not entirely bleached away. She wanted to know if I knew anything about it.' She looks at her hands. 'He always wanted everything bleached. He was mental about hygiene. Had to bleach the floors, every day. All the work surfaces. The bathrooms. The toilets. Bleached all his white shirts.'

'That why your hands . . .?'

'He wouldn't let me wear gloves. She said it's too late to see me today but they would be over tomorrow and that I might have to go to the police station.'

Talk about jumping the fucking gun. They can't just go from finding a bit of blood to assuming someone's been stabbed, Gareth I mean, that's what they must think. 'He could have nicked himself shaving, cut himself on a broken glass or something. I mean, for heaven's sake, you could have dropped the fucking Sunday roast down your own T-shirt.'

'It wasn't a bit of blood,' she says. 'It was quite a lot of blood. Spattered. It's hard to get rid of blood. That's what Susan said.'

Thirty-Six

DS Clarke

DS Clarke can see the blue-and-white police tape as soon as she turns into Oval Road, and the two forensics vans parked either side of the silver Lexus, also taped off, outside the house.

An officer she's never met before is under the bonnet of the Lexus, and another newbie is holding one of those inspection mirrors under the passenger side.

She smiles to herself. She's about to tell the officer that she doesn't think he'll find Gareth James under there, but then doesn't. Not the time for levity.

It's hard to get rid of blood, she thinks. Most people think all you do is get a bit of bleach and you're sorted. But you need to get the right bleach. Chlorine bleach makes the bloodstain disappear, but the forensics team use Luminol and then it's back, clear as day. You have to use oxygen bleach to properly get rid of blood. With hydrogen peroxide in. Really buggers up evidence, does oxygen bleach.

DS Clarke nods to PC Chapman who's standing like a sentry by the front door, strides over the doorstep and onto the black-and-white tiled floor, now patterned with the muddy treads of many police boots.

'Shouldn't we have . . .?' she starts.

'Documented,' calls a voice from the bottom of the stairs.

'Come through, DS Clarke. We're waiting for you.'

Josie Byron, DS Clarke's most trusted Scene of Crime Officer is suited up, and turns to face DS Clarke in the doorway of the kitchen.

'The markers represent the extent of the blood evidence,' she says. An area, a metre across, has been sectioned off in the centre of the kitchen and running alongside the cupboards beneath the work surface.

'What about on the drawers?' asks DS Clarke.

'Getting there,' comes the reply.

'Best guess?' says DS Clarke.

'You know I don't do best guesses.'

'Something, though?' says DS Clarke. She knows that face.

'Well,' says Josie Bryon. 'A crime definitely took place, I'm 99 per cent sure it's human blood. The spatter pattern is not clear yet. You'll have to wait on it.'

DS Clarke nods. 'And?'

'And it's been badly cleaned up.'

'That's it? Badly cleaned up? Done in a hurry?'

DS Clarke had been hoping for more.

'Or done by someone who just wasn't bright enough?'

DS Clarke thinks about Clare and Gareth. Neither fit that bill.

'What about if they were really bright? says DS Clarke.

'That's what I thought. Given the amount of cleaning fluids they have in this house . . .'

'What,' says DS Clarke, frowning, 'You think it was left deliberately?'

'I'm saying it's an option.'

'Or they were in a hurry . . .'

'Or they were too confident.'

'I'll await your report. Thanks, Josie,' DS Clarke says quietly. 'Call me on my mobile if there's anything else.'

When DS Clarke gets back to the office, the report on the T-shirt is waiting in her inbox.

DNA profile from Clare Chambers (43872641)

289, Oval Road, Camden

'Have you seen the DNA result?' shouts PC Chapman, from her desk.

'Reading it now,' she calls back.

In this case, all the bands present in the profile obtained from the T-shirt are not represented in the profile of Clare Chambers.

The results from the DNA profile . . .

'Great,' says DS Clarke.

'What?' says PC Chapman.

'It says the result of the DNA profile obtained from the T-shirt is approximately twelve million times more likely to originate from someone unrelated to Clare.'

'Really? Twelve million?'

'Yeah.'

'So probably not her then,' PC Chapman says, sitting down in the chair opposite.

'Probably not . . .'

'Or her dad.'

'Unless, of course, her dad wasn't her dad,' says DS Clarke. 'We do know her dad *was* her dad, right?'

'Yes, they've been DNA matched.'

'Good that they've given us something to work with though, right? We've got someone's DNA. Possibly Gareth's.'

'What about the kitchen floor?' says PC Chapman.

'Human, but no DNA report yet.'

'So, we've got significant signs of a violent crime, but no perpetrator and apparently no victim, except Clare – who doesn't match.'

DS Clarke returns to her inbox.

'If we believe we have a crime, then we must have a perpetrator and a victim. What about if there were two victims?'

PC Chapman's eyes grow wide.

'What, another victim? Someone else?'

'Why not?'

'Because Clare would have said.'

'Would she? You seem very confident, Dawn. Clare doesn't seem to be able to remember anything much about the night before she turned up at the station. Or the days or the weeks before that. I'm not sure we know who Clare really is.'

'With the greatest respect, Detective Sergeant . . .'

DS Clarke, still scrolling through her inbox, interrupts.

'Never trust a person who starts a conversation with that phrase. With the greatest respect what, Dawn?'

'Look, you've run far more cases than . . .'

'Yes, Dawn, I have. Hence, when I hold up a red flag, you need to take note. Just because criminals appear nice, doesn't make them innocent. Some of the nicest people I've ever met have ended up being guilty.'

'Really?'

'Well no, not really – but you catch my drift.'

'I'm only saying that . . .'

The phone rings, and DS Clarke is almost grateful because Dawn, bless her, is actually starting to annoy her. It's hard to think straight when everyone around you is . . .

'Sarge, it's Walker. I've just got back from the wedding shop as instructed. Would you like me to bring in my report or email it?'

'Bring it in now, Walker. Chapman and I are both here.'

DC Walker hands DS Clarke one printout and another to Chapman. She's trying to appear efficient.

'At approximately 11.03 hours, I visited the The Wedding Boutique in Chiswick High Road, London W4 5RG. I met the owner, Ms Meering. Ms Meering . . .'

'How old?'

This process is too drawn-out for DS Clarke.

'Who?'

'Ms Meering?'

'Oooh, I don't know, quite old.'

'Mid-sixties? Mid-fifties?'

'Early fifties,' she nods.

'Middle-aged, then,' says DS Clarke.

'Right. She says she has owned the lease for the shop since 2001, and that previously she had leased premises in New King's Road, with a similar business.'

'Are you just going to read out the whole thing?' DS Clarke says to Walker.

She nods and continues.

'Ms Meering sells bespoke wedding dresses. She says that brides-to-be book an appointment, try on different styles, select a style, then a dress is created from scratch. Ms Meering says prices range from two and a half grand for a simple, man-made fibre dress, to up to fifty grand for an Italian silk dress.'

'Can we cut to the chase, Walker?'

'I am,' she says, nodding again.

'Ms Meering remembers a couple matching the description of Ms Clare Chambers and Mr Gareth James. She particularly remembers Mr James as she says she spent more time with him than Ms Chambers, who was trying on gowns with her assistant. She remarked that Mr James was a charming young man who had offered to give her some advice regarding the interior design of the store. She said that he had commented that he was an architect but had also studied interior design. She said that he had called himself "The Full Package" and she laughed and said that she had agreed. I asked if she was always this familiar with grooms; Ms Meering said that she had been joking.'

'And she thought that was funny, did she?' DS Clarke says, looking up at Walker.

She nods and continues to read from the printout.

'She was unable to confirm what date the couple had come into the shop. She said that they had walked in off the street, and that it was evening time, just before she shut shop, which was unusual as most brides-to-be make an appointment and go when there's daylight. So they can see the dresses better,' she said. 'The light is better during the day, you see,' she added. She goes back to reading.

'She said it was also more normal for a bride-to-be to bring a friend or a relative – the mother of the bride, most usually, but that Mr Gareth James had revealed Clare had no living relatives. She seemed most disturbed by that.'

'What does that mean? "Disturbed"?' says DS Clarke.

'She asked if Clare was in some sort of trouble.'

'And did she ask about Gareth?'

'No, but she did say that she saw him a few weeks after the initial meeting.'

'Presumably when he went to collect the dress?'

'No, she said she had bumped into him socially. "Purely by chance",' she said.

'Did she actually say "Purely by chance"?'

'She did,' says Walker, snapping shut her laptop, with a per-functory smile.

'And?'

'And I left, saying that I would call her if I had any further questions.'

'Walker. Where did she bump into him socially? For heaven's sake.'

'Is that pertinent . . .' begins Walker, then nods and turns to leave.

'What do you think?' DS Clarke asks Chapman, once Walker has sidled out and closed the door.

'I think that there's something a bit odd about a woman who chats up bridegrooms.'

'Not as odd as a bridegroom who chats up a fifty-year-old shop owner, even if she scrubs up like a dream, while his fiancée is trying on wedding gowns. Tell me you've got something good on Gareth's laptop. Tell me we are getting sodding somewhere with this case.'

'I've brought you a memory stick. Take it home with you. Maybe the cats can help.'

Thirty-Seven

Clare

Mrs Henry woke us up.

God knows what time.

I didn't hear the door.

Sally answered it.

Said to let us know that DS Clarke was on her way with Celia.

It's not even eight o'clock in the morning.

But I'd rather get it done with.

'Look,' says Sally. 'Why don't you let me come in with you, so I can help you if you feel upset or anything?'

'I haven't done anything wrong. Why would I get upset? It's just stressing me out.'

Babe.

I've got this friend.

He could give you some vitamin shots to help calm you down.

'I know you haven't done anything wrong, but it doesn't sound like . . .' She runs out of steam.

'Doesn't sound like what?'

'Look, all I'm saying is that if you want me to be around, I can be around, and if you find you are getting freaked out, I can be waiting for you with a pizza or something, doughnuts, coffee, neat vodka, cigarettes . . .'

'Cigarettes?' I say, giving her a face.

'Well, she's a freak, that Kitty, and you know it. About as much use as a cock-flavoured lollipop.'

I pull a face.

'She's not that bad,' I say, trying to imagine a cock-flavoured lollipop.

'I'll admit she gets my knickers in a twist,' she says, 'but I have my reasons. I don't like her.'

'She has more of a life than we do,' I say. 'Going to dance class. Shopping! Hanging out in bars. All the stuff I used to do when I was young.'

'Says the ancient twenty-four-year-old!' laughs Sally.

Prashi's eldest bangs on the door.

'Mum says whoever it is that's visiting you is here!' she calls.

You know what I've noticed as well.

You forget stuff.

So, like yesterday, I told you to clean the floor, with bleach.

And you know what, I think you forgot to use the bleach.

Standards, babe, standards.

My face must have registered something.

'You haven't done anything, so stop looking so damn glum and get down there and be confident,' Sally says.

She looks better without her makeup.

That's what Gareth always used to say about me.

Said I looked like a hooker in lipstick.

Even if it was just lip salve.

What's that scab doing on your lip?

You look like a smack addict.

What do you mean?

Babe, I never even touched you.

I never will touch you, either, with a face like that.

Go put some lipstick on or something.

Cover that thing up.

Is it a sore?

Have you been sucking dick again?

'Hello, Clare, it's good to see you. I've brought Celia with me, she's just getting a coffee.'

I don't know what to say to Detective Sergeant Clarke.

Susan.

I feel like she's switched sides.

At first, she was all nice. Now she doesn't even like me, let alone believe me.

She puts her bag next to the table. A proper briefcase. Like official. She has files and forms and stuff in it.

And her laptop.

She sees me looking in her bag.

'You OK? Finding your feet here?'

'I'd rather be at home. Have you found Gareth yet?'

'No, not yet, Clare. He's still top of our priority list.'

She's lining her stuff up on the table. Straightening things.

'Checked the hospital CCTV again yet?'

'Yes,' she says slowly. 'We have someone on that. As I've said numerous times.'

Rustling unnecessarily in her bag.

'But they still haven't found anything?'

'We don't believe he was there. There are over five hundred cameras. There's no one meeting his description.'

Taking things out of the bag, then putting them back.

'I love the way you say you don't *believe* he was there. Not definitive, is it? Pathetic. You're not getting very far then, are you?'

'Shall we not start out this way, Clare?'

She drops a file on the floor and bits of paper go everywhere.

'I'm not trying to give you a hard time,' DS Clarke says. 'I'm trying to find out what happened.'

'I told you what happened.'

No one will ever believe you, babe.

You don't even know when you're lying.

'I know you did. And as I told you at the station,' she sighs, 'and again at the hospital, we need evidence. And at the moment, the evidence is not stacking up.'

'I hate that phrase.'

'Not adding up?'

'And that one.'

'Do you mind if I record our conversation?'

She pulls out a tiny tape machine.

'What for?'

'It can't be used in evidence. It's an informal chat to help us figure out what's going on.'

'It sounds formal. You look formal with your tape-recorder and everything. Aren't I supposed to have legal representation or something?'

'You can have that if you want. That's your right. But I'm not charging you with anything, Clare. It's just an informal chat. And Celia is here.'

'Not charging me,' I say, trying to take that in. Why would she be charging me?

'No,' she says.

I shrug.

Fine.

I think that.

I don't say that.

Celia comes into the room, balancing two mugs of coffee and a ring binder.

'Now, Clare, I haven't made you a coffee, my love, because I know you're not a big fan, so let me go and get you something else. A tea? I brought some lemon and chamomile? Rosehip? Or I've got a carton of Ribena in my bag?'

Smiling, nodding, smiling, nodding.

Rosehip tea!

'Neat vodka?' I say, thinking of Sally.

Wishing she was here.

Celia's cardigan has a sheep on the pocket.

A white fluffy cloud with a black face and two black legs.

Is it normal for a grown woman to wear a cardigan with a sheep on the pocket?

Do they wear these things to try to disarm you, in some way?

'Nothing, thanks,' I smile.

Susan starts fumbling with the recorder.

'Clare understands that we need to tape this for evidence, but that it's an informal interview,' Susan says to Celia.

Celia's looking at the floor.

'We are here to try to help you, Clare, work out what happened over the last few weeks,' Susan says, looking directly at Celia and unzipping her laptop from its neoprene case.

'Do the last two years not count, then?' I say.

'And the last two years,' says Susan, tapping the keyboard, bringing it to life.

Back in control.

'So, for the tape, Clare,' she says. 'This interview is being audibly recorded. We are in the Rose Room at York Gate Women's Refuge, London NW1 4QG. The date is the fifteenth of April 2019 and the time by my phone is ten past nine in the morning. I am Detective Sergeant Susan Clarke, Community Support Adviser at Camden Police Station. Also present is Celia Barrett, acting caseworker for Clare Chambers. Do you agree that there are no other persons present?'

I look at her.

What is she doing?

Why am I being treated like a criminal?

You're a worthless piece of shit.

'Do you agree that there are no other persons present?'

'Yes,' I say.

'Please state your name and date of birth.'

'I thought you said this was informal?'

Celia shifts uncomfortably in her seat.

She runs her finger around the neck of her sweater.

Too high.

Too hot.

Itchy.

Something.

'This is informal,' she says.

'Please state your name and date of birth.'

'You know my name and date of birth.'

'For the tape,' she says, sounding bored, tired, exasperated, furious . . . all those things.

'Clare Chambers, twenty-sixth of March nineteen-ninety-six,' I say.

'You'll have to say it louder,' she says, resting her elbow on the table and her head in her hand, like she's waiting, waiting . . .

'Clare Chambers, twenty-sixth of March nineteen-ninety-six,' I say, louder.

'Since we last saw you, Clare, we have completed a thorough forensic investigation of the property at 289 Oval Road, Camden. This property is in your name, is that correct?'

'You know that's correct,' I say.

'Yes or no, for the tape,' she says, looking at her screen, and conspicuously not at me. 'During our investigations traces of blood were found on a unisex T-shirt in a laundry room at your home. The traces do not match your blood or that of your father. Do you know how the blood got there and whose it might be?'

'No.'

'Are you able to inform us of the whereabouts of Gareth James in order that we can establish his blood type and rule him out of our investigations?'

'You know I don't know where he is! I just asked *you* that! This is ridiculous.'

'Do you know his blood type?'

'I'm not even sure I know his real name!' I shout. 'Look, Detective Sergeant Clarke, you seem to have changed your tune here. Last time I saw you, you were trying to help me! Arrest Gareth for consistent, long-term abuse, you said. That's what *you* said. Now you seem to be saying he is the victim!'

'Clare, calm down. CALM DOWN!' Celia gets up and starts trying to pat my shoulder. 'Let's get you that cup of—'

'Oh, fuck off, Celia. You! Susan! What's going on? Explain to me what you're doing.'

Susan looks pained.

'Clare. There is too much blood on that T-shirt for us to pretend that something serious hasn't taken place there. Now, either you know about it or you don't.'

'I don't.'

'You're sure?' she says.

'Don't you think I'd know if someone had died in my house?'

Babe, it's like this.

Take the tablet, it'll make you feel better.

Here.

Take it now.

'OK, let's hold that thought for a minute. Celia, get her some tea.'

Celia is getting up.

Then sitting down again.

Up and down.

Pulling faces at Susan.

'Yes, now, Celia! Forget the tape,' Susan says, getting even more annoyed.

'But you said . . .' says Celia.

'Get the fucking tea!' Susan shouts.

'For the tape,' I say.

Susan gives me a long, hard stare.

'Here's the problem, Clare,' she says, when Celia closes the door.

She's talking quietly.

Not for the tape.

'Number one, we have evidence of too much blood, way too much blood. Number two, we have a whacking great wedding photo of a very happy couple. Number three, Gareth's journal is packed with information that is entirely at odds with what you've told us. *Entirely.* Number four, he's got a whole mountain of emails that back up his side of the story.'

Did I tell you, I used to work for the CIA?
    Yeah?
    I still do.
    I'm a sleeper.
    I'm a lone wolf, that's what they call me.

'And what is his side of the story?'
    'The emails appear to be to his various friends, many based in the US and Australia. Asking for money, basically.'
    'True to form.'
    'Money for you.'
    'Me?'
    'He says his new wife has been ill and he needs money for her medication, plus she's spending money like it's going out of fashion.'
    'His new wife?'
    'You.'
    Celia comes back in with a rosehip tea.
    It smells like sherbet.
    Hot raspberry sherbet.
    'I'm spending money like water, am I?!'

'Profligate. Says you've had depression, an eating disorder, problems with substance abuse, and that you're self-harming.'

'Self-harming?'

'Trying to set fire to yourself, that kind of thing.'

It's not that I want to hurt you, babe.

It's just that I like to watch you hurting.

And you do want me to be happy, don't you?

You do.

Yes, you do.

'And you know that's not true, right?'

'I believe that *you* believe it's not true,' she says.

'You're not pulling that stunt on me again,' I say.

'You need to help me here, Clare. Explain to me what has gone on.'

I nod.

'Clare. You need to help me.'

I nod again.

You want me to be happy, right?

You're my wife.

That's what wives do.

Make their husbands happy.

'The wedding photo doesn't help your case.'

'I told you about that. I explained to you all about that.'

'Clare, we've been to the shop and interviewed the owner.'

'Well, good, and . . . ?'

'And the lady remembered your visit and commented on how charming your partner was.'

She's reading this off her laptop.

'And so that makes me a liar?'

'Why are you getting angry, Clare?'

'I'm not angry.'

You're out of control.

That's the trouble, you can't control your emotions.

'She said that Gareth told her that you were being treated for being . . .' she looks at her laptop again '. . . bipolar. That makes you . . .'

'Manic, hypomanic, depressed, intolerant, aggressive?' I interrupt.

'Yes,' she says.

'He got it out of a book,' I say. '*Living with Bipolar Disorder* by Lynn Hodges. My mother had it. Died from it. Well, she committed suicide. But I've always thought she would still be here if she'd got the right help. They didn't know what it was, back then. He's always loved that book. Especially the bit about how bipolar occurs "five times more often in a person who has an affected close relative".'

'So, you haven't been diagnosed as bipolar?' says Susan.

I shake my head.

'For the tape?'

'No. I have not.'

'And your doctor would back that up, would he?'

'What, Stephen?'

'Dr Stephen Short. Psychiatrist.'

'Stephen's not a psychiatrist. He's a nutritionist. He specialises in managing mood swings with natural herbs and supplements. He gave me vitamin shots and supplements. St John's Wort. Kava Root. DHA. Omega 3 Fatty Acids.'

'Consultant Psychiatrist MBChB, FRCPsych, Dip Psychotherapy.'

'Well, maybe he did that too.'

Vitamin shots changed my life, babe.

    Gave me so much energy.

    And you need something for your mood swings.

    Supplements.

    I've noticed you seem a bit low.

'We can simply go and ask him, Clare,' she says.

    'I wish you would,' I say. 'I can't wait!'

Steve's a great guy. We go back, me and Steve.

    Remember?

'OK,' she says, looking at her laptop again.

    'OK what?' I say. 'Looking for some other shit to fling at me?'

    'It does you no favours being aggressive,' sniffs Susan, flicking her eyes up from the screen. 'The journal is perhaps the most damning piece of evidence, for you personally.'

'How can something he scrawled in a notebook constitute evidence?' I say. 'He could have made it all up.'

'It's written evidence, apparently collated over a period of time, which describes a long-term pattern of abnormal behaviour characterised by unstable relationships with colleagues and friends, unstable sense of self and unstable emotions.'

'Sounds like a textbook.'

'That's not what it says; that's what it has been assessed as, by our psychology expert, Emma. You met her.'

'Emma. I remember. Iron fist in a silk glove.'

'I'll read you an extract, if you like.'

'Please, go ahead, read me an extract.'

'Celia, you read it.' Susan looks at Celia who nods. Susan settles back in her chair and folds her arms, looking at me.

'October fourteenth, 2018. Today I was so upset to discover that my lovely Coco hasn't been taking any of her anti-psychotic medication.'

Anti-psychotics!

'For god's sake! They were vitamins, I told you.'

But they made me feel too sick. Too sick.

They're both watching me. Susan nods at Celia and she continues.

'I hate to admit it, even to myself, but she's becoming increasingly out of control. All I said to her was we needed to go buy groceries. She had an episode and refused to leave the house.'

All the while Celia is reading, Susan keeps her eyes fixed on me, seeing how I react.

'I haven't been to a supermarket in seventeen months,' I say.

'She even refused to get dressed, though Jesus knows we've got enough clothes from Net-a-Porter.'

Net-a-Porter. I wish.

'He won't even let me use a computer,' I whisper, almost pleading, 'in case I'm on some dating website looking for a boyfriend.'

They both look blank.

'When I told her I would have to go get the groceries myself, she doused herself in paraffin and threatened to set herself on fire. This is the fourth time she has done this. It's only a matter of time before something dreadful happens.'

'Something dreadful,' repeats Susan. 'Doesn't sound like the psychopath you keep describing. . .'

Fuck.

I don't understand.

I can't remember.

'I spoke with Stephen. He has been so kind. He explained that the symptoms of bipolar are brought on by seemingly normal events, but going for groceries seems like about the most normal thing in the world. I don't know what to do. Stephen says he's going to prescribe some Ritalin for the depression. You have to take it regularly to prevent episodes of extreme anxiety. I don't know how much longer I can go on like this. She's so aggressive. So violent. Stephen says that's all part of it.'

I can't catch my breath.

Celia stops reading and looks up.

'Clare – look at me, Clare,' says Susan.

'Just because it's written down doesn't make it true!' I gasp.

Because this is too frightening.

I can hear him laughing.

I'm plausible, babe.

You know what that means?

It means women can sniff out a good lay.

'I mean, you don't honestly believe that, do you?' I say. 'He doesn't even sound like that. He would never have said: "I don't know how much longer I can go on like this." Psychos don't admit defeat. When did you ever hear a psycho talk like that?'

'Clare, you're the only one who says he's a psychopath. Everyone else—'

'Who is everyone else, exactly? Some woman in a dress shop that he could have shagged for all I know? He shagged almost every woman he met.'

'Everyone says he was a really nice guy. Very charismatic. There were a couple of barmaids in the—'

'I'll bet there were. And they loved him, right? Got it.'

I feel sick.

'Why would I douse myself in paraffin, DS Clarke? Why would anyone douse themselves in paraffin?

'Or ruin their hands with bleach?' she says.

'Bleach?' I say.

'Bleach,' she says, looking at me oddly, and reads from the screen.

'January twelfth, 2018. Clare wants me to go get some household bleach. She says that the house needs to be sterilised. All

the surfaces. Plus, the floor. Says she even wants to sterilise my shirts. I come back with a bottle of bleach, like the normal stuff you get at the grocery store, and she goes mental and says I have to go buy industrial quantities of the stuff so she can get the house spring-cleaned. I buy her gloves but she won't wear them. It's like she wants to hurt herself. I'm so worried about her hands. Typical bipolar. She can't help what she inherited from her mother. I love her so much. I just hope she's going to get better with my help.'

'Jesus, tell me you're not believing this shit,' I say, starting to cry.

Not sorry for myself.

Just frustrated.

Hot.

Too hot.

Sick.

Babe. Can you hear me? Babe?

Did you especially like the bit about the gloves, babe? What did you think, babe?

And the bleach? Only a really fucked up person buys that much bleach. A fucked up person with an awfully big cleaning up job to do.

Babe. Can you feel them closing in on you?

'Go away. GO AWAY!'

I'm shouting. I can't breathe.

'Clare?' Susan says. 'Clare! Celia, get her some water. She's having a panic attack.'

'GO AWAY.'
'CALM DOWN. CLARE!'
'GO AWAY! LEAVE ME ALONE.'

I'll always be right here with you, babe.

I'm sick.

He's here.

In my fucking head.

'GO AWAY!'

'I'm not going anywhere, Clare,' Susan says.

'What?' I say.

She doesn't understand.

I shake my head.

'Not you. *HIM.*'

Thirty-Eight
Sally

When I saw Clare legging it up the stairs, half of me wanted to leg it up there right behind her, and the other half was thinking, well, at least I can get half a bloomin' chance to talk to Sue without anyone seeing, if you know what I mean. Then when I saw Sue, white as a sheet, walking through reception like a zombie, I thought, well, this ain't gonna get me very far.

'Forget it, I'm knackered,' she goes.

'What do you mean, forget it? I need to talk to you. I didn't even speak to you all of yesterday.'

'You'll have to come to me,' she goes. 'At the station.'

'I thought it weren't safe for me to put my nose out the door, let alone come to the station.'

'I'll send Chapman. She seems to like it up here,' she goes.

'When?' I say, grabbing her by her arm.

'Sal,' she says, 'just give me a couple of hours, right. That girl's doing my head in.'

'What, Clare?' I say.

'No! Cinder-fucking-rella,' she goes, shaking off my hand. 'Who'd you think? Somebody's messing with my mind here, and when I find out who . . .'

'It's not Clare,' I say as she's going out towards the front door. 'She's been tricked. That guy's a psycho. Seriously. She's lucky to be alive.'

'Well, someone's a psycho,' she says. 'One of them, that's for sure.'

'Look, I've known you a long time, Sue,' I say. 'You can trust me. She's not lying. She's a great girl.'

'How to spot a psycho number one: emotional manipulation!' she says.

'It's not possible to emotionally manipulate me,' I say. 'I've been round the block too many times.'

'Not as many times as I have, Sal. Listen,' she says, and stops trying to race out the door and looks at me properly. 'You should see how spotless that house is. The wedding picture. If you saw his laptop – stuffed with emails to his friends saying how happy he is with his gorgeous wife. If you saw the amount of documents he's downloaded about how to treat bipolar – all the meds, plus all the fucking tree roots and flowers and shit that's never going to work in a trillion years and the journal . . .' She runs out of steam.

'How to spot a psycho number one,' I say.

She turns on her heel and strides out. I watch her climb into the passenger seat, and Chapman drive her away.

'I didn't know you two were friends,' says Kitty, swinging on the banister at the bottom of the stairs.

'Ah, Kitty,' I say. 'Not tap-dancing today?'

'Contemporary jazz,' she goes. 'Where's Clare?'

'Listen, Kitty. Can we have a quick chat about Clare? You see, the thing is, I don't know if you realise or not, but I don't like you, not at all, not even slightly, not one bit. I think you're cold and manipulating and you're up to something and I don't know what it is, but really, girl, whatever your game is, just quit, will you?'

'I don't . . .' she says.

'Don't bother, Kitty. I'm not interested in hearing anything you have to say.'

'I'm sure. What I was about to say, before you so rudely interrupted, was that I don't give a shit what you think. However, I *am* interested in why you and Policeman Plod are so matey. Go way back, do you? Clare know you're mates, does she? Bet she doesn't. All her little secrets being passed on to who knows . . .'

I brush past her and go back up the stairs.

'I won't tell her. But if I need a favour, I'll be asking.'

'Don't be fucking ridiculous, Kitty. That shite doesn't work on me.'

'So now Kitty knows,' I tell Sue later, at the station, after Chapman has come back and picked me up and dumped me in the underground car park at the back.

'Little tramp.'

Sue's office is also at the back of the station. I wouldn't usually be allowed in there, but I'm zero risk to them, I guess, which once upon a time would have made me feel a little dull, but I guess once upon a time I wasn't.

'What I don't understand is how she managed to get into York Gate in the first place – Kitty, I mean.'

'Played the system, that's how,' Sue goes.

'Surprise, surprise,' I say.

'To be fair, it didn't go totally her way. She cried wolf once too often.'

'What d'ya mean?'

'She used to hang out in some student bar in Manchester. She'd get off her face, like all of them do, but she got into the habit of sleeping with the students then running to the police saying she'd been raped. And the story was always the same from the lads; that she'd been up for it at the time, but next morning she'd gone mental on them.'

'What, so she didn't get raped?'

'Well, not to start with – not in the way she described, anyway. She'd cry rape then she'd get paid off by the lads' parents just to keep it out of court. However, one night it seems she comes into Greenheys nick and she tells the copper she's been raped, again, and he sends her off home. Tells her to stop wasting police time. The copper'd seen her before. Wasn't about to take any more of her crap.'

'Is this before or after she was in the looney bin?'

'You mean the child psychiatric unit. After. She'd just got out. Gone to live with her granny, poor woman. Anyway, the copper sends her home and she goes straight up to A & E and tells them the same story, gets tested. Turns out this time she had actually been raped, by three of the fourteen lads she'd accused in the first place. Seems like they were very pissed, saw her out on the pull and thought, "Been accused of it, may as well get our money's worth". So, they all got sentences, and the copper got early retirement.'

'She's such a conniving piece of work.'

'She told the court that she felt "at risk" from the other eleven men she's accused, so they gave her free accommodation at a women's refuge, for a year. They had to, really. Save face.'

'And she chose York Gate, cos it's in the middle of London and she gets to treat it like a hotel?'

'Yup. In a nutshell.'

'I don't think she'll say anything to Clare, not yet, cos she'll wanna keep it as a bargaining chip. Terry used to do that. Might be best to come clean with Clare, though, don't you think? She's gonna blow a gasket if she thinks I've been feeding you stuff.'

'Well, as it turns out, you're defending her rather than snitching on her anyway.'

'She wouldn't hurt a fly, Sue, honest she wouldn't.'

'I'm not so sure. And you haven't seen the journal.'

'You can't show it to me?'

'No, I can't,' she goes. 'Not at all,' she says, opening the middle drawer on her side of the desk and pulling out a large leather book, posh black leather like you get in shops in Bond Street that make wedding invites and the like. It's smooth. Like a baby's bum. Padded.

She pushes it over the desk and turns it to face me.

'See what you make of that,' she says. 'I'll be back in an hour. Anyone asks, say you're assessing the grammar.'

'His English is probably better than most of the exam papers I get to look at,' I say.

'Shame your expertise doesn't do anything for your accent,' she says, closing the door behind her.

'Ditto,' I shout back.

The cover of the journal is plain, so I don't know why everyone is calling it a journal.

But then, on the first right-hand page, in the middle, written in black fountain pen, it says, JOURNAL, and it's been underlined with a ruler and there's a small smudge at one end. So that's why everyone is calling it a journal, because he's calling it a journal.

Blimey, that's what they call grandiosity, and bloody typical narcissist, if you ask me. I've read a lot about narcissistic personality disorder over the years. And borderline. And psychopathy. Especially psychopathy. After Terry.

And then, after that, all the way through, every date is handwritten, in the same black ink, with the same fountain pen, with an italic nib I'd guess, and roughly the same amount of words, in the same large curly script. Controlled.

April 3rd 2017

For more than 25 years, I've been keeping a journal. I started when I was about nine, squirrelling away thoughts, hoping that someday I would be able to look back and laugh at my young mind . . .

Nah, as Big Debbie would say. Grandiose, but these aren't the words of a narcissist. Too much empathy. I flick through some more pages, and there's more of the same.

April 28th 2017

There's no stopping me with this journal. I've worked out that I've accumulated 10,000 journal-writing hours in my lifetime and I truly believe it has saved me on many occasions. It has become my therapist and my dear friend. Someone I can turn to in the darkest hours when I have toxic feelings and emotions that . . .

Nah. Again. Doesn't sound like a narcissist or a psycho. Doesn't even sound like a man, for that matter. Too self-aware for a man. I flick to the back.

February 21st 2018

Today I found out that Coco hasn't been taking the medication that Doctor Short recommended and I can see that her moods are swinging out of control. It's the worst I've seen her. Talked about our wedding plans.

Says she wants just me and her. No relatives. No friends. I think she won't do it if it's not just me and her. She chose a dress. It's Italian silk. The best I can afford. Actually, I'm not even sure if I can afford it, but Jerry said he can loan me a couple of thousand till August. She tried on every dress in the shop, I think. That really made her smile. Like old times. Before she got sick.

March 9th 2018

My wedding day. I Gareth James, do solemnly swear that I take thee, Clare Chambers . . . Today was the happiest day of my life — just me and Coco and a couple of witnesses we dragged off the street. I managed to book this tiny register office in West Yorkshire. Really quaint and romantic. Coco looked divine in her silk dress. Like an angel. My angel. I've never seen her so happy.

March 26th 2018

I had a bout of serious depression about five years ago and I discovered I was completely unable to absorb vitamin B-12 into my bloodstream. As much as a third of the population cannot absorb B-12 from food or supplements due to a lack of intrinsic factor, or, as in the case of older adults, a lack of stomach acid. Intrinsic factor is a protein secreted by the stomach that joins vitamin B-12 in the stomach and escorts it through the small intestine to be absorbed by your bloodstream. Without intrinsic factor, vitamin B-12 can't be absorbed and leaves your body as waste. Without intrinsic factor, vitamin B-12 can't be absorbed and leaves your body as waste.

He repeated a sentence there. Odd.

I was totally unable to sleep. Despite eating food sources and taking B-12 supplements my B-12 levels measured extremely low. Fortunately, injections restored levels which I have continued to maintain via sublingual B-12 supplements which are inexpensive (they dissolve under the tongue which allows for absorption directly into the blood through the extensive capillary system under the tongue).

Took Coco to see Dr Short and he's gonna sort her out with some shots and some B-12 supplements, like I used to get.

Nah, nah, nah, different style altogether.

Sue walks back in.

'You want a cup of tea?' she says, going out again.

'There's something not right about all this,' I say when she returns and plonks the mug down in front of me.

'Tell me about it!' she goes. 'Clare told me a very different story about the wedding dress shop, for a start. She said they went there soon after they first started going out. He says it was six weeks ago. She says they never got married; he's got a bloody great wedding picture above the mantelpiece.'

'Does the picture over the mantelpiece look two years old?'

She gets out her phone. 'Impossible to tell. The veil doesn't help. What do you think?'

I shrug.

'She does look happy. I mean, it looks like she's having the time of her life, just like he said. What did your lot say about the book?'

'They're digitising it.'

'How?'

'Some poor sod is copying it word for word. Emma said that the style changes throughout. Said if she couldn't see it was the same handwriting, she'd think it was different people.'

'Multiple personalities?'

'You're getting good at this. Yes, I thought that, but Emma says if it's multiple personalities you'd see a change in the handwriting. Everything would change, not just the tone of voice.'

'Psycho, then?' I say.

'Or an honest guy trying to help his sick girlfriend.'

I'm about to interrupt but she stops me.

'I want to believe her, Sal,' she says.

'Something's so fishy, it smells like Albert Dock,' I say.

'That could just be my tea,' says Sue. 'You should go back.'

'Aren't you supposed to be telling me about Terry?'

'Oh yeah, sorry.' She shrugs. 'His mum told a couple officers that they were the C word yesterday, but apart from that . . .'

'Still got her faculties, then.'

'Still got a mouth like a fishwife, more like,' says Sue.

'Fishwife means something else now. Means the wife of a man who's a homosexual.'

'Really?' says Sue. 'Who knew?'

'I looked it up on Urban Dictionary, and they do the definition and everything, then they show the word in common parlance, you know. And it said, hang on while I remember it, it said "Melissa is married to Steve, but she's a fishwife, cuz (spelt C-U-Z, by the way,) cuz everyone knows Steve sucks cock like a hoover".'

Sue spat her tea onto the desk she was laughing so much. 'You have to be kidding me. It said that in a dictionary?'

We stop when we've drunk our tea and Sue's put the book back in the drawer.

'How long is it going to go on, do you think?'

'Listen, Sal, Terry's not the sharpest knife in the drawer, is he? He'll surface. And when he does he'll go back inside and we'll start again. He'll get an extended sentence. Another five years, maybe. Then, after that, we go through all this again.'

'Would have been better to get him killed,' I say.

'You don't think that.'

I don't tell her that I do, that it would have been better for me, for my life, to have had him wiped out. Back then you could have got it done for two hundred quid.

'I have to say, you're in the safest place. Look how quick the fire services got there. All for an aerosol!'

'Cigarette.'

'You what?' Sue says.

'Kitty.'

Thirty-Nine

DS Clarke

DS Clarke doesn't like to work Sundays and as a rule she doesn't. She gets her washing and ironing done for the week. Sorts the recycling. Does a shop if she can be bothered. Gets the car cleaned if she hasn't managed to persuade one of the lads at the car park to do it.

But this morning DS Clarke decides to go into work.

That Kitty girl is trouble, she thinks, worrying that Sal might have some explaining to do if Clare gets wind of their friendship.

She pings an email to PC Chapman, asking her to look further into her background.

'Not now,' she finishes the email. 'Tomorrow is soon enough.'

DS Clarke is also struggling to work out how to get hold of digital data and realises that what she really needs is someone at least twenty years younger than her to help.

'Hi, Mark? You wouldn't be able to put me through to IT, would you?'

PC Mark Corkett is on reception.

'I'm sorry, there's no one in IT today, sarge. It being a Sunday. Strict nine-till-fivers, those guys, Monday through Friday.'

'OK, thanks, Mark. Of course.'

Who needs IT anyway, she thinks.

'SECTION 22(4) OF THE REGULATION OF INVESTI-GATORY POWERS', DS Clarke reads off her email. 'Google Inc, C/O Custodian of Records, 1600 Amphitheatre Parkway, Mountain View, CA 94043.'

She scrolls down.

'Describe the communications data to be acquired specifying, where relevant, any historic or future date and/or time periods sought'

Her phone buzzes.

'Sarge. Thought you'd like to know that the IT department ARE in today. They're re-platforming and they're at critical, so they've all been called in.'

'Critical what?'

'I don't know. It's only amber though, not red. So, you should be all right.'

'I have no idea what you are talking about, Mark.'

'It means . . . well, it means they're here, sarge. That's all you need to know.'

'Who's in charge?'

'Tom.'

'Tom Boring, the world's geekiest geek with the wife he bought in Thailand?'

'Bohrer.'

'Whatever. Can you get him in here?'

It's all very well, she thinks, Sal saying that Gareth's not the type to write a journal, but what the fuck – she's not even met him.

Note to self, stop swearing.

Is swearing still swearing if it's only in your head?

A tall, gangly youth with crooked teeth and no smile whatsoever, puts his head around her door.

'Tom. Hi. Thanks for stopping by. Did you get my request about the laptop?'

Good grief, she thinks. He really is the most unfortunate-looking bloke. It was the children in the main office who said he bought his wife. To his face. He doesn't dispute it.

'Yes, DS Clarke. We got that on Friday. Ticket number 38729. Reference 42317, Clare Chambers.'

On a trip to Bangkok, apparently.

'So, Tom, how's it going?' she says.

No one would willingly marry that.

'For our own records, Detective Sergeant Clarke, could you please describe the communications data that you require, specifying, where relevant, any historic or future date and/or time periods sought.'

'What does that mean exactly, Tom?'

'WYSIWYG, Detective Sergeant Clarke!'

'Wizzy what?'

'WYSIWYG, Detective Sergeant Clarke. What you see is what you get, DS Clarke. Specify what you want and that's what you'll get.'

'You've got the email addresses?'

'Yes.'

'Go away and find out anything you can then.'

'The DCG Grade 3 – SPoC will require reasons for requesting the data. Full disclosure.'

'We've filled out the form, Tom. Isn't that enough?' DS Clarke reads off the form. 'Explain the reason for requiring this data, and we've put: "The above email addresses relate to evidence in a serious crime. A laptop is held in evidence containing emails to and from the above addresses. The owners of these accounts may have crucial information and could potentially, be important witnesses." Does that cover it?'

He leaves. Without a nod or a goodbye or anything.

DS Clarke has a surprised look on her face.

Her email pings.

It's from PC Chapman.

'I know you're at work,' it says in the title box.

Her phone buzzes.

'DS Clarke? It's Chapman.'

'Chapman, thanks,' she says. 'Look, sorry to bother you but did anyone do a background check on Kitty? You know, Little Miss Tricksy at York Gate.'

'No. Emma Tudor confirmed that she was diagnosed narcissistic disorder last year.'

'What's her interest in Clare, then? And Sal?'

'Oh, she's only interested if someone's getting more attention than her. She's nuts. Narcissists feel superior consciously. So, they like, tell themselves, *all the time*, that they are better than anyone else. But deep down they feel extremely insecure, despite how self-loving they look on the surface. It's usually something to do with their parenting. Neglect, you know. You don't get born that way. She can't really be blamed.'

DS Clarke thinks to herself that lots of people get scarred by their parents, but they don't all turn into . . .

'And did Emma have any further stuff on Clare?'

'Clare's diagnosed PTSD. That's what Emma Tudor says. It's completely different.'

'How completely different?'

'She's got all the symptoms. Negativity. Feelings of distress. Avoidance of conversations. Feeling distant. Bursts of anger. All the doctors agree.'

'What about hearing voices – is that typical PTSD?' says DS Clarke.

'I think that's something else,' says PC Chapman. 'I think that's called psychosis.'

"Hmm. So properly nuts."

Forty

Clare

'Come for a fag.'

I don't know how she got in. I don't even care.

'Come for a fag. I've got menthol.'

Tell her to fuck off.

'Fuck off.'

'You'll feel better! I've got Diet Coke.'

Tell Kitty to fuck off.

'Kitty. Fuck off.'

'Stop being a dick. You'll feel better with a Coke and a fag. Get up and shut up feeling sorry for yourself.'

She yanks the dressing gown that's over my head.

'The alarms will go off again.'

'We can get up on the roof. No one will know. Come on.'

'The roof?' I say, sitting up.

'It's a nice day. Why not?' she says.

She's carrying a towel and wearing a red bikini top, cut-off denim shorts, mirrored aviators and a white cotton peaked cap with 'I came to break hearts' sewn on it in pink letters. Her ponytail is clipped through the hole in the back of the cap, and looks like a My Little Pony tail. All cutesy. If you had to guess you'd think she worked in an American carwash in some dodgy eighties film.

'Want some?' she says, applying another layer of red sparkly lip-gloss over her mouth, then holding out the tube. 'It's SPF 50.'

'What about the rest of you?' I say, looking at her glistening pink skin, covered in oil.

'I wanna get brown, don't I?' she says.

I shrug.

'Come on. Wear shoes. The attic is full of mice shit.'

Kitty has removed the entire contents of the airing cupboard in her bathroom, including the shelves.

It's all lined up on the floor of her bedroom.

In between skinny pink G-strings, and mounds of preformed bra cups.

And plates of half-eaten food.

'Not surprising about the mice,' I say, nodding at the plates.

She shrugs.

She's covered the boiler with a towel and squeezes past it to a half-door, with wooden steps behind.

'Attic,' she says, taking off her cap and sunglasses, making sure I'm following.

She dips down through the doorway so I can only see her pink Converse, which run up the steps on the other side.

The small amount of light in the attic comes in slim, diagonal shafts through the cracks in the tiled roof, criss-crossed by wooden roof joists that look like they need replacing.

It's empty, just dust and droppings, from mice and birds, I guess.

'Come on, it's this way,' says Kitty, climbing up a short metal ladder, and through a trapdoor.

The roof is a long strip of asphalt behind a low wall, which runs along the side of the pitched red slates.

It's not ideal for sunbathing. You can't even lie side by side.

'You can bring a towel up too, next time,' she says, lying down flat on hers, undoing her shorts a bit to expose her stomach more.

'Diet Coke,' she says, unhooking one from a pack of six that she's stashed under a magazine and a T-shirt.

'Fag,' she says, flicking open a white and green packet and handing me a white cigarette with a silver band around it.

Posh cigarettes.

Minty.

I prop my back against the roof.

Just enough space between me and the wall to cross my legs under me.

Face out over the wall.

Camden rooftops.

Look nice in the sun.

There's the market.

The canal.

That building Louisa said I should get a flat in.

A long time ago.

Sun on my hair.

Breeze.

Warm for May.

I'm trying to work out where my house is.

Wonder where Gareth is.

Breathe out slowly.

'Met someone who knows you,' she says.

Just like that.

'Oh yeah?' I say.

Heart thumping.

Hey, babe.

Don't tell me you forgot me for a minute.

'A man.'

I take another drag on the cigarette.

Another mouthful of Coke.

'Described you completely. Even got your dressing gown right.'

Bathrobe.

Tell her it's a fucking bathrobe.

'Got your hair right. Fair. Your build right. Thin. Your height. Model height by the way.'

'Yeah?' I say.

Your tits are still saggy.

'But he said your name was Coco.'

Because you look like a Coco, babe.

You ain't no Clare.

I told you, Clare is like a shit name.

Someone like me wouldn't go out with someone called Clare.

'Must have the wrong person then,' I say.

PANIC.

PANIC.

CAN'T BREATHE.

'You know what, I think I'm going back down.'

'Hey, don't go. Finish your cigarette. I need some company.'

'I'm not feeling so good. Bit hot for me,' I say.

Can't breathe.

'Wear my cap,' she says. 'I bought it online. Rihanna has the same one.'

I pull her cap on.

'Do you see this mark on my leg?' she says, suddenly sitting up. 'Do you think it's a bite or like eczema or what? Do you think I should show Mrs H?'

There's a small circle of red skin on her calf. About the size of a polo mint. It looks dry and itchy.

'Go to Boots,' I say. 'It's just ringworm.'

Breathe.

'Shut up,' she says. 'SHUT UP! Ring fucking worm. I've got worms?'

'Ringworm is just a fungal infection. Like athlete's foot.'

'I've got a fucking worm.'

She's freaking out.

'Do I need to get it removed?'

She's standing up, bouncing from one foot to the other like she's been bitten by a snake or something.

I start to laugh.

'What!' she says. 'What's so fucking funny?'

'It's not a worm, you moron. It's an infection. Put cream on it, it'll go in a day. Two days max.'

'How come you're the world expert on ringworm?' she says, sitting back down and picking at the skin on her leg.

What is this cream? Babe?

This cream.

Anti-fungal.

What you got that's fungal?

I thought we agreed no more shopping on your own.

Give me your key now.

NOW.

KEY.

Don't you fucking lie to me, slag.

Don't mess with my fucking mind.

What infection have you got?

Says here it's for thrush.

You got thrush you dirty slag?

It is PRINTED ON THE OUTSIDE OF THE FUCKING BOX.

Thrush.

THRUSH.

Don't lie.

DON'T LIE.

There's nothing on your arm.

That's just a spot on your arm.

You've got thrush, ain't you?

Ain't you?

You got thrush cos you've been fucking all those guys at work.

I know what you get up to.

I see you.

I know what you do all day.

Pretend you're working.

Pretend you don't even like these guys.

Give me your phone.

GIVE ME YOUR FUCKING PHONE.

GIVE ME YOUR FUCKING PHONE AND YOUR FUCKING KEY.

You dirty bitch.

DIRTY BITCH.

Who's Simon? I'm going to kill him.

Remember that, babe?

'GO AWAY.'

'Hey, don't take it out on me,' Kitty says, pinching off a piece of dry skin between her scarlet-painted nails. 'Not my fault some guy wants to know if you're OK. Even if he did get your name wrong.'

'Look, Kitty,' I say, starting to feel faint.

Need to get downstairs.

'Seemed more interested in Sally.'

'I think you've got all this confused,' I say.

'Look, I met this guy out front, from the squat at the end. When I told him we was a refuge, that this whole thing is a refuge, he said that he thought there might be a girl here called Coco. I said there weren't any girls called Coco. And then he described you. Well, actually, it was the dressing gown that did it.'

'What'd he look like?'

'He was old. Like a drunk. Said he saw you in the police station. That you smelt of paraffin. He called you the girl with the bare feet.'

'I don't remember anything about the police station.'

Feels like a dream.

'Said he helped you, cos you were falling over.'

'Some tramp guy?'

'Yeah, he's some tramp guy all right. But he's not stupid. God knows how he ended up like that.'

'I don't really remember much about that day to be honest,' I say, steadying myself by resting my hand against the wall. 'He's in a squat?'

'At the far end. They're all squats down there. As I say, though, he was more interested in Sally.'

'What, my Sally? Sal?'

'Said there was another girl in the station at the same time. Called Sally. That's what he said.'

'Sally's hardly a girl.'

'That's what I said. He said, "It's all relative." Dunno what that means. Anyway, he said that she was looking after you in the station. And that maybe you might know where she was cos he met someone who was looking for her. Her brother. Long-lost brother. She's been missing for years, apparently, and this guy had come all the way from Liverpool to find her. After all those years. Sweet, eh?'

'Sally wasn't at the station. He's got the wrong person.'

'It was definitely her. From Liverpool, ain't she? Hasn't been back in twenty years. She told me that herself. And he said she's been friends with the policewoman at the station all that time. That Susan woman. They go back. Best friends forever. That's what he said.'

And I don't want to believe her. But it all adds up. Sally and DS Clarke best friends.

And that's the thing, babe.

Just when you think you can trust someone, they fuck with your brain.

Forty-One

Sally

I saw Barney today, staggering down the road out front of the refuge, off his face it looked like, with his massive coat pulled up round his ears, doing Dr Zhivago or something, like he hasn't even noticed that it's nearly summer.

PC Chapman was giving me a lift back from the police station, you know, and I saw him right outside and when we stopped I thought I might as well say hello because what difference does it make anyway, whether some old dropout knows where I live or not, whatever Sue says.

He didn't see me at first, he was so busy sticking his nose over the front wall, looking through the windows, so when I said, 'Barney,' even though I said it quietly, he nearly jumped right out of his skin.

'So, this is where you've been hiding yourself, is it?' he says, when he's recovered himself, slurring more than I remember.

'You all right there are you, Barney?' I say, slightly shocked by how rough he's got in a matter of days. He wipes his nose on his sleeve.

His eyes are half closed.

'You living round here, then, Barney?' I say, and he looks around him, like he's surprised where he is, then looks up at the sky, like he's surprised that's there too. He picks a scab on his face, a little purple scab by the side of his nostril, but all his skin looks red and mottled, like corned beef, nothing like it did before.

'So, you're looking well,' he says, like he just woke up. 'Been nice seeing you, girl,' he says, and wanders off up the road.

'You still on the programme?' I shout after him. 'Barney, you still on the programme, are you?' But I knew he weren't still on the programme.

He waves his arm in the air, not turning round.

PC Chapman slams the car door.

'Bad timing,' she says. 'He was asking about you the other day at the station. Saying he hadn't seen you. You shouldn't let anyone know where you are, Sal. You never know who he might speak to.'

'Don't look as if he could string more than two sentences together if you ask me,' I say. He wasn't like that the last time I saw him, and if you were to ask me I'd say that if he *is* still on the recovery programme, he's topping up on something else. Told you it never worked.

'Well,' I say to Chapman, 'we're back home, safe and sound now, aren't we? So there's nothing for you to worry about.' And I flash my key fob at the panel by the front door and it swings open.

'You want me to come in?' she says.

'I think I can manage from here, just about, but thanks for the lift,' I say as she walks back down the front path.

Security buzz me through the next door, and I'm only just in reception when Kitty appears, out of nowhere, and it's like she's on uppers or something.

'I've been scouted!' She's frantically brushing her hair with her head upside down. 'And it's a really big deal, probably international sessions and everything. Met this totally cute guy called Axel in the pub at lunchtime. He's not an actual scout, but he knows everything about modelling and he has all the contacts and he wants to meet me tonight to discuss getting a contract with Storm or something. Just got the call,' she says, flicking her head over so her hair forms a halo of golden static. 'Graduated' golden static. 'I'm gonna get a portfolio together and we're gonna go on some go-sees.'

'What's a go-see?' I say, cos that's got to be made up, like the rest of her story. No doubt about that.

'You go see people,' she sneers, as if everybody knows what a go-see is. 'You think this jacket makes my bum look big?' she says, turning around to show me her bum, and she looks over her shoulder, pouting her glittery lip-gloss.

'Enormous,' I say, walking off in the opposite direction.

'Good,' she says. 'Oh, yeah, Sally, I told Coco, by the way. It *is* Coco, ain't it, Sally?'

I ignore her. Little bitch, I think, but I don't say anything, I just keep on going.

'Last time I saw Clare, she was talking to herself. No, hang on, she was SHOUTING AT HERSELF,' Kitty calls.

The front door buzzes again and she flounces off down the path, her hair bouncing along like she's in a TV commercial.

She was right, though, when I get up to our flat front door, I can hear Clare talking to herself before I even open it.

Clare is sitting on the top of the wardrobe, in her bedroom. She's tucked herself into the corner, folded herself up really small. She looks like a tiny bird that's terrified and broken its wing.

'Nice weather up there, is it?' I say, because I don't know what I'm supposed to do with someone on the top of a wardrobe, and I want to try and get her down safely. I mean, what do you say to someone who's sitting on top of a wardrobe? I'm at a bit of a loss here.

'Fuck off! You're not here. Fuck off. I can't hear you,' she says, real quiet, but threatening.

I'm worried that she's going to fall off the wardrobe, or worse fall off the wardrobe and through the window, and break her neck or something. But that's not the really weird bit. The really weird bit is she sounds like a proper mad person, like she's got the devil is inside her.

She won't look at me.

'Clare, why don't you come down and we can talk about everything?'

She stares out the window, big eyes, from behind her drawn-up knees, but she doesn't look at me.

'Clare,' I say, but she doesn't answer, doesn't even acknowledge.

'CLARE!' I shout, and she glares right at me.

'I hate you,' she says. 'I fucking hate all of you.'

'I know you know about Sue. Detective Sergeant Clarke,' I say. No movement.

'I want you to know something. I haven't told her anything you wouldn't want me to tell her and I have been your friend from the start and will continue being your friend, if you'll still have me. I need you, right now, so please don't give up on me, and I'm sorry for lying to you, because, to be honest, I don't know why we decided not to tell you 'cept that I was thinking I could help you more this way. But, looking at it from your point of view, I must just seem like a snitch. Seriously, I'm not and I hope you can forgive me.'

'YOU LYING BITCH!' she yells, suddenly leaping from wardrobe onto the chair next to it, and throwing herself into the bed, pulling the duvet over her face.

'I know you must—' I start.

'YOU LYING BITCH, GET OUT!' she yells again, sliding off the mattress and jamming herself between the wall and the bed.

If I'm honest, in a situation like this, I don't think there's much point in arguing because I think I'd feel the same if I were her. I can't quite get my head around why Sue and I thought it was a good idea in the first place, not to tell her we were friends, but I guess it didn't come from me. The whole thing, that Sue thought I'd get more out of her if I was her 'friend' rather than Sue would as a police officer? Well, let's face it, that's shit. Plus, the police don't appear to have done much, do they?

'YOU'RE JUST THE SAME AS THAT BITCH POLICE-WOMAN,' she shouts after me as I close the door. 'SHE DOESN'T BELIEVE ME EITHER.'

*

Later on, I make a cup of tea, and I make her one as well, even though she doesn't like tea. I knock on her door quietly and put it next to her bed with a couple of the chocolate Hobnobs she likes. And I say sorry, whisper it; I don't even know if she's awake or not cos she doesn't move when I go in or when I leave.

Not long after that she comes out of her room and sits down on the sofa, with a face that looks swollen and blotchy the way my face does when I cry for a week. She doesn't look at me, just faces the window with a rolled-up tissue dabbing at her eyes.

'You wanna face mask?' I ask gently.

'What for?' she says.

'Make you less, um blotchy?' I say. 'It's aloe and cucumber. Cooling,' I say.

'Don't like cucumber,' she says.

'You don't eat it,' I say. 'You put it on your face.'

'Does it smell like cucumber?'

'No, it smells like apricots, what do you think?'

'Don't like cucumber,' she repeats.

'Well, shove some cotton wool up your nose and pretend it's apricots. It's organic,' I say, flopping down next to her with the sachet, 'so it hasn't got any nasty stuff in it.'

''Part from cucumber,' she says, scrunching up her eyes. 'Can you put it on me?' she asks and it reminds me just how young she is and how all she really needs is a mum. She swivels round and flips her legs over the back of the sofa, so her face is on the seat. I cut off the top of the sachet and squeeze the contents onto a thick wad of cotton wool, moving her hair off her face, and gently wipe the green goo over her forehead. It's seriously the most cucumbery smell I've ever smelled in my whole entire life, and I've used this one about a million times and never even noticed it, but by the time it's right under her nose, the cotton wool is over her mouth and she can only mumble in protest. She looks like . . . I can't think of his name . . .

'The Incredible Hulk!' I say.

'What, not a Disney Princess?' she goes.

'That's when you take it off,' I say

'I've always fancied being a Disney Princess – ever since I was a little girl.'

'You're not supposed to move your mouth,' I say, 'you gotta leave it on for five minutes and then you can peel it off,' I say. 'And that's the most fun ever, cos it takes all them blackheads out of the pores on your nose.'

'MMMMmmmmm, MMMMM, mmmmm, mmmm' she mumbles, which roughly translates to, I haven't got any blackheads on my nose.

'Everybody's got blackheads on their nose,' I say, 'you wait and see.'

She shuts up and I go and stand by the window, thinking about how Barney has obviously slipped off the wagon and I wonder if he's really living in the squat up the road. I wonder how much Kitty knows and isn't saying, and I wonder what it would be like to get on one of the trains going out of Euston and disappear to some island off the coast of West Scotland, where it would probably rain the entire winter and be full of midges the entire summer – so that's that little dream out the window – and I wonder what's gonna happen to Clare.

'I saw Gareth's journal today,' I tell Clare.

'He doesn't have a journal,' she says. 'He's not the sort. Seriously.'

'You're not allowed to move your mouth,' I say. 'Here, let me peel it off.'

I sit back down next to her on the sofa and start flicking up the rubbery edges of the mask.

'It's black leather and it's handwritten with an ink pen, like a proper fountain pen.'

'Mont Blanc,' she says, without moving her lips.

'He had a fountain pen?'

'Pride and joy. I bought it for him as a wedding present,' she says, still without her mouth moving.

'I thought you—' I say.

'He told everyone it was a wedding present. Well, anyone who would listen.'

'Friends?'

'No, he didn't have any real friends. People in shops. People at the pharmacy or at the doctor's surgery. He'd whip out that pen at the drop of a hat.'

I'm peeling the mask from the top down and it's pulling over her eyebrows where the rubber has got stuck in the hairs.

'So apparently he's been writing it every day for nearly two years and it says things like how the journal has become his best friend in his darkest hours.'

She sits up. 'You have got to be kidding me. Gareth doesn't speak like that.'

'Says he was only marrying you because you had an extreme fear—'

'– of abandonment. Yeah, I know. Let's see—' she says, pulling my hands towards her.

'Loads of blackheads,' I say and laugh.

'Oh, my absolute God,' she says, staring. 'You're not kidding. *Loads* of blackheads.'

'Says that you are bipolar and that he is treating it with meds or some shit like that.'

'That's not right! I just had vitamins from Stephen. He's really nice. He's this Harley Street specialist.'

'He's a Harley Street specialist in personality disorders,' I say.

'Yeah, Sue told me that. And that he'd prescribed anti-psychotic drugs. But that's not what he was doing with me. He said that the vitamins would cheer me up, improve my mood. Just vitamin shots and mineral supplements.'

'Did you talk to him on your own?'

'No, we always went in together. Gareth and Stephen are friends. He said they went way back.'

'And you weren't in the least suspicious of that?'

'What, are you saying I'm a moron? Join the queue,' she says, looking in the mirror, picking off the remaining bits of green rubber. 'I'd stopped taking the vitamins anyway.'

'Meds!' I correct her.

'Meds,' she agrees.

'Why?' I say.

'Because whenever I had them, I'd lose track of time.'

'And it never occurred to you that something was going on?' I ask, wondering if I'm pushing her too hard.

'What, like he was drugging me off my head? Maybe,' she says. And two fat tears gather in her lower eyelids and splash onto her cheeks.

'We need to undermine the journal,' I say.

'What's that mean?' she says, wiping the tears away.

'I mean that there must be things in there that we can prove aren't true.'

'Like what?'

'Like your wedding. He talks about your wedding day – at a registry office in Yorkshire.'

'I've never even been to Yorkshire.'

'The wedding photo. You say he took it in the shop, in the changing room.'

'It even looks like a selfie, don't you think? I think it does.'

'I don't know. It looks quite nice to me. Sue doesn't think it looks like a selfie.'

'He must've taken about a hundred shots. So he had plenty to choose from. Anyway, people see what they want to see, don't they! She's already decided I'm guilty, even though she's got nothing on me.'

'Sue's a good one, Clare. Honest.'

'Yeah, it really feels like it.'

'I mean it. Her heart is—'

'Look Sally,' she says, getting up and walking to the window. She has her back to me. She's so painfully thin I can see each one of her ribs through her T-shirt.

'You might think Sue is the nicest person on the planet and she might be, but she's no match for Gareth. He is the most manipulative person you could ever meet. And all this shit we're going through now? He's set it all up. He's probably *still* setting it up. Maybe this was his plan all along. Make me look bad so he gets off scot-free. And then he'll be able to go and do this all over again, somewhere else, to somebody else.'

Forty-Two

DS Clarke

DS Clarke sees great potential in PC Chapman. Noting Barney's interest in Sal, and following up, that's good policing. What is he doing hanging around there anyway? That's what she's thinking as Chapman clicks open her seatbelt and leans in to open the car door. She's an old-fashioned style of copper. Even down to her oh-so-sensible shoes. She observes quietly. PC Chapman slams the door behind her, looking up the road and down. Calmly. Methodically. She's instinctive. DS Clarke sees a bit of herself in Chapman.

DS Clarke makes a mental note of details wherever she goes. It's a habit. What she means by mental note, is really a mental note – it's as though she's writing stuff down in her head, word for word, which makes recalling it easier later. Take now, for example. The street seems to degenerate with every step. At the north end, where they left the car, nearest the bridge towards Chalk Farm Tube station, the front doors are freshly painted in bright colours with shiny brass door handles and matching letter boxes. The paving slabs are smooth and evenly laid. The trees have been clipped. It's past going-home time and there's the smell of a dinner drifting from open kitchen windows – something easy for the kids, fish fingers and peas, while a pot of something more sophisticated bubbles away in the slow cooker. There's a smart red bike, with white and red striped tyres, pushed up against a dark green bush.

A door opens and a young woman emerges, fair hair scraped back; she pretends not to notice two female police officers walking past. She lowers her eyes, wipes her wet hands on the back of her jeans, picks up the bike, and takes it inside. The windows vibrate in their oak frames when the door slams shut behind her.

The further south DS Clarke and PC Chapman walk, so the chinks begin to appear. There's flaking paintwork, a half-missing picket fence, cracked concrete paving slabs and loose kerb stones. DS Clarke is wondering how the council draws the line between 'worth maintaining' and 'not worth maintaining'. And if some poor unfortunate person trips on these uneven slabs, are they not as eligible for compensation as the more fortunate with the smooth pavements?

The front gardens are rammed with wheelie bins, overflowing with black bin bags. There are multiple buzzers instead of one gleaming doorbell. There are panels of safety glass in the beaten front doors, woven through with criss-crossed wires.

DS Clarke is beginning to wish they had some backup.

'Did you tell Sal we were visiting Barney?' she says.

'No, course not,' says PC Chapman. 'I don't think it's even occurred to her. She's known him for years. Got a bit of a soft spot, I reckon. She doesn't see him as trouble.'

'Course she doesn't,' says DS Clarke. 'She doesn't think anyone is any trouble, apart from Terry. How'd you say you got the address?'

'Pharmacist. Barney's quit the programme,' she says quietly, over her shoulder.

'Which makes him even more trouble. Talking of pharmacists – have we got an appointment with our vitamin doctor yet?'

'Tomorrow,' she replies.

'I'm keen to see the whites of his eyes,' says DS Clarke.

'How come?' says PC Chapman, slowing down. 'I think this must be the one.' She takes a left and kicks a crunched-up beer can off the tarmac path leading up to a front door, blonde ponytail swinging behind her.

Except there's no front door.

'You here, Barney?' she calls into the dark rectangle behind the empty door frame.

'Oy, Barney Pickard!'

No reply.

There's a smell of fresh urine and rotting food.

'We've come for a visit, Barn. Shove the kettle on, there's a love!'

A window slides open, then slams shut, somewhere out the back, where it's hidden in shadow.

'You sure about this?' PC Chapman says under her breath.

DS Clarke is most definitely unsure.

'Well, of course I'm sure,' she says confidently. 'A couple of middle-aged women, walking into a squat full of criminal drug offenders . . .' says DS Clarke.

'Speak for yourself, grandma,' Chapman whispers.

'Oh, we've got a grandma here, have we?' whispers a voice right in DS Clarke's ear. A dot of orange, glowing in the corner, behind the sitting-room door, lighting up a dark face.

'Jesus fucking Christ, Ryan! I'll be lucky to make it to my next birthday at this rate!' breathes Dawn, like she's run out of air.

'Can we get this straight once and for all,' he smiles. 'Is it no fucking swearing or lots of fucking swearing?' He laughs then abruptly stops.

'Where's Barney, Ryan?' asks DS Clarke, catching her breath.

'All right, grandma, he ain't here, right!' he says, a cigarette in the corner of his mouth. The ash silently falls off the end, onto what was once a carpet.

'We'll just see if he's upstairs, shall we?' says Chapman, but she's lost the swagger in her voice. Ryan's weak but he's still, what, six foot two?

'You got a warrant then, have you?' he says, no more smiling.

'For a squat, Ryan?' DS Clarke says, folding her arms. Taking control.

'It's home to me,' he says.

'We'll just have a quick look in here, shall we?' Chapman, squeezes past DS Clarke towards the back of the house, where there was probably once a kitchen.

The innocence of that ponytail, golden in the grey, glowing in the gloom. Black greasy fingers, cracked nails, angry bruises wrapped in bloody grey bandages. She doesn't scream when he slowly wraps his hand around her ponytail, and then yanks her head back. She just gasps, and puts her hands up to the sides of her head, trying to hold in the roots of her hair, as he pulls her back towards him and drags her small frame up to his. Her black hat skids towards the front path. Her shoes are kicking against the hollow skirting board. Her elbow hits the door frame. She gasps again.

As soon as he feels DS Clarke's arms twisting through his, pinning his shoulders back, he drops Chapman. No struggle. The smell of sweat and skin and old beer.

She still doesn't scream. Just lets out a gulp of air and runs to the open door.

'You gonna arrest me now?' he says to DS Clarke. 'You gotta arrest me now.'

DS Clarke lets go of his arms and pushes him against the wall of the sitting room.

'I assaulted a police officer – you gotta arrest me.'

DS Clarke slowly shakes her head.

He raises his arm and takes a step towards her.

'I'm assaulting you, you daft bitch!' he says, trying to smack her face. 'Arrest me!'

He strikes out at her, but she deftly catches his hand and holds it, steady.

'Is that what you want?'

'What do you think, grandma, eh?' he shouts in her face so that spit sprays on her cheek. 'What do you fucking think?'

She relaxes her hand and his arm drops.

'Anything's better than this,' he whispers, tears slipping from the corners of his eyes and he slides down the wall onto his knees and buries his face in his coat.

'Tell Barney, I wanna see him,' DS Clarke says, picking up Chapman's hat and striding out of the squat.

'Now!' she yells.

'Oh, and by the way,' she says, coming back up the path. 'You ever touch one of my officers again, and I'll do worse than bang you up.'

And she turns on her heel.

Forty-Three

Clare

Kitty is shouting through the door to be let in.

It's not even 7 a.m.

'Go away,' I say.

'You're the only person I can trust,' she says.

'No, you can't,' I say. 'I'm not trustworthy at all. I'm asleep.'

'I need to talk to you, just for a sec . . .'

I open the door. She stares at me.

'You've got some sort of green shit in your ear.'

'Good.'

'I've met this model scout and he says I have a real future.'

'Oh yeah?' I say.

'He says I just need to get some shots done. Says he knows some top people and that he'll do me an enormous favour and put me in contact with the best, but I need to have a few pictures of me, with like different hair and makeup, and different kinds of poses, to see how photo-ready I am.'

'Did he say photo-ready? Like oven-ready?'

'No, it was a way longer word.'

'Great, let's do it later?'

I try to shut the door.

'No, it's urgent.' She bundles into the room and unpacks her makeup bag on the floor next to the mirror.

'He wants to see something by lunchtime. He wants to send them over to Mario. How about I just do my makeup and you tell me when it looks great?'

'OK, but can't you just do it somewhere else.'

'But here is fine!'

'No, go away,' I say. 'Come back in an hour and I'll help you.'

'You want some of my "Love It to Bits" Smarties McFlurry?'

'No. Go away. See you in an hour.'

'You want tea?' Sally asks.

'It's like Piccadilly Circus in here,' I say. Sally's standing there in her dressing gown.

'You want tea or not?' she says with a sigh, looking at Kitty.

'Yeah, go on then. Never thought I'd start liking tea.'

'You wanna put the bathroom cupboard back together when you have a sec, Clare? It looks like a shit . . .'

'Hi,' interrupts Kitty. 'This is my Dolce look. What do you think?'

'What's a Dolce look?' says Sally.

'Dolce & Gabbana. Sexy Italian label,' I say.

'If that means Flamenco slut, yeah, you've really got it,' says Sally.

'I wasn't asking you, witch,' says Kitty, out of Sally's earshot.

'It looks great,' I say. 'You're a natural with an eyeliner pen.'

'Can you take my picture then?' she says. 'On the roof?'

'Kitty, I'm not going on the roof. Let's just do it here.'

'It's way too hot in here. And there's no space,' she sulks.

'Well, did he ask for full length or not?'

'Head shots,' she says.

'So, we don't need space,' I say. 'Just stand there. The light's good.'

The soft daylight and the watercolour flowers on the curtains and my dressing gown are at odds with her thick foundation and hard scarlet mouth. Her pupils are like pinpricks.

'I think you should be more natural,' I say. 'You look like you're trying too hard.'

She thinks I mean her pose. Which I do, but it's not just that.

'This is exactly the same as Kim Kardashian does it.'

'Yeah, and she looks like she's trying too hard, too.'

I take some pics with her phone and flick through them.

'Let's have a look,' she says.

'Let me take some more first,' I say, standing on my bed. 'You look better when you don't pose.'

'Let's have a look first,' she says.

'Keep doing that. Just being natural. Close your mouth. Your teeth look yellow.'

'Just give me back my phone,' she says, jamming her lips together. Getting angry.

'I can take some more,' I say, carrying on clicking.

'Fuck off, Clare. Give me back my fucking phone!' She tries to grab it.

'God,' I say, 'I'm only trying to help you.'

'I say when you help and when you don't' she says. 'You're not the one in charge here, Coco.'

I stop.

'Don't call me that.'

'Coco. Coco. Coco.'

'You are fucking weird. Get out, Kitty.'

'What about my next look? I need to do American leisure.'

'Go away. Really, go away.' I push her out of the bedroom.

'But what is American leisure?' she says, jamming her pink sneaker in the door so it won't shut.

I push her. Not even that hard. Though she acts like I just tried to stab her or something.

'You abused me! YOU ASSAULTED ME,' she shouts. And slams the front door.

The pest man must have been because the airing cupboard door is open and all the shelves have been stacked against the radiator. I slam the door shut, before a horde of mice come charging down from the attic.

'I hear you assaulted Kitty,' says Sally, handing me a mug of tea.

'News travels . . .'

'She has a nasty habit of being assaulted. I'd like to have a go myself.'

'She told Mrs Henry?'

'She's made a formal complaint, but honestly, no one took her seriously, particularly when she's off her head, which she is, if you ask me, and if she stays down there with Mrs H much longer and she gets a whiff of it, then Kitty'll be digging an even bigger hole for herself. What's with all the photos?'

'It's the modelling thing.'

'What'd you attack her for?'

'I didn't attack her. You know what she's . . .'

'You shouldn't let her get to you.'

'She kept saying my name was Coco. Said some tramp from the police station told her.'

Your name IS Coco.

'What tramp?' says Sally, looking away.

Looking confused.

You don't even look like a Clare.
  It's common.
  I don't do common, babe.

'Clare!' says Sally. 'What exactly did she say?'

'I was on the roof with Kitty . . .'

'You were on the fucking roof with Kitty?'

'Shut up, if you want to hear. I was on the roof with Kitty and she said that she'd met a bloke from one of the squats down the other end of the road who asked about me, as in Coco, cos he remembered me from the police station. I don't remember any of that.'

'You don't remember being at the police station?'

'No, not really. You were there; he said, you were. I don't remember anything much from that day really.'

'Yes, I was there, but what did Kitty say next, that's the important bit.'

'She said that this tramp bloke had asked her if I was at the refuge, because she told him it was a refuge, and he asked her if there was another girl called Sally.'

'Girl!' says Sally, looking half-pleased. Then she frowns. 'What'd he want to know for?'

'I dunno, Sally, maybe he fancies you.'

'Don't you start.'

'No, wait, she said something about how he'd bumped into someone who knew you. A relative of yours. A brother. He was looking for you because you'd disappeared. I think that's what she said. Yeah, she said . . .'

Sally rushes into the bathroom.

'Sally, where are you going?'

She's knelt over the toilet.

'Sally. Sal, what's the matter? He's only some junkie or something. Sal . . . Sal . . .' I rub her shoulders. 'Shall I get Mrs Henry? Sal?' Frothy tea and purple jam. 'Sal I'm going to get Mrs Henry.'

'Why didn't you tell Sally what Kitty said before? It's not like you haven't had time,' Celia says, hugging her own stupid cardigan.

'I don't know. I forgot!'

This looks like a mothers' meeting.

Mrs Henry is hunched over a coffee mug.

Sally is cradling a cardboard sick bowl.

Celia is fussing over everyone.

I don't even know why Mrs Henry is having a go at me. I'm only trying to help here.

'I'm astonished that you could forget something so important.'

'I'm astonished that the police still haven't found Gareth or Terry. Join the club.'

'Where's Kitty now?' says Sally.

'She's at her dance class,' says Mrs Henry, not looking up. 'I hear you assaulted her this morning, Clare.'

'I pushed her out of my room, Mrs Henry.'

'She's made a formal complaint.'

Sally coughs. 'Can I stop you all, just for one second?' she says.

We all stop and look at Sally.

'Do you mind if I explain what's going on here? Firstly, Kitty is not going to be at her dance class, she is with a model scout who has promised her the world. Secondly, when she does come back, chances are she will have taken a massive dive, even if *Vogue* have booked her for their next twelve covers, because she will be coming down off whatever she was high on this morning.'

'High?' says Celia. 'I thought you didn't . . .' she says, looking at Mrs Henry.

'She . . .' says Mrs Henry.

'Wake up and smell the coffee,' says Sally, dabbing at the corner of her mouth. 'Third. What is third?' she continues, screwing up the tissue into a ball. 'Oh yeah. Today's news. So, one of the lads from the police station, probably Barney, possibly one of the others, has been contacted by Terry. And that Barney knows where I'm living. What we don't know is if he's told Terry that yet. Where's Sue?'

'DS Clarke is on her way, but she's had to divert to the hospital,' says Mrs Henry. 'Something about Chapman.'

'I believe she was already looking to speak to Barney . . .' says Celia.

'We need to find out what Barney has said,' says Mrs H.

'Barney won't have said anything, if it was him,' says Sally. I think she's sweet on him. 'Barney's a good guy. Known him for years.'

'And Barney is not the threat here. It's Terry,' says Mrs H. 'In situations like this you have to be extra vigilant,' she goes on, stating the bleeding obvious, if you ask me. 'Let's not get distracted by Barney. Do we even have a description of Terry?' she says. 'All I've got is the cutting from the paper that's in your file, but that's from more than twenty years ago. I'm assuming he doesn't look like this anymore.' She hands the cutting to Sally, who passes it to me without looking down.

'LIVERPOOL MAN FOUND GUILTY OF MURDERING WOMAN MISTAKEN FOR WIFE' it says, in bold *Daily Mirror* type.

Two photos of blonde women, side by side, pretty, young, almost identical if you didn't know, and a picture of a bungalow with a picket fence, and a dark green garage door.

The house is symmetrical, made of honey-coloured brick with a grey roof and a glass conservatory on one side.

And a man in the garden. Curly hair. Set mouth. Defiant jaw.

Sally watches me as she retches into the bowl. She wipes her mouth again.

'It was only at the start he mistook me for Hayley,' she says. 'Came in through the patio windows and got hold of her from behind and had the knife right up to her neck before I walked in. Then he saw he had Hayley and not me and I saw the thought pass through his head, should he push her away and chase after me, and you know what he said?

'He said to me "Guess what feels better than killing you?"'

'And he pushed the knife harder into her skin and he said "Watching you, while I kill your best friend, that's what," he said. And I begged him not to do it, begged him to let us go, or just kill me but not to kill Hayley, White Wine Hayley. She looked so fucking scared. So fucking scared. Her eyes—'

She throws up again.

And then Kitty walks in.

'You won't believe!' she says. Then, without waiting for us to reply, 'He hates my fucking pictures! Says I look like a slut.'

'We're in the middle of something, Kitty,' says Mrs Henry. 'Would you mind?'

'Says the pictures are really good but that I'm not right for fashion. Wants to know if I've got any friends. So I told him, I said to him, I live in a fucking refuge, with a load of fucking misfits who deserve to have had the shit kicked out of them. I wish you were all fucking dead.'

She slams out of the room like a whirlwind. Sally sighs and leans back in her chair, looking up at the ceiling. A tear follows a channel through her foundation down her cheek. She wipes it from the corner of her mouth.

Forty-Four

Sally

I don't mind admitting that I could have slept all afternoon, but then Prashi's youngest daughter knocks at the door and thank God Clare was there, because my face has swollen up from being sick and crying and I'm quite sure I'd have scared the pants off her if I'd answered it.

'Mrs Henry says there's a man here to see Sally and he's not allowed in so she'll have to go and sort it out.'

'Thanks,' says Clare. 'Did you hear that?'

The urge to throw up comes back hard.

'Tell her I'll be down in five,' I say, holding my mouth. I've only just woken up and still feel sick, but now I feel even worse, and I'm dehydrated too, so I'm drinking tap water like there's no tomorrow, which I never do in London because they put all sorts of shite in the water here, including fluoride. If I want extra fluoride I'd eat toothpaste, wouldn't I?

'Are you OK?' says Clare, through the bathroom door, which I open a crack and see she looks like she's about to jump out the window herself.

'Yes, I'll be fine,' I say, patting my face with water. 'Terry wouldn't be fool enough to come up the front door. Neither would his family. So, it'll be Barney, I guess. Or Ryan.'

'Do I look like I've just done ten rounds with Frank Bruno?' I say.

'I don't know who Frank Bruno is, but if he's a boxer, yes,' she says.

'Thanks,' I say.

'Here, put some of this on,' she goes, giving me some lip salve and mascara.

'We're in the wars, you and me, aren't we?' I say, putting on my jacket.

'Who d'ya think's here,' she says. 'You want me to come?'

'It'll just be Barney,' I say. 'If it was Terry we'd be hearing police sirens by now.'

'You can hope,' she says. 'Not if Detective Sergeant Useless is on duty.'

'Don't be getting at her,' I say, pulling my boots on and heading off down the stairs. 'She'll save the world one of these days.'

'One psycho at a time,' she shouts after me.

Barney is standing outside the front of the refuge. He has his back to me but I'd recognise that coat anywhere. Mrs H is talking to him from the front door. You won't believe it, but she is actually laughing, and I don't think I've ever seen her laugh, which only goes to show the charms of Barney, even if he is a tramp junkie.

'. . . because we don't let any guests in, particularly if they're male,' she's saying. 'Not even the Dalai Lama.'

I don't hear his reply.

'Well, you're not because you don't have the orange robes.'

'I'm in disguise,' he says, and he sees me over her shoulder, in the lobby.

'And a very good disguise it is too, Mr Lama. Sally, don't come out here. You don't have to come out,' she says. 'Stay where you are and Barney can speak to you through the door.'

Mrs H wanders into the front yard, picking weeds out of the cracks in the concrete. Gving us some kind of polite privacy.

'Sally, I just wanted to tell you that it's all OK,' he says. He's sitting on the wall and I'm leaning on the door frame. Awkward like a pair of teenagers.

'Calm down, Barn,' I say. 'You OK?'

'Yeah, Sal, just happy to see you. You OK?'

'Yes, Barney. Don't worry. We're all perfectly safe here.'

He's twitchier than usual and he sees me looking for tics.

'You still on the programme, Barney?'

'Miss Parton,' he says. 'You know I wouldn't let you down, now don't you.'

He takes in a deep breath and I can almost hear him telling himself to calm down.

'I didn't tell him. That's what I came to say. You know, didn't tell him anything. He tried like. You know. But what I always say is, "Honour among thieves. Respect among the downtrodden", that's what I always say. Don't I always say that, Sal?' he says, looking round at Mrs H.

'What didn't you tell him?' I say, pulling the door shut behind me so I can hear him better.

'I was at the pub, you know, the one by the market,' he says quietly, so Mrs H can't hear. 'We were all there, we were, you know me and Olly and Ryan and the rest.' Mrs H has wandered to the end of the path and is looking up and down the road like she's searching for a lost cat, or waiting for the postman, but I know she's keeping her eyes peeled for a convicted murderer.

'Got my benefit through, you know, like normal. And we was sitting on the tables outside and there was this guy sitting near us, having a smoke. Seemed nice enough, you know. And I asked him where was he from, like you do, and he said he was from South Liverpool. And then he said Aigburth Road. And he said the Dingle. Posh end. Best place in the world.'

I want to be sick.

'And I said, "That's just what my friend Sally said, must be good this Dingle. Think I'll take a trip there myself," I says to him. And he goes mental, like. Grabs me by my collar like he's gonna throttle me.'

Mrs H is getting twitchy herself now, like he's making too much noise.

'Barney, you should be telling this to DS Clarke, not Sally,' she says, but he doesn't stop.

'And then he gets all calmed down, and that's when he says he's your long-lost brother, like, you know, and at the time,' he says, 'at the time,' he nods, looking up at the sky, 'I thought, it all sounded, you know, right, like . . . true and everything,' he says, looking me in the eyes, then looking away. 'So anyway,' he says, looking up the street, like he's suddenly in a bit of a hurry, 'I just wanted you to know. And, you know, I didn't tell him.' He gives me a weak smile and shifts his foot, just a little.

'What didn't you tell him?' I say, breathing as shallow as I can so I don't throw up.

There's a long silence.

'That girl all right, is she?' he says, like he didn't hear what I said.

'The girl with the bare feet? Coco?' I say, thinking back to what Clare looked like when she first stumbled into the police station.

'She didn't die, then, from drinking the paraffin?'

'It wasn't paraffin,' I say. 'He told her it was, which is almost as bad as giving her the real thing, if you think how she must've felt.'

'Some people are sick in the head.'

'Yup, some people sure are sick in the head,' I say. 'He had this game he played with her,' I say, checking that Mrs H is out of earshot. 'It was called the matches game, and he used to tie her up, pour paraffin over her, then flick lit matches at her to see if she'd set on fire.'

'You are fucking joking me,' he says. 'How does anyone come up with shit like that? What's up with him?'

'Psycho. There's a lot of them around, Barn. You should watch out.'

'Nah, you don't have to worry about me, girl,' he says. 'I'm tickety-boo, me. Keep on taking the jungle juice and all. On the mend, as they say. Hey, Mrs, can I just give her a hug?' he says.

'No,' Mrs H says. 'Sally, go back inside.'

'Look, Mrs, I'm not a murderer. I'm her friend. And I just wanted to make sure she's alright.'

'I don't recommend that.' Mrs H looks at me frowning, but he's already squeezing the life out of me, wrapping me in his coat. The smell is just about enough to knock you off your feet.

'You had a wash recently?' I say, trying not to cough.

'There you are, you see,' he says to Mrs H. 'She loves her old friend Barney, don't she? Don't you love your old friend Barney?' he says to me.

She gives me a look and nods her head towards the door. 'Come along now, Sally,' she calls as she buzzes through the front door and disappears into the foyer. Barney watches her carefully then suddenly lurches forward again, spreading his arms wide.

He leans in and squeezes me tightly and just when I think he's going to squeeze all the actual breath out of me, he bends down and he whispers in my ear, 'Sal. Take this for me, will ya?' and I feel something drop in my pocket. 'I can't trust myself with it. I've already got through half of it and now it's driving me mad. You're the only person I know who will keep it safe. If I have it, you know what I'll do with it, and for once in my life I want to do the right thing.'

And then he lets me go, before Mrs H has even had time to turn around.

'Don't we all feel better for that?' he says, starting off up the street, in a bit of stagger. 'Be seeing you, Sal. And you, Mrs. Very nice to make your acquaintance, I'm sure,' he says.

I put my hand in my pocket and in the corner of it is a roll of notes. And for all his talk, all his honour amongst thieves, I know what he must have done to get it.

'I vote we don't tell Sue, about the hug,' I say to Mrs H, trying to stop her nagging at me about how irresponsible I am.

'I vote you do as I tell you next time, Sal,' she says. 'I don't know what you were thinking. You know I'll have to make a report.'

'Maybe you can be a little economical with the truth in your report?' I say.

'Maybe you've put me in a situation where I'll have to be,' she sniffs.

'You're way too cautious in life; you should try living a little,' I say, thinking I'd get on to Sue and tell her about Barney, only this roll of cash in my pocket is not so much burning a hole as setting fire to my entire jacket. I need to get rid of it somewhere safe.

'And you should try not putting your life in danger, or mine,' she shouts down the hall. 'Or anyone else's.'

'Now you're in trouble,' says Clare, following me up the stairs with a Pot Noodle in her hand. 'Did you assault Mrs Henry?'

'Eating that shit will kill you,' I say.

'There's loads of nutrition in a Pot Noodle,' she says. 'They said I had to eat a bit of what I fancy, and I always fancy a Pot Noodle. Besides, being poisoned by a fast food snack sounds like quite an attractive proposition, considering some of the other options.'

'Shh, a minute,' I say. 'I need you to help me.'

She closes the door to our flat behind her and leans against it.

'What?' Clare says, staring at me and stirring her Pot Noodle with a fork.

'If you needed to hide something, like something really important, that you didn't want anyone to find, even big nose Kitty, where would you put it?' I say.

'Big or small?'

'Small,' I say, holding up the roll of fifty pound notes.

She raises her eyebrows, but nothing else, no questions, no nothing, just like you'd expect from a best friend, and opens her bedroom door.

'Easy,' she goes.

'What, in here?' I say. 'What d'ya mean, easy?'

'Didn't you ever hear that story about the prawns? This bloke. I don't know who he was. He traded his wife in for a younger model. Some girl who looked exactly like his wife, but thirty years her junior. Well, on the day the wife had to move out – her home remember, her soft furnishings and scatter cushions – she takes down her lounge curtains, slides out the curtain pole, twists off the ends, then fills the hollow pole with Sainsbury's Taste the Difference Extra Large Atlantic Prawns.'

She snorts. I snort.

'Then she hooks back the curtains and ta dah! Three days later, the worst smell in the world and no one can find it for months. Years even. They had to move out in the end.'

'You're kidding!' I say.

'Not kidding.'

'I love the fact that they were so specific. Sainsbury's Taste the Difference Extra Large Atlantic Prawns.'

She hops on her bed, unhooks the metal curtain pole, totally wrong for a bedroom but they must have inherited it from somewhere, and unscrews the knob on the end.

'What you got in there?' I ask, because the whole way she did it was too practised, too streamlined, like she'd done it before.

'Well, you may as well see, since you know everything else,' she says. And she pulls out a dirty piece of cotton wool and wrapped up inside it is something shiny.

'Gareth's,' she says, dangling a gold heart locket and chain in her hand, and my jaw is virtually on the bloody floor. 'Or rather, Gareth's mum's.'

She slides her thumbnail into the side of the locket and it flips open. Inside there's a tiny photo of a woman holding a baby.

'Is that him?' I say.

'I dunno. It's a baby!' she says.

'My auntie used to have a locket like that', I say, 'Is there an inscription?'

'No,' says Clare, 'Not that I could see.'

'Let me look,' I say. I push my nail into the side of the locket and after some coaxing, the back clicks open. Inside there's an inscription.

'For Geraldine, to celebrate the birth of our son, Gareth Marlon, on this 14th day of October, 1981, With my love.'

'Gareth Marlon. Gareth Marlon what?' I say.

'Dunno,' she says. 'He never said anything about his family.'

She folds the locket back into the cotton wool and shoves it into the curtain pole, with the fifty pound notes. Her back's still turned away from me when she whispers, 'Fancy you hiding cash.'

She comes and sits down next to me on the sofa. It's late afternoon and the train tracks are wobbling in the heat.

'Like you've got a leg to stand on,' I whisper back. 'What the hell are you doing with Gareth's mother's locket – and while we're on the subject, why on earth haven't you given it to the police, you absolute moron?'

'I didn't know it had his name in it, did I? What we gonna do?'

'I dunno,' I say.

We just sit there, with our arms folded, wondering which sack of shite to open first, when one more bowls in: Kitty, back on cloud nine.

'Look,' she goes, slightly taken aback that Clare and I are sitting in the darkest part of the room with our arms folded like it's the most normal thing in the world, not saying anything because we've run out of things to say and things to do and things to think about, because nothing's normal; in fact, everything is so not normal it's almost funny.

'Look,' she goes again, frowning, like we're the weirdos. 'Can we try some more photos? Axel says, maybe if I do some without makeup, he can send them to Mario in the morning and Mario'll get back to us really fast but he needs them ASAP.'

'Not now,' says Clare.

'Not ever,' I say. 'Go away, Kitty.'

She slides over the back of the armchair and plops into the seat, ponytail swishing.

'He said your photography is amazing, Clare. Said the pictures were top quality, it's just I had too much makeup on and he'd like to see something more natural. Said maybe we should shoot outside. Like we could go on the roof, like I said before. He said, if you like, he could show your shots to a photographic agent to see if they thought you had talent because he thinks you have a real eye. A real eye for composition. I think that's what he said.'

'Fuck off, Kitty,' says Clare.

'Same,' I say.

Forty-Five

DS Clarke

In the car park at Camden Road Police Station, DS Clarke, PC Chapman and DC Walker were heading in different directions. DS Clarke was planning on visiting Ms Meering at the wedding dress shop, although, God help her, she has better things to do. PC Chapman intended to pay the doctor on Harley Street a visit and DC Walker was waiting on an urgent call back from someone whose name Joanna has forgotten.

'She said it sounded urgent,' says DC Walker, with her phone pressed up to her ear. 'She said the lady was in a highly agitated . . .' She stops to listen.

'It was Mrs Vocking of . . .'

'Oval Road,' finishes DS Clarke. 'What'd she say?' she barks at DC Walker.

'She said . . .' She stops. 'Joanna, if she said it was urgent, you must surely be able to remember what she said! Oh, OK.' DC Walker ends the call and looks at DS Clarke. 'Mrs Vocking said there was something in the garden.'

'What? A bird? A plane? What?'

'A knife. She says she saw a knife in next-door's garden. She saw a knife in next door's garden glinting in the sun.'

'Let's go!' says DS Clarke. Her visit to Ms Meering at the wedding dress shop would just have to wait until tomorrow.

DS Clarke has already seen the garden and forensics had already checked it, although in fairness, it won't have been with the same level of detail as in the house. They were looking for bloodstains. Indoors.

'Mrs Vocking, is it?' DS Clarke says to the frumpy woman who answers the front door of the house next to Clare's.

'Harriet.'

'Harriet, hello. I'm Detective Sergeant Susan Clarke. I'm investigating . . .'

DS Clarke tells Mrs Vocking as vague a story as she possibly can. And yes, Clare was fine, and yes she was sure that Gareth was fine also. And, yes, surely they would indeed both be home at some point. Yes soon.

'Such a nice girl. Knew her father,' Mrs Vocking was saying.

'Could you tell us how you came to discover the knife?'

'Oh, well, I was upstairs, just sorting out the bedding in the spare room for my daughter, she's coming to visit today, and I happened to look out of the window and saw a glint, you know, in the sunlight. So, I went out into the garden, not to be nosey or anything, and I looked over the fence, as you do, and there it was, large as life.'

'And you haven't been into the next-door garden, Mrs Vocking?'

'Harriet. Call me Harry. No, I haven't.'

'So, you haven't touched the knife? Can I just be very clear on that point?'

'Oh no, I haven't touched anything.'

'OK, Harriet, I'd like you to stay in your garden, while I go next door, and I'd like you to point out to me where you think the knife is. Can you do that?'

'Yes, I believe I can.'

'Good. Just give me a minute while I get through the back gate.'

DS Clarke and PC Chapman retrace their steps.

PC Hall is standing with his back to his patrol car, leaning against it, looking up and down the street like a proper copper. He straightens up when DS Clarke and PC Chapman emerge from Mrs Vocking's property.

'All right, PC Hall. Got the key?'

'Yes, sarge. I've opened up already.'

'Good, OK, stick with me. You got the forensic packs?'

'Yes, sarge. But forensics are on their way. They wanted to see the scene before we move anything.'

'Well, good. Even better!'

DS Clarke is aware that forensics will want to search every inch of the garden. Every blade of grass needs to remain exactly as it is. The incongruity of the outside and the inside of this crime scene strikes her as odd. This garden is overgrown, uncared for. People who keep smart houses usually keep smart gardens, she thinks.

'OK, Mrs Vocking. Please could you point to where the knife is?' DS Clarke calls over the fence from the patio behind Clare's house.

Mrs Vocking's head suddenly appears above the faded wooden fence.

'*It's over there, in the far corner,*' she shouts. '*Under the bud-dleia davidii.*'

'What's one of them?' whispers PC Chapman.

'No, no, the buddleia. Yes, right there. You see?'

DS Clarke stands on the low wall next to the patio. Tucked under an overgrown bush that looks like one of those overgrown weeds you see on a railway track, there's a kitchen knife, half wrapped in newspaper. The handle is hidden. But the blade, eight inches long, DS Clarke guesses, is maybe one-third showing, and what is visible is mostly covered with dried blood.

'How'd we miss this before?'

'Sarge, I wasn't on the search detail.'

'I'm not blaming you, PC Chapman. I'm just asking, how did we miss this before? Forensics are either half blind or . . .'

'They couldn't have missed it, sarge.'

'No, they couldn't.'

And if they did, DS Clarke thinks to herself, my head's on the block.

At the side gate, DC Walker and PC Hall are talking in low voices.

'How about . . .' says DS Clarke, 'you two stay here while Chapman and I take a little trip to the doctor?'

'Sarge,' nods PC Hall.

Dr Stephen Short is of average height, in his forties, DS Clarke guesses. He's thin and wiry under a clean-cut beige flannel suit, with large brown eyes. In fact, he's not bad looking, she thinks, although too thin for her preference, if she could ever admit to herself that she had one.

'Dr Short,' says DS Clarke. 'I believe one of my team has spoken to you on the phone?'

'DS Clarke,' he smiles, choosing to ignore PC Chapman. 'There seems to be some confusion at your end, am I right?'

DS Clarke makes a point of introducing PC Chapman.

For which PC Chapman is grateful, but it's most probably lost on Dr Short.

He nods at her, without the least embarrassment.

Dr Short's practice is at the smart end of Harley Street. His room is light and airy, and the main surgery has been painted with a sky scene, clouds and birds and rays of sunshine. DS Clarke hates that kind of thing. You're paying good money for medical advice, not some art installation, she thinks.

'Do you mind?' says DS Clarke as she places a tape recorder on Dr Short's desk.

'As a matter of fact, I do,' says Dr Short, switching it off and pushing it back across his desk. He looks rather grand, sitting there in his high-backed leather armchair, the sort of man who can dispense great wisdom, with enormous confidence.

'Purely for the record,' says DS Clarke, her hand hovering over the record button.

'That's what I'm afraid of,' he smiles, pushing the recorder away. 'I'll need my lawyer present if you want an official state-ment. I had been led to believe this was a little "chat",' he says, making little quote marks in the air with his index fingers.

DS Clarke hates that kind of thing too.

'There is some confusion actually, Dr Short, though I'm not sure whose "end",' and she makes little quote marks too, 'it emanates from.'

Dr Short throws back his head in laughter.

'Bravo, bravo, Sue – if I may call you that.'

'No, Dr Short, you may not call me that,' says DS Clarke. PC Chapman's eyes nearly pop out of her head. 'You may call me Detective Sergeant Clarke. While we are currently enjoying an informal meeting, it would be highly inappropriate of you to call me Sue in a more official situation, for example, down at the station, which is where this conversation may eventually lead us, so Dr Short, let's just stick to formality, shall we?'

He draws the palms of his hands together, in a prayer-like gesture, and lets the tips of his fingers rest gently on his lips.

'Go ahead, Detective Sergeant Clarke,' he says.

'You are Dr Stephen Short, of twenty-three Harley Street, London W1G 6AD.'

He nods.

'And you have been treating Ms Clare Chambers . . .'

'No, I have not!' says Dr Short, bringing his hand down with a slap on the table edge.

'You have been treating Ms Coco . . .' begins DS Clarke again.

'I have been treating *Mrs* Coco James for the past eighteen months,' says Dr Short.

'Mrs Coco James is also known as Ms Clare Chambers.' DS Clarke gives Dr Short a brief, forced smile. 'And you also know Mr Gareth James?'

'I do indeed, known him for years. Great guy. Great, great guy,' he offers rather too readily, without being asked.

'And you've been treating, Clare, Coco, whatever we choose to call her—'

'For Bipolar Disorder,' he interrupts. 'As I told your colleague on the phone.'

'Not for nutritional problems and vitamin deficiencies?'

'Look,' says Dr Short, getting a little hot. 'I don't know where this story is coming from, but Coco knew full well that she was coming here for her emotional instability. She was diagnosed with Bipolar Disorder. I predicted a while back that, with her symptoms, and without taking the correct medications, she was heading for a full-blown psychosis, and if she is saying different to that, well my diagnosis is quite . . .' His voice trails off and he shakes his head.

'DS Clarke,' he says, suddenly standing up. 'We have got off on the wrong foot. Let me explain a little more fully what is going on here. Your colleague mentioned on the phone that Coco has been saying that she was on a course of vitamins for mood swings. With Coco, we are talking about Bipolar Affective Disorder – you may know it better as manic depression.'

DS Clarke nods.

'You're an intelligent woman,' he says. 'You know as well as I do that giving someone a vitamin shot, or a mineral supplement isn't going to touch the sides of Biopolar Affective Disorder. The girl is, frankly, delusional,' he says.

'Was she originally referred to you, Dr Short? It would really help to know that,' interrupts PC Chapman.

DS Clarke nods.

'No, Gareth's a really old friend. We knew each other in high school.'

'And you saw Clare as a personal favour to Gareth, is that right?' says DS Clarke.

'Yes, that's correct, although I kind of felt I'd bitten off more than I could chew with Coco,' he says, nodding gravely.

'Oh really?' says DS Clarke, taking out a pen and pad.

'Yes, do write this down,' says Dr Short, trying to take control, thought DS Clarke. 'Her symptoms are paranoia, extreme mood changes, high mania and low depression, displayed as impulsive behaviours, agitation, feelings of worthlessness and suicide, hearing voices as well as believing she has super powers.'

'What kind of super powers?'

'That she can feel no pain. She regularly self-harms. Gareth had a hell of a time, poor guy. She attacked him many times. She even tried to set herself on fire. More than once . . .'

'And hearing voices?'

'So she said. In the last six months alone, we've tried Lithium, Sodium Valproate, Olanzapine and Quetiapine,' he says, 'though not all at the same time,' he says and smiles. 'Without Gareth as her full-time carer, I doubt she'd still be here. Without the strict dosage required to manage her illness, well, that's what prevented the onset of mania.'

'Well, thank you for that, Doctor Short,' says DS Clarke as she gets up to leave. 'Just one thing occurs to me . . .' She smiles, that tight-lipped smile she reserves for people she really doesn't like. 'How come she's fully functioning now, when she's not on her strict dosage?'

'Well, I-I don't know, I'm sure,' says Dr Short, momentarily undone.

'Perhaps it's the vitamins she's taking,' she says, smiling again.

'You do know you're dealing with a highly manipulative individual, don't you, Detective Sergeant Clarke? She seduces people into believing her. She plays the victim. But watch out. It's all just a game to her.'

'Do you happen to know where Mr Gareth James is now, Dr Short?'

'No, I'm afraid I don't. I'm actually very concerned about him.'

DS Clarke and PC Chapman exit the building and climb into the waiting Vauxhall Astra.

'Do you know what Dawn?' says DS Clarke. 'I think I'm getting a little bit bored with our little friend Coco.'

Forty-Six

Clare

'Susan, what ya doing?' says Sally.

Susan's just walked into our sitting room.

'Clare Chambers,' she says, standing outside my bedroom door, 'I am arresting you on suspicion of the murder of Gareth James. You—'

'Sue, what you doing?' shouts Sally.

There are two officers with her. I haven't seen them before. Two male officers and Celia.

'... do not have to say anything, but it may harm your defence ...'

'Sue, you're making a mistake!' shouts Sally.

'... if you do not mention, when questioned ...'

They come right over to my bed and haul me up.

'... something you later rely on in court. Anything you do say may be given in evidence. Do you understand?'

'Sue, you don't have to put handcuffs on her. She's a kid!'

They yank my hands behind my back and clip some hand-cuffs on me.

Babe!

You hear me, babe?

What's that remind you of, honey?

Gareth's laughing at me.

'Do you understand?' she shouts in my face.

'Take her to the station, PC Corkett, I'll follow you there.'

'Let her put her fucking shoes on!'

'Come on now, Clare, put your . . .'

You don't want to go out without your shoes on, babe.

Think of your feet.

'Clare!'

What's everyone saying?

I can't hear.

Falling down the stairs.

Kitty's face.

Staring.

'. . . gonna be back soon . . .'

Down the stairs.

'. . . doesn't know yet,' says Celia.

'. . . need to do my pictures!'

'Go to your room, Kitty,' shouts Mrs Henry.

Through reception.

Prashi starts crying.

Abigail and Sian.

By the door.

Whispering.

'She didn't do it!' yells Abigail.

The front door buzzes.

Dark outside.

Buzzing stops.

Click.

Back of car.

Click.

No air.

Radio buzzing.

Voices.

Celia.

Looking out the window.

Given up.

Click.

'Your name is Clare Chambers.'

I nod.

A different room.

'Please answer for the tape!'

'Yes, I guess, but . . .' I say. She interrupts. There's a camera in the corner. And a policeman by the door. Eyes forward.

'You were born on the 26th March 1996.'

She looks at me. Cold.

I nod again.

'For the tape!'

'Yes.'

'You have been arrested and brought here today because we believe that you may have had something to do with the disappearance of a Mr Gareth James, of 289 Oval Road Camden, NW1 4BS.'

The policeman by the door is watching out of the corner of his eyes. Our eyes meet and he blushes.

'Do you wish to speak to a legal adviser now, or have one present during the interview?'

She's eyeballing me.

Babe. Tell Susie Sue you don't need a legal adviser, babe. You haven't done anything.

Only guilty people get legal help.

'Clare?'

She sighs.

'No,' I say.

'No, what?' she says, looking round the room to see if everyone else is as exasperated as she is.

'What was the question, again?'

'Do you wish to speak to a legal adviser now, or have one present during the interview?'

'I don't need a legal adviser. I'm innocent.'

She raises her head sharply.

God, Susie's a right fucking bitch!

'No, for the tape,' I say, before she can.

She breathes out slowly.

'At the conclusion of this interview, I will give you a notice explaining what will happen to the tapes and how you and or your solicitor can get access to them.'

'OK,' I say.

She clicks on her keyboard.

'On the tenth of April, there is evidence that a crime took place at property 289, Oval Road, Camden, NW1 8BS. Traces of blood were found at the property, specifically on a white T-shirt and also in the kitchen area. There is evidence that an attempt had been made to remove the blood, using household bleach.'

Boring fucking bitch.

'Receipts,' she says, looking up again, 'from HP Dunlop hardware store on Mount Pleasant Road, indicate that four five litre bottles of household bleach were delivered to the address on the twenty-seventh of March, twenty-eighteen. Is that correct?'

I shake my head. I don't know about any bleach. Bleach was his thing.

Tell Susie Sue to get on with it.

'For the tape, Clare is shaking her head. We found traces of bleach on your skin and on your dressing gown.'

Bathrobe, babe.
Tell her it's called a fucking bathrobe!

'Did you use the paraffin simply to mask the smell of the bleach, Clare. Is that it?'

I shake my head.

'We found a receipt for the four bottles of bleach hidden in your bathroom cabinet. Do you deny knowledge of this?'

That was me, babe.
They need to be detecting. It's what they do.
Bet Susie Sue was wetting her pants over that.

'This morning we located an eight-inch carving knife, in the garden of the property, with traces of blood that match the blood found in the kitchen and on the T-shirt, which we believe may belong to Gareth James.'

Yadda yadda yadda
Just say yes and you can get out of there.

'And we have spoken to Dr Stephen Short, of 23, Harley Street, London W1G 6AD, who confirms that he has been treating you for eighteen months, for Bipolar Disorder.

Good old Stevie.
Atta boy.

'He's a nutrition doctor . . .' I say.

'A Harley Street Psychiatrist,' Susan says. 'There's a big sign on the front door.'

Susie's just bullshitting you, babe.
  She's playing with your mind.

'Let me tell you what I think happened that night, shall I, Clare?' she says, pulling out a chair and sitting facing me. 'Let me tell you what the circumstantial evidence suggests happened.'

It's just a game, babe.
  Someone has to win.
  Someone has to lose.

'From what Dr Short says, Clare, Coco, whatever it is that you choose to call yourself, you have recently been forgetting to take your medication, either deliberately . . .'

And we think deliberately don't we, babe?

'. . . or otherwise, which makes you unable to control your emotions.'

You're weighing me down, babe.

'. . . so, you experience frequent emotional ups and downs . . .'

And you never know when to shut up, do you?

'. . . and become impulsive and suspicious. Dr Short reports that you believed that, despite having recently married you, Gareth was going to leave you for someone else . . .'

I WISH.

I think that.

I don't say that.

'. . . do you have a comment you want to make, Clare?'

Don't tell Susie Sue anything.

I shake my head.

'. . . and according to Dr Short, it would be perfectly within your scope to believe that the only way to stop him was to kill him.'

'And do what with the body?' I say.

Make it into chicken tikka masala? I love a chicken tickka masala.

He's laughing.

'You tell me, Clare.'

Oh, just tell her to fuck off.

'Shut—' I start.

He's doing my head in.

'Clare? Shut?' says Susan.

She sure as hell don't miss a trick, babe.

'Go . . .' I start.

Because he's still doing my head in.

Baby, baby, baby.
    I'm all you've got.
    They don't give a shit about you.
    I told you they wouldn't.
    Told you no one would believe you.
    They just think you're mental.
    Babe.
    You actually are fucking mental.

'CLARE,' shouts Susan, so suddenly that all of us jump out of our skins.
    'DO YOU HEAR VOICES, CLARE?'
    'NO!' I shout back.
    'No, I don't,' I say more quietly.

Babe.
    You can tell her about me.
    It's OK.

'No! I don't hear voices. Not at all.'

Except mine, babe.

'Clare!'
    I say nothing.

Remember our song, babe?

I can't breathe.

'Clare, can you please breathe normally?'

You know the one.

There's no air.
'Clare, you're deliberately hyperventilating, Clare. Stop it!'

Now, how does it go?

'Celia. She's passing out. Get her water. Quickly now. Someone get her some tea with sugar. Clare!'

Oh, can't you see . . .
You belong to me . . .
How my poor heart aches . . .

'CLARE. Why are you humming?'

Every step you take . . .
Every move you make . . .

Darker.

Every vow you break . . .

Sliding off the chair.

'Celia! Get a medic in.'

Don't take me back to the hospital!
I can't get the words out.

Every smile you fake . . .

'On the floor!' says Susan. 'She's fitting!'

Every claim you stake . . .

Darker.
Shaking.
'. . . faking!'
'. . . can't fake this kind of reaction. Breathe, Clare, come on!
Clare, slowly now, slowly.'

I'll be watching you.

Forty-Seven

Sally

Sue's returning my call. About sodding time.

'You can't sleep either,' I say.

'No,' she says. She sounds low.

'Sue, I need to talk to you about Terry,' I say, before she can get a word in.

'Is she OK?' she says.

'Yes, she's fine,' I whisper.

'She's there, is she?' she goes.

'Yes. She's here.' And I think to myself, I don't know where else she'd be, it was you that dropped her off.

'What, in the same room?'

'No, of course she's not in the same room. I wouldn't be talking to you if she was in the same room, would I? She's asleep. I don't know what you guys gave her, but she's out cold.'

'She had some kind of breakdown. She was singing to herself at one point. Talking to herself, and that was before they gave her the drugs. They just sedated her and took her to the hospital for a check. We decided that York Gate was the safest place for her, for now. She's hypoglycemic. You should make sure she eats more. I thought you were on that.'

'Maybe you should go easy on her,' I say, because when they brought her back in, even Celia said she thought they were way too harsh.

'I think I was too tough,' Sue says quietly.

'I need to talk to you about Terry!'

'Sal, I'm at a loss to know what to do. On the one hand, she makes a totally convincing victim and Gareth sounds like the archetypal psycho. But without a walking, talking Gareth, that doesn't work. And then Gareth, he also makes a convincing victim; blood everywhere, abandoned personal belongings, no sign of him in all the usual places, the emails, the journal, the knife . . .'

'Knife? You didn't tell me about a knife.'

'Found this morning. In the garden.'

'Clare's garden? How come you missed that before.'

'I don't know . . .'

'Maybe someone put it there . . .'

'Oh, come off it, Sal. I've heard enough conspiracy theories for one day.'

'Just saying . . .'

'And Clare looks like the archetypal personality disorder. But she's not daft, Sal. She's an intelligent girl. More intelligent than we've given her credit for, I think. What if she killed him, hid the body and then came crying to us to make it look like she's the victim? Has she been starved, or is she anorexic? Is she emotionally unstable or emotionally manipulative? Is she terrified of being abandoned or a killer? What's to say she didn't plan this whole thing? Maybe she's bipolar, maybe she's not. Maybe she's a narcissist. Maybe she's a psycho.'

'And maybe she needs help!'

'Psychopaths who go around killing people don't deserve to be helped.'

'Some people would argue that point with you, Sue. They can't help how their brains are. But that's not her.'

'I'm not bothered about their brains, Sal. I'm bothered when they go around killing innocent members of the public.'

'And Clare's just that – an innocent member of the public who's been set up.'

'I hear she attacked Kitty again?' she says.

'You are actually kidding me,' I say. 'Kitty makes all that stuff up. She likes causing trouble.'

'It's been recorded that Clare acted highly aggressively towards her. Twice.'

'*I* act highly aggressively around Kitty. She's an animal.'

'I'm being pressured to charge her. Either that or have her sectioned.'

'What?'

'You heard. The boss says we need to get some results – after all the shite with Liverpool prison, I need to get some results in one of these cases.'

'Has anyone actually *looked* for Gareth, properly?'

'We're looking for a body now. If you'd seen what the Luminol spray picked up, you'd understand.'

'But you don't even know if it's his blood.'

'No, but the distribution pattern suggests a violent attack. It's type O. She's type A. It's human. It's the same blood on the knife and her prints are all over the handle.'

'Did she give you his name yet?'

'Gareth James doesn't come up anywhere. It's as though he never existed.'

'She has a locket that she stole from him. It's got his name in it.'

'Hang on, hang on, hang on. What locket?'

'She said she found a suitcase that was all packed. She said she told you that.'

'She did. Not about a locket, though. There's no sign of a case, by the way, so we don't really believe any of that.'

'She said that underneath everything, in the case, was this old tin box, and it had an American passport in it, in a different name, not his, she couldn't remember what, and other stuff, like the cutting from the paper, from when she handed the cheque thing over to the cancer charity, and she didn't know he had that either, and this gold locket, wrapped up in cotton wool, and she took it, and she hid it in the hem of her dressing gown, sewed it in.'

'How come she's kept that to herself? Something as important as that?'

'Well, A, she doesn't trust you, and B, she didn't realise there was an inscription. I would have thought she would have told you that today.'

'She didn't string two words together today.'

'Because she was scared, that's why.'

'Oh, come on, Sal. Emotional manipulation. Classic.'

'I've seen it.'

'You've seen the locket?'

'Yes, I've seen it. It's gold. Dunno if it's real gold, and it's a proper locket on a chain. I found the engraved bit.'

'If that's true, why hasn't anybody told us?'

'I haven't even spoken to you, not until now. And I only found out about it last night so stop giving me a hard time.'

'The inscription. It said his name. It's Gareth Marlon, born 1981.'

'And you didn't mention it at the beginning of this phone call because . . .?'

'I'm telling you now.'

'Goodbye.'

'Goodbye. Call me back . . .'

'Goodbye.'

CLICK

I've just sat down by the back window when my phone vibrates again.

'Have you found him?' I whisper. 'Admit it, I'm a genius.'

'What?' says a man's voice.

'Who's this?' I say, knowing it's not Terry, that's for sure; he doesn't sound anything like this.

'Sally, I need my money back,' says the voice. 'Meet me out the front.'

'What the fuck, Barney, are you kidding me?' I say. 'It's the middle of the night. Where'd you get my number from?'

'Meet me out front. I'm desperate!' He's starting to shout, and his voice is echoing around my sitting room.

'No, Barn. I can't. It's too dangerous. I'll get caught,' I hiss. 'You do realise, if I get caught giving you money it'll look like something else. Besides, I can't get out, you've seen the security here,' I say, and jab the phone off.

Soon as I put the phone on the table it starts vibrating again. I switch it to silent, pick up my mug and go to the window. I can see Barney's coat huddled into the bush of a house opposite.

The phone lights up again; I see Sue's name flash across the screen.

'Marlon?' she goes. 'Who calls their kid Marlon?'

'Marlon Brando's mum?'

'Apart from Marlon Brando's mum.'

CLICK

It's past 2 a.m.

I'd forgotten about Barney for a second. You see, the trouble with people like Barney, well junkies, really, is that they lie. And because they've fried their brains they forget what they've lied about. They are so busy not telling you something that they tell you it.

So if you had lost your dog, say, and there was this junkie who had stolen your dog, sold it and used the money to buy a wrap – not a chicken and mayo wrap like you get from Marks, you understand, but a wrap of drugs, that sort of wrap – and you didn't know he had stolen your dog, and you went over to him to ask him if he'd maybe seen your dog? Before you'd even said anything, even opened your mouth, he'd say to you, 'I promise I didn't steal your dog.' And if they were really off their heads, they'd say to you, 'I promise I didn't steal your dog, sell your dog then use the money to buy a wrap.'

My phone buzzes. Sue.

'What now?' I say.

'There was a Gareth Marlon Sullivan born in Delaware in 1981,' she says.

'Great!'

'But he disappeared in 2009. Believed to be dead. I've left a message with Pennsylvania State Police department.'

'Right,' I say.

'Another dead end,' she says.

'You could wait until the Pennsylvania State Police department call back.'

'Sal. You're going to have to come to terms with some things.'

'Oh, get off yer stage, Sue,' I say.

'You don't need to feel embarrassed. Psychopaths are very accomplished at gaining people's trust.'

'Psychopaths don't become so emotional that they pass out.'

'No, but they can hold their breath, Sal, long enough to look like they're passing out.'

'Don't be ridiculous.'

'Sal, *you* sound ridiculous, defending her when she's obviously guilty as fuck.'

I don't say anything.

'I'm not embarrassed,' I say.

'No,' she says.

'I'm not ridiculous either,' I say.

'No,' she says.

'I'm sorry, Sal,' she says. 'I'm going to bed.'

CLICK

The phone lights up again, immediately.

'I thought you'd gone to bed,' I say

'What was it you wanted to tell me about Terry?'

'What if he knows where I live?'

'What makes you think he might?'

'Nothing . . . It was something Kitty said.'

'Well, I wouldn't worry about her. She's not right in the head.'

'It's just that . . .'

'Now listen. Chapman told me Barney was outside the refuge the other day, when she dropped you off.'

'I'm worried, Sue.'

'Okay, well, if you're worried, I'm worried. You can't trust junkies. Stay away from the windows. We'll get some extra security down there.'

'I—'

'Talk to you in the morning,' she says as the call clicks off.

Forty-Eight

DS Clarke

Despite not having slept, Detective Sergeant DS Clarke gets into work early.

PC Chapman is already sitting at her desk, predicting a shit storm.

'Chapman!' snaps DS Clarke. 'Meeting, now, bring your coffee. Number one, check how PC Hall is getting on outside the refuge. I sent him up there last night. Sal got spooked.' She hangs her coat on the back of her office door, closing it behind her.

PC Chapman starts stabbing numbers into her phone.

'Not yet!' says DS Clarke. 'Number two, get Emma Tudor down here. I need to go over what happened with Clare yesterday. We need to decide if we've got enough to section her.'

PC Chapman nods and writes it down. Not the day to argue.

'She could be lying through her teeth,' says DS Clarke.

'You think?'

'You don't?'

'No, actually, I don't.'

'If you're so sure she's innocent, find some fucking evidence to support her,' says DS Clarke, flipping open her laptop. 'Go,' she snaps again.

'What are you not telling me about, Sal?'

'I'm not not telling you anything,' she shouts back through the door.

DS Clarke scans through her emails. Nothing from the Pennsylvania State Police department.

PC Chapman pokes her head back around the door.

'That was quick!' says DS Clarke, without looking up.

'I haven't spoken to her yet, but I just got this off Joanna,' says PC Chapman.

'What is it?' says DS Clarke, looking up.

'It's an incident log from Transport for London, for Clare's car. Taken in January this year.'

'And? Read it to me.'

'Mr Kalid Abbasi, Parking Officer, made a complaint, about a Lexus IS, registration blah, blah, blah. In Clare's name. Insured only for Clare.'

'What's the complaint?'

'*Enforcement Officer Notes.*

'*Lexus IS registration WR14 JGD*

'*At approximately 14.05, I was attempting to issue a penalty charge notice (PCN) to the above vehicle parked illegally in a residential permit area on Wimpole Mews, W1. There was a female seated in the front passenger seat of the car, but no driver was present in the vehicle, so I went ahead and issued the PCN, placing it under the wiper blades on the driver's side.*

'*At approximately 14.08 an unidentified male came up behind me as I was issuing a ticket for a car further up the road, and attacked me by kicking me in the thigh. He called me a "Paki bastard". He had what I believe to be an American or Canadian accent.*

'I asked the male attacker to "back off", which he did. The attacker was very angry. When the attacker opened the driver door to the car, I then asked him to give me his full name in order to process an official report. He slammed the door of the car and walked towards me in a threatening manner, telling me to "Fuck off home to Paki land." I believed he was going to kick me again so told him again to "back off".

'The attacker then opened the passenger door of his car, shouted at the woman to move over, pushed her, and sat in the passenger seat himself. The woman was young, possibly twenty. She switched on the engine and manoeuvred out of the space, with great caution. I then saw the male punch her in the side of the head. She braked hard, so the car lurched. Then the engine revved. I ran towards the car shouting "Get off her" but as I came alongside the car she drove off at speed. As she reached the turning into New Cavendish Street, I saw the attacker strike her on the left side of her head again, and her head banged against the driver's window.'

DS Clarke stares at PC Chapman

'Well, you'd better follow up with Mr Abussi.'

'Abbasi.'

'Yes, him.'

'Oh, hang on, hang on.'

'What?'

"Supporting Evidence: the officer's bodycam shows a male attempting to kick the officer but not actually making physical contact. Hence the offence was not followed up. The footage was archived.'

'Put Walker on it. We may actually have something.'

'Sarge.'

'This could finally make her story stand up. Chapman, call Walker. Oh, and call Mrs Henry. Make sure they're on alert.' DS Clarke calls after her.

Forty-Nine

Clare

There's the clank of bottles and a rustling of bags, then a sigh, before someone bounces onto my bed.

'You look like shit, but I need to find some good angles for my pictures.'

Kitty is in my room, AGAIN.

'How did you get in? Have you actually got another key?'

'You left my old one on the side the other day. I took it for safekeeping.' Like she's done me a favour. 'I've got you orange juice. And coffee.'

'What time is it?' I say, beginning to remember all the shit from yesterday. DS Clarke treating me like I'm the nut job. Feeling like a nut job.

'Seven,' she says. 'Ish.'

'What's ish mean?'

'Six.'

'Why'd you get up so early?' I say.

'S'not that early. McDonald's opens at five. I think this angle is nice,' she says, taking a picture of me, with a pillow half over my face.

'Don't take photos of me, Kitty.'

'Why not?' she says. The phone is clicking, over and over.

'Because I say so.'

'Because why?' she says.

'I don't need a reason,' I say, lashing out and whipping the phone out of her hand.

'And that's what I mean,' she says. 'Highly aggressive assault.'

I've had enough of her.

'If I was going to assault you, Kitty,' I say, kicking her off the bed, and landing on the floor next to her. Her head hits the skirting board and I put my hand around her neck.

'If I was going to assault you, Kitty,' I say again, 'highly aggressively. You'd be fucking dead, kid.' And I squeeze her throat between my fingers.

'Clare!' shouts Sally from the door.

'She's a fucking headcase,' I shout back, and jump back in bed.

'Psycho, I just want some pics,' Kitty whispers. She's staring in the mirror. Rubbing her neck. Looking at the red marks carefully, one by one, like they're trophies.

'Sally will do them, won't you, Sally?' I say.

'How're you feeling, Clare?' says Sally.

'Like shit.'

'They sedated you. You'll feel like shit for a while,' she says.

'Clare, if you'd just take some pictures, I'll go,' Kitty says, picking herself up. 'She was only play-fighting.' She grins at Sally. A fake grin.

'Yeah, I was only play-fighting,' I say, rolling my eyes at Sally, thinking I do actually want to kill her . . .

'Careful, Clare,' Sally says, like she's thinking something.

Then she turns to Kitty.

'That's not what you'll tell Mrs H, though, is it? In about, what, seven minutes . . .?' says Sally, looking at an imaginary watch on her wrist and turning on her heel. 'Try and shut up. Both of you. Some of us are trying to sleep. I haven't had a wink all night.'

She wraps a cardigan around her shoulders and peers out of the window to the street below. Then she checks her phone and disappears back into her own room.

'Jesus Christ, Kitty,' I say. 'OK. Stand in front of the wall. Then go away.'

If she'd just fuck off with her stupid pictures, I could go back to bed. I've got the headache from hell. I've got a policewoman trying to stitch me up. I've got so much shit . . .

She stands where she'd stood before, next to the bed. The light is clean and bright.

This time her face is bare – she does look better without makeup, but she looks about twelve.

'He says I look better with no makeup,' she says.

'He's right,' I say.

Click.

'Like a blank canvas waiting for someone to turn me into a masterpiece,' she says, checking her pout in my mirror.

Click.

'Said I'd be open to interpretation without makeup. Mario likes to see the real girl,' she says.

Click.

'Which agency?' I say, thinking it all sounds like the usual fashion bullshit.

'Storm,' she says. 'He asked me if I have a passport. If I like to travel. If I'm happy travelling. I said I do, and I am. It's easy to get a passport, right? I mean, like, I can get one tomorrow. He says he can get me out to Milan, tomorrow. Says he has this friend who owes him a favour, and he'll help me because I'm really special. He said that. That I'm really special. Asked me if I speak Italian. I said I do.'

'Do you?'

'Of course. I have a friend who's Italian.'

'But do you speak it?' I say, flicking a piece of blonde hair out of her face.

'Not fluently, but nearly fluently. I mean, it can't be that hard. Stefano is one of the stupidest friends I've got. What's that on your chest?' she says, changing the subject.

'It's just a scratch,' I say, covering it with my T-shirt.

'Is that one of the burns?' she says.

'I don't know,' I say, conscious of the fact that my lower legs are uncovered.

'What about that bruise?' she says. 'How did you do that again?'

'I don't know,' I say, 'just clumsy, I guess.'

'Haven't you gone yet?' says Sally, coming out of the bathroom.

'Everyone here says you did all that to yourself,' says Kitty.

'Yeah,' I say, wondering who everyone is, in Kitty world.

'Yeah, like you deliberately burned yourself just to get in here.'

'Right,' I say.

'And that you killed your husband.'

Sally pushes open the bedroom door.

'I heard that you fucked half of Manchester then cried rape!' says Sally. 'So why don't you fuck off.'

Nice one, Sally.

'Hey, Kitty, let me ask you one thing,' I say, as she's trying to pick up all her stuff with Sally pushing her out the door. 'When you go and get your McDonald's in the morning, do you get a sausage and egg McMuffin and then plant the wrapper in the bin and say it's Sarah's?'

'Yeah,' she says. 'So?' she says.

'So that whole story about Sarah getting McDonald's every morning was just you making it up.'

'So?' she says again. 'She's fat, ain't she? Must be shoving something down her throat.'

'You're weird,' I shout as she leaves.

From behind the front door of the flat, I hear her shout, 'Yeah, but I didn't kill my husband then set myself on fucking fire, did I?'

Sally's bedroom door slams. I wonder if she's cross with me because Kitty woke her up.

I try to go back to sleep but all I can think about is all the things I'd wished I'd said to Susan.

Like how she was underestimating Gareth.

Psychos are clever.

They've entirely deluded themselves – makes it easier to delude everyone else.

It's well after lunch when I surface again.

The sedative is wearing off.

Sally is in the bathroom.

I would have had a shower but I can wait.

'You want a pizza?' I shout through the door.

'Thank God you didn't suggest Pot Noodles,' she says. 'And how about we get a couple of salads as well, or we could go down to Marks.'

'What about Gareth?' I say.

'Or Terry?' she says.

She thinks I'm only thinking of myself. 'Sorry, Sally. I didn't mean to be selfish,' I say. 'It was all so shit yesterday. I don't even know what happened . . .'

'I'm starving,' she says. 'Let's get a pizza and a tomato salad and a spinach salad.'

'And some dough balls,' I say, 'with garlic butter.'

We sit at the back of the dining room because it's sunny.

And it was warmer for a change and we would have left the window open but there's a cold breeze in the shade and two of the children are kicking a ball around in the garden, yelling at each other.

It isn't a proper football. They aren't allowed a proper football in case it breaks the glass.

The thing with pizza is that you always want one and then as soon as you have had one slice, you're full.

'I can't believe I let you talk me into a vegetarian again and now you don't want any more,' says Sally, shoving the salad across the table. 'Eat some of that before you waste away in front of my very eyes.' But she keeps staring at her phone and slamming it back down on the table face down, like she doesn't want me to see it and she keeps not looking me in the eye and I wonder . . .

'Have I done something to upset you, Sally?' I say.

Something's not right.

'No, love. You haven't.'

'If I had, would you tell me?' I say.

'Sure I would,' she says. 'Now eat some salad.'

The front door buzzes.

Then the inner door clicks.

Kitty storms down the hallway, sounding like she's going to murder someone.

We sink back in our seats and Sally does that face like an 'eek' emoji.

Last thing we need is a Kitty attack.

She storms up the stairs without coming into the dining room.

'You really have to watch what you're eating,' Sally says. 'If you're hypoglycemic you should see the doctor to make sure you're not diabetic, because fainting is definitely one of the signs, and I read in a magazine that if you don't eat regularly, then you can feel faint but if you have glucose tablets on you, then as soon as you feel—'

Kitty comes crashing back down the stairs.

'Why are you hiding down here?' she shouts. 'You're deliberately avoiding me!'

'Calm down, Kitty,' Sally says. 'We're not—'

'Not you, HER,' she yells, pointing at me.

I stand up, with a dough ball still in my mouth. I switch it to the inside of my cheek.

Mrs Henry comes running out of her office.

'Kitty, what is all this about?' she says, trying to slow Kitty down by holding her arm. 'Kitty!'

'DON'T ASSAULT ME OR I'LL HAVE YOU ARRESTED!' she shrieks at Mrs Henry.

Mrs Henry backs away, behind Kitty, then motions to the two security guys with a nod of her head.

Kitty has her mobile in her hand and is waggling it in my face.

'You did this *deliberately*!' she says. 'You bitch!' She's right up to the table now, shoving her phone in my face.

Sally hasn't moved from her seat.

'What have we done now?' she says quietly. Calmly.

'Not you, her!' she says again. 'Axel doesn't like *any* of the pictures of me.'

'Come along, Kitty,' says Mrs Henry.

'Says I have a common face. Common! Says that in Milan they like more "editorial" looking girls.'

The two security guards are now standing behind Mrs Henry.

'Says I'd do better in Manchester, where they do all the online shit. Or Bradford. Fucking Bradford. Who goes to fucking Bradford?'

One of the security guards starts moving towards her.

'And then guess what he says?' she shouts.

Mrs Henry has her hand on Kitty's elbow.

'He says "who's this girl, she's amazing!" This girl has a real future. And he's looking at the pictures of you. In bed. Looking like a fucking beached whale. With your face all blotchy like a junkie.'

Mrs Henry guides her backwards, slowly, and she doesn't even seem to notice. The security guard is on the other side. She doesn't notice that either.

'And he says, "tell me where she is, she's just what they're looking for in Milano." He said Milano like he's fucking Italian. What the fuck does he know?'

They're still gently guiding her backwards towards the stairs.

'I said to him, you don't want her. She's wacko. She's a proper psycho,' Kitty shouts from the bottom of the stairs. 'I said to him, she killed her husband,' she yells. 'So, don't expect a contract any day soon, COCO. It is COCO, isn't it? Cos you ain't gonna get one. PSYCHO.'

She's still screaming as they turn the corner and help her up the stairs.

I slowly remove the dough ball from my mouth and leave it wet on the table.

Fifty

Sally

I've let her go upstairs on her own.

I don't feel like pizza either.

I empty the salad into the box, pick up the soggy dough ball and go into the kitchen.

Part of me feels like I want to scoop her up as if I'm her mum or something, and part of me feels like I never want to see her again.

When she was sitting on top of Kitty, I thought she was actually going to kill her. If she's playing me, she's doing a really great job. Maybe Sue's right, maybe she is just acting the emotional victim. If I told Sue what she'd done to Kitty, she'd definitely get her sectioned.

If I told Sue what Barney had done to me, she'd definitely get Barney banged up, and throw away the key. And me sectioned for not telling her. But I'm not just going to throw him under a bus. He's got a good heart – for all his problems.

My phone vibrates and I'm expecting my five hundredth missed call from Barney when I realise it's Sue.

'We've had to pull out PC Hall from outside the refuge,' she barks, as if she's in a hurry. 'I just haven't got anyone available right now, Sal. I'm getting pressure from upstairs. But I've spoken to Mrs Henry and she's put the security team on high alert. That should be fine for now. I'll get someone else down there later. They'll be there before it gets dark.'

'Thanks, Sue, I'm not going anywhere.'

'Keep away from the windows.'

'I am keeping away from the windows,' I say, with my nose pressed up against one, drawing pictures in the condensation from my breath.

'I hear our Kitty has had a meltdown,' she says, changing the subject, thank God.

'She's actually mental,' I say, walking into one of the empty rooms and closing the door, thinking: at least she didn't try and strangle anyone like Clare did.

'How's everything else?' she says.

'Same old, same old,' I say. 'I've been emailed some stuff from work. That will keep me busy at least.'

'It won't last forever,' she says. 'He's not smart enough to stay underground for too long.'

'Hey, Sue, I was thinking. That journal you had. Did you ever get anywhere with it?'

'Not really,' she says. 'We're going back over it. Oh, but there's some traffic warden report we got from TFL this morning about a man refusing to give his full name in January and the registration number matches Clare's car. We're following it up. We might have some evidence to support Clare's story at long last. But why'd you ask about the journal? I need it to help urgently, Sal.'

'OK, well, the thing that struck me about the journal was not so much what was in it – which was mainly rubbish, by the way – but how it was written. Been nagging in my brain. The style kept changing, so one minute it was official sounding, another minute it was like emotional first-person stuff. When I read exam essays, I have to look out for that kind of stuff. When a voice changes. I mean, you do realise he could've just nicked the whole lot off the Internet, don't you? It's dead easy to check; all you do is use this bit of software and it checks it automatically – it's called Turnitin. Get one of your lot to have a look.'

'What's it called again?'

'Turnitin, one word like T.U.R.N.I.T.I.N, but you say it like it's "turn it in".'

'OK, great, thanks.'

A phone rings in the background.

'I've gotta get that,' says Sue. 'Call you later.'

I go up to our flat but there's no sound from Clare's room and half of me is convinced she's thrown herself out the window. I'm determined not to mother her, so I last for at least fifteen minutes before I poke my head round the door and see she's just fast asleep. That's all I need to know.

I do some work, and when I can't stand reading any more terrible teenage grammar, I go for a cuppa.

In the kitchen, Derek, the older security guy is making a coffee.

'Been told to keep an eye out for your ex.' He winks at me. 'Be OK love.'

I take a mug down from the cupboard.

'How's the boyfriend?'

I feel my cheeks getting hot and quickly squeeze out the teabag and throw it in the bin.

'Never thought I'd get a blush out of you,' he shouts as he heads back to the desk.

'He's not my boyfriend. Hey, Derek . . .' I go up to the desk, scanning the road outside.

'Did you, by any chance, give Barney my number?'

'Who am I to stand in the path of true love?' he replies. 'But don't tell the boss, eh?'

'No, I won't tell the boss,' I say, wondering how much cash Barney would have got for that piece of information.

Prashi is late with the girls again but no one is really that worried because the news is on the TV and Donald Trump has said something stupid again and the press are acting like a pack of rabid dogs. Aiysha is knitting, with four needles at the same time, and I don't even begin to understand what that's all about, Sian has a pile of magazines on her lap that she's nicked out of the doctor's surgery and has settled in for the night with an out-of-date Easter egg from Marks and a box of Maltesers, Abigail has her laptop open and is shouting at her emails, Sarah is studying a book about diets and Big Debbie has lined up seven bottles of nail polish, four nail files and a bottle of pink nail polish remover along with a fat bag of pastel-col-oured cotton-wool balls, all in straight lines, and is slathering Shea Body Butter onto her hands like she's trying to preserve Tutankhamun's mother or something.

'I don't know why *this* even constitutes national news,' says Aiysha. 'That's what I don't understand. There are some very real things going on in the world at present, and the lead headline on the six o'clock news is about an overprivileged chinless wonder with a massive sense of entitlement marrying some American.'

'Isn't she divorced?' says Sian, not looking up, as the footage shows some supermodel type stepping off a private jet in giant sunglasses and a white skirt that hasn't creased despite her hav-ing flown halfway around the world; if it were me, I'd have spilt my tea all over it before we'd even taken off.

'She *looks* divorced,' says Sarah, picking something out of her back teeth with a match.

'How does someone look divorced?' growls Big Debbie from her table by the window.

'In fairness, she does look like she's been round the block a few times,' says Abigail, looking over the top of her screen.

'You look like you've been round the block a few times,' says Big Debbie, leaning around so she can see the TV.

'I'm not marrying into the monarchy,' says Abigail. 'Well, not yet anyway.'

'They wouldn't have you,' snorts Sian.

'It'll be no life for her,' I say, 'because she'll never get a moment's peace from the press, for driving the wrong kind of car, or getting her hair done wrong, or wearing a dress that makes her look too fat or too thin, or . . .'

'Oh yeah, sounds like a fucking nightmare to me,' says Big Debbie. 'All them dresses. All them parties. All that fucking hairspray. I'd be lost to know what to do with myself. Oh, Prashi's back.'

She must have walked past the window. The front door buzzes. It buzzes longer than usual, but I guess Prashi has lost one of the girls to a dandelion in the front garden that needs blowing or a shoelace that's come undone and needs tying, or something that little girls do when they don't really want to come home yet, because it's way more fun out in the sun than it is stuck in here, in the dark cold shadows.

'And now to international news . . .' the newsreader says.

From where we are sitting in the TV room, you can't see the front door, or the lobby, or the door into reception, but you kind of get used to the sounds of what's normal – like when the buzzer stops buzzing, it's usual to hear the inner door click as the security boys release the bolt, then the sound of voices returning, usually laughing or complaining, sad to be back, glad to be back. Safe and sound.

But the buzzer has buzzed for too long.

And then there's a pause.

Then a click.

Then silence.

It feels wrong.

Suddenly, none of us are watching TV anymore.

Mrs H is walking backwards from reception, slowly, slowly, white as a sheet, so she is level with the entrance to the TV room, her left hand, the one nearest the doorway, slightly raised, hand outstretched, like she's mentally saying 'stay, stay, stay'.

'Well,' comes a voice, a strong accent, a man's voice. 'Ain't this nice!'

I haven't heard that voice in over twenty years, but it still turns my blood to ice.

'AIN'T. THIS. NICE.'

Everyone turns to look at me.

Abigail is nearest the door and can see furthest up the hall. She closes her laptop and her face falls into the shadows.

'So. Where's my girl? Anybody seen my girl? Five foot two, eyes of blue,' he sings. 'You in charge are you, lady? You seen my Sally, have you? Sally! SALLY!'

Mrs H stands there, stiff as a board.

There's a shuffling sound and she takes half a step backwards.

'He's got Jay, Prashi's youngest,' whispers Abigail. 'Prashi and her eldest are with security, but he's got Jay and he's got a knife.'

Big Debbie picks up the control and switches off the TV. The blue light in the room disappears.

'Who's in there?' he says. '*Has anybody seen my gal,*' he sings.

'He's coming. He's got a knife against her neck,' whispers Abigail again.

'SALLY, DARLIN'. YOU IN THERE, DARLIN'?' he shouts.

I'm stuck to the chair. I can't move, but silently the other women move to the corner opposite Abigail, the other side of the doorway. Aiysha, Sian, Sarah. Big Debbie sits staring at her nail polish bottles like she's in a trance.

Mrs H is still keeping her hand where it is, 'stay, stay, stay'.

'There's no one here,' says Mrs H. 'You've come at a time when the residents are at a class. Now just let Jay come over here to me. If you let—'

'What you think? I just got off the banana boat?' says Terry. 'SAAAALLLLLYYYYYY.'

'About ten feet,' whispers Abigail again, edging further back into the shadows.

Big Debbie stares at me. Then shakes her head.

'He'll kill you whatever you do,' she whispers.

I get up. It's now or never. Just do it, I tell myself.

'THERE SHE IS!' shouts Terry as I walk through the archway into the hall.

Mrs H goes paler, stiffer.

'Five foot two, eyes of blue, HAS ANYBODY SEEEEEN MY GIRRRRRL,' he sings. Jay's eyes are huge under her headscarf and the knife he is holding is horizontal against her throat. She stares at me, two big tears appearing in the corners of her eyes, and when she shuts her eyes tight they fall, leaving shiny channels down her dusty face.

'Pleased to see me, Sal?' he says, stopping suddenly. 'You don't look pleased to see me, girl. Still look like my girl. Only just though, eh, Sal? Twenty years hasn't been kind, has it, love? Put on a few pounds—'

'Look, um, Terry,' I say.

'Look, um, Terry,' he says. 'Look, um, Terry. Seriously, Sal? Is that the best you've got for me? Your husband? After twenty years? Twenty years, ladies and gentlemen! I ask you!' he says and spins around to check Prashi and the security guards are still behind him.

'Ex-husband,' I whisper.

'Oh? Ex-husband, is it, Sal? Ex-husband! You'll always be my wife, Sal. Always. You mean the world to me. Couldn't wait to see you again. Number one priority you were on my bucket list of things to do when I got out. Number one. Visit Sal. Say Hi to Sal. Go and give Sal what she's got coming to her.'

'Could you just let Jay go?' says Mrs H. 'She's just a child. Her mother—'

'Shut up, bitch,' says Terry, without taking his eyes off me.

'Jay is eleven years—'

'I said shut up, BITCH,' he says, jamming the knife harder against Jay's neck. More tears fall from her eyes.

'Does this remind you of anything, Sal?' he says. 'Does it, girl? White Wine Hayley, eh? Remember her. What a good-time girl she was. Weren't she, Sal? Always had one-too-many that White Wine Hayley. Lovely blonde hair as I remember. Much like your hair was. At the time, eh, Sal. Not now, Sal. Don't look like that now, does it? Bet you wish you'd died instead of her, eh? Least then we'd remember you when you was pretty. Not like now. You look like an old sow.'

He spins round again.

The two security guys look afraid. Derek is there. His face is grey and drawn.

'You didn't press the alarm, did you?' says Terry. They shake their heads, the younger one and Derek. 'Cos you know I'll kill her before the police get here, don't ya? And then I'll kill you both. Understand?'

One security guy nods. Then the other.

'Can I ask you?' he says, backing up, fast, with Jay's head still pushed against his stomach and the knife against her neck. 'Can I just ask you two, man to man, as it were,' and he's still backing up so he's level with the security desk. 'Do you think Sally here, with the grey hair, do you think she looks like a fat old sow?'

The two security guys look blank.

'Do you? *Do you think she looks like a fat old sow?*'

They nod.

'Say it then. Say, "Sally looks like a fat old sow".'

One of them mumbles something.

'Now, who heard that?' he says, pushing Jay forwards again. 'Did anyone hear that. Hands up if you heard that?'

No one moves.

'See, gentlemen. No one heard that. Let's see if anyone in this room down here heard that.'

Abigail goes out of the TV room, hands up, like she's in an episode of *NYPD Blue*.

'So! There's another one! Who do we have here, then?'

'Just me,' she says. 'And I definitely heard everything.'

'Don't play the smart arse with me. Anyone else hiding in there?' he says. She flicks her eyes to me.

'There's no one else. Just me. And the telly,' she says.

He stares at her and she shrugs.

'Go on then, Sal. You back into there. Think we need some quiet time, you and me, and this lovely little girl. So young and innocent . . . bit like White Wine Hayley, really, eh, Sal?'

As I back into the TV room again, the girls are all lined up against the side of the wall, flat, petrified. Apart from Big Debbie. Big Debbie is crouched over, right by the door. I've got to admit, at first I thought she was having some kind of seizure or something, but then I see, out of the corner of my eye, that she has her arms above her head, and she's watching for Jay's feet as Terry edges her in through the archway. Jay can see Big Debbie now; her eyes swivel sideways, then to me, then back to Big Debbie again, like she doesn't understand, and all I want to tell her is it's all going to be OK, but even I don't really believe that, can't really believe that. Terry is staring at me, right into my soul, to see if I know something he doesn't, something that will give it all away.

And then I see Clare over Terry's shoulder, standing on the stairs, facing me, looking like the girl with the bare feet, the desperate girl in the police station, hair stuck to her head, rings under her eyes, dressing gown wrapped around her tightly, confused, afraid, tears streaming down her face, with a vacant look, as if, at that very precise moment, she's just stopped caring about anything else.

'Don't die, Sally! Don't die, Sally! DON'T DIE, SALLY!' she screams. She can see Terry and the knife and Jay.

Terry freezes and slowly twists his head.

She drops down one step, as though she's in a daze, and then another, like she's sleepwalking, and I follow her with my eyes, and she keeps on screaming and howling like there's an animal inside her. Terry drags his eyes from her to me and back again. And Mrs H is moving in slow motion towards her, and she's still screaming . . .

Then right next to me, there's a click sound.

Big Debbie. She makes this weird kind of click with the side of her mouth.

At the same time as I look down to see where the click is coming from, I catch sight of Abigail's laptop in Big Debbie's hands, grasped tightly, her fingers turning white against the harsh purple of her nail varnish.

Terry turns back, contorts his mouth into his usual sneer, pushes Jay that extra inch into the TV room and in one movement Big Debbie brings herself up and around like a fucking shot putter, and puts all her weight behind that laptop, smashing it into Terry's forehead before he's even managed to see it coming. His neck snaps back and his legs fly out from beneath him, throwing Jay forwards into my outstretched arms, as his body smacks to the floor and a dark pool begins to form around his head.

Silence.

Even Clare shuts up.

A bubble of blood appears between his parted lips then pops leaving a spray of drops on the grey stubble around his mouth.

An alarm sounds and in the distance a siren whines, gradually getting louder as it approaches.

The security guards start shouting into their phones.

Jay starts to sob and Prashi starts to run and Clare starts to fall and Mrs H goes to catch her.

'You fucking broke my laptop,' says Abigail, crouching down and putting her arms around Big Debbie's shoulders.

Big Debbie falls into her.

'I really hate it when men say you're fat,' she says.

Fifty-One

DS Clarke

The Wedding Boutique in Chiswick High Road is triple-fronted. The window frames are arched and painted white. There are two front doors, each with brass door handles. So far, so very weddingy.

A woman in leather trousers and a fringed suede jacket staggers up to the left-hand door. DS Clarke clocks the five-inch stilettoes. The pavement is raised at that point, with stone steps and a handrail leading to a handful of designer shops. There's a tree, one of those London plane trees, with overgrown roots, so the concrete slabs around it are uneven. Not the ideal path for five-inch stilettoes.

She's busy with a bunch of keys, undoing locks at the bottom, the top and the middle of the door. Her shiny beige leather-clad bottom is exposed like a full moon.

DS Clarke has a particular opinion on middle-aged women in leather trousers and high heels.

'Ah, Mrs Meering,' says DS Clarke, trotting up the steps in her Doc Martens.

The woman straightens, pulls down her jacket at the back and turns.

'Ms,' she says, pushing open the door.

Ms Meering has thinning fair hair with highlights, lowlights and a lot of mousse to give it lift at the roots. She's had work.

'I'm DS Clarke,' says DS Clarke. 'I believe you've already met one of my colleagues, DC Walker. I just have a few more questions . . .'

'Look, I know you people work incredibly hard . . .' Cheshire accent. Can't miss it.

'. . . it's just that I have clients in half an hour and the heating's been off all night, and my assistant Sandra isn't here today and there's no milk. So, can you perhaps refer back to whatever your constable got from me and not waste my very valuable time? No offence. Sorry to seem rude,' she says, beginning to close the door behind her.

She's missed with her lipstick. She has a wobbly line around the edge her lips and some sparkly gloss in the middle. Some of the sparkly gloss is on her teeth. DS Clarke rubs her own lips together. Lip salve she's had since at least 2010.

'My Detective Constable did make some useful notes, Ms Meering – can I call you Colleen? – but there are a couple of things outstanding, and I'm quite sure you'd much prefer to answer here rather than down at the station.'

Her hands fall to her sides, and she exhales noisily.

'Look, Police Lady Clarke. I'm done with answering questions about Gareth . . .'

Gareth already!

'*Detective Sergeant* Clarke. Actually, Colleen, my questions were about Clare Chambers *and* Gareth James, but since you seem to be so forthcoming about *Gareth,* perhaps we can start there. May I sit?' she says, and eases herself onto a chintz, over-stuffed cushion in the window seat.

Colleen Meering looks at DS Clarke blankly.

'Is this the dress that Clare Chambers bought?' DS Clarke taps on her phone and shows her the image, Clare grinning under a veil, Gareth looking over her shoulder, all smiles. Only the shoulder of the dress is showing.

'That's the dress she selected, yes,' says Colleen. But there's something in the way she said it.

'So, they put in an order and collected the dress at a later date?'

'Well no, that's what should have happened.'

'But?' says DS Clarke, giving her an encouraging fake smile. 'You did them a favour, did you? Is that it?'

Her phone starts buzzing. She ignores it.

'Yes. Kind of,' says Ms Meering.

'And why would you do that?'

Ms Meering is blushing. 'You're blushing, Colleen. Why's that?'

She's silent.

'Did they pay you in cash? Was that it? Under the counter?' says DS Clarke.

'No,' she says. Too quick. 'No, he didn't pay. Not even a deposit.'

'So, they didn't order a dress.'

'No, they did order a dress, but he cancelled it. Asked me not to say,' she whispers.

DS Clarke shakes her head like she can't believe her ears.

'Hold on,' she says. 'So there never was a dress. Just a dress she tried on.'

'Um, yes.'

'And Gareth told you not to tell anyone, if you were asked? Is that it?'

'Yes, that's it. That's it!' she says emphatically.

DS Clarke raises her eyebrows.

'And why would you agree to do that, Colleen?' she says. 'You're an upstanding member of the community, I'm sure. Why would someone like you, Ms Colleen Meering, living in Chiswick, running a profitable little business, with a nice three-storey overlooking Ravenscourt Park, why would you agree to tell a lie to the police. Which, let me remind you, is a criminal offence?'

Colleen Meering is staring at her feet. Her face is the colour of a beetroot. And when she raises her head and looks at DS Clarke, it's clear that she's about to cry.

'He made me promise,' she barely whispers.

'In return for what, Colleen?' says DS Clarke softly.

She says nothing. And then she lifts her chin, and juts it out.

'Opportunities like Gareth don't come along every day, DS Clarke,' she says. 'I'm sure you understand that. Frankly, he was too good-looking to turn down.'

DS Clarke's phone buzzes.

'He was charming.' Ms Meering shrugs.

'That's it?'

'Very attentive. Unusually so.'

DS Clarke's phone goes off again. She clicks through to the call. It's Mrs Henry.

She listens and her heart starts to race.

'Tell me she's all right!' she says into the phone. 'Ms Meering, I've got to go.' And runs down the steps back to her car.

Fifty-Two

Clare

Mrs Henry says it's wrong to celebrate somebody being cracked on the head. Specially if it's your ex-husband.

Sally says it's every bloody reason to celebrate. She says she's gonna go off to get some sparkling wine.

Because she can now.

Because she's free to do what she wants.

Free to go home too, if she wants to.

But Detective Sergeant Clarke says she has to wait. Says you never know where his brothers might be hiding. Right outside for all we know.

Says she'll get PC Chapman to get the Prosecco.

Says it's not really police business, going out buying Prosecco for refuge residents. But that she can turn a blind eye, 'Just this once, mind.'

'Given the circs,' she says.

The ambulance has been and gone.

They tried to say I had to go. To get checked.

But I was like, fuck that.

I'm not missing out on all the fun.

And Detective Sergeant Clarke said that wasn't really the attitude.

And that a serious crime had been committed.

And Sally nodded sombrely.

And then nudged me in the ribs when Susan wasn't looking.

We've all been herded into the dining room.

Mrs Henry is waiting outside the TV room with a bucket of soapy water and a mop to get the bloodstain off the floor. But there's some bloke with a flash camera taking pictures of it from every possible angle.

'Crime scene!' he'd barked at her.

Suddenly we've all gone quiet.

'FUCK ME SIDEWAYS,' shouts Big Debbie, out of nowhere. We all nearly die on the spot.

'I've only gone and broken a fucking nail,' she says.

'You've broken a fucking nail?' says Sian.

'On that fucking laptop!' says Big Debbie.

'Is that it? I thought at least the Pope must have died.'

'I'm going to have to file the lot down and start again,' she tuts.

'It was worth it,' says Sarah, trying to join in.

'I don't think he were worth my nail, actually, that scumbag,' growls Big Debbie.

'We must thank the Lord for small mercies,' says Sarah.

'Jesus, once you and the Lord get together we know we're all in trouble,' says Big Debbie.

'I wish they'd hurry up with that Prosecco,' says Abi. 'I'm parched.'

We fall silent again. Sit there, in a daze, while the police buzz in and out of the security gates, their heels click, click, clicking up and down the hall.

Cerise, Rose and Magenta have all been cordoned off by Mrs Henry, so the police can conduct their interviews.

Everyone will be interviewed.

That's what she says. Before they've had their Prosecco, she says.

Whatever you did see or didn't see, it's all important, she says.

And another room has been given over to the ambulance service. The one at the back, Fuchsia. Everyone is being checked for shock, she says.

'You come first,' says Mrs Henry, looking at me as though I'm the biggest victim.

'Don't you think . . .' I mouth at her, and nod my head sideways towards Sally.

Sally has turned puce.

She's not said a word for half an hour, at least.

'She's in shock,' she whispers, nodding, putting her arm around Sally's shoulders and gently helping her out of her chair.

'Come along, Sally. Let's get you checked first,' she says.

Sally's tears are falling like rain.

Terry got carted off in the ambulance.

Under police guard.

Prashi and the girls have gone too.

And Big Debbie's a hero.

He's not dead or anything.

Terry's not.

Well, not yet he's not.

Everyone agrees it couldn't have happened to a more deserving man.

When PC Chapman gets back with three bottles of Prosecco, I go to the kitchen with Abigail to find some cups.

It's dark in the kitchen.

We don't bother to turn the lights on.

Somehow it feels better in the dark.

Different to how it's ever felt before.

Safer.

'Plastic beakers or mugs?' says Abigail, standing in front of the open kitchen cupboard with her hands on her hips.

'Mugs,' I say, noticing the poster and the scribble in the corner. 'Wasn't totally the same shit today, was it?' I say to Abs.

'Nope,' says Abs. 'That was totally different shit.'

There's a felt tip on the side. One of Prashi's girls must have left it there.

I kneel up on the counter and scribble out the comment. Then line the mugs up on a tray.

And then the door swings open suddenly, and bangs against the wall, making the kitchen cupboard doors slam, and the mugs on the tray rattle against each other.

'Is Sal in here with you?' shouts Susan. She looks like she's about to explode.

'She's in with the nurse,' I say.

'I'll give her "in with the nurse",' she says, and swivels on her heel.

By the time I've reached the kitchen door, Susan has disappeared into Fuchsia, and the nurse, looking slightly crestfallen, is coming out.

'I don't care if she's in . . .' I hear before the door slams shut.

There's the sound of raised voices.

We can all hear them and catch snippets of sentences '. . . Barney . . . Ryan . . . Heroin . . . Terry . . .'

So much for soundproofing.

Mrs Henry opens the door a fraction.

'SHUT IT,' shouts Susan from inside.

No one feels like Prosecco anymore.

Then the door clicks open.

'I told you to steer clear of him, didn't I?' she shouts. 'You and your little romance.'

'It's not a romance!' shouts Sally from inside the room.

'Mrs Henry!' Susan yanks open the door and strides into the hallway.

Mrs Henry is standing right next to the door, like a sentinel. She looks like she's about to kill herself.

'In!' shouts Susan, slamming the door behind her, but the door misses the catch and creeps open again, and more of the conversation leaks into the hall.

'Mrs Henry. Were your ears burning?' shouts DS Clarke.

'Were they? No. What were you saying? I thought . . .' Mrs Henry murmurs, flustered.

'What would you like to tell me, Mrs Henry, about Barney?' says DS Clarke.

'He's just a bum, you know, a junkie who's squatting at the end of the road,' says Mrs Henry.

'Oh, believe me,' shouts Susan. 'I know *exactly* who Barney is. What I'm asking is why he's been hanging around here, spending time with this idiot? I've just been informed by the security team that he was trying to hug her yesterday. Didn't I tell you to watch out for them? Didn't I expressly ask you to keep me informed?'

The door opens wider and now I can see Sally and Mrs Henry sitting, looking like they're in the headteacher's office.

Mrs Henry looks up. 'He's been hanging around trying to look through the windows. He turned up yesterday afternoon. To see Sally. He was off his face. Very agitated. Sally came to the door—'

'It's too late to tell me now!' shouts Susan.

Mrs Henry's eyes widen. Then she looks at her hands.

'We know that one of them, probably Barney, was asked by Terry where Sally was living,' she says quietly.

'NO SHIT SHERLOCK,' yells Susan.

'And you were going to tell me this when?'

Mrs Henry shrugs like a schoolgirl.

'And Barney has been hanging around here.' And you didn't formally report that. EITHER! all day

Sally has buried her face in a bundle of Kleenex.

'Surely the issue wasn't about Barney, it was about Terry,' says Mrs Henry.

'And I thought I was running this case!' says Susan, looking out of the door to see who is listening – all of us – and slamming the door shut.

Five minutes later it slams open again and Susan marches down the hall to security where Derek's eyes are widening by the second. He stands up. To attention.

'And Barney was waiting outside tonight, wasn't he? You saw him. You knew he was there!'

Derek is staring at the floor. Sally and Mrs Henry are limping down the hall after Susan.

'If he *was* there, maybe it was because he was trying to stop Terry,' whispers Sally, starting to cry again.

Mrs Henry is trying to console her.

She may as well have thrown a grenade with that little line. Sue looked like she was going to explode.

'I'm furious with you both,' says Susan. 'You put your own lives in danger. You put everyone else's lives in danger! What did I tell you both about trusting addicts?'

'It might not have been. . .' says Sally.

'Oh, shut up Sal. Stop being so fucking naive. C'mon, Chapman. Let's go and find out what exactly Mr Barney Pickard has been up to!' she shouts.

She strides off down the hall, like she's got the devil in her pants.

Fifty-Three

Sally

You could've heard a pin drop when Sue slammed out of the front door, seriously. I mean, we were all in a complete state of shock cos none of us had ever seen her lose her rag like that before.

I'm not saying she shouldn't have lost her rag, because she's right that I put them all at risk and I'm sorry that I put them all in that situation. But she's a policewoman. Just saying . . .

'Look,' I say to everyone in the TV room when they let us back into it and Mrs H has washed the floor, 'I'm sorry.'

They're all there, all of them; Big Debbie with her pots of nail polish lined up like nothing has happened, Abigail and Sian, looking thick as thieves as usual, Prashi and the girls, who've had enough for one lifetime to be sure, and little Clare, tear-stained and dirty, looking like a hopeless child.

'Look,' repeats Big Debbie, slapping her file on the table, 'I don't know about anyone else, but I don't get to smack some murdering bastard in the face every day,' she says and she thinks for a minute then smiles a broad smile '. . . *and get away with it!*'

Everyone laughs and Abigail starts clapping, quietly mind, but clapping, and then we all start clapping.

'I'm quite sure that Chief Constable Whatnot is right to be having a total blowout hissy-fit about something-or-other that none of us quite understand, least of all our Sally here, *but . . .*' she waits for the noise to settle down '. . . I, for one, would like a *drink!*'

We all cheer, and Abigail grabs a bottle and starts unpeeling the foil top. Mrs Henry pops her head around the corner and tells us to shush but gives us a wink, and Sarah is handing around mugs. In no time we've all got a drink in our hands.

'When you were crouching down,' says Abigail, giggling and slurping out of a *Frozen* mug, 'you reminded me of something.'

'*Crouching Tiger, Hidden DRAGON?*' says Sian, nodding like she really means it.

There was a pause, and we all looked at Abigail.

'Erm,' says Abigail, and we all screech our heads off, like a pack of hyenas.

'Watch yourself, Abi,' says Big Debbie, laughing. 'I pack a powerful punch.'

'I'll bet Terry will vouch for that,' says Clare giggling.

And they all look at me cautiously, to see if that's OK to say, or if it's too soon to make a bit of a joke like that, him being my ex and everything.

I start to cry, and Abigail shakes her head at Clare but I'm not crying about that; I'm crying cos I'm so sorry about Jay, and

I know I did it all wrong and they are the nicest people in the world. Then we have another round of drinks and a group hug. Because that's what women in a refuge are like. That's how they are, after what they've been through.

Mrs H comes in with her serious face on. She's had a call, she says – they haven't located Barney. That'll be what the police will have said. Located. Not a word she'd use normally. And she closes the curtains, not that that will do much good since they're like old rags; you can see right through them when it's dark out and the lights are on inside.

And the swish of the curtains and the set of Mrs H's jaw takes the wind out of our sails, and we settle down, staring into the bottoms of our mugs.

Big Debbie's talking about the time she represented England in the World Student Athletics championships, doing discus and shot, and how she did a heave (that's what she said; I mean, I don't know the terms) of 17.01 metres which was a personal best, but got beaten in the end by a South African girl who weighed nineteen stone, but it was muscle. Sarah's all ears, Clare nudges me and winks. Then Mrs H pulls up the chair next to us, in the corner.

'You've had quite a day.' She looks at me steadily, like she's trying to work me out. 'I think you'd better think about going up to bed.'

'You'll be throwing me out tomorrow,' I say. 'I've got used to it here, used to having people around me.'

'Perhaps with Terry back inside you can start to live a more normal life again,' she says.

'You'd think,' I say.

'Well, there'll be some semblance of normality back in your life.'

And I think, what the hell does she know? Terry's brothers will be blaming me for all this and what the hell was Barney actually doing? I check my phone. But there are no missed calls.

Fifty-Four

DS Clarke

DS Clarke is striding up Regent's Park Road in a fury that she's only felt a few times in her life. She can't decide who to be angry with first. Sally for being stupid, Terry for being a monster or Barney for selling Sally out.

PC Chapman has gone to pick up the car from around the corner, so, for now she's on her own and she's not even slightly unhappy about that.

'Dawn, I'm not scared of a couple of off-their-heads addicts,' she'd said to PC Chapman. And that was three minutes ago, so Dawn should be here any second. In fact, Sue thinks, that could be her car now. But it isn't.

Somehow, the street looks worse tonight. The street lamps have stopped working from about halfway up, some kind of act of defiance by the council, as though they are trying to punish the squatters by switching off the lights. The squatters won't care – they prefer the dark.

Ryan is sitting on the pavement outside the squat, his back against the low front wall, head between his knees. As DS Clarke's footsteps slow, he lifts he chin and juts it out to rest on his knees.

'Oh, it's you!' he whispers.

'Where is he?' says DS Clarke.

'Come to arrest me?' he whispers. 'Too late. 'Can't you see I don't need any help right now, grandma?'

'How much have you had, Ryan?'

He doesn't reply. A line of spit connects the corner of his mouth to the moth-eaten collar of his coat.

'Who were you expecting, Ryan?'

'I have a very busy social calendar,' he grumbles.

'Who else?'

'None of your business, grandma.'

'Where is he?' she says again.

Ryan doesn't answer. His head has sunk back into his collar. She kicks his shoe and his foot slides forwards. His knee drops to the ground and his head jerks up out of the coat again.

'What is it?' he whispers, his throat hoarse.

'Barney?' she says, tapping her foot. 'Remember him?'

'You must've missed him. I don't know where either of them are . . .' he trails off.

'Who was the other visitor?' says DS Clarke, stepping past Ryan as he sinks back into his oblivion.

'I don't suggest you go in, grandma. Not unless you want your throat slashed.'

She steps over Ryan's legs and walks up the pathway and into the front hall.

'Barney!' she shouts. 'Get on down here.'

There's no reply. Just a scraping sound on bare floorboards.

'*Barney!*'

Nothing.

Only the sound of her own breathing, then the sound of Ryan groaning as he struggles to stand up and starts stumbling up the path behind her, blocking what light there is and plunging the hall into darkness.

A car door slams.

Footsteps running up the road.

'Sarge. SARGE!'

'Chapman, what is it? I'm in here.' Her voice sounds thin, even to herself.

She edges backwards out of the hallway, turns sideways past Ryan, holding her breath so she doesn't smell him, and turns to face Chapman on the pathway.

'Sarge! I think we need you back at the station . . .' She's out of breath.

'Did something happen, Chapman? Is everything all right?'

'*Is everything all right, Chapman?*' mimics Ryan from behind her, as he flips a lighter. '*Oh, Chapman, save me, save me!*'

'It'd better be good,' she says, under her breath, holding Chapman's shoulders in an attempt to calm her down.

'Sarge, Tom Bohrer has come back. Bohrer from IT. He got that Crime Prevention Data request back about the email addresses. You know, the ones on Gareth's laptop.'

'And? What's so urgent?'

'They're all registered to 289, Oval Road.'

'Shit! All of them?'

'All of them.'

'To who?'

'Mr Gareth James. He's the registered owner of all the email addresses.'

'Sending messages to himself. Smart. He's smarter than we thought. A lot smarter . . .'

Chapman's phone buzzes.

'Sarge, there's news from the hospital.' Chapman's eyes glow in the glare of her phone.

'Now what!' says DS Clarke.

'Terry Mansfield died ten minutes ago . . . What shall we do, sarge?'

'I guess we go give Clare and Sal the news . . .'

Fifty-Five

Clare

'I thought you'd gone!' shouts Sally down the hall to Susan.

Sally's a bit drunk.

Susan's talking to the security team at the front desk.

Chapman is standing next to her, looking out of breath.

Derek is putting on his reflective coat.

He takes up sentry duty outside the front door as Susan comes down the hall to talk to us.

'We haven't found Barney yet,' says Susan. 'You will stay away from the windows, and you may not use the front exit. Not until I say so,' she says, looking from one pale face to the next. 'If anyone sees him outside the building you must let security know immediately. In fact, I would recommend that we adopt a code red until further notice.'

Sally mouths at me, 'What's a code red,' and I try not to giggle.

'Sal, it's about Terry.'

Sally shuts up and the blood drains out of her face as Susan sits down next to her, perched on the edge of the plastic chair.

'Sal, he's dead. Heart attack.'

'I see,' says Sally quietly, twisting her hands together.

Susan nods, slowly. 'A massive heart attack. Obviously they did everything they could. But I imagine that we all feel it's for the best,' she says. 'You know it is.'

Sally shrugs.

'It's over,' Susan says.

'It's over,' Sally repeats. 'Fucking 'ell,' she says. 'That's it then, right?' she says. And I smile at her, because that's kind of the best news, really.

'I have some other news,' Susan says, looking directly at me.

'What?' I say, my stomach somersaulting. By her face I can already tell it's gonna be bad.

'Well, Gareth . . .' says Susan.

'What about him?' Sally says, interrupting, her voice impatient, the wine talking again.

'Well, the good news is that all the email addresses that Gareth was contacting, his friends who were helping him get through his "difficult life" and lending him money? They're all registered under his name,' she says, with a half-smile.

'Is that good?' I say, thinking: because I always told you he was a manipulative bastard.

'It makes your story add up,' says Dawn, over Susan's shoulder.

'My story always added up,' I say, and Sally pats me on the arm.

'Be thankful for small mercies,' she laughs, 'and more Prosecco.'

'Don't you think you've had enough?' says Susan. 'Maybe—'

'Oh, give me a break an' all, Detective Sergeant I'm-in-Charge! We deserve a bit of a laugh.'

'Did you tell her about the journal as well?' Dawn says to Susan. 'Did you pick up the message I left earlier?'

'No, what did it say?'

'That the Turnitin software showed up that 57.3 per cent of the journal was copied directly from online sources.'

'What's that mean?' I say to Sally, who's looking unusually triumphant.

'It means that I'm DA MAN!' says Sally, high-fiving Susan.

'Someone get me a mug,' says Susan, looking relieved.

'It's youth speak,' says Mrs H to Sian, who's staring at us, looking confused.

'So, you know the journal was a load of bollocks?' I say.

They all nod. And I feel hot tears explode from my eyes like in kids' cartoons.

Then someone says, 'Where's Kitty?'

No one has seen Kitty since she had her meltdown and the sedative must have worn off by now.

It does seem weird she hasn't shown her face, what with all the sirens and alarms going off. Not like her to miss a drama.

Then I remember her sitting on the side in the kitchen, waiting for her toast while the chicken was on fire.

'Perhaps leave her alone,' says Mrs Henry. 'She's had a bad day. Those fashion people are so shallow. Say anything, do anything to get the next big thing. I'll check on her later.'

Susan says it's way past her bedtime and gives us all a hug. Halfway down the hall she comes back and tells us that we must all still be vigilant, that Gareth and Barney represent a real threat. Sally just nods, and looks like she might keel over any minute.

Prashi starts talking about going to bed. Her girls are going to wake her up in about five hours. But then Aiysha, whose eldest saw her drinking a glass of wine earlier, insists that they should have a nightcap and they're back in the middle of the action. Abigail and Sian are laughing so hard they'll have sore heads in the morning.

Sarah is boring the pants off anyone who will listen about how she's afraid of spiders. And how she got into the Italia Conti Stage School in 1978 but her mum and dad wouldn't let her go. Said it was too full of common people. Bad influence.

'And that's why I'm fat,' she finishes, slamming down her Minnie Mouse mug and spilling half the remaining Prosecco on the table.

'Nah,' slurs Big Debbie, 'you're fat because you eat too much,' she says. 'Same as me.'

And Sarah starts to laugh.

Mrs Henry tells them to shush.

All the lights are off.

In the end, we're the first to go up but in fairness, Sally's the most pissed.

'I can't believe it,' says Sally.

'What? That Sarah was invited to go to the Italia Conti Stage School? Gareth went there,' I whisper.

'I meant about Terry,' she says, trying to negotiate the stairs. 'But I don't believe that either.'

'He said he did,' I whisper, still thinking about Gareth. 'Said a lot of shit. I was asking him, one day you know, what he was going to do with his life. How he was going to contribute, to humanity, and, oh yeah, help pay the bills.'

Sally snorts, misses a step and falls onto the handrail.

'Pretty simple question,' she slurs.

'You'd think,' I say.

We reach the first floor.

There are dimmed lights on the landing.

'First off he said he'd like to start a rock band. And then he told me he had plans to leave for LA soon. Said he had some friends who were opening a fashion store and they needed his eye.'

'Because there's nothing he doesn't know about fashion, right?'

'And then, like one minute later, he said he was thinking of applying to Juilliard to do a Masters.'

'What's Juilliard?'

'It's like the best music conservatory in America.'

'Didn't know he was that good.'

'He wasn't. He could manage a pretty good Celine Dion in the shower.'

'Even I . . .' Sally starts, laughing loudly at the same time, and I shush her, but there's so much noise coming from downstairs that I'm sure we aren't disturbing anyone, and me shushing her made her laugh all the more.

I clap my hand over her mouth and she bites my finger. I scream.

Sally has to cling on to the handrail and sit down for a minute.

'So anyway, then he fixed me with a very serious look and said, "I'm going to tell you something now which is entirely private, and you will not tell a soul. I think I'm going to a Buddhist monastery retreat in Bhutan for a year."'

Sally can't get up. I think she's about to pee herself she is laughing so hard.

'You've got to tell Sue,' she says, gasping. 'She'll be on the next plane.'

She stops laughing.

'What?' I say, concerned, wiping tears of laughter from under my eyes. 'What? What is it?'

She's frowning.

There's a smell of something wrong.

I don't know why.

It's just not the usual smell you get at the top of the stairs.

I don't know what it is.

There's light spilling from our flat door, down the stairs.

The front door is open, and as we get higher up the stairs, we can see all our stuff is everywhere.

We pick our way across the sitting room.

The bathroom has been smashed up.

The shower curtain pulled down.

The sofa cushions have been slashed.

The mattresses are ripped open.

And every bottle of shampoo and shower gel, deodorant, perfume, splatted and crunched into the carpet. Bits of mirror reflecting the light.

The pages from magazines and books are flapping.

All our clothes are torn and Sally's suitcases have been flung against the window.

'Fucking Kitty,' I say. '*Fucking Kitty!*'

'She wouldn't,' Sally says. 'Not even Kitty.'

'Of course, she would. She's so fucking furious about that modelling shit! I'm going to fucking kill her!' And I stumble across all the crap on our floor, towards her front door.

'Clare, let Mrs H handle it. Let's just go—'

'KITTY! KITTY, I KNOW YOU'RE IN THERE!' I yell.

I'm about to hammer on the door, when it drifts open and I fall into the room, catching hold of the handle to steady myself, pulling myself up, looking up ... And there's Kitty. Hanging where a pink fringed lampshade used to be, white plastic light flex wound around her neck, chin on chest, graduated blonde hair falling forwards, eyes glazed, bulging, skin grey, arms straight, nails chipped, slowly, slowly, slowly turning, the flex creaking, and her tiny bare feet not quite touching the fallen chair beneath them.

And a familiar voice says, 'Hello, Coco.'

Fifty-Six

Sally

I'm not shitting you, I just heard a man's voice, and all I can think about is running because that's the kind of huge sodding coward I am.

My heart is thumping so hard I think it's going to fall out and I'm still drunk from the bloomin' Prosecco and the stairs are dark and surely someone else is going to hear him?

From the doorway of our flat all I can see is Clare, on her knees, coughing and throwing up onto the carpet of Kitty's flat.

And then suddenly there's the sound of heavy footsteps and a man is silhouetted in Kitty's doorway who lurches out and grabs me by the arms, dragging me into the room.

My knees scrape against the wooden floor and I can feel the skin ripping and he kicks the door shut behind me.

Gareth.

Thick wavy hair, fake tan, model-style muscles, bluey-white teeth, enormous sense of entitlement, yellow suede slip-on shoes with no socks.

'I'm watching you,' he says, dropping me like a sack. 'I know about you,' he says, sitting back on a chair. 'Kitty doesn't like you,' he says, picking up the gun that's lying next to the chair and aiming it at Clare. He pulls out some underwear from the back pocket of his jeans, a red bra and pants and loops it over the nose of the gun.

'Didn't,' I say, 'she didn't like me. She's not in a fit state to like anyone now!'

Kitty is slowly, slowly spinning and the light flex is groaning under her weight and her straightened hair is wafting like she's in a gentle breeze, even though she's not.

'Well observed,' he says. 'She didn't like anyone much. And her whining was off the fucking scale. You're next,' he says, motioning upwards with his head. 'Coco, take off the shit you're wearing and put that on.' He tosses the underwear with the gun.

Clare wipes the corner of her mouth on the back of her thumb.

'Smells like you've been drinking, babe,' he says. 'You know I don't like you drinking. Messes with your meds.'

Through Kitty's bathroom door, I can see the airing cupboard wide open, the shelves stacked neatly against the side of the bath and the towels and sheets piled on the toilet seat. Kitty must have let him in.

The sitting room is sweating, and humming with the smell of sick, but Gareth's shirt is ironed, pristine, powder blue without a whisper of perspiration, and he's as calm as you like, sitting back in his chair.

'Where's the necklace, whore?' he says to Clare.

She's starting to take off her pyjama bottoms, the ones with the pink rabbits, and she stops and stares at him, one foot in one foot out.

'The locket. Where the fuck is it?'

'I don't know,' she says, flicking her eyes at me.

He sees her.

He misses nothing.

'Babe,' he says with a sigh, lovingly outlining the contours of the gun with his forefinger. 'You have no idea how much you fucked up the whole plan by stealing that, do you? All those fucking meds you took you didn't need to. All that planning. Plane tickets. Months of planning, babe. You fucked it up. So, the locket.' He leans back. '*I* know you have it. *You* know you have it. And now it seems, *she* knows you have it. So, where is it? Stop fucking with my time.'

'I don't—' she starts.

And I say, 'If she says she doesn't know, she doesn't know.'

'Don't you fucking start!' he shouts. 'Shut up! Get on your knees and shut up,' he yells, loud enough to be heard downstairs, I think. I hope.

I struggle on to my knees on the carpet. Clare drops her white pants to her ankles, kicks them away, then starts to put her foot into the red pants. She overbalances and takes a step towards Gareth.

'Easy, babe, you don't wanna hurt yourself,' he says, getting up and yanking her arm, so she falls forwards even more. She's a tangle of legs and pants and I can see that the burns between her legs are still angry and purple.

'Naughty panties, making Coco fall,' he says, settling back in his chair again, resting his arm behind his head, watching her trying to pull up the red pants. 'And the top,' he says.

Tears are streaking down her face.

'Babe, you look ugly enough not crying. Stop now or I'll give you something to cry about.'

She wipes the tears with her fingers.

'You wanna know where you slipped up?' I say.

'I don't slip up, Miss Marple,' he says, not moving his eyes off Clare, half smiling at her bare breasts. She tries to hide herself but that makes him smile more.

'The journal,' I say. 'It was pathetic. Stealing all that stuff off the Internet. So obviously not one person – one minute you're a fucking doctor, next minute you're an emotional wreck, next minute you're soooo in love,' I say.

He lurches out of the chair and smacks me so hard across the face with the gun that I land on the wooden floorboards, head first, and everything is black. I hear Clare gasp and then another sound of metal hitting skin and he's smacked her across the face as well.

'I heard you talk too much. Shut up,' he hisses.

He breathes out slowly through his mouth, staring at the gun in his hands, thinking, thinking.

'Where's the locket, babe?' he hisses at Clare, and he towers over me, and he wraps his hands around my throat and starts squeezing, looking at Clare. Squeezing.

I try to speak but I can't.

I can't breathe.

'Where's the locket?' he says again to Clare, relaxing his grip.

Clare's face is criss-crossed with the tracks of her tears.

'It's in my room,' she says, haltingly, staring at me, not blinking, and if I'm supposed to have a plan, I don't, and if

I'm supposed to read her face and know *her* plan, I can't. And anyway, she looks like she doesn't have a plan either.

'Clare . . .' I whisper.

'Shut the fuck up!' he says, kicking my leg as he walks past. He pushes her out the door and motions for me to follow. In the other back pocket of his jeans is a clear plastic bottle of blue paraffin.

From the inside of our flat there's a banging sound, like the water boiler is going nuclear or something. We all stand on the landing, outside our open front door, listening, Clare nearest the door, silently crying.

'What the fuck is that?' he hisses at me.

'It's just the hot water,' I say. 'It always . . .'

There's a clank and a thud and Barney falls out of our bathroom, coughing, into the sitting room, glancing at me, gazing around at our trashed flat, pictures fallen off the walls, chairs tipped up and slashed, shards of mirror glittering.

'Sal, girl,' he says, smiling, when he sees me at the door, putting his hands on his hips. 'Sorry, Sal, but I need my money. Urgent,' he says, with a grin and a shrug. He looks better than I've ever seen him. Well, like he used to look before he began living on the street. His cheeks are pink instead of his eyes. 'Tried to call you earlier,' he says, giving me a glance, but shaking his head and laughing. 'Looks like I missed the party of the century.' He's talking fast, frenzied, like he does when he's high. Gareth is standing in the shadows in the hall behind me, with the gun in my back.

'The girl with the bare feet,' he says to Clare, looking her up and down. 'Looks like most of your clothes fell off, again.' His eyes rest on the burns between her thighs and he almost imperceptibly winces. 'You really do need to get your head around the concept of wearing clothes, you know. I reckon you'll feel a lot warmer,' he says, looking around. 'Saves on vitamins and stuff. I need my money, Sal,' he says, his hands shaking like they do most of the time, 'I don't know what game you've got going on here, love, but I need my money.'

'Hey,' says Gareth from behind me. I stiffen and I watch Clare's shoulders tense. 'I'm Axel, Kitty's boyfriend. Your mates back at the squat must've told you about me, right?'

'Oh, yeah, right,' says Barney. 'Yeah, Ryan did mention something about you. Said something about the attic. Axel, you say?' he says, flicking his eyes at me, meeting my gaze, like he does when he's off the drugs. 'Are you in on the party too, Axel?' Barney smiles.

'Well no, not exactly,' says Gareth, cool as a cucumber. 'There's been a bit of a row and Kitty can't find her necklace and it looks like Clare and Sally here know a bit about it.' He pushes me and Clare further into the room and kicks the door behind him.

'Sally-Ann Parton! Turned into a common thief have you?' says Barn, with a giggle, which is weird because he can see I'm not smiling back. 'Must be something to do with the company you keep. Can't wait to tell your sergeant friend. Well, it looks like someone has been trying pretty damn hard to find something in here. But look, I'm in a hurry. Can you get my money, girl?'

'The necklace and your notes are in the curtain pole, in the bedroom,' I say, staring in disbelief at Barney, trying to fix him with a look he'll understand. Clare seems to wake up for the first time, and stares at me, and Gareth stares at her and Barney stares at him.

'Tell you what,' says Gareth to Barney, 'you go have a look for us both, while I make sure no one disappears from here. Don't want to upset Kitty any more than we have to, right, ladies?'

He sits down on the end of the sofa, brushing aside the socks and magazines. Clare nods mechanically.

'You just unscrew the end. Right-hand side,' I say, half shaking my head, thinking it's a fine time for Barney to give his system a break, only to go half stupid, cos anyone can see this situation calls for something like a code red at the very least.

'You'd better not be lying,' says Gareth quietly, as Barney opens Clare's bedroom door.

Her room is the worst mess, cos there's nothing much left of it, except a few pieces of wardrobe and shards of mirror. The only thing hanging is the curtain pole. He was busy while we were all messing around downstairs.

'Yeah, you'd better not be lying, Sal. I've got a lot riding on this. I don't know why you didn't give it back when I first asked you, bitch,' Barney says. I start to speak, because he knows that I couldn't have . . . and then I think: he would never call me a bitch. Barney just wouldn't. Ever.

'Even *he* thinks you're a bitch, bitch.' says Gareth quietly, under his breath. Smiling.

Barney has unscrewed the curtain pole and he comes back into the room, holding the curtain pole in one hand and his roll of notes and a screwed-up piece of cotton wool in the other. He loops his arm around the curtain pole, jams the fifties in his pocket, unwraps the cotton wool and holds up the gold locket on its fine gold chain.

'Give it here,' says Gareth.

'This it? Looks old,' Barney says, holding it up to the light.

Gareth is gazing at the locket. Mesmerised.

'Pass it,' he says, coldly. 'Now,' he says.

'Looks like real gold,' says Barney, spinning it around a bit. 'Worth a bob or two,' he says.

Gareth is tensing with every word. 'PASS IT!' he shouts, and in one swift movement, Barney folds the necklace back into the cotton wool and lobs it across the sitting room, arcing over Clare's head.

Gareth catches it with his left hand, still staring at Barney, and for a few seconds he holds it there, smiling to himself, satisfied, aware of us staring at him, and relishing every moment of his triumph.

As he looks down and opens his hand, the cotton wool folds back and he lifts his other hand leaving the gun resting next to him, and he presses the side of the locket. Just as the locket clicks open, I see a tiny movement in a triangle of mirror resting by the bedframe. In the reflection of the sitting room I can see the door behind Gareth nudging open, just a fraction.

'So, we've got what we come for.' Barney breathes out slowly. 'So, let's get out of here, before them coppers came.' He nods his head towards the bathroom.

Gareth smiles, a broad white American have-a-nice-day-now grin. 'You go ahead, Barney ... I'll be done in a minute. Tell Ryan not to wait up.'

'Nah, come on, mate,' says Barney, really friendly like. 'We can go through this way,' he says, beginning to pick his way through the torn clothes and empty shampoo bottles.

Gareth levels the gun at Barney and waves it towards the bathroom. 'As I say, you go ahead,' he says, more menacingly this time. 'I've got a game to play with Coco before I go. I've even brought refreshments,' he says, tapping his back pocket. 'Haven't I, babe?' And he slips the bottle out of his pocket and shakes it in front of her, twists off the lid. Her eyes have glazed over as though she, Clare, that funny little girl who doesn't like cucumber, but loves Pot Noodle, who doesn't eat gluten but loves a pizza, who showers too long and wishes she was a Disney princess – she's no longer inside that twisted body as paraffin is dripped onto her hair.

The door behind Gareth moves a fraction again. I'm watching it in the mirror, moving my eyes towards it, to get Barney to notice. And Gareth notices instead, sees me looking in the bedroom, and screws the lid back on the bottle

'Don't wanna waste it, babe, do we,' he says. 'Bitch,' he says, striding over to me. 'What you up to?' And he's moving towards the bedroom slowly, with the gun outstretched. 'Is there someone else in there?'

Barney looks confused, shrugs a shrug, and hangs his head like someone who is beginning to realise that he can't think of a way out this time, and just as Gareth crosses the threshold of Clare's bedroom, there is a small, polite knock at our front door. Gareth looks at me as though I'm doing something to trick him.

'It'll be Prashi's daughter,' I say, quickly. Clare smacks her hand over her mouth and stifles a whimper and sinks lower to the carpet, every vertebra in her spine showing through her papery skin.

'We'll have made too much noise,' I say, nodding, 'and her mum will have sent her up to tell us to shut up, cos that's what she does,' I say, and he starts to train his gun on the door, and I say, 'She's only seven, for fuck's sake,' and I push myself up off the floor, knees aching, skin smarting, and he starts lowering the gun to the height he imagines a seven-year-old to be. I stagger forwards to stand in the way, between the gun and the door, and he raises the gun higher and points it at my head and smiles.

'It's all right, Jay,' I whisper, leaning on the door frame. 'It's OK, love, we'll shut up now, I promise, you go back to . . .' I say, and I bring my eye to the crack in the door, looking down to where Jay would be, and there's Sue's shoes, and a whole load of other shoes crowded onto the landing between Kitty's room and ours, '. . . bed,' I say, looking over my shoulder at Barney, crouched with his hands over his head, and Clare curled up on the floor with her hand still over her mouth and her hair in a pool of paraffin, and Gareth across the room, smiling, with the nose of his gun pointing at my head.

'Aim high,' I whisper, and in the second that follows, in slow motion so that it feels like minutes, the door sweeps open, squealing on its hinges, and bounces against the magnolia painted wall, and I'm grabbed by the shoulders by so many hands, and flung through a crowd of police marksmen whose rifles are clicking, clicking, clicking as they range around the flat, tumbling forwards into the sitting room, until they come to rest on Gareth, whose smile slowly slips as he swings his head left and right, looking for the quickest way out, and then all the action stops and the room falls silent and there are like a million officers in the way so I can't see what's going on.

'Gareth Marlon Sullivan,' it's Sue talking, 'I am arresting you for the attempted murder of Clare James. You do not . . .' and there's a heavy thud, '. . . have to say anything but it may harm your defence . . .' and a groan and a gasp of air, '. . . if you do not mention when questioned something which . . .' and a click and a scrape as someone's shoes are dragged across the floor, '. . . you later rely on in court. Anything you do say . . .'

And soon footsteps thunder down the stairs as nine Specialist Firearms Command officers take Gareth Marlon Sullivan away.

'Hey, girl with the bare feet,' I hear Barney whisper, 'Clare, are you all right?'

And I drop to the floor because I haven't the strength to walk and I crawl from the landing on my hands and knees. I can hear orders being given to the medics to bring stretchers, and make it snappy, that it's three females and one male, and I think there's only two of us and then I remember.

Clare doesn't reply. Her spine is still curled over her pathetic bruised limbs. I can see her fingers moving, scratching, picking at the skin on the side of her thumb, and I roll her into my arms and try to warm her damp, cold skin.

Then I hear myself saying, 'What, Barney? How?'

'Ryan told me. Well, Ryan's state told me. He's off his head and he had to've got the money to buy his stuff from somewhere. I had to bloody crawl all the way along the attic from our place. I hate the bloody dark,' he says. 'And mice,' he says.

'What do you think we should do?' I say.

'I think we should get you patched up. You got blood coming out your head. And then we should get us all the fuck out of here,' he says, and a medic wraps a blanket around Clare and the colour begins to come back to her face and Barney helps me up off the floor and gives me a hug and squeezes me tight.

'Right,' I say, from inside his coat, same smell that's about to knock me off my feet.

'It was me that called the police,' he says.

'You did?' I say.

'Honour amongst thieves,' he says.

I put Clare's dressing gown around her shoulders and guide her through the door, placing her hand on the handrail, pressing her gently against the wall of the stairs. We're going down slowly, step by step, my arm looped about her shoulders, Barney in front to catch her fall, and she's staring into nowhere, and there's dribble coming out of the corner of her mouth, and her hair is dripping, same as the day I first met her.

Fifty-Seven

DS Clarke

The door buzzer goes.

'Sarge, we're here.'

And five minutes later it goes again.

'SARGE, ARE YOU ALL RIGHT?'

'I already told you I'm fine,' she snaps, adding extra concealer under her eyes. She's had precisely two and three quarter hours sleep.

It's 09.02 and DS Clarke's car, with PC Hall behind the wheel, is pulling up in Harley Street outside a door with a brass plaque that reads 'Dr Stephen Short, Consultant Psychiatrist MBChB, FRCPsych, Dip Psychotherapy.'

'Thank you, Hall,' says DS Clarke. 'Did you call ahead? I do hope so. I expect Dr Short will be really pleased to see us.'

'You'll need this, sarge.' Hall places a printed card in her hand.

DS Clarke ignores the receptionist's protests completely and opens the door to Doctor Short's office.

'Ah, Dr Short. Thank you so much for seeing us again at such short notice.'

'I do have patients . . .' he begins.

'I daresay,' says DS Clarke, checking the card. 'They'll have to wait. I am here to arrest you, Stephen Christopher Short, on suspicion of impersonating a medical doctor without the required qualifications, aggravated identity theft, furnishing false information to the Drug Enforcement Administration and distributing controlled substances without a licence. You do not have to say anything, yet it may harm your defence if you do not mention, when questioned, something which you later rely on in court. Anything you do say may be given in evidence.'

'I see,' he says, examining his buffed fingernails. 'I see,' he says again. 'May I just get my bags?'

'That won't be necessary, Mr Short. My officers can fetch your things. We'd like to take you straight to the station, if you'd be so kind. We have colleagues from America on their way. It appears you've been impersonating a medical doctor for some time.'

'Can I just say,' says Mr Short, looking ashen, 'if I'm being taken into police custody, I would imagine you know the full horror of Gareth Sullivan or James. Can I please request that I am afforded the utmost security?'

'You don't have to answer any questions, Mr Short, but can I ask, what made you support Gareth James' actions in relation to Ms Clare Chambers?'

'Because he would have killed me if I hadn't. And he's threatened to reveal my status for years. I've a thriving practice here. I'm good at what I do, believe it or—'

'Even though you're not qualified,' interrupts DS Clarke.

'Yes! Gareth made me do everything. Supply her with the antipsychotic drugs. Pretend that they were vitamins. I even gave him pints of my own blood for God knows what – anything to get him away from me.'

'We have him,' she says, and watches his reaction.

He stops and looks up.

For a second there, he looks relieved.

'You're sure?'

'Yes, we're sure. Aren't you sorry?' I say. 'He was your friend at some point, wasn't he?'

'A psychopath doesn't have any friends, Detective Sergeant.'

Sally and Clare are sitting in the day room.

They each have their own seat on the sofa, but in the crack between the two cushions, Sally is clasping Clare's tiny, chewed fingers.

The TV is on with the sound turned down.

They are both pale.

Nearly grey.

Staring at the TV but with their heads somewhere else.

'Ladies,' says DS Clarke, pulling up a chair. 'You look like an old married couple.'

Clare blushes and pulls her hand away, instantly chewing on her thumbnail.

'Want some news?' says DS Clarke.

'You've brought George Clooney with you?' asks Sally.

'No. The Delaware police have been on the phone. A missing presumed dead Gareth Marlon Sullivan was on the international wanted list for holding a woman captive in her own home for three years, then murdering her and burning her remains. He had been previously charged with one count of kidnapping and one count of rape, but he jumped bail and then disappeared.'

'Wonder why he didn't kill me?' whispers Clare, like she's almost afraid to know the answer.

'I thought about that,' says DS Clarke, 'and I think it's because he was hoping to just disappear this time. If stuff had come out about you, Delaware might have pieced it together. But a murder scene and no body, no ID? They would never have got to hear about it. And he'd have got off with all your money.'

Clare chews her thumbnail.

'We should celebrate,' says Sally. 'Fancy some Prosecco?'

Clare pulls a face like she's going to be sick.

'Joking,' she says.

'I'll have a cuppa, though,' says DS Clarke and their eyes meet and they both grin, with tears in their eyes.

'Thanks,' Sally mouths at DS Clarke.

'Sorry,' DS Clarke mouths back.

'Would a *Frozen* mug be all right for sarge?' says Sally, crying and laughing at the same time as she heads for the kitchen.

Acknowledgements

In an attempt to highlight the depth of friendship that develops between women in extremis in my books, I have a habit of focusing on the very worst with men. I'd just like to point out that, unlike my male characters, I'm fortunate enough to now have nothing but excellent men in my life – my darling dad, my patient and brilliant husband, and my adorable boys. Thank you to them and the many fine men in the world who outbalance the very few bad.

Want to read
NEW BOOKS
before anyone else?

Like getting
FREE BOOKS?

Enjoy sharing your
OPINIONS?

Discover

READERS FIRST
Read. Love. Share.

Sign up today to win your first free book:
readersfirst.co.uk